I0806112

THE UNSELECTED JOURNALS OF *Emma M. Lion*

VOL. 7

BETH BROWER

THE UNSELECTED JOURNALS OF

Emma M. Lion

VOL. 7

Rhysdon Press

contact@rhysdonpress.com

Published by Rhysdon Press
Printed in the United States of America

Publishers Cataloging-in-Publication data. Brower, Beth.
The Unselected Journals of Emma M. Lion, Vol. 7: Beth Brower; p.cm.
ISBN 978-1-957492-01-8 Fiction Historical 2. Fiction. I. Title.

Second Edition
10 9 8 7 6 5 4 3 2

978-1-957492-01-8

Text was set in Baskerville

Emma M. Lion

would like to dedicate these pages to

The Nieces

PREVIOUSLY MENTIONED PERSONS OF INTEREST

Emma M. Lion – *Myself, obviously. Owner of Lapis Lazuli House.*

Niall Pierce – *Photographer. Avenging Angel. Much yet to…discuss.*

Young Hawkes – *Vicar and Reprobate. Knower of things. Keeper of secrets.*

Duke of Islington – *Will battle for his friends, not only against.*

Archibald Flat – *Still a General Plague on mankind. Yet, one must endure.*

Cousin Matilde – *Archibald's older sister. Dragon of a woman.*

Lady Eugenia Spencer – *Aunt with engagement plans for Arabella's Season.*

Damian Spencer – *Errant cousin. Currently…I've no idea, actually.*

Arabella Spencer – *Beauty of* The Season, *will become engaged…to someone.*

Parian – *Valet, Butler. Less unpleasant than he was.*

Agnes – *Maid, Cook. Scottish. Impressively capable and earnest.*

The Roman – *Still not seen in person. However, he thinks I'm lovely.*

Mary Bairrage – *Good chum. Employed by telephone company and Prof. Fletcher.*

Jack Hollingstell – *Confidence man in my debt. Terrifying thought.*

Roland Sutherland – *Childhood nemesis turned gorgeous Sun God.*

Saffronia March – *Artist. Family friend. Fellow St. Crispian.*

Ben Chambers – *The Pirate. Waspish and insulting owner of The Hound.*

Lady Trewartha – *Gracious Hostess. Lives in Baron's Square.*

Reprobates Ten – *Striker, Capper, Quality Jones, Sargent, The Boy, Mastiff, Charlie Cross, Odysseus, Night Watchman, & Mighty Nigel Hawkes.*

Mr. Penury – *Banker endeavouring to find me work.*

Mrs. Penury – *My serious banker's silent yet delightful wife.*

Professor Fletcher – *Widower. Masculine. Cuts own hair. Terrible glasses.*

Victoria Braithwaite – *Prominent name on my Enemies List.*

Lady Sheridan – *Aunt Eugenia's friend. Society Matron.*

Charles Goddard – *Tall. Skinny. Flagpole! My Unintended Intended. Sigh.*

Lord George West – *Potential husband for Arabella. Mourning his sweet pea.*

Annalise Clifford – *A fresh acquaintance, introduced at Lady Sheridan's tea.*

May Northgate – *A fresh acquaintance, also introduced at Lady Sheridan's tea.*

Maxwell Stuart – *January 31st 1861 – July 27th 1880*

March 1st

"~~*Good morning, Niall. I spent half the night thinking about…*~~"
"~~*Weather is such a pleasant thing to find in the morning…*~~"
"~~*Morning, Pierce. We agreed to speak about the, um, why don't you begin…?*~~"
"~~*Pierce, you devil…*~~"
"~~*Seeing as how you are* quite *accomplished in the art, I was wondering, idly, how many women have you previously kissed?*~~"

I've yet to come up with a suitable greeting for when I see Pierce this morning.

Disaster is pending.

Cheer up, Emma. The very worst that can happen is Pierce decides to leave—taking his room and board monies with him—while I and my insufficient funds are flung into the street. To beg.

I would hazard St. Crispian's to be a generous place.

Even Islington might stoop to toss a coin or two.

I'm less cheerful already.

And tired.

Volleys of rain came down half the night. Gusts of wind like cannon fire shaking the windows, as if the storm were being thrown against Lapis Lazuli by the handfuls. Warlike and belligerent, only a thin roof between myself and each clap of thunder. The battle raged until dawn, water streaming off the roof and down the window like an extra sheet of glass, distorting the grey morning.

All this spectacle, and yet it was the sound of Pierce moving through the rituals of his day on the other side of the wall that shoved me from an atmospheric awareness to the heart-pounding, unequivocal state of being wide awake.

I heard a meow.

Then the cadence of Pierce's reply but not the words themselves.

Tybalt meowed again and Pierce laughed.

It was so tremendously endearing that I pulled the blanket over my face with a sigh.

After Pierce had gone downstairs, Tybalt came through his curtain into my room, finding me curled in a half-circle. With a chirp he jumped onto the bed and settled against me, purring. I untangled myself enough to reach out a hand and pat him on the head.

The rain continued to fall.

Storms are ominous portents in literature, but when I forced myself from the rumpled tousle of my bed and looked out the window, there was no gloom or ill fate to be had, as if the strong-handed rain had only been intent on washing away the soot and grime and dust of a long winter.

It was not gentle, but it was good.

And I was glad for it.

Now I'm feeling almost eager to see Pierce. To speak with him.

Even if I don't know exactly what I wish to say.

Heavens, it's warm for a March morning.

Later

Foiled.

Utterly!

And by a Pirate, no less. How does one compete against a man with a wooden leg?

One does not.

It isn't that I'm not worried for Chambers.

I am.

After breakfast, I'd meant to go straightway and knock on the door of the studio, having found one passable sentence. "It would appear we have some unresolved feelings between us. Tea?"

I can see my gravestone once I've died of the subsequent mortification.

Emma M. Lion
Not Equipped to Navigate Her Own Life

Rather, I'd paced the breakfast room and tried to breathe. (I had worn one of my nicer morning dresses, and the corset was biting.)

"What are you doing, Miss?" Agnes asked when she came in to clean.

"Composing myself, Agnes. And striking several false notes, I think."

She frowned.

"Are you taking music lessons?"

"No, Agnes. I am not."

Feeling more than a little foolish, I left the breakfast room and crossed the hall with as much confidence as I could manage. It was not as much as I'd have liked.

I saw that Pierce's studio door was ajar.

Was this a tentative invitation?

A welcome not wishing to convey expectation?

An accident?

I lifted my hand and…

A knock sounded on a door. Urgent. Angry.

The knock came again.

It was not the door of Lapis Lazuli House.

It was at the door of Lapis Lazuli Minor.

I could hear Pierce walk across his studio, enter his small excuse for a hall, and open the door. "Chambers!"

A muffled reply.

"What have you— Here, let me help you. Careful now, put your weight on my shoulder. What the hell have you done to yourself?"

"I need something. Give me something, anything."

"We need Fairchild."

"No."

"Don't be a daft fool. Watch your step here."

I backed away from the door, one step, two, not wanting to be caught in the middle of whatever it was that Chambers was needing.

"Did you do this on purpose?" Pierce asked him.

"Of course not. At least, I don't think so. It wouldn't stop, the pain. Burning up my body like fire. I tried to get out, walk until I couldn't feel anything and, well, you see what happened."

"You look exhausted," Pierce said, the gentle turn of his voice a surprise. "Here. Let's get you settled. Careful. On the blanket so as not to get mud on the sofa. It's Emma's."

A dismissive snort.

"Drink this," Pierce said. "I'll fetch Fairchild."

"Don't call Fairchild."

"If situations were reversed, what would you do? Oh, that's right.

They have been. You tied me to the bed and went for a doctor."

"You're a right ba—"

"Save it, Chambers, for when you're in your right mind. You'll enjoy it more."

A bitter laugh. "Help me get back to the shop. I've work to do."

"Not in that state."

"I have to—"

"I'll help with your shop. It's Saturday and I've no appointments. Now, if you want to go back to your room, I'll help you, but I'd advise against it. You're better off resting here."

"Sometimes I hate you."

Pierce laughed.

I retreated to the drawing room, and I'd no sooner entered when I heard the studio door close.

And lock.

A rather long walk, I should think.

March 2nd

There is blood on my boots. I didn't realise it until early this morning when I opened my exhausted eyes, and there they were on the floor as if *I'd* been the one shot.

I should explain.

Last night, long after Pierce and Dr. Fairchild had helped Ben Chambers down Whereabouts Lane and I'd spent several hours hiding at Thornfield Hall with a man whose only secret was keeping an insane wife in the attic, I blew out my lamp and went to sleep.

The disruption came a few hours past midnight.

At first it was a whispered call, then a scuffle, and the sound of something hitting the stone of Lapis Lazuli, all the while my mind was prodding my body awake.

I convinced myself out of bed.

Pulling a robe over my nightdress, I went to the window and peered down. In the deep blue of the street were three figures. I pushed my window open an inch to listen.

"Which room is she in?"

"How should I know?"

"Throw rocks at all of them?"

"No, no, that angry fellow might wake up."

"Angry fellow? You mean the old man?"

"No. The photographer."

A guffaw. "You're such a trout, Sargent. He's a good enough sport at The Cleo."

"He told Quality Jones where to go right enough."

"Quality Jones was puffed out of his blooming mind."

A laugh.

"Try that window there."

An arm cocked back, and I thought it best to intervene.

"Ho there!" I whispered down. As if we were at sea.

"Ho there!" rose a rambunctious cheer.

"Shhh!" I motioned. "Quiet down!"

"E of A! Your service is needed," shouted a Reprobate.

"It's past midnight," I hissed.

"Quarter past two, if you must know."

"We need your assistance."

"Is it truly necessary?"

Reprobate: "It's life and death."

Reprobate: "But come quickly."

Reprobate: "No time to lose."

"Is Hawkes with you?"

"Hawkes!" they all shouted in unison.

"Yes," one answered. I think it was Charlie Cross. "Or he will be. He *has* to be, you see. But we need your services."

"This all sounds like a very bad idea."

The street lit with three grins.

"Very!"

"Wonderfully so!"

"But essential. Absolutely essential."

Urgency being required, I closed my window, pulled my old black (rather grey now) coat over my nightdress, and then my new black coat over that. Next came a pair of warm stockings and my boots. I splashed water on my face, tied back my hair, wrapped my mother's pink and green shawl around my neck, and pocketed the front door key before descending as quietly as I was able.

Cousin Archibald snores.

As does Parian.

A relief it is, to have my room in the garret.

Letting myself out the door and motioning for the three Reprobates to quiet down as I locked it, I glanced about—no lights in any of the houses—and followed them up Whereabouts. I was in the definitive company of Sargent, Charlie Cross, and Odysseus.

"Where are we going?" I asked as we were crossing the Diagonal.

"Primrose Hill," answered Sargent.

"Why?"

Odysseus: "Insults and injury."

Sargent: "Armed conflict."

Charlie Cross: "We only do this sort of thing in the street if it's a full moon, you see."

"Please clarify what the dickens you speak of, gentlemen."

Charlie Cross took my arm and pointed heavenward. "It's a waxing crescent," he explained. "There's nothing for it. We have to shoot in the park."

"Shoot?" I replied. "Oh heavens, you don't mean a duel?"

"Of course we do," Sargent said. "Night Watchman got tangled with The Boy, and The Boy is restless and a whip tongue for all that. So Watchman called him out. You're needed to be the Fifth."

"You mean Second?" I asked.

"Not at all; Odysseus is the Second, I'm the Third, and Charlie here is the Fourth. But we're without a Fifth. That's you."

"Duels are so old-fashioned," I attempted. "No one does them nowadays."

"Nonsense," Sargent replied. "They're terrible good fun. We've had dozens upon dozens and only lost half a finger."

"Whose!"

Odysseus held up his left hand. I could see that he did not have an entire little finger.

My stomach dropped. "This is a horrible idea. Where's Hawkes?"

"The other set have gone Hawkes Hunting."

"Is he anyone's Second? Or Third? Or Fourth?"

The three of them laughed like I'd said the most ridiculous thing.

"Of course not, E of A, Hawkes turns around so as not to witness."

"And have you sent for Dr. Fairchild?"

"Nah," replied Sargent. "We so rarely need a leech. We've Hawkes. He's as clear a head as any Pickled Herring. Why, when Mastiff shot me in the leg, Hawkes didn't even look up from his book. He simply asked if a bone had been hit. When I said it hadn't—which was confirmed by my Second, Third, Fourth, and Fifth, of course, because I was deep in my cups—Hawkes held up a bottle of spirits and clean bandages and said, 'Best wrap it up then and stay off it for a few days.'"

"I'm not certain I believe that, Sargent."

At which point we'd come out onto the grass of Primrose Hill and my stomach was feeling inside out. When we crossed the lawn to join the other Reprobates, I could see Hawkes, fifteen steps away, doing his level best to see the words on the page of his book.

I left the jollified (and imbecilic) Reprobates and confronted their tenth member.

"Hawkes," I stated.

He looked up at me. "Miss Lion. Having a pleasant night?"

"I was, until I realised I was walking into a duel with what I assume are inebriated young men who seem to shoot at one another with uncomfortable frequency."

I received a long, unblinking look from my vicar.

I tried again. "How often does death by idiocy threaten?"

He smiled. "Does your question encompass all Reprobate activity, or is it isolated to duels?"

I blinked.

Once.

Twice.

I replied, "Let us suppose that, yes, I'm speaking only of Reprobate shooting Reprobate. We'll leave all other forms of foolishness and violence aside."

"Tonight marks the one hundred and thirty-ninth formal duel."

"Heavens!"

"An average of fourteen a year. So you might deduce," Hawkes said, I swear it was a touch dryly, "that death by idiocy is my near constant companion."

"No wonder you became a vicar. The amount of required prayer alone…"

The faint moonlight helped his smile push aside the darkness.

Hawkes.

"Well"—I settled into the idea—"as it has been a while since my literature has reviewed the customs of duelling, shouldn't there be a doctor on the premises?"

"I think we'll manage," Hawkes said. "If something were to happen, Fairchild can be roused easily enough."

We turned to look at the Reprobates, two loose groups bickering like crows.

"What are they doing?" I asked.

"There is a disagreement regarding the terms."

"The terms? But aren't duelling terms usually where, when, and who? Factors which are all accounted for."

Hawkes crossed his arms, his book held in his left hand, a finger still marking his place. "If a Reprobate sneezes out of turn, there must be compensation made. If a Reprobate challenges another Reprobate during the proceedings, there must be disciplinary action taken. If we're all arrested, there must be a scapegoat. Important details to be considered, Miss Lion."

It was in that uncanny moment that I felt a sneeze coming on.

"Is there anything I ought to know as a Fifth?" I asked, rubbing a finger under my nose to avoid paying whatever compensation would be demanded.

"Stand in your line, diagonal formation, and answer the question when asked. That's all."

It wasn't long before the Reprobates began to organize, the two groups separating as Night Watchman and The Boy stood in the centre, each fussing with his pistol.

"What a horrible decision I made getting out of bed," I breathed out.

Hawkes, for his sins, smiled again.

I was called over. "E of A! Where is she? There she is, with Mighty Nigel Hawkes. Come on, there's your place."

I was brought to the end of a line of Reprobates and given a bell.

"You see anyone who looks like Scotland Yard—"

"Scotland Yard?"

"—ring three times and run for it."

"Understood."

So there we were, all sorted, The Boy and Night Watchman standing back to back—the former with a cigarette in one hand while holding the pistol lightly in the other.

"Oh dear," I murmured.

"Lay aside your unease, Miss Lion," Charlie Cross said. "Not too many duels before you'll grow accustomed."

It was not, I admit, a comfort.

I glanced towards Hawkes, half turned away, still trying to read in the moonlight.

"Go on then, Hawkes," someone called.

"Put the book away!"

"Hawkes! Stand forth!"

Bless that Reprobate of a vicar, he kept reading, turned the page, and then took in at least another paragraph before closing the book with a snap and folding his arms, holding the book against his chest.

He looked at us all with calm resignation, then asked, "Temperature?"

"Balmy," Odysseus stated. "For March."

"Time?"

"Three o' one, on the dot," said Sargent.

"General temperament?"

"All in all, we've a reasonable state of mind," said Charlie Cross. "No drinks, er, not too many drinks between us."

"Moon?"

I was unceremoniously elbowed. "What?" I whispered back at Charlie.

"Moon," he said. "You must call out what sort of moon!"

"Oh." I glanced up and in my haste cried out, "Waning crescent!"

A groan went up around me.

"What's she thinking?"

"You would think it was her first duel."

"Steady on, E of A!"

Charlie Cross elbowed me again and whispered, "It's waxing."

"That is to say waxing crescent, gentlemen."

A rumble of approval.

"Sins?" Hawkes said, an eyebrow raised.

"Let's not weigh ourselves down with too many details, Hawkes," The Boy said, the end of his cigarette bouncing with his words. "Time for pistols."

"Ready!" called Mastiff. "Pace!"

The Boy and Night Watchman each sauntered a haphazard ten paces as I leaned towards Charlie Cross and said, "I don't think duels are supposed to be so…informal."

"Brace yourself!" This was again Mastiff. "Shoot!"

Night Watchman and The Boy both turned, levelled their pistols—I had *fully* expected them to be pointed towards the sky—and pulled their respective triggers.

The Boy did not flinch.

Night Watchman crumbled.

A general groan went up.

A groan!

As for myself, I may have screamed.

Hawkes bent his head, possibly asking God for patience.

"The idiot moved!" The Boy said, tossing his cigarette onto the ground and walking towards Night Watchman. All the Reprobates were rushing over.

They stood round in a circle, looking down.

"Does it hurt?" Sargent asked.

Nothing.

I, at this point, had pushed my way through and collapsed onto my knees beside Night Watchman.

"Are you—!"

But before I could finish my sentence, Night Watchman groaned and rolled onto his back, his left hand grasping his right arm. "You winged me, you idiot!"

"You shouldn't have moved!"

"I'm supposed to throw a game of Watch, Watch, She Goes at the club tomorrow!"

This began a rumble of complaints.

Horrified, I tried to remove his hand from the wound, the blood warm on my own hands, only to realise Hawkes was kneeling next to me. As collected as ever, Hawkes took a handkerchief from his pocket, pried Night Watchman's hand from the wound, and studied it.

The Boy, crouching down, lit a match so we could all see.

Hawkes frowned, fingers prodding. "A middling graze. Arm will be fine. Coat will not."

A general outcry went up as Hawkes tied the handkerchief around Night Watchman's arm and helped him sit up.

"You went down for a graze!"

"When Charlie was shot in the leg, even he balanced on his other one until he fainted!"

"My finest moment," Charlie Cross said.

"A *middling* graze," Night Watchman defended.

I almost put my head in my hands, then realising they were covered in blood, I took a deep breath and wiped them on the grass. I was shaking.

"You'll get accustomed, E of A," said a Reprobate.

"Nothing to worry over."

"'Course not."

"Leave Miss Lion alone," Hawkes ordered quietly. "Anyone who grows accustomed to shooting a gun at a person is a fool."

"Does he mean us?" someone whispered.

Silence. Then, "Hawkes the Fox has spoken!"

And general laughter as Night Watchman was helped to his feet, he and The Boy shaking hands.

"Oi! You there!" came an angry call from across the park.

"Oh dear," I said. "Is this when I ring the bell?"

"Well, boys," Sargent said. "It's every man for himself!"

They scattered, Odysseus helping Night Watchman along.

A whistle sounded as two constables began running from the opposite side of Primrose Hill.

"Miss Lion, shall we?" came Hawkes's voice. He put his hand in mine and pulled me away. I held the clapper of the bell with my fingers as we took half a dozen quick steps. And as if by magic, we were in shadow, standing quiet against the trunk of an oak tree while the two constables, puffing out their desperate breath, raced after the Reprobates, cursing all the while.

Yet there were no Reprobates to be found.

The constables disappeared into St. Crispian's.

"Hawkes?"

But he was gone.

I'd not even felt him release my fingers.

Later, I found a peppermint in my coat pocket.

When I went to church, there was nary a Reprobate to be seen.

Hawkes excepting.

Islington, however, was there—dark hair perfectly coiffed, hazel eyes clear.

"You look like you slept well," he said as I sat down beside him.

"Good morning, Islington. I did not, actually, but I thank you."

His spine as stiff as his collar, Islington—master of the side-eye—delivered his signature look. "Dare I enquire?"

Looking ahead, I gave my head a very Hawkes-like single shake. "I doubt you would wish to know."

"Keep your escapades," he said.

Truly, that is what he said.

As if I do such things all the time.

Which I don't.

Usually.

I turned to look at him and said, "An escapade or two is good for the soul. Even yours."

He managed a simultaneous scowl and guffaw.

"Yes, Islington. Yours. Now, the service is about to begin. Do behave yourself."

Hawkes's sermon was on loving one's neighbour, according to the Gospel of Mark.

Which puts me in an awkward position. Ought one love their neighbour? According to the Gospel of Emma, it's very difficult to know. My mind flashed back to the drawing room, Pierce cutting the distance between us, and his hands around my waist…

My cheeks flamed a shocking pink. I know this because Islington looked towards me, away, then back with a questioning expression. "Are you unwell, Lion?" A pause, then he murmured, "Or merely convicted by the guilt of your escapades?"

Closing my eyes and gritting my teeth, I lifted my boot and firmly planted it on Islington's shoe. The yelp was controlled, indistinguishable from the general rustle of the congregation. But I could hear it and the accompanying hiss.

"Must you have?" he managed.

I lifted a finger to my lips in solemn disapproval and pointed towards Hawkes, who was telling me that, yes, I *was* supposed to love my neighbour.

He said nothing, however, about it happening in the drawing room.

Later

> *I WAITED A WHILE TO TRY AND CATCH YOU AFTER CHURCH, BUT THEN I NEEDED TO GO HELP BEN CHAMBERS.*

I'm disappointed I missed you.
After the service, Islington and I sat in glorious argument.

REGARDING?

Violence in church. And then I asked Hawkes if his fellow Reprobate had recovered from being shot.

BLOODY HELL. IS HE ALL RIGHT?

Hawkes seemed very well.

I MEANT THE REPROBATE WHO WAS SHOT.

It was a friendly duel. "Cause pain but never maim" is the motto, apparently.

How was your time with The Pirate?

LONG—BEN NEEDED TO BE SORTED.

Did something happen to make him out of sorts?

HIS LIFE.

I HAVEN'T BEEN AVOIDING YOU.

Nor I you. I was reading in the drawing room, but then it grew so late I came upstairs.

IT IS LATE.

TOMORROW THEN?

Tomorrow

March 3rd

My reflection this morning seems young, uncertain, and—I fear—unexpectedly prudish. A very bad omen. My dress looks particularly sweet and inexperienced. My features carry nothing of what one would call sophistication. And my hair has suddenly decided to cooperate, falling into the most demure and subtle twist, nary a stray curl.

Far too prim.

Perhaps this is Divine Retribution for my having attended a duel.

Pierce was not in his studio. Neither was he in the breakfast room. Agnes provided the answer to his whereabouts when I stepped down into the kitchen.

"Why Miss, how fetching you look, styling your hair just so! My mother says that when a girl knows how to style her hair with nary a loose lock, she is become a woman."

I considered Agnes, thinking several choice things before saying, "I'm afraid there was nothing to be done."

Pouring my tea, Agnes puckered her brow. "I'm not sure what you mean?"

I sighed.

Despite the knot tied with a bow in my stomach, I drank my tea as I imagined what I would say in today's attempt to speak with Pierce.

"*I have come to discuss in a very adult manner that rather blistering kiss we shared in the drawing room. Have you any comment on the matter, or should I begin? I've drawn up a list of resulting emotions. Perhaps you've done the same?*"

We've not been in the same room since it happened. And all the minutes since feel taut. What if it's uncomfortable? Or painfully awkward? Or Pierce has realised he's made a dreadful mistake and is trying to walk it backwards and pretend that nothing occurred?

Nothing feels worse than disaster that trips over the heart.

Agnes ~~drew~~ yanked me from my thoughts with, "Mr. Pierce told me to tell you he's working at the British Museum all day. He said that if you liked the idea of a diversion, you could find him there late morning, and the two of you could go for tea. Or he would discuss business this evening."

Business.

Business?

"Did he, Agnes? And how did he sound?"

"Sound, Miss?"

"Yes, did he sound as if he wished, that is, *expected* me to go to the museum, or was the suggestion made from…moral duty?"

Agnes, having just toasted a muffin on the skillet, was generous with the butter. (Too generous if our fate be the gutter.) "I don't understand, Miss. My mother says one's moral duty is as plain as day."

I closed my eyes. "His tone, Agnes?"

"A bit grumbly, it being early. Do ya ken? But after breakfast he came back to say, 'Make certain Miss Lion knows she's under no obligation.' He then said, 'Pull yourself together, Niall.' Which is how I knew he wasn't talking to me. My name's Agnes." She placed my breakfast in front of me. I opened my eyes to find her staring. "Miss Lion, are you ill?"

"No, Agnes. Thank you."

And so I've returned to my garret in a noble attempt to study half the morning away. Skipping over *Mixing in Society*, I've reached for Plutarch, thinking that with twelve great men to distract, who needs to think of one walking about the British Museum?

How Things Stand in Ancient Greece

Theseus is heading to Athens, having just discovered he is the son of Aegeus, King of Athens. A ship was offered. All he need do was travel to the coast, get on a ship, and sail the Mediterranean (or would it have been the Aegean?) to the famed city. (How is it I don't have an atlas on hand?)

But did the great Theseus accept such accommodation?

No.

He decided to travel by way of the Peloponnese—filled with cutthroats and brigands—because he wished to prove himself the equal of Hercules.

Self-assured, indeed.

Perhaps he had a tendency towards seasickness?

Ah, look at the time. I leave for the British Museum with great hopes that, when I return, Theseus arrives in Athens in one piece.

I've just glanced to see if my hair has recovered its usual, unruly form. Unfortunately, no. I look a vestal fashion plate. I've even tried to tug a few strands out of place. To no avail. The demure curls only add to the overall effect.

Time now to fetch my coat and gloves.

Later

Pierce was right, I did enjoy my walk across London. The city was full of movement and the sort of noise that makes a day stand on its own two feet. Then I arrived before the museum, and the pillars looked so smug I almost turned right around.

A clear sign I was not quite myself.

I usually adore a well-constructed pillar.

I digress.

Uncertain which hall of the museum exhibits brooding photographers, I allowed myself to wander. After taking in an array of Greek statues and downright gawking at the Rosetta Stone (imagine being intelligent enough to decipher such a thing), I girded my loins (awful phrase, that) and asked a guide where one Mr. Pierce, erstwhile photographer, might be.

Enquiry made, I was led beyond the exhibits, through a corridor where a collection was being sorted, and then into a room with several windows, a table in the centre.

There stood Pierce, studying a piece of pottery in his hand.

My lungs tightened.

Pierce looked farther away than he really was, as if I were considering him from the outside of a window. For a brief moment, I saw a stranger. A man who catches the eye. Dark hair, tall and capable, quicksilver eyes, features sharp and dangerous. Very much the avenging angel. Admittedly, my heart pounded like an inconsistent drum.

He looked up. A second passed before any response played on his face. Then the lines of half a smile pushed up, eyes narrowing in uncertainty.

I could feel an identical mask on my own face and the tension of the drawing room all over. Like static and thunder. As often happens when confronted with an opaque situation, words rushed to my tongue, their weight building before spilling over into nonsense.

I meant to say, "You appear to be busy."

I meant to say, "Good morning."

I said, "You appear to be morning."

Tragic.

My perception of self includes a belief in general capability.

In that moment, I was questioning said belief.

"Good, that is," I rushed. "And it is morning. Good morning. You are…here."

Pierce's uncertain, slanted smile relaxed. He looked down at the shard in his hand, then back up at my face. It was so very charming.

"You seem anxious," Pierce said.

"Not at all. Yes. Perhaps I'm not feeling quite myself. I've been… Ever since…"

His expression stilled.

"I didn't mean…"

"Emma," he said, "take a breath. How about we go for a drink or tea or something. We can…moot."

He then took his own advice and took a breath.

As did I.

"That would be lovely," I said, stepping closer to the table he stood behind. "What have you been asked to photograph?"

"Newly acquired pieces for the Roman collection. I—"

Just as he was to explain, someone walked into the room from a door to my left.

A woman. Holding a stack of papers to her chest.

"Mr. Pierce, I have asked you to please wear the gloves provided when handling the artifacts." Her tone was one of studious long-suffering.

My eyes moved to the unused gloves at the far end of the table.

Pierce set the pottery back on the table. "My hands are clean."

The woman pushed a pair of spectacles up the bridge of her nose. "They are clean to the measure that you do not have dirt or ink on your fingers, but the human body releases oils, and I try to keep the artifacts in pristine condition."

Pierce gave a nod and reached for the gloves. When he spoke, he did not sound contrite. "Forgive my absent-mindedness."

"Only use the gloves," she stated. "Please."

After a pause, Pierce replied, "Certainly."

I tried to keep from smiling by pinning my cheek between my teeth.

A tense exchange over a piece of ancient Roman pottery was exactly what I needed.

I could feel my feet beneath me again.

She was younger than I'd first thought. A year or two below thirty? Plain, not due to her face but her clothes and how she'd arranged her simply braided hair, which was blonde, with a streak of white above one of her temples. She stood an inch taller than me. Her glasses nearly distracted from them altogether, but she had large, cornflower blue eyes. After a look in my direction, she tilted her gaze back to Pierce.

"You are not to have visitors while working."

Pierce's response was to stare in silent challenge.

"She is not on the approved list," the young woman pressed, indicating me with a sharp incline of her head. "Unless I missed the name?"

"Didn't you satisfy your urge to badger me earlier with those tiles?"

"Those particular Roman tiles can only be shifted by Dr. Green or myself."

"And yet I'm the one who knows best how to work with the light."

"You can direct, Mr. Pierce, but you cannot touch. Do you need me to show you how to put on those gloves?"

"Yes, please," came Pierce's sarcastic response, "as I've never come across the invention before."

"I'm beginning to wonder."

My spirits rose even further. Clearly these two had locked horns more than once. Her brittle maneuvering in combat, with his disbelief and clenched jaw.

Highly enjoyable.

A lock of my hair even loosed itself.

The young woman returned her spectacled gaze to me.

"Mr. Pierce, won't you introduce us?"

"Miss Sarah Kingsnorth—it is miss, isn't it?" Pierce replied with an edge. She delivered a look of steady irritation. "This is Miss Emma Lion. Miss Kingsnorth is in Acquisitions. We've worked together before."

"Miss Kingsnorth," I said, holding out my hand. "A pleasure. Truly."

"Miss Lion," she replied in her straightforward tone. We shook hands. "Unfortunately, the only name on Mr. Pierce's list is one Benjamin Chambers. Your name has not been approved."

"I can't say I'm too put out by that," I replied. "I'm not likely to trust myself with a two-thousand-year-old piece of…anything."

"We were about to leave, in any case," Pierce said. "I'll be gone an hour, then return."

Miss Kingsnorth raised an eyebrow above her brass spectacles. "Mr. Pierce, I did tell you the timing of this commission was sensitive."

"You did."

"So perhaps you stay, in hopes that we might finish within the week. We have a great many artifacts to catalogue and only so many hours of daylight."

"I'm aware," Pierce stated, "and have taken all that into consideration. I have something important—"

"Pierce," I interrupted, "our business can wait for another time."

"Wonderful," Miss Kingsnorth said.

Pierce flattened the line of his mouth. "I know how to time my work, Miss Kingsnorth."

She tightened her grip on the stack of papers she was holding. "Mr. Pierce, so do I, and I'll thank you to stay. Good day."

She turned and walked out of the room.

His eyes followed her. "She's a peach."

"I like her," I said, with a brighter smile than the one I brought with me.

Pierce's laugh was unconvincing.

"In another life," I said, gazing at the artifacts on the table, "I would *be* her."

"Heaven forbid."

"So it seems."

"I'm sorry to have asked you to walk all this way," he said, looking at the work before him.

But I wasn't. And I told him so. "I'll wander the museum and swoon. Over artifacts, that is. Not…"

He looked at me.

~~Unsure what to say, I stepped up to him and, standing on my tiptoes, kissed his cheek.~~

That is what I considered doing.

Instead, I said, "It may be best we speak later, in any case. Without you being pressed by work. I… I don't want to make a mess of anything."

He tapped his finger on the table before him, his gaze still fixed on my face. "Nor do I."

"It's settled."

He made a gesture of stubborn agreement.

"I'll ask Agnes to keep supper warm?"

"Yes, then we can— Ah, dammit. Ben Chambers asked for my help this evening."

"Speaking of your assistant."

"Occasional assistant. You see, he's had a large order of stock come in, but he fell and injured himself, and I—" He lifted a hand in defeat.

"Of course you should be helping him," I replied. "And it was nice to see you, nonetheless."

An apologetic smile. "You as well."

I left. Feeling him watch me leave.

The Egyptian Hall calmed my nerves.

Upon returning to St. Crispian's—decidedly not thinking how well Pierce looked with Roman pottery strewn about him—I stopped by Everett's on King Henry's Road and bought half a dozen pastries. Then, walking to Traitors Road, I set about trying to find the location of one Night Watchman. For if one cannot discuss a kiss surrounded by antiquities, one ought to console the wounded after a duel.

A given, I should think.

It is mostly men who live on Traitors Road, and many a man I did see, but nary a Reprobate.

I walked up and down.

Twice.

Several hats were tipped in my direction.

Finally, I stepped inside The Cleopatra. Gibbs looked up.

"Miss Lion," he welcomed. A far cry different from the greeting I received last July.

"Gibbs." I smiled. "Do you know if Hawkes is in his room, perchance?"

A shrug. "No idea."

"He's at the church," a man called from ~~his cups~~ his table.

"There you go. Scottie says he's at the church," Gibbs repeated.

"Thank you. Much obliged, er, Scottie."

I turned and nearly ran square into a man coming in through the door. After a badly coordinated dance, we were both free; he to his pint, I to the church.

Entering, I looked about the empty chapel and then towards the old vestry.

It was possibly a very foolish thing, speaking with Hawkes, as he does scrutinize the soul. But sacrifices must be made so one can do a little good in the world. And the pastries were not going to eat themselves.

I knocked on the closed door.

"Come in, Emma," Hawkes said. I frowned—Hawkes's uncanny talents on full display—and went in.

Hawkes was not at his desk. He was not near the window. No, he was standing with his back against the north wall of the room directly across from the door, his desk and chair abandoned to his left. Arms crossed, head bowed, eyes closed, right foot lifted so as to be anchored against the wall at his back.

"Hello, Hawkes."

A nod. But he neither raised his head nor opened his eyes.

I sat in the chair in front of his desk, placing the boxed pastries near a few written out pages (a sermon?), before I settled back and linked my gloved hands across my lap. Hawkes, his expression pulled tight for a few concentrated seconds, released himself from whatever prayer or contemplation or worry in which he was engaged. Pushing himself from the wall with his right foot and rubbing his eyes, he ran a hand absently through his hair while claiming his own chair on the other side of the desk.

He looked across at me. "Good day?"

It was a question, not a wish.

"Always the hope," I replied, trying not to tip my hand by thinking of Pierce. "Might I enquire after Night Watchman?"

A shadowed smile crossed Hawkes's face. "Up all night at a club, if Striker is a reliable source."

Really?

I took umbrage. "Here I was picturing him languishing in bed! At dear expense, I've purchased pastries. I've practically turned myself into the Good Samaritan, Hawkes."

Hawkes looked at me with his cloudless blue eyes. "There's the rub," Hawkes said. "To add insult to injury, Night Watchman did not return to St. Crispian's this morning. I believe he's in Mayfair, at a cousin's house."

I frowned. "Day-old pastries are not ideal."

"Few things are."

"Then, Hawkes, we find ourselves with only one thing to do." I opened the box and slid it equidistant between the two of us. "Shall we?"

It was all approval, the way he smiled.

March 4th

AS IT HAPPENS, I AM BOOKED SOLID ALL WEEK. BUT I AM FREE THE EARLIER HOURS OF THE EVENING.

So you will be at dinner?

YES. IF THAT'S ALL RIGHT.

Preferred. Would that you could stay longer.

A CLIENT HAS INVITED ME TO HIS CLUB. I ACCEPTED BEFORE WE FOUND IT SO BLOODY IMPOSSIBLE TO SPEAK WITH ONE ANOTHER. I'D THROW HIM OVER, BUT A PROFESSIONAL REPUTATION IS HOW I EARN MY KEEP.

Will you be regaled with hunting stories?

GAMBLING, MORE LIKE.

THIS EVENING, THEN?

This evening.

Later

I've been sitting in the garret window, telling Tybalt about Theseus sailing to the island of Crete to defeat the Minotaur. Because when earth-shaking personal occurrence meets inevitable yet unachievable confrontation, it seems only right to hide among the Greeks.

They managed to get through many an eventuality.

We shall see if I can do the same.

And now something is happening down on Whereabouts Lane.

Removers have arrived at houses number 34 and 36. They seem to be emptying both places with abandon.

Wonderful, as Theseus, Tybalt, and I could use the diversion.

It's just shy of a ruckus—the doors flung open, a man I recognise as a neighbour I've seen buying stamps at the Reed and Rite running frantically between them, giving instructions. His hair is uncombed, and his necktie is wilted, depressed as silk can be.

What, I wonder, is all this about?

Later

What have I done that is worth the universe meddling in my and Pierce's personal affairs? And from what realm is the meddler sent? Dear me, it was awful. Tragic enough, the way I fussed before the mirror, attempting to find something that was appropriate but not too formal. (What a ruinous thing a kiss can be.) I've been known to arrive at dinner wearing a skirt and blouse or one of my faded dresses. Pierce has certainly witnessed every variation on the theme. And yet there I was, frantically holding everything Madame Tasset has ever made up and frowning at my reflection. Thinking I ought to look like a mature individual, I decided to risk something formal and chose my sea green gown. As if that were normal of me to wear in my own dining room.

It is not.

(A peek inside the pages of *Mixing in Society* confirms I am Most Decidedly Failing the expectations for a young woman of my age. Alas. Alack.)

Agnes only had a moment to help me into my dress before rushing back down to the kitchen. "Oh, Miss, I couldn't be happier. The Society of St. Crispian's Senior Servants promotes such ideals. I think I smell the fish burning!" She was gone before I could look in the mirror and plainly see I had made the wrong decision. Knowing I would never extract Agnes from her rightful kingdom minutes before the meal was served, I tried to manage the job myself.

It is, I'm afraid, a gown not easily managed on one's own.

I was trapped.

(Why is Parian not a woman?)

There was nothing to do but own up to the foolish impulse.

My cheeks burned scarlet as I attempted to arrange my hair. I placed the lion pendant around my neck.

I feared it was going to be a catastrophe.

And it was.

Only not the sort I'd been anticipating.

When I passed Parian in the hall, he eyed my dress in question.

"Someone in this house must uphold standards," I stated as I marched into the dining room.

Sitting in his place at the table was Pierce—not having changed into evening clothes as it is a Thing We Do Not Do—reading a newspaper. He lifted a hand to his chin, in thought.

~~It nearly did me in~~.

He looked up. And stood. Eyebrows tilted in question. "Are we supposed to be formal this evening?"

I sighed. "This was my rather embarrassing attempt to properly, well, I thought wearing something nice would add solemnity, or something… Then I panicked and wished to change, but Agnes was gone, and I was trapped."

"May I help you with your chair?"

I waved him off. "No," I grumbled, sinking into said chair and—pulling my skirts out of the way—shifting forward in a crab-like manner. The entire process was much slower than it ought to have been and provided ample time to reflect on the adult I have become.

Pierce grinned, sat, and began folding his newspaper and setting it aside. He then looked at me again. "Solemnity was the aim?"

"Obviously"—I blew a lock of hair away from my face—"it isn't working. No, do *not* laugh. I'm embarrassed enough as it is."

"You're not managing solemnity, I'm afraid, but charm, certainly."

"Yes, well." I took a breath. "A nice idea, in theory."

It was then that Parian entered, and we began our meal.

Pierce and I were too polite as we began to eat, asking after one another's day.

Very domestic.

Flat.

Uncomfortable.

It wasn't going to do and we both knew it.

"I think—"

"Shouldn't we—?"

We smiled, mine accompanied with a resigned sigh, his with a softer sound.

"Please," he gave me the floor.

I pressed my lips together and fussed with my napkin, then I opened my mouth to say—

The door also opened.

Cousin Archibald walked in.

He was carrying a book, our missing solemnity comically found in his person as he puffed his chest and walked the length of the table, sitting in the far chair and looking first at Pierce then myself.

I cleared my throat. "Cousin Archibald, have you not already dined?"

A nod. "And after weighty consideration, I've decided we would benefit from a reading this evening. As we all share the same roof, I feel it imperative we be on the same page, as it were, regarding the silkworm."

Pierce stilled.

"The silkworm, cousin?" said I.

Archibald raised both eyebrows and opened his book as if lecturing at the Sorbonne. "*Chapter One: The History of the Silkworm. As with any story of love and betrayal, the history of the silkworm is as exhilarating as it is moving. All experts can agree that...*"

Pierce and I looked at one another across the table in what I wish could be labelled joint disbelief but was resignation borne of what was becoming painful experience.

"*...silk is composed of both reverence and sensuality...*"

Blood rushed into my cheeks, and Pierce, dropping his gaze from my face, lifted his fork—more weapon now than silverware—and stabbed a carrot, eating it stoically. I did my best to follow. No longer hungry as I suffered through descriptions of the ideal climate for the silkworm being compared to a bedchamber for the innocent bride.

"*...she is to be coaxed gently...*"

It was too much for my inexperience.

All appetite gone, I abandoned my silverware on my plate, pushed it away, and rested my elbows before me, hands clasped in the attitude of prayer. Pierce, gripping his glass of wine as if it could save him, leaned back. Our gazes locked—all thought of possible discussion having fled before the simple, painful truth that we were captives of a worm.

There was an attempt made.

"Cousin, I really believe we should—"

"*The folds of such a garment are an apt comparison to sunlight, the ebb and flow of an unsullied lake, and excellent penmanship.*"

It was painful.

Torture of the keenest cruelty.

And so I did what any honourable prisoner would do: made way for my fellow captive to escape.

"Mr. Pierce," I said quickly when Cousin Archibald paused for breath, "knowing you have another obligation, let me excuse you now so that you won't be late."

"What, what?!"

Bless Pierce. He did not wish to leave me languishing in the dank, damp prison of *The History of the Silkworm.*

I widened my eyes in the international signal for: *Save yourself before it's too late!*

Giving a single nod, Pierce placed his napkin on the table and reached for his newspapers, looking at me when he said, "Thank you, Miss Lion, for the enlightening and diverse experiences I find at your table." Pierce then nodded to Cousin Archibald. "Mr. Flat." He stood. "I wish you both a good evening."

"But the mating rituals! What what what?!"

Pierce, however, was ~~out the door~~ swiftly out the door.

Later

YOU FELL ON YOUR SWORD. I OFFER MY THANKS.

I refuse to confess that chapter three was, in fact, very interesting.

March 5th

It is the one-year anniversary of my arrival in St. Crispian's.
What glorious assumptions I had for my life.
Stepping off the train at St. Pancras.
That beautiful tang of freedom falling forward.
Financial ease. A large library. Calm after the storm.
And here I am, one year later…

A year is such an odd packet of time. It seems so ordered: a dozen months, a handful of seasons. Deceptively even. Make no mistake, it will go awry every which way. Balance? Impossible. Control? Not worth mentioning the word. Some days cling and others run, many shifting just enough to incommode but give no great variety. And then out of the pedestrian blue comes an explosion which reduces all plans to smithereens. The reward for making it through? Getting to do it again.

For good or ill.

When I weigh the last twelve months, I affirm my year tipped towards the good, which may mean I'm either a blind optimist or one who values the profound mingled with the absurd.

Or both.

If I were to summarize the last year in a single dash across the page? However ill-fated in the fiduciary arts, I am blessed in my friends.

So be it.

For now.

Once I find my Dissolute Viscount, I will be flush with both friends and funds.

And one year later my journal is ink-stained and fat, the binding stretched to the delightful ease of a book that has been opened over and over. Due to The Great Burning of 1882, it is now one of the few written artifacts of my life. I am uncertain how many weeks will consume the final pages, but with my (some might say) inane desire to record my days in profusion, something must be done.

Off to The Hound I go to scout out an eventual replacement. I wish myself luck.

Later

So skilled is Ben Chambers in incivility, I've decided it is his one divine gift.

I'd no more than pushed through the door of The Hound—mistletoe removed, brass bell in place—when I was greeted with a firm, "No."

I glanced towards the counter, then about the room, my eyes finding him up the bookshelf ladder, managing the top shelf.

"I—"

"No," he snapped, looking down, his eyepatch askew as if he'd hastily forced it into place.

"Mr. Chambers, you don't even know what I'm going to ask you."

"Are you selling raffle tickets?"

"No."

"Do you represent any sort of society?"

"I— No, of course not."

"Are you here to purchase an item?"

I brightened. "In very fact, I am."

"No," he stated, turning back to his work.

"But—"

"This is a gentlemen's shop."

"Yes, and—"

"No exceptions."

"Balderdash."

He glanced up. That is to say, down.

"Balderdash," I stated again, giving my confidence a tonal flourish. "The Hound is a shop that sells items often *used* by gentlemen. Now, if you were to try and make the argument that gentlemen are, indeed, your only custom, then I would argue that you've sold to Mr. Flat on more than one occasion. Which leads me to believe that what you mean is this shop is exclusively for males. And while I find the idea preposterous that magnifying glasses, books about foreign places, and numismatic pursuits are solely male interests, I also argue that you sold me a dictionary."

"A damaged dictionary."

"Yes, well, I think we can both agree that damaged items still hold value."

He stilled.

It was then I grasped what I had said and to whom I had said it.

Chambers tugged at his eyepatch from unconscious habit, balancing on his one whole leg. "That's the biggest pile of horse—"

"Mr. Chambers." I held up my hand. "Please. I wish to buy a journal—a simple, well-crafted journal—as I will soon have completed this one." I gripped my journal, as if for protection. "The Reed and Rite did not have the *right* one, and I thought—"

"You thought wrong. Go away."

I quirked my mouth to the side and let out a deep breath. "Then I will resort to less-than-noble means."

He laughed. "Like what?"

"I'm not above manipulation. In this instance." I looked heavenward a moment. "Well, in this and a few other instances, but I only use it in dire—or justified—circumstances such as this."

"Manipulation does not work on me."

"It works on everybody."

"I'd like to see you try." Such dripping challenge, I couldn't wait to prove him wrong.

"Surely consideration—"

"I have none."

"Dignity requires—"

"Dignity doesn't exist."

I frowned. "All right. I invoke the name of Niall Pierce."

"What?"

"You heard me. I come as a…a friend of Niall Pierce, and as his landlady, requesting your help."

He shook his head, but when he spoke, there was a catch in his voice. "That's your grand invocation?"

"Pierce would want you to help me. I'm certain."

The Pirate's mouth looked like it had been sewn together, he pressed it so tight. Half a shake of the head, a slam of a book back into its place, and he went about the tricky business of easing himself down the ladder, careful of his peg leg. (I was, it must be admitted, impressed.) Once on the floor, perspiring for his pains, he limped past me without a word, seeking refuge behind the counter.

Although there were no visible marks from his fall, Chambers did seem frayed around the edges. Vulnerable, perhaps.

A thing which I forgot to remind myself when he snapped, "Is that it?"

"Pardon?"

"Is that the journal you're replacing?"

"Yes."

He held out a hand. An expectant hand.

As if I would casually toss it across the counter.

I gripped my journal tighter.

Ben Chambers absently lifted his fingers to the spider web of scars on the side of his face. "It doesn't bother me in the least for you to take your custom elsewhere."

He folded his arms.

I planted my feet. "I wish to purchase a journal here."

"But you won't allow me to do my work."

It was ridiculous and I told him so, followed by, "Is not your work to sell the goods of your shop?"

"My work," he argued, "is to curate. I curate my shop. I curate my displays. I create careful collections. This includes books of all kinds. I," he placed a hand on his chest, "am perfectly happy turning you away. Suit yourself. If you'd like to buy a new umbrella or a stationery set"—he flicked his hand as if he were brushing away a swarm of mayflies—"be my guest. But I will not allow a book *of any sort* to leave my shop if it is one sliver below the expectations I have set for myself. So you can either hand me that abomination of personal indulgence or leave my shop. Which will it be?"

If anyone else had delivered such a speech, I would have been moved. I would have raised my hands in applause and said, "Bravo! Standards at last."

The Pirate, however, had irked my less-than-sterling character.

"Then I expect Something Exceptional," I said in a clipped manner, setting my journal firmly on the counter between us.

Abomination of personal indulgence, indeed.

The Pirate waited long enough to give himself the advantage, then reached for it.

My stomach tightened.

He picked up my journal, the side of his thumb moving along the worn, black leather of the bottom edge. Turning it over in his hands, Chambers studied width, height, the simple pattern of three raised lines across the back of the spine. He tipped it up to look at the top then the bottom, finally running his finger along the ink-stained edges of the pages themselves. He moved to open the book.

"Certainly not!" I cried, my hand shooting out to reclaim my property. He leaned back enough for my fingertips to miss the journal balanced expertly in his hands.

"Do give me the courtesy of treating me as a professional," he growled.

"Yes, but that— I haven't— I don't— There are a good many things written there."

Chambers blew out of his nose in amusement. "Obviously."

"Is it so ridiculous a wish to not want to share my private reflections with a stranger?"

"Why would I *want* to read them?" he said forcefully. "What could you possibly have written that would not be a waste of my time? We all have criteria, Miss Lion, and I am convinced your scribblings are far below mine."

My eyebrows knit as if tugged sharply with a thread. "I do not claim to be a modern Pepys by *any* stretch of the imagination, but if you envision that what you hold in your hand is merely accounts of afternoon tea and scandal page gossip, you would be grossly in error. Seeing as how All Hell Breaks Loose in my life on a regular basis, I find the record in your hand to be vastly entertaining. In parts." It was here I faltered atop my metaphorical soapbox. "I do record what was had for tea on occasion. Which, I wager, even Samuel Pepys must have done from time to time."

The Pirate had listened to my impassioned defence with no reaction.

And then, "So you've not actually read Pepys."

"What I've read and not read is a sore subject," I answered, thinking of my father's worn *Pepys*, now who knows where.

He opened my journal.

Like a jealous God waiting for inevitable sin, I watched the line of Ben Chambers's sight and my journal with equal hawkishness. But Chambers wasn't paying attention to the words on the page. No. He began by taking a single page and rubbing it between his fingers. His acerbic expression could not altogether cover the calculations of his trade, and for a moment, the sooty, filth-covered window that is his usual dour expression was wiped clean enough to let the light through. Interest. Challenge. Art.

After considering the paper, he fanned the pages and studied how they fell. Words and names and exclamations written in my own hand were visible as he flipped the pages back and forth. He paid no mind. After all this, seemingly satisfied, he opened to the date of the very first entry.

Here his eyes did linger.

March 5th

I've arrived in London without incident. There are few triumphs in my recent life, but I count this as one. My existence of the last three years has been nothing but incident. The train billowed its way into St. Pancras Station five minutes early…

I flung a hand across the counter and covered the page.

"Excuse me!" I said with indignation. "Were you *reading*?"

Ben Chambers adjusted his eyepatch. "Trains don't billow," he said.

My mouth dropped open as I gave him a disbelieving stare. "Firstly, that is very, very bad form of you to have done! Secondly, of course trains don't billow, but their smoke most certainly does!"

"Then why didn't you write the smoke of the train billowed?"

"Because I was painting a picture."

Chambers grunted. "Paint it right or don't paint at all."

"You…are a horrible human being."

"Finally," Ben Chambers smiled meanly, "something in which we have perfect accord. How long will it take you to finish…this?"

"Well, I'm not sure. A month?"

"When you've a dozen pages remaining, you can leave this here at

The Hound, and I'll see what I can do."

He tossed my journal onto the counter and turned away as if our business was concluded.

I stood fuming.

He began sorting something or other behind him.

I cleared my throat.

I cleared my throat again.

He turned around to face me. "Was there something else?"

"Why would I ever consider leaving my journal with you?"

The question did not warrant an expression that made me feel like an imbecile.

However, that is what I received.

Accompanied with, "Because if I am going to do a job, I do it *properly*. This"—he tapped his finger on the worn, black cover—"is hideous. It needs to be rebound. The paper, I will grant, is good quality. Very good. Which is why I agreed to this ordeal in the first place—"

"Ordeal?"

"—and have not escorted you from the premises. But if you think I'll let this monstrosity remain, you have come to the wrong shop. You need a custom binding, one for all your journals going forward. I wish to think on the design."

"You've already given me a custom binding."

He recoiled. Which I thought was *a bit much*. "That binding is for your library. Unless you are claiming this"—he picked up my journal—"an equal to Dante, Shakespeare, and Dr. Johnson."

I flushed.

He continued, "A personal journal should be just that, *personal*. With a thoughtful, bespoke binding."

"I can't argue with that," I graced.

He glared. "So your current journal will be rebound. It's non-negotiable."

"Can't I wait as you rebind it?"

"It isn't my preferred method," Chambers stated.

"My life isn't always my preferred method, and yet here I am, day in and day out."

And then, surprise of all surprises, he laughed. And it wasn't too sharp or too clipped. "I have work to do," he said, flipping through the ledger on the counter. "Go scribble away in your little book about things you believe to be conundrums."

"Odious of you, after we two actually achieved a pleasant moment."

"Maddening, isn't it?" he replied.

"Quite."

Then he squinted his ~~eyes~~ eye in thought and ordered, "Open your journal to New Year's Day."

"Is that a command?"

"Do you want me to help you?" he snarled.

I opened my journal to the first of the year. "Don't you dare read another word."

But Mr. Chambers wasn't looking at what I'd written on the page, he was studying the binding. Then the man—if it can be believed—said, "Well done."

I am not a creature that minds praise; however, I wasn't certain what I'd done to deserve it from St. Crispian's resident misanthrope. "Well done how?" I asked suspiciously.

"You split the year between signatures." He was pleased.

"Meaning?"

"Do you know what a signature is?"

"I assume you're not meaning the writing of one's name?"

The slow shake of his head was more displeasure than correction.

The man is such a snob.

"See how your journal is made up of a series of folded sections sewn together? Each of these sections is a signature. You—miraculously—ended the year between signatures. This means I can bind *1883* as one journal. This second journal will comprise your writings of *1884*."

"But how can you be sure *1884* won't be shorter or longer?"

"Miss Lion," he looked up at me with condescension, "do I tell you how to go about your business?"

I frowned at him. "I don't think you can wholly claim you never have, but for the sake of this insulting exercise, I will answer no."

"Do me the courtesy of believing I know exactly what I am doing."

"Hmm," I answered in my best Islington. "Funny, you invoking courtesy."

"Come back when you've only a dozen pages left. Bring that…"

"Abomination of Indulgence. Yes, I know."

Chambers delivered me one of his jaded smiles. "We understand one another. Good day."

"Good day."

I left.

My reward for having endured with grace under fire was to return home and find a freshly printed, perfectly folded copy of St. Crispian's *Gazette* on the sideboard in the hall. The headline of the first story read, "*Traitors Road exceeds 100 bachelors! Ought an exterminator be called?*" and with great satisfaction, I settled in Hawkes's chair (nearer the fire) to enjoy the fruits of my labours. (I mean the receiving of the *Gazette*. I've absolutely nothing to do with how many bachelors live on Traitors Road. At least, not that I'm aware.)

Later

Pierce has been occupied in his studio all day. Even through tea. Afterward, he hastily changed his clothing and slipped a note (found later) through the wall.

> *I'VE BEEN SCOUTED TO TAKE THE PORTRAITS OF AN ENTIRE GENTLEMEN'S SOCIETY. THE OVERTURES ARE THIS EVENING OVER DINNER AND CARDS. IT'S PROFITABLE WORK. I LOOKED FOR YOU EARLIER, BUT YOU WERE OUT. BAD LUCK.*
>
> *SPEAKING OF DINNER, ISLINGTON HAS INVITED US TOMORROW, IF YOU'RE NOT ENGAGED. HE ASKED US FOR EIGHT O'CLOCK. I WOULD NEED TO MEET YOU THERE.*
>
> *I'M SORRY TO HAVE MISSED YOU THIS AFTERNOON.*

I've just replied with,

> *Dinner with Islington sounds like an improvement over our last. Let us pray he does not own* The History of the Silkworm.

And so the inevitable has arrived.

Dinner at Islington's.

The four of us together for the first time since *Late Evening in the Drawing Room with Rain Falling Outside.*

Also known as *Pierce and I having Kissed.*

Also known as *I would much rather have spoken with Pierce before facing the four of us together.*

I am, admittedly, nervous. Nervous the memory of it will be burning on my face. Nervous that Pierce and I have tampered with something rare—that blissful, golden alchemy—and only curse follows.

What if we've…

What if they…

What if things are irrevocably changed?

March 6th

Last night, while pulling at my worry like a loose thread, I witnessed something peculiar. There was a pile of rubbish placed on the pavement in front of number 34. I'd assumed the man living there meant for the removers to…well, remove it in the morning. But as I was worrying over ~~the four of us at Islington's~~ noble thoughts such as the charitable organizations which must be supported, the door of number 34 opened.

From my vantage point, it appeared to be a door in some fey world for the way the light spilled onto the lane. And then my neighbour, his shadow mimicking every panicked action, rushed down the steps to the rubbish pile and pulled out a framed painting that had been obscured by a few tattered cushions. Holding the portrait before him, he uttered what seemed to be a fervent apology and then, arms wrapped full round, pressed his cheek against the canvas.

Tybalt, hearing the cries, had leapt up from the floor and peered out of the window. His feline tendency towards discretion at all costs did not approve of the spectacle. He was, however, very drawn to the rat-shaped shadow that darted from the rubbish pile.

Now, this morning, the rubbish pile is gone, and I find myself ~~mildly~~ reasonably curious as to what is happening across the lane.

It *has* been a few months since I've paid a visit to Mrs. Morrow of the Watchers of Whereabouts Lane. Perhaps I ought to ask her what she knows.

Later

That did not go as anticipated.

Silly. To not have expected a tax on my own life for enquiring about that of another.

Alas.

When I went to see Mrs. Morrow, I was shown into the parlour by a sharp-eyed maid.

Mrs. Morrow greeted me with, "Good morning, Miss Lion."

"Mrs. Morrow," I said in return.

"Please sit."

I did.

"Do you come here on business?"

"I do. Of sorts."

"You want to know what is happening with 34 and 36 Whereabouts Lane?"

"The houses directly across from Lapis Lazuli."

"Yes. The Happy-Sad houses."

I leaned forward. "Pardon?"

"Those two houses have a history of hosting either the very happy or terribly sad. You noticed Mr. Bray, who has occupied *both* these five years, I'm sure?"

"The gentleman who has forgotten to comb his hair these last few days?"

"Yes. He has extraordinary teeth."

"I hadn't noticed. Strange, as I like to think I'm more-than-usually observant."

"Everyone believes so." She smiled congenially. "And almost everyone is wrong."

"Oh."

"As for Mr. Bray, the back and forth was too much. Elated one month, desperate the next. He blamed his living in both houses. We gifted him a basket from the Watchers of Whereabouts, poor man."

"Of course." I accepted a cup of tea. "But why did he not live in only one of the two?"

"Sometimes we are too sad to trust in anything, even happiness," Mrs. Morrow replied.

I gave a slow nod. "Do you know who intends to take his place? Or will the houses remain empty?"

"I've heard 34 will be taken by a niece."

"A niece? His niece?"

"All I know is she is *someone's* niece. She has a husband and two small children. They return to this part of the country in six weeks or so. Number 36 has yet to be let."

"Are any cats coming with said niece?" I enquired on Tybalt's behalf.

"A dog, if it's any consolation."

I sighed. "It will be to some."

"The husband's work seems to be the law."

"How litigious."

"Quite," she replied. "From what I understand, there is money. A medium, round, pleasant sum that keeps their accounts as plump as a baby. He works, but there is no scraping by."

"Lovely dream."

"She comes from more money than he, a healthy dowry, but they are from the same class, which is often important."

"I can imagine." I wished to ask how she could possibly know so much about the future tenants of our lane, but refrained on the grounds that I wasn't certain I wished to hear the answer.

We finished our tea in companionable silence as we looked out of the window.

Upon finishing, I set down my cup and saucer and said, "Thank you for the visit, Mrs. Morrow."

"At tat tat," she said as I moved to stand, as if practicing to be a drum major.

"The Information gathered at this house comes with a price, Miss Lion."

I swallowed. "A price?"

"We watchers work hard. This sort of knowledge does not feed itself."

In my experience, gossip usually does, but I said nothing except, "What can I do for you?"

"There are rumours. Would you please illuminate one of them?"

I answered with a wary, "Illuminate?"

"Something about a studio door propped open after business hours, something about words exchanged with a duke after church services, and something about a midnight tussle with the fountain, or was it with the vicar? I don't recall which." She placed her hands primly—one over the other—on her lap and looked at me, expectant. "I should hate to get any of it wrong."

Fool, Emma, you be.

You know you live the sort of life that would not bear up well under scrutiny.

Of any kind.

Considering the current happenings in my relationship with

Pierce, I thought it best to leave that door untouched. An argument with Islington could be reported most Sundays we are both in attendance, but I suspect she was speaking of February, when I ran after him and yelled his Christian name. Loudly. In the street.

As for Hawkes and the fountain, I've been rather pleased it has not yet come to light. Until now, it seems. I almost selected the incident with the fountain, thinking that surely Hawkes could weather such gossip.

But then I hesitated.

Mrs. Morrow is an expert in her field. Had she provided the three options as a test, a way of marking what I would avoid? Do the women of Whereabouts carry such Machiavellian tendencies? (I fear they might.) And so I decided I would say something about Pierce, most dangerous piece on the board, to throw her off the trail. And then thought, what if she expects me to defend my most vulnerable position? Does that leave me to settle on Islington? But will she be waiting for me to choose the middle of the road?

The only option was to admit, thereby dismissing, all three.

"I am afraid you have stumbled on three things which did happen. Mr. Pierce, under Mr. Flat's dedicated and silk-robed observation, needed a door—his being held for ransom by the Whereabouts Lane Committee. Following Christian practice, when one has two doors, ought not one lend the second to a neighbour? I think so. Now, it *is* true there were words exchanged with Islington after a church service, and good reason for it. He tends to disapprove of perfectly wonderful things, like opinions. As for Hawkes and the fountain, we were gathering monies for the poor and he practically saved my life. I freely lay these at your feet as they ought to be noised abroad. The first and last as examples of Christian duty, the middle as a warning to those of high status."

She watched me shrewdly.

"Is that payment enough?" I said lightly. "I really must be off. When one has an Archibald Flat on one's hands, it is best to be vigilant."

This earned me a look of clever appreciation. "Very well, Miss Lion. And remember that information offered freely and at random brings its rewards."

"I shall remember."

Emma Considers if Her Misdirection Be a Sin
An Imaginary Conversation

Emma: "Forgive me, Hawkes, for I have sinned."
Hawkes: "Again, Miss Lion?"
Emma: "I am afraid so. Intentional misleading by telling the truth."
Hawkes: "I see."
Emma: "Is it so very bad?"
Hawkes: "There are spiritual concerns: heaven, hell, and the like."
Emma: "Oh dear."

Later

When I arrived at Islington's this evening, Crosby answered the door and said, "Welcome, Miss Lion. The men are in the library."

The men.

As if the number meant nothing.

How many men?

Two? Three?

Aren't butlers supposed to be meticulous?

"Wonderful," I smiled, feeling ill. To postpone the inevitable, I stalled with, "Is the Countess of Alwick on the premises?"

"Yes, Miss. She is ensconced in the Rabbit Room." Crosby paused then, and with a very butlerian beetling of his brow, he added a very unbutlerian comment. "Having taken umbrage with something His Grace said, I believe she is writing a fictional duke's wretched demise into her book. But it was not *I* who spoke." He touched his finger to his nose knowingly.

I blinked.

Crosby resumed his usual manner as if he'd said nothing but, "Please, Miss Lion, no mud on the floor."

My smile blossomed into something irreverent. "Thank you, Crosby. A much-needed uplift."

He moved his head just so and, giving a serviceable clearing of his throat, motioned me towards the corridor and my ~~fate doom destiny~~ tangled reality.

I walked down the corridor towards the library door. It was ajar, a ribbon of light marking the wall. I could hear the throw of voices back and forth in short, amused conversation. Someone laughed. Islington, *I believe*. Then came an answer in a lower register. Pierce.

"Arguable at best," replied Islington. "What say you, Hawkes?"

"*We know what we are, but know not what we may be*," he quoted. And the Shakespeare was so very grounding, I decided right then and there that, should my courage ever fail me, I would kidnap Hawkes, take him to a faraway place, and make him quote Shakespeare all the day long.

Then Pierce's voice again and a rejoinder from Islington.

"Where's Lion?" I then heard Islington say.

"She'll be here soon, I'd guess," Pierce replied. "I thought I'd be delayed, so we arranged to come separately."

My stomach tried to force a retreat.

My brain made a remark about fleeting courage.

My heart ached for the very real possibility that I would open the door and find everything changed. Find that Pierce and I had tampered with lightning only to scorch the rare camaraderie we four had claimed. And the precarious nature of the entire affair would come crashing down on both our heads.

I placed my hand on the door handle and pushed it the rest of the way open. I may have uttered a prayer.

"Good evening." My own voice sounding thin in my ears.

"Finally," Islington said. "I need someone with enough sense to take my side."

My eyebrows shot up. "Are you speaking of me?"

"Don't look a gift horse in the mouth."

"I shan't."

"But neither should you let it in at the gates," Pierce said.

"I shan't do that either." I looked at him, willing normality into the exchange. Pierce was not in his evening kit but in a professional, clean-cut black coat and trousers. He'd had his hair trimmed, adding to his sharp appearance. Our eyes connected, he smiled and then looked away. Hawkes, sitting in the chair behind Islington's desk, one foot crossed over his knee, was reading. He looked up at me, then went back to his book.

"Mrs. Knowlls has apologised profusely," Islington said, pouring me an aperitif, "but there was a small disaster in the kitchen. She's sent for Agnes and assured me that all will be sorted within the half hour. I told her none of us minded in the least."

"My Agnes?"

"Agnes is a dear," Hawkes murmured from the desk.

"Your Agnes," Islington replied. "Sit. I've been trying to tell Pierce that an acting troupe should be established that is wholly dedicated to the performance of Shakespeare."

"Too one dimensional," Pierce argued.

I sat on one of the sofas flanking the fire. Pierce sat at my side, Islington on the sofa opposite. "I second the motion, without question," I answered. "I would join. And run away with them."

"Emma Lion as Coriolanus," Islington said, trying not to look too amused at his own jest.

"Hamlet," said Pierce.

"Henry V." Hawkes closed his book and walked over, sitting beside Islington and diagonally from me. Which led to Islington and Pierce exchanging favourite accounts from the Hundred Years' War.

And there I sat amazed; we four had remained intact. The alchemy bore no bent shape or off-balance measure. We were as we always were. And the fact that I could feel my heart beating in response to Pierce's easy attitude—his low quips, fingering his glass in thought as he listened, a self-assured shrug—but not tip off balance, felt like a miracle.

At one point, when I'd sent a snipped comment in Islington's direction and he had batted it back with equal play, the lines around Pierce's eyes were left more pronounced for him having smiled. I glanced at him, then away.

It held.

We, the four of us, held.

I let out a slow breath of relief—Pierce and Islington having moved on to discussing an article in *The Times*—and so it was Hawkes who looked up from his book and frowned in interest.

Before I could think what to say, a harried footman opened the door and announced dinner was finally served.

Wonderful.

The food, the company.

All of us seemingly content to be where we were.

Silence among friends forms a pleasant shape. I know this mostly from the nights Mary and I both lay reading in our beds at Fortitude, with a forbidden candle lit. Tonight held one of these silences until Islington, waiting for his plate to be cleared, looked about at all of us and said, "Turner?"

"Moody," answered Pierce, taking a drink. "Damn good at what he did."

His gaze turned on me. Having little to say regarding Turner of my own experience, mostly because I've seen so few of his paintings, I stole an opinion. (Fault Thirty-Five on Cousin Archibald and Matilde's list: propensity towards thievery.) "My father always said that Turner understood unspoken but universal law. This gave him a scope large enough for the world to fit into. He said Turner's expansive vision is why he could paint the sky so well."

Islington nodded. "He was certainly born under a star for understanding the skies. The portraits of him as a younger man seem to convey an understanding of his own genius."

"Arrogant?" This was Pierce.

"Is seeing clearly arrogance?" I asked.

"A visionary then," Islington offered.

I glanced across the table. Hawkes's gaze was unfocused, despite him listening. "What would you add Hawkes?"

"I never answer Islington's questions," he replied. Then, "But I have seen the portraits of him when he was young."

"And?" enquired Pierce.

"Most of us are afraid of the shadow our destiny casts. He didn't seem to be."

When it came time to leave, Pierce, Hawkes, and I stepped out into the square, the scent and press of early spring evident even in the late hour. We were in easy company with one another, Pierce walking between us with his hands in his pockets, his limp softer than it has been of late. Hawkes and I, passing the fountain, exchanged the edge of a common glance.

We walked down Sterling, and upon reaching the Diagonal, Hawkes did not turn up towards Traitors Road and his flat beside The Cleopatra but, rather, continued with us down to Whereabouts, listening intently to Pierce describe a chemical process he was experimenting with in his work. Stopping before Lapis Lazuli, Pierce and Hawkes naturally wound up their conversation.

There was a pause.

"It's late." I stifled a yawn.

"An early start ahead," Pierce replied, arms crossed, head bent.

"It has been a long week," I said.

Pierce laughed. "That it has."

And Hawkes, who had his book beneath one arm, hands in his pockets, purple scarf about his neck, considered me.

Then frowned.

Then glanced towards Pierce.

He drew his eyebrows together, lifted one in cautious comprehension, and looked back at me.

It may have been the shadows and hazy gaslight, but I swear the line of his mouth twisted, part amusement, part curiosity.

"Goodnight then," he said quietly. And without saying another word, he continued down Whereabouts towards King Henry's Road.

"Sometimes," Pierce said slowly, as we watched the figure of Hawkes seemingly disappear, "I get the feeling that Hawkes knows things that are impossible for him to know."

"I suspect he often does."

Pierce's gaze flicked over my face. He smiled at me.

I smiled back.

With Hawkes gone, the feeling about us changed shape, pulling Pierce and I into an orbit that had been previously eclipsed by the alchemy of we four.

I almost said something—that we could talk now, tonight. But a curtain just up the street shifted, and I knew we had an audience watching.

"It would be best if you and I both entered our respective doors," I murmured. "With an air of having spent our evening in the company of a vicar."

Pierce glanced up the street, then nodded.

"I've been worried," I stated with no preface, even to the surprise of myself.

Head down, hands in his pockets, Pierce turned slightly on his heel until his face was mostly concealed in shadow, waiting for me to illuminate my meaning.

"I've been worried it wouldn't feel the same between the four of us. But it did. And I'm glad for it."

Pierce looked up at my face, the light glancing off his eyes in a flash of silver. He waited a breath before answering. "I noticed that as well."

"A good thing."

"A very good thing," he answered. Then one of his rueful smiles. "It's been a hell of a week."

"Yes." I smiled in return. "Our days have been at complete odds. Are you finished at the museum?"

"My work with them will be stop and start. I'll also have several portraits in the coming weeks for the gentlemen's society."

"So you got the commission?"

A pleased expression. "I did."

"Congratulations."

"Thank you. Tomorrow I *will* be here, in studio. My late afternoon should be free. Are you?"

"Sorted." I nodded militantly.

He laughed.

The curtain up the street moved again. "That's our second warning. Goodnight, Niall."

And I was up the stairs and into the house, closing the door behind me.

Agnes was still awake; I could hear her telling Parian about Islington's kitchen—"Two stoves of the *highest quality*, Parian. And the pantry! Here, have another biscuit."—and I left them to it, going upstairs, pausing on the second floor to see a light shining out from one of Cousin Archibald's rooms, then up to the garret.

I did not light my candle or the lamp atop my green bookshelf.

Instead, I went straight to the window.

Pierce still stood on the pavement, arms crossed, staring at some unfocused point before him.

What was his line from Whitman?

I too am not a bit tamed, I too am untranslatable.

Watching him from the window, I felt both relief and uncertainty. He isn't pushing me off. I must have been more worried than I'd realised that he might be deliberately avoiding our conversation.

But no.

He wouldn't.

That isn't like Pierce.

March 7th

My mother once told my father that if he used the phrase *All Hell Breaking Loose*, it just might.

Prophetic.

At exactly midday, My Doom arrived at Lapis Lazuli.

I was sitting in my window seat practicing Latin when Aunt Eugenia's unmistakable carriage stopped before my front door. As the horror of what I was seeing registered in my mind, trunks and cases were already being unloaded. Arabella was the first to descend, followed by Aunt Eugenia.

"Agnes!" I yelled. "Parian!"

Flinging *Latin Phrases for the Unrepentant* onto my bed, I was down all the staircases as if the very hounds of hell were ~~after me~~ swarming my front door.

"Stop that racket!" yelled an irate Cousin Archibald as I pounded past the second floor.

The racket did not stop until I arrived in the hall—breathless, hair askew—just as the bell sounded. Parian came from inside the drawing room, a dust rag in his hand.

"Miss, shall I get the door?"

Nodding, I put a hand up to my waist and pulled half the oxygen from the hall into my lungs.

Parian had scarcely opened the door before he was pushed back, the hurricane force that is Aunt Eugenia filling the hall. She began giving orders as trunks and hatboxes were carried inside. Arabella floated in mere seconds after, fresh and unruffled, the eye in her mother's storm.

"Aunt Eugenia! Arabella! What a surprise."

"Emma," Aunt Eugenia said, the last half of my name an octave higher than the first half. "Disaster has struck."

"I daresay it has," I stammered.

"We left Spencer Court this morning with the intention of arriving at Spencer House, where we would settle ourselves for *The Season*. This Most Important Season of Our Lives. And what did we find?"

I couldn't imagine, so I ventured, "Rats?"

Aunt Eugenia yanked her chin up. "How vulgar an answer. What we found was that the servants sent ahead had been delayed by a broken wheel. Arabella and I were left to enter with only our driver and footman."

"A tragedy, Ma'am."

"Stuff and nonsense. The tragedy was the roof."

"The roof?"

"The roof. Leaking for days."

I looked at Arabella. "The entire roof?"

"The garret is puddled," she said with her honeyed voice. "One of the rooms below, also."

"That...that's all?" I looked back at my aunt. "Surely the repairs can be—"

"I will not subject myself to the hammering and yammering of workmen, Emma. I will not! Arabella and I will stay here until everything at Spencer House is set to rights." And with that proclamation, Aunt Eugenia moved past me, throwing a command at a rather agog Parian. "Tea, I should think. Here in the drawing room. The cook will need the time to sort out a luncheon to my liking."

I realised, when I looked back at Arabella, that my mouth was hanging open.

"Terribly cosy," Arabella said smoothly in return, her complexion like roses and cream.

"You fiend," I hissed. "Arabella!"

She stepped closer, bent down, and kissed me on the cheek. "There are limits to how often I can sway Mama in either direction. I find myself needing to reserve my skills for times of true crisis. Don't pout, Emma, we will have such jolly fun."

"*You* will have such jolly fun," I muttered.

Arabella smiled and led the way.

I followed, casting about for any aspects of my life that would prove dire were Aunt Eugenia to encounter them. I realised there wasn't anything that did not fit that description.

Flashes of my clothing, comportment, household organization, Cousin Archibald, the occasional shooting of Reprobates, barraged my mind.

And then the *tour de force*.

Pierce.

Tall. Sharp. Mysterious. At times inebriated. Pierce.

I lifted a hand to my stomach.

"Are you ill, Emma?" Arabella asked from the pink chair.

Aunt Eugenia—removing hat and gloves before enshrining herself on the green sofa as if she meant to never leave—sniffed. "A pale countenance when one is expecting guests is the height of incivility."

"I wasn't expecting anything," I said, sitting in Hawkes's chair, an acidic taste in my mouth. "Now, Aunt. I am happy to accommodate you and Arabella, but as Lapis Lazuli House is not prepared, I do believe you would be much more comfortable in a hotel. Claridge's? Or say, Brown's?"

"Brown's." Aunt Eugenia wrinkled her nose. "I realise, Emma, the Great Sacrifice I am making by staying here while Spencer House is set to rights. However, this is the most crucial Season of Arabella's career; there is much to discuss. If you are not properly trained, my work will be double. We can spend our days refashioning your general comportment. In addition, I've yet to meet Miss Dowd. Where is she?"

Ah.

Ah.

My unsettled stomach twisted.

Arabella—divine goddess amused with mortal struggle—shifted towards me expectantly.

I straightened my spine. "I'm afraid, Aunt, Agnes Dowd is away due to a personal matter."

Aunt Eugenia looked unconvinced, which led me to elaborate further. "A funeral, actually. For a much beloved…cocker spaniel."

Aunt Eugenia wrinkled her nose. "I've no patience for a Spaniard, no matter from what region he hails."

It was my turn to wrinkle my nose. "Oh, no, Aunt! I'm not speaking of someone from Spain—which to me seems like a country of very fine people. A *spaniel* is a breed of dog."

My Aunt closed her eyes and lifted a hand to her heart. "To fuss over every living thing! Why, I wouldn't attend the funerary services of most humans."

"Technically it isn't fuss over a living thing, Mama," Arabella inserted comfortably from her throne, "as the spaniel is dead."

Aunt Eugenia waved her off, her sharp gaze still on me. "Then I look forward to an interview tomorrow."

"She might not be home tomorrow, owing to—"

"If she is not returned tomorrow, I would think her a very lackadaisical chaperone, indeed! I will send a note to Lady Sheridan; we will arrange for a new chaperone this afternoon."

I was sinking in the maelstrom that was my life.

"Now that you mention it, Miss Dowd *is* only away for one night, this night, tonight, you see. And will return tomorrow as she puts her supervision of my person above grief, any grief, friend or…fowl."

Aunt Eugenia's frown creased in several places. "I certainly hope she does."

I gulped. If Aunt Eugenia realises I don't have a chaperone, my autonomous life will be over—coming of age, regardless.

"Well," she huffed.

"I'll go check on tea," I managed.

Dignity prevailed until I'd closed the door behind me. Alone in the hall, I fell back against the door and closed my eyes. Catastrophe. Disaster. ~~Just deserts~~. Unjust deserts. Cruel fate.

Taking a fortifying breath and whispering that I must pull myself together, I looked about. The first crucial task was to ensure my aunt and my photographer never find themselves in the same room.

I needed to blockade his door. But with what? The sideboard was too heavy to move and too obvious. There was, however, the chiffonier in the dining room, the perfect width and just shorter than me in height. Rushing into the dining room, I flung open the doors of the chiffonier. Only linens. Nothing that could break. Wonderful! Brushing my skirts out of the way, I steadied my feet in place and pulled.

Nothing happened.

Rushing to the other side, I again planted my feet and pushed.

It moved an inch.

Cursing the high-quality piece of furniture, I tried again, a wave of desperation rising from my already unsettled stomach. "Steady on, Emma," I calmed. "You've done much worse. Far worse. And are alive to tell the tale."

It's true.

Running to the breakfast room, I stole a small carpet and then returned to the dining room. Hefting one side of the chiffonier, I squeezed the carpet beneath, then lifting the other side, I pulled the puddled carpet through. Once on the carpet, I was able to push and pull the chiffonier into the hall inch by miserable inch. I could hear Aunt Eugenia and Arabella speaking with one another and prayed that it be a long, engrossing conversation.

It was when I was almost to the studio door that it swung open. Pierce, reading a newspaper, sauntered into the hall.

Sauntered. As if the world were not ending.

Abandoning my efforts, I rushed around the chiffonier and flung myself at him, pressing my hands against his chest and marching him backwards.

He was, to say the least, startled.

"Get. Back. In. There," I grunted as I forced him back.

Pierce did his best to oblige, his limp causing a near stumble.

"Am I being banished?" he asked, catching himself.

"What?" I looked up at his face. "No. I've an aunt in the house. And an Arabella. An infestation of relatives, as it were. They are staying the night. Or two. Or three. Which means *you* do not exist."

Pierce registered the information, then barked a quiet laugh. "Yes, Captain," he said, voice low. "I'm assuming this means we will not…" He made a motion between the two of us.

"No! Absolutely no considering what happened until she is gone. We must stop thinking of each other altogether. She'll know. And then all will be lost." I pushed him another step back into his studio.

"Which implies you *have* been thinking of me."

I opened my mouth, cheeks pink. "I admit to only a reasonable amount of thought."

"I admit to more than that."

It was then I realised my hands were still on his chest, rising and falling with his breath. I looked from them up to his face, then I pulled away.

I wondered…

Dear me.

"I'm sorry. I didn't mean…" I then bit my tongue so as not to narrate the moment further.

"Emma! I demand you return immediately," rang Aunt Eugenia's voice throughout the hall.

"Need help with that?" He glanced over my shoulder at the chiffonier.

"Only if you promise to close and lock this door after you do. Hurry!" I whispered in panic. I moved to the other side of the chiffonier, intending to push while Pierce pulled, but he wrapped his hands around the corners and simply slid it into place. I watched his hands as he squared it against the threshold; long fingers, capable and scarred. I could feel the memory of their weight. The sensation seemingly relegated to glorious memory, due to our inability even to discuss the matter. "Thank you," I breathed out, avoiding his eyes, the chiffonier safely between us. "Thank you. Now close the door and lock it. If we see one another on the street, we are circumstantial acquaintances, nothing more. Nothing. More."

I could feel him studying me as if I were a photograph. Then, "Good luck to us all," he said before closing the studio door.

The lock went home.

"Steady on," I whispered, then returned to the drawing room.

Of course, I was met by my aunt demanding What In Heaven's Name I'd Been Doing.

"Only instructing Agnes to hurry," I smiled. "The kitchen was very warm."

"The kitchen, was it?" Arabella drawled.

"The kitchen," I repeated, sitting down again, the remnants of electricity racing around the palms of my hands.

The next hour was spent hammering out accommodations. After Agnes brought a robust tea—pushing back the need for luncheon by a few hours—she and Parian raced upstairs while I jousted with Aunt Eugenia.

"Arabella and I will both sleep on the third floor."

"Parian has his room on the third floor, Aunt. I will not displace him. There is an empty room next to his that would be serviceable if you *cannot face the stairs*." The last half of that sentence being a direct quote.

In the end, Parian moved his things up to the fourth floor, and

Aunt Eugenia and Arabella were settled on the third.

"Violet trim, Emma? Ghastly! Sometimes I entertain the idea of thinking better of you, only to confront a revulsion like this."

I am now hiding away, doing my best to assuage the headache that seems to have crept upon me without my realising. As for Agnes Dowd? I've half wondered if Saffronia or someone else in St. Crispian's could play the part. But no. Engaging with Aunt Eugenia on any front is not for the amateur. It requires professional training.

There is only one thing to do.

Send for Jack.

Later

That worm-ridden, conniving, self-satisfied serpent!

Later

It is late. Everyone in the house is asleep. Save Agnes.

And I—out of desperation—am preparing to meet Jack.

The long and the short of the matter is this: Having hailed Toff as he was running messages past Lapis Lazuli, I offered him a glazed petit four, then proceeded to ascertain if he knew how to find someone discreetly in London.

"Confidentiality assured, Miss. Who's it you're looking for?" he asked, licking his fingers.

"A man named Jack. Jack Hollingstell. He'll likely be found in a less reputable neighbourhood."

Toff, good boy that he is, nodded. "I've a friend who lives across King Henry's. He can ask around."

I handed him the message for Jack, and we shook hands on the deal.

Jack,

I need to speak with you. Urgently. Life and death.

Emma

The rest of the afternoon was spent managing Aunt Eugenia while Arabella rested for dinner. No need to record the sordid details. Early afternoon passed. Late afternoon. No message from Jack. When it came time for our evening meal, all four of us—Cousin Archibald included—were seated at the table.

The meal was one of Pierce's favourites, I noted with a dismal tug in my chest.

I worried Aunt Eugenia would mention Miss Dowd, and my fate would be sealed. I also worried how Cousin Archibald and Aunt Eugenia would get along. I needn't have. He has recovered whatever wits he'd lost when robbed—too bad, as the thought of having a hermit in the dining room was beginning to grow on me—and is as snivelling, cutting, and whining as ever. Aunt Eugenia had no patience for him until the conversation turned towards my comportment, and then one would have thought they were bosom friends reunited after a long absence.

"I noticed there is now a very heavy piece of furniture in front of your salon door," Arabella said when the elder relations were discussing my abysmal lack of sophistication.

"A pleasant touch, I thought," was my reply.

"Hmmm. You see, I've been hoping that while Mother is otherwise distracted, I might be properly introduced to your…tenant?"

"Shh," I whispered. "Expect nothing of the kind."

"But I do. Speaking of expectations, are we to meet Miss Dowd tomorrow?"

"I'm working on it."

Parian entered. "Forgive me, Miss Lion. There is a boy at the door—"

"Thank you, Parian!"

And I bolted.

Toff wore a satisfied expression.

"Is he coming?" I rushed out the words.

"I was told to tell you that as he has business at The Drunken Duck, you are to come to him."

Images of me flinging myself about that stage danced across my mind.

"I couldn't possibly."

"He said I'm to say"—and Toff screwed up his face to make certain he was remembering correctly—"'Peach cream, I'm a busy man. Come to me or nothing at all.' And he promised a hackney at a quarter to midnight."

I may have growled.

Toff, evidently pleased with this unusual addition to his day, grinned. "Also, you're to look nice. If you come dressed like a bluestocking, he won't even bother. The dress needs to be red or purple, he says."

"Oh he does, does he? Can you get a message back to Mr. Hollingstell before then?"

Toff nodded.

"Tell him he's the worst sort of vermin, that his requests are beyond ludicrous…and to have the hackney wait on King Henry's Road."

"Emma!" came Aunt Eugenia's shout. "What could you possibly be about? In my day…"

I ignored the rest of the sermon, sending Toff back to the kitchen for payment in both coin and baked goods before returning to the dining room.

"Forgive my absence," I said, sitting down before my now-cold fish. "I have a friend who is ill. Soon to be much worse," I added under my breath.

There now.

Complete silence in the house.

It is twenty to midnight, time to sneak down to King Henry's Road.

I am not considering the terrible ramifications of my choice should things go badly.

For a chaperone of Aunt Eugenia's choosing would be worse.

Later.

Or rather, early. Much too early.

I've just returned home.

Dawn is breaking.

Neither Aunt Eugenia nor Arabella are early risers.

So much the better.

I Record the Whole

The hackney waiting on King Henry's Road had the same driver who delivered me to The Drunken Duck on my last infamous visit.

~~A small comfort.~~

A foolish comfort.

It was not to the back-alley door I was delivered. Oh no. It was to the crowded and well-lit front entrance. The letters of The Drunken Duck as bold as the brass from which they were wrought. A man stepped forward to help me from the hackney. He was nondescript, so quiet one hardly paid him any attention at all.

"Miss Lion?"

"Yes, hello. And you are?"

"Need Ta Know."

"Ah. Well, pardon."

"No, Miss." He gave me his arm. "The name is Need Ta Know."

I blinked as he moved me through the patrons in the foyer. "Am I to call you Mr. Know?"

"Need Ta is just fine."

After leaving my black coat with the attendant, we passed through a fine set of doors and were met with a wall of smoke and boisterous laughter. The dimmed dance hall took its shape: tables filled with patrons laughing, arguing, gawking at the stage. The dancers had nests in their hair again. I instinctively reached up to pat my own. But it was not in the main gallery we remained. We went up a set of stairs and down a long corridor that connected the building next door. Need Ta Know pounded on a door with his fist. A porthole of a window opened.

"Eh?" came a voice.

"Brummell's got noffin' on us."

The porthole closed and the door opened.

Dear me.

Just as much smoke, just as many people, someone at a piano playing a popular tune, but the atmosphere could not have been more different. I was, for the first time in my life, in a gambling hell, and not the kind that nice, polite men of influence such as Roland attend.

I clutched the arm of my guide.

"Only relax, Miss. Tonight you be Mr. Jack's charm, so noffin' can touch ya."

I made a sound of jaded disbelief.

"But ya do need ta swag a bit more, duck. It's time for a litta play-along, if ya drift my way. Jackio needs a charm who can handle the moment. Ya see?"

"I see," I replied, swallowing. "Mr. Need Ta, if you can't find Jack when I'm through with him, I might have tossed him into the Thames."

Need Ta Know chuckled and patted my hand as he led me through the gaming tables. "Now don't go sayin' such fings. I account for Jackie's whereabouts, ya see. And if you say you gonna toss him in a riva, I gotta toss you in a riva. Ya see, Miss?"

"Heavens. Are you his body man?"

"I is what I is. Go on now." He nodded towards an open door.

Thoughts of Aunt Eugenia squelched any other hesitations, and I straightened my shoulders, lifted my chin, and walked into the room.

I Do Not Report The Following With Pride
However: "*Truth is Truth to the end of reckoning.*"

Whereas the larger room of the gambling hell had been full of noise and music, this back room was pensive, the air pulled tight. There was a crowd—mostly men, but some women as well—surrounding a single table. It was difficult to see. I inched my way forward. A man against the wall was watching me rather than the game. He touched his ear, then cracked his knuckles. I grimaced at the sound.

"Gentlemen," said a familiar voice, "my lucky charm has arrived."

(Honestly.)

(I bite my thumb at the scoundrel.)

A little reshuffling and the table before me became fully visible.

There sat Jack holding court, dressed in the cleanest cut of evening clothes I'd ever seen him wear, hair coifed with the shine of pomade, predator eyes bright. On the table was a wager of pound notes, coins, jewellery, a watch, and what appeared to be a deed of some sort. And across from Jack sat the man with the scar across his cheek. The one to whom I'd given the ruby bracelet.

I gritted my teeth.

"Hello, sweets," Jack said without standing. "I could use a bit of luck just about now, and you always come through." His eyes surveyed my red gown as he motioned to an empty chair at his side. "Do me the honour?"

All the women in the room had rouge on their cheeks and colour on their lips. I looked bland and, well, innocent in comparison.

When I mentioned this to Jack later, he laughed. "You looked *ingénue*. It was charming."

To which I replied, "*Il est trop tard pour semer les pois*."

"I have no idea what you're talking about," Jack replied.

"Yes, well, my French is rusticated."

But that exchange happened only once we'd fled.

Quite literally.

I digress.

I sat beside Jack, each curious gaze sticking to the back of my neck, and he leaned towards me with a whisper. "The mighty Miss Lion has sought me out. What's the special occasion?"

"I am going to dispose of you, Jack," I whispered in return. "They will never find the body."

Jack grinned. "I like the dress."

The man across the table cleared his throat. "Your play, Jack," he said in his rasping voice. "Lucky charm or no lucky charm."

"What's the rush? You have a wife to run home to?"

Half the room snickered. Half did not.

A jest to which I was not privy.

I looked at Jack's opponent.

He was watching me.

I wished I'd thrown off Jack's order and worn my dullest, most conservative grey afternoon dress. I felt vulnerable. The man held a foul-smelling cigar loosely, his hand adorned with large, jewelled rings. I returned his appraisal long enough to imply I was not frightened (I most certainly was), then returned my attention to Jack, who was considering his cards. They were playing a game I did not understand. It was not whist.

"Euclid," the man across the table said, still looking at me.

This comment drew my attention back to his face. He remembered me then. And my geometrical stammering.

"I'm impressed," I lied.

"I never forget a face," he answered.

"Nor I," I lied again.

"What was it Jack said your name was?"

"He didn't."

"Let's have it then."

Jack tapped the side of my shoe with his.

"Marigold," I answered.

"You've come far." He put his cigar out in an already ash-strewn dish at his elbow. "From stumbling about a stage to Jack's lucky charm."

"One might say Jack is *my* lucky charm," I brazened.

"Careful, now," Jack said in an easy tone, considering his cards. "Rumours might start that I'm not running my own operation." And with that, he tossed a roll of pound notes on the table.

I pictured that same roll of pound notes in my account at the bank.

So beautiful it almost brought me to tears.

The man with the scar eyed Jack's raise and then pulled something from the interior pocket of his jacket. Stones blinked as he draped a bracelet—a diamond bracelet—across the substantial wager. Comments rippled through the room. Jack cocked his head, a smile dangling off the side of his face, before reaching out and lifting the bracelet with a single finger. It hung like a young snake. Placing his cards face down on the table, Jack reached for my wrist. I thought about twisting away, but in a matter of two movements, the bracelet was secured, cold against my skin.

"You haven't won that yet," the man with the scar said.

Jack tossed a pair of rings tied together with a red ribbon—a man's ring of plain gold and a woman's ring, ornate, with one large emerald and two side diamonds. The man with the scar gave the smallest sign of recognition, the scar on his cheek more striking as his complexion reddened. Jack's latest wager had struck a nerve.

Men began banging their fists on walls, the sound swelling to a unified drumbeat throughout the room.

Jack's opponent eyed him with a slick smile. After half a beat, he turned over his cards.

Queen of diamonds, queen of hearts.

Jack laid down his hand.

Ace and king of diamonds.

Cries erupted all around the room. I couldn't have heard my own voice if I'd shouted, but Jack pulled me close and yelled right into my ear, "Be so good as to gather my winnings?"

I wanted to wring Jack's neck.

I wanted to not touch anything on that table.

I wanted the diamond bracelet off my wrist.

I decided the first and third of these desires could be accomplished by acquiescing to the second.

Standing, I opened my reticule—neither classy nor seedy enough for the night's work. Jack and his opponent both watched in equal measure. I gathered the notes, then the deed, the coins, and finally I placed the watch and jewellery on top before snapping it closed. Jack stood, a dangerous smile on his face. "Keep tight hold of that," he whispered through his smile.

"Yes, but I really need to speak with you about—"

But Jack, his hand on my arm, was whisking me out of the room and into the rest of the gambling hell. There was some racket behind us, but we didn't turn. Noise spilled from the tables around us, gamblers glancing as we passed. Jack led me to a pokey corridor on the other side of the room, where suddenly the wall…well, opened. We were through it, the panel back in place, in seconds, a thunder of footfalls running past where we stood concealed.

Despite the dark, I swear I could *hear* Jack's smile.

His hand moved down to mine as he said, "Time to run for it."

"I—"

At this juncture, I feel I ought to record that this episode in no way represents the life I believe I am presently living. While dancing on the stage of The Drunken Duck ~~might be~~ ~~likely~~ is beyond my usual purview, backroom high-stakes gambling hells followed by a pleasant amount of exercise is far beyond what I consider *Emma's Usual Scrapes*.

But there we were, thundering down a hidden staircase, me doing my best to keep my heeled boots beneath my person, one hand clutching Jack, the other gripping my reticule. Two flights down and we were met with a puddle of shadows standing at the bottom, looking out of a greased-over window.

"Haskins?" Jack said, out of breath.

"All ready, sir."

I gawked. There stood another Jack, a young man similar in appearance. Same clothing, same manner.

What was most surprising, however, was the Emma who stood beside him.

She was not so exact, but in a half-the-night-gone back alley, it was difficult to tell the difference. She wore a red dress.

I nearly stepped on Jack's foot. To make a point.

I did not.

It was not the ideal moment for moral instruction by corporal punishment.

(I do, however, anticipate such a moment will come. I will beat Jack. Soundly.)

I watched the alley with my scoundrel companions, as if I knew what they were looking for. Jack made a signal. The false couple was out of a door, her hand in his, running for a closed carriage. We watched them climb in. She giggled.

I wrinkled my nose in distaste, vicariously stained. "Really, Jack. I never!" I hissed.

As the carriage sped away, three shadows separated themselves from the dark, following.

"Are those *his* men?"

Jack gave no answer. We waited. At length, a fourth shadow peeled itself from a doorway and sauntered after the rest.

"That's our cue," Jack said. He was handed both hat and cane as an ornamental comb was slipped into my hair, a necklace placed around my neck, and a long cloak was tied over my shoulders. We now looked like we'd just left the opera. Jack wove my arm through his and led me to a door opposite.

"Let's see if our luck holds," Jack grinned. We slipped into the darkness.

(How dramatic it all sounds.)

Crossing the alley, we entered a passage between two buildings letting out into a mews where a hansom cab waited.

I entered with nary a giggle.

Imagine.

Jack followed, throwing himself beside me as the hansom lurched forward.

And we were away.

In the silence that preceded my yelling at Jack—

> "Jack, how could you drag me into something like this!"
>
> "You were splendid, peach cream."
>
> "I did not ask to meet with you so I could join the criminal underground!"
>
> "Forgive me, sugar, but what exactly is it you think I do?"

—I had a moment to reflect on how much I enjoyed my freedom and how little I wished to go to the gaol. I am shackled by Aunt Eugenia enough as it is.

"I assume you're taking me home?" I said after ~~we'd~~ I'd stopped yelling.

"In a roundabout way, yes. I've not yet had the signal we're not being followed."

"We're being followed!" I tried to spin around, but Jack's iron grip kept me in place. "Relax," he said, sounding like he was taking far too much of his own advice. "Our job is to look rich and tired and pleased with ourselves. Now, what is it you need?"

Tossing my reticule at Jack—he caught it neatly—I crossed my arms. "The nerve, Jack."

"I'd say you've got plenty of that yourself. Anything else?"

I dug my gloved fingers into my arms so as not to add battery to my list of charges for the night. "I need a chaperone."

"Whyever for? I've always been tickled that you don't have that particular albatross around your neck. You're a rare bird."

"No. I mean, yes. That is, temporarily. The thing is…" And I explained my coming to London last March, Agnes Dowd, Aunt Eugenia, and the leak in the roof at Spencer House. "If I do not have a dull, grey chaperone in her early forties with a mole on her face arrive at my house, having just come from the funeral of a beloved cocker spaniel, my freedom will come to an abrupt end. Despite my quite legal age."

Jack sat looking out of the window, his left hand absently opening and closing the clasp on my bulging reticule. The top of the carriage was hit three times. Jack lifted his cane and replied with a double tap. The carriage turned, changing course.

"Done," he said at length.

I balked. "What, no bargaining? No striking a deal?"

When he answered, it was quietly, "I am in your debt, Miss Lion. You know this."

With his words came the feeling of his mother's frail hand in mine, asking me to promise to watch out for Jack. I had to resist the urge to squeeze it back. How much did she know, truly know, I wonder? Tonight has certainly opened my own eyes to how deep Jack is in these games he plays.

"Thank you," I replied. And then, "Although that is the *second* time my coat has been abandoned at The Drunken Duck."

He smiled, then slipped the reticule into a secret compartment below our seat.

"I will need that back, you realise."

Jack did not answer. We drove in silence until we reached St. Crispian's. But instead of stopping at or turning up Whereabouts, the carriage came to a stop at the base of Traitors Road. Peering out of the window, I could see house lamps glowing in the deep night.

"Why are we—"

"Turkish delight," Jack said as he descended and then offered me his hand, "if by any chance this aunt of yours is to see you approaching Lapis Lazuli House, your greatest position of strength is to come from the top of the neighbourhood, on foot. You can claim attendance at a St. Crispian's party. The Lady Trewartha, for example. The Countess of Alwick. Miss Saffronia March, perhaps?"

"How do you know of all these people?" I said as I ~~stepped~~ clambered down onto the street beside him.

"Because as slapdash as you think I am"—he offered his right arm and I took it—"I am thorough. Besides, if we walk up Traitors, we can gawk at the lamps. A thing I seldom have time to do. It's my busiest time of night, you see."

"I absolutely cannot walk up Traitors Road with you at this hour. Anyone might see us! All of Islington's prophecies come true. I've been told I would ruin myself, but in the end, it will be you, won't it, who ruins me?"

"Tell them I'm your cousin." And he removed a pair of spectacles from his left pocket and placed them on his face, somehow managing to look as trustworthy a young man as you'd ever find. He then pulled the hood of my borrowed cloak over my head.

"Is this very small dash of charm how you keep people from wringing your neck?" I asked.

Instead of answering my question, Jack pointed to a lamp of a raven in flight, light pouring out from his open beak. "I'm partial to that one." Grudgingly, I pointed across the street to an open book with light spilling off the pages. And so we continued, admiring, noting. Halfway up the road—not a soul to be seen—I showed Jack the fox holding the bird in his mouth.

While his eyes considered every detail, I considered him.

An inconvenient thing, seeing the corner of his mouth shift upward at the sight of something enchanting. "What you dragged me into tonight was abhorrent, Jack, but in this moment, one would almost forget you're a lying, cheating, thieving, plundering—"

"Don't accuse me of things you haven't seen me do."

"My imagination has no qualms filling in the blanks, Mr. Hollingstell."

By the time we came to The Cleopatra, we were, unfortunately, grinning, arm in arm.

"Good evening, Miss Lion."

I jumped.

There was a figure on Pierce's bench.

"Oh!" I said, startled. "Hawkes!"

And then, for reasons unbeknownst, I hiccupped.

Not my finest hour.

"Bless you," he said, as if I'd sneezed.

"I— You're sitting…here." I released Jack's arm. "In the middle of the night. As good a place as any I suppose. I'm… I needed fresh— *Ah*. That is to say, I've been out on a matter of business. Do you remember Mr. Hollingstell?"

Hawkes stood.

Jack extended his hand. This time Hawkes shook it.

"Mr. Hollingstell," he said.

"Vicar. A beautiful night."

"It is," Hawkes replied.

And we three stood there trading only silence.

It persisted long enough for Jack to rock back and forth on his feet.

And then, all at once:

Said Emma, "Rather late, I should think."

Said Jack, "Are vicars often out all night?"

Said Hawkes, "Care to sit awhile, Miss Lion?"

…followed by enough of a pause for us all to register what we'd said.

"Thank you, Jack, for seeing me home. I think I'll sit with Hawkes."

"Whatever suit you wish to play, sweets." His light-fingered hand touched my shoulder. "Keep the cloak for now, I'll see your coat returned. Along with your reticule. Empty, of course."

"Er, thank you?"

He lifted my hand to his lips, kissed it, then, spinning on his heel, hands in his pockets, Jack tossed the words, "G'night, Vicar," over his shoulder and walked down Traitors Road.

Hawkes watched him go.

I, having seen enough of Jack, snuck a glance at Hawkes. What was I looking for? Disapproval? Censure? "Abysmally foolish, I suppose, walking Traitors with Jack at a time like this."

"Not tonight," Hawkes said.

He then looked at me. Not disapproval, not censure, but the faint outline of something else.

I believe it to have been caution.

Hawkes stepped past me—his shoulder brushing mine—and sat back down on the bench. And it was as if the night released a long breath, wrapping around the dark spires of the church, complementing the glow of the lamps along Traitors, enveloping Hawkes as a necessary ingredient of the spell.

I sat down beside him.

"A quiet place, when one can't sleep," Hawkes said.

"Yes," I murmured. Then, "Hawkes, I should explain. You see, I've a rather trying—"

"You don't have to explain anything to me, Miss Lion," he said.

I opened my mouth to reply, but before I could, he began softly,

At length a pleasant instantaneous gleam
Startles the pensive traveller while he treads
His lonesome path, with unobserving eye
Bent earthwards; he looks up—the clouds are split
Asunder,—and above his head he sees
The clear Moon, and the glory of the heavens.

I closed my eyes. A rest. A balm. A baptism of poetry after the smoke and tawdry exchanges of Jack's world. Hawkes knows how to speak moonlight as well as anyone.

"Coleridge?" I asked.

"Wordsworth."

Was Hawkes the pensive traveller?

I did not ask.

Hawkes placed his ankle over his opposite knee, crossing his arms, slouching a bit more against the worn bench. He lifted half a magician's smile as he looked up. Not wishing to disturb the magic, I sat longer than I ought to have, drawing my borrowed cloak snugly, relaxing against the bench, closing my heavy eyelids for only a moment.

It was when the predawn birdcall began that I realised I'd fallen asleep on Hawkes's shoulder. He'd sat unmoving, book of poetry open before him, hands blue from cold.

I made a sound at the stiffness of my muscles and said, rubbing my eyes, "How long have we been here?"

"A few hours," Hawkes replied.

I yawned. "How very rude of me."

"Not at all."

Uncomfortable in my gown despite the warmth of the cloak,

I shifted, yawned again, and blinked my eyes at the silver light of earliest morning. "Surely someone has seen us by now."

"No one has passed this way. No one has come to their window. Besides," he spoke in a faraway tone, "St. Crispian's gives me all benefit and no doubt, however undeserved."

My smile was a messy, wrinkled affair.

Hawkes closed his book and looked at me. His blue eyes a more complicated shade, like the predawn ocean. "*Innocent sleep*," he quoted. "*Sleep that knits up the ravel'd sleave of care. The death of each day's life. Sore labor's bath, balm of hurt minds, great nature's second course. Chief nourisher in life's feast.*"

I sighed. "Shakespeare at daybreak. Hawkes, you are too good to me."

He smiled and lifted a hand to his already rumpled hair.

Standing, I claimed my balance, shook out my skirts, and did my best to pin my hair into place.

"Good morning, Hawkes," I said in farewell.

"Good morning, Miss Lion."

The slight morning breeze caught his hair and the upturned lapel of his blue coat, making him look like a moving painting. I noted these details, then turned and walked past The Cleopatra and around the corner, down the Diagonal before turning right onto Whereabouts Lane. Walking up the front steps of Lapis Lazuli, I took the key out of my corset and unlocked the front door, closing it quietly before taking off my shoes and tiptoeing up the stairs to my garret. I decided to sit and wring out the night in words as I don't feel I can sleep.

I've just realised the necklace and the bracelet are no longer on my person. Jack had, with his light fingers, taken them both.

The ornamental comb in my hair remains.

I've now left The Duck with a nest and an ornamental comb.

Perhaps next time I'll acquire a hat.

I placed the comb with the crown and sceptre from the Reprobates—and their bell that I've still not returned since the duel. I am forming quite a collection.

March 8th

One would have thought that after such a night, I would be half dead to the world.

Argumentum a contrario. I am bright-eyed and awake.

Seeing no reason to believe that a debauched life of midnight gambling offers such rewards, I've decided that the magic resides with Hawkes.

Later

Jack did it!

Bless his slithering soul.

My entire morning was spent entrapped (entrapped I say!) in the drawing room with Arabella, Aunt Eugenia, and Cousin Archibald, my two elder relations discussing in detail the letter that he and Matilde crafted regarding my many faults.

"I see you only did half a job," Aunt Eugenia sniffed after reviewing the copy he had kept for himself.

"You must allow for the overwhelming nature of the task," replied he. "Especially as I was lately injured." He indicated his three-year-old scar.

Arabella lounged in my pink chair, entertained.

I sat in Hawkes's chair, bouncing my knee and watching the door.

It had only just occurred to me, O Emma of Little Planning, that if Cousin Archibald were present when my chaperone ~~arrived~~ *returned*, the game would be quite up.

It was imperative I dislodge the man.

But how?

"Stop fidgeting, Emma!" Aunt Eugenia commanded.

"Hmm, yes," Cousin Archibald said, smoothing down his few remaining hairs. "That goes with number thirty-six. Excessive movement. What, what! And number twenty-seven! A trying presence."

Arabella smiled.

I made a face in return.

I'd considered several options for removing Cousin Archibald (i.e., arson, hysterics) when my mind was illuminated.

"Cousin Archibald, would you mind retiring from the drawing room?"

"I have every right," he snivelled, "to enter this room when and how I will."

"Only, as I don't have a mother, I mean to ask Aunt Eugenia some questions, some rather *female* questions."

"Why I never!" Aunt Eugenia said.

"What, what?" Cousin Archibald said. "No such thing will happen under this roof."

I clenched my jaw. "Only, you see, my—"

"How dare you!" he cried, his face purpling. "The indecency. You...you, you hoyden!" He ripped the paper of my recorded faults from Aunt Eugenia's hand and marched straight out into the hall, slamming the drawing room door behind him.

"Emma!" Aunt Eugenia was enraged. "How vile. I'm ashamed of you!"

The next step of my plan required me to step lightly. I did not want to lie exactly. Only give an impression which may or may not be accurate. Muddle. That's it. My intent was to muddle.

"I apologise, Aunt. It was unconscionable to reference the realities of female life, however," I lifted a hand as she opened her mouth to discourse on the subject, "I suspect it likely that Cousin Archibald might be susceptible to fleas and nits. He was, after all, robbed coming home from the train station. He was also robed, but that is beside the point. Why, he could be infected with anything. Knowing that, I could not allow him to continue in your presence. I think it best you avoid him altogether for the duration of your stay. That is why I saw fit to drive him from the room. However indelicate."

Aunt Eugenia had stood rather abruptly when I'd said the word fleas.

"Why I never!" she both whispered and thundered at once. She began shaking out her skirts and touching the back of her neck. "I want your maid in to clean this room immediately! We will move to the salon."

Ah.

Ah.

The image of Pandora's box being opened by my own hand flashed across my mind.

A sobering and somewhat disappointing realisation when one understands they are their own worst enemy.

"I am certain the drawing room is not infested, Aunt."

"A chance I Refuuuuuse to take," she said, stretching the word as far as she could. "Once your maid has put everything to scrutiny and tidied the room, we may return. Until then, the salon it is. I assume that purple sofa is still serviceable?"

"It's plum," I said, dejected.

"That matters not a whit."

"We cannot use the salon, Aunt."

"Whyever not?"

"Because I am renting the salon to my tenant."

In times of pending catastrophe, one tends to consider the minutest details, the prelude to everything crashing upon one's head—or so it seems from my personal experience. In this instance, Aunt Eugenia's eyes bulged in such a particularly round manner that they looked like the bottom of two glass bottles.

"What do you mean, your *Tenant*?"

Forcing myself to remain in an attitude of casual explanation, I lifted my shoulder. "You do recall how Mr. Flat created Lapis Lazuli Minor several years ago? The far sliver of the house? I'm certain my mother wrote of it to you. There happens to be someone letting it just now, and for an additional profit. As I've…that is to say, it was agreed The Tenant would let the salon as well."

"Why I never!"

"You most certainly would not," I replied, somewhat cheekily.

"We shall just have to take the room back," Aunt Eugenia commanded. "I might reside here well up to three days! Having only one room to sit in leaves me very put out."

"Would that we could, Aunt, but I am afraid it is not possible. Perhaps it will follow that your roof will be repaired sooner than we might think."

"I demand you tell me who this Tenant is at once!"

Arabella smiled demurely. "Yes, Emma, do tell?"

While maths was never my strong point, it was simple arithmetic to understand there was a right way and a wrong way to solve this equation.

"Cousin Archibald arranged the situation, of course. You may have seen the gentleman's name in the society papers? A Mr. Niall Pierce, photographer of the wealthy and important."

Aunt Eugenia stood stock still, as if my words hadn't had time to yet be absorbed.

I was expecting a small reaction—something akin to the eruption of Mount Vesuvius. What I received instead was the opposite.

"Do you mean the man who photographed Lady Vancott and her daughters?"

Her interest was piqued. She puffed her chest in a self-important manner.

I have no idea if Pierce has photographed Lady Vancott (& daughters), but seeing it brought such a level of interest, I decided to assume he had.

"The very one!" I smiled. "He's done a number of society portraits. Well, not a *number*. Mr. Pierce is exclusive, Aunt. It is no Simple Thing to convince him to accept one's business."

"What a feather in your cap, Emma, that he keeps his studio here," added Arabella. "One could almost consider you his patroness."

"I wouldn't go that far—"

"Quiet!" Aunt Eugenia waved her hand in my direction. She sat back down. "This is fortuitous. I am pleased, quite pleased. I've been meaning to have Arabella's portrait taken. Clever of you to have thought to accommodate me so. How convenient!"

After a blank stare, I felt the straight line of my lips bend as reluctant sound was forcing its way out of my mouth.

"Don't look like a lizard, Emma. Young ladies shouldn't be so reptilian. Unless one's a Sandoval. They cannot help it. The entire family should remove into a pond."

"Aunt," I recovered, "Mr. Pierce's schedule might be—"

"Nonsense. Invite him to dinner this evening. He and I can discuss an arrangement."

As terrifying a thought as any.

"Aunt, I think—"

"Invite the man to dinner, Emma. I insist."

One cannot die on every hill.

I carefully walked back down this one. "I shall send Parian over with a note."

"Of course, you will. I'll not have Lady Vancott holding anything over my head."

It was then the door opened.

I was expecting to see said Parian. Instead, I was greeted by a face I knew well despite having never seen it in the flesh before.

Agnes Dowd.

My Agnes Dowd.

The one I'd spun out of desperation and a desire not to be chained to convention.

She stood ramrod straight in muted brown, wearing a dismal hat with one sad-looking black feather. Robust but not rotund, her face—as Aunt Eugenia would later proclaim—the correct shade of forgettable. Brown eyes, overbearing nose, a mole just where it ought to be.

"Miss Dowd!"

"Good day, Miss Lion. I trust my absence has not been too much trouble."

"Indeed, no," I stood. "Aunt, let me introduce my very proper chaperone, Agnes Dowd. Miss Dowd, my aunt Lady Eugenia Spencer."

Miss Dowd came walking over to Aunt Eugenia, who offered her hand. I'll never again smirk when I read a novel whose heroine waits with bated breath. For there I was, the very same. But Miss Dowd knew just how to take Aunt Eugenia's hand. Gentility without remarkability. Polite manner without beauty. As for the costume details? Sheer brilliance. There was even dog hair on one side of her drab and appropriately four-years-out-of-date skirts.

Well done, Jack!

"I have long looked forward to our meeting," Miss Dowd said in judgemental monotone. "I understand the weight of the burden Miss Lion must be to you."

Aunt Eugenia closed her eyes in agreement. "My sister married an Irish painter. One can only expect so much."

"I have often felt that if all painters were gathered into a compound in the South of France, we might purchase their works by catalogue without having society disrupted by any unnecessary and excessive feeling. Heinrich von Angeli excepted, as he did paint our beloved queen. Long may she reign."

Aunt Eugenia, her vision expanded by what ~~could~~ ~~would~~ should be possible if all narrow-minded aristocrats banded together, made an effort not to stare. Her mouth jogged open and closed in great energy before she said, "Miss Dowd, I find you to be a woman of excellent judgement. Please, sit here beside me on the sofa. I've long had thoughts regarding Keeping the Arts At Bay."

"It is the only way," Agnes Dowd answered as matter-of-factly as any spinster morally determined to wear brown.

Arabella and I exchanged a look. She was impressed, something Arabella seldom feels and on principle never shows.

My answering smile was dazed.

Suddenly the price of helping Jack did not seem as steep as I'd believed it to be.

By the time I was called into the conversation, Miss Dowd was saying, "Miss Lion, I do hope you've reviewed the chapters in Judges I marked, as well as the society pages in *The Times*. As one can fall in either direction, it is best to stay centred and silent." This last remark to Aunt Eugenia, who was glowing in approbation.

"You ought not mind, Miss Dowd, that I've chaperoned Emma into society without your accompaniment. I see now how your influence at a dinner or a ball might keep Emma checked in essential ways."

Miss Dowd frowned. "Lady Spencer, I am merely the fibre in Miss Lion's social dietary requirements. It's best for me to remain at home, a steady companion. The champagne of your instruction is what Emma needs in the upper echelons of society."

I did my best.

Truly.

However, the laughter erupted with no warning.

I slapped my hand across my mouth, wide-eyed, tears glistening.

Attempts to contain myself resulted in what sounded like a death rattle.

Aunt Eugenia's answering look was grim. "I can see a few days without chaperonage has left you quite the heathen, Emma. Perhaps you would like to leave us. You might go send Parian to invite The Photographer to dine with us this evening. I daresay the fresh air will do Parian good. He looks like a half-spent candle. There now, take Arabella. I don't believe in young women remaining in the room after making noises." This last sentence was said to Miss Dowd. Then back to us. "Off you go. Miss Dowd and I must Discuss my expectations for *The Season*."

Glancing at Miss Dowd, who gave me nothing more than a firm look, I was encompassed by a feeling of safety and well-being. Two words I'd not expected to associate with Jack. Standing, I took Arabella's hand and pulled her from the pink chair. "Come along, Arabella. Let us find Parian."

I sent Parian with a note to Pierce…

Meet me in the back garden. I've terrible news that should be delivered in person.

…and while he delivered it, Arabella and I sat at the kitchen table while Agnes fussed over the menu she was reinventing for the next few days, and I tried to explain Miss Agnes Dowd.

"But Miss, you don't have a chaperone."

"Well, I do, Agnes. In spirit. It's highly biblical. Now. Let's simply pretend she's been here all year. I promise to explain everything later, but if you don't want me having to move to Spencer House while you and Parian look elsewhere for work, I advise you to be patient—and silent—until I can."

It was not blackmail.

It was a lesson in action and consequence.

Agnes wrinkled her nose. "I can wait, Miss. I'm relieved. Very proper of you. Even if her name *is* the same as mine."

"So very proper, Emma," murmured Arabella.

I made a face.

When I'd gathered enough time had passed, I excused myself—"You are to remain *here*," I ordered Arabella. "And if your mother decides to enter the kitchen for any reason, scream."—and slipped out of the kitchen door.

~~Pierce was waiting in the garden, hands in his pockets, looking down, his hair falling forward in the way that might tempt one to take their hand and…~~

Pierce was waiting in the garden. Hands in his pockets. Looking down.

That is all.

He glanced over as I closed the door behind me. I took the stairs from the kitchen door up to ground level.

"Your garden needs a good sorting," he said.

"Are those the words of a volunteer?" I asked, stepping around some self-satisfied mud.

"If you would like the help."

"It turns out, I do need help but in a different matter entirely. I need you to flee the country so I can't extend my aunt's dinner invitation to you this evening."

At this point I had stopped close to where he stood. My arms crossed, I was looking down at my shoes and his, standing on the detritus of winter.

He is right. The garden does need sorting.

"Why am I extended an invitation for this evening?" Pierce asked.

"The Vancotts are to blame. And you, I suppose, for being determined to take photographs of high society."

"You mean Lady Vancott and her daughters?"

Aha! I didn't lie after all!

I looked up. We made eye contact. Something pleasant somersaulted. "My aunt is wanting you to do a portrait of Arabella. She demands you take it while she is in residence here."

"I'll not likely have time," he replied, as if it weren't the comment of a man about to lose his head.

"That is for you to say. But do stay in her good graces this evening. And don't be overly familiar. And do try to appear less handsome than you are, however gothic."

I earned a smile at the word handsome and a puzzled look at the word gothic.

"It's a compliment," I said. "Handsome men are like beautiful architecture."

"I can't tell if you're simply nervous or wretched at giving compliments."

"Both, likely. And now I must return before I am found out—" And as I took a step back, I slipped.

Pierce caught me.

Grabbing my elbows and holding me up—"Steady on"—until my footing was secure.

"Thank you," I breathed out. Finding purchase, I eased up straight, feeling his pressure on my elbows. Then, as he released his grip, I reached back my left hand and took his, to step over the puddle on the path.

"Do you have your footing now?" he asked.

But I was not thinking about feet. I was thinking of the way that as he held my hand, his thumb had moved lightly over my knuckles. It felt like seeing something so beautiful one must stop to stare.

"I think so," I said, sounding breathy in an unfortunate and unflattering way.

Dismal, considering the moment.

Back on the stone above the stairs and safe from a garden seeking revenge, I turned towards Pierce, to say thank you.

He had not yet pulled his hand away.

Neither had I.

And for the smallest moment I thought…

I leaned towards him.

Pierce pressed his thumb against my hand.

A throat cleared at the kitchen door.

I spun around. There stood Arabella, an eyebrow raised in superior amusement, her perfection out of place beside the quirky back door at the bottom of the stone stairs.

I cannot say who it was that let go.

I do not remember.

Only that a sense of hesitation remained after I'd clasped my own hands before me. "Hello, Arabella. You remember meeting Mr. Pierce? I've just confirmed that he…well, that is to say…" I looked over my shoulder. Pierce was again standing with his hands in his pockets, an indiscernible line running through his expression. "Are you free to join us for dinner this evening, Mr. Pierce?"

"Yes," he replied.

"Wonderful. We shall all suffer together." I smiled, went down the stairs, grabbed Arabella's wrist, and pulled her into the kitchen, ~~shutting~~ slamming the door behind us.

Later

It has not been a day of pleasant anticipation.

Later

Who would have guessed—in a thousand variations of a thousand years—that Pierce would so evenly manage Aunt Eugenia?

I suppose, on further reflection, anyone who has ever met him.

With Aunt Eugenia invading Lapis Lazuli, dressing properly for dinner was non-negotiable. So this evening Arabella and I readied ourselves in the garret. She looked crushingly perfect in soft pink. The fabric—a silk damask patterned in gold thread. It must have cost a year of most middle-class lives.

Or more.

I wore Arabella's old dress—my finest.

"The shimmer will please a certain guest, I should think," Arabella said as she was pinning my hair. In that moment I could hear Pierce enter his room on the other side of the wall.

My eyes widened, and I lifted a finger to my lips. "Shh!"

She smirked. "Is that him, darling?"

I flicked a finger at her wrist, and she laughed.

Arabella had not yet finished with my hair when a note was pushed through the wall.

ANY INSTRUCTION YOU WISH TO GIVE?

"Oh, this is delicious," Arabella said, intercepting the communication. "You actually *do* send messages through the wall."

"Arabella, hand it here."

Taking a loose piece of paper in hand, she picked up my fountain pen.

We could hear Pierce moving about his room, getting ready.

"Arabella!" I hissed.

"Mr. Pierce," she dictated, "It's devilishly convenient of you to be so handsome, as we both need—"

But I had wrested the pen from Arabella's traitorous hand before she could finish. Then I crumpled her half-written missive and tossed it into the rubbish bin. Arabella went to sit on the chair near the window seat, watching as I took up my pen to respond.

Only be prepared for absurdity. And possible emigration if things go as terribly as they very well might.

I THINK WE'LL MANAGE.

Did I tell you Islington required a stiff drink after such an encounter in January?

His soul still bears the scars.

When Pierce's answering laugh could be heard—muffled, but sound enough—Arabella and I looked at one another, a flush rushing to my cheeks. Arabella, leaning into the comfort of the cushions with all the confidence of a ruling monarch, looked at me as if she knew everything.

Aunt Eugenia was waiting with Miss Dowd in the drawing room—the former having dressed for dinner with the latter's help—their aperitif being sloe gin. Not knowing if this was Aunt Eugenia's doing or that of my chaperone, I swallowed it, literally and metaphorically.

When the front bell sounded, Parian was at the ready. Through the open door of the drawing room, I saw Pierce enter the hall dressed in his nicest evening kit, hat in perfect condition. It was taken—as were his gloves—by Parian before Pierce entered the drawing room.

Aunt Eugenia stood expectantly. "The Photographer, I presume."

Before I could manage the introduction, Pierce stepped forward, considering Aunt Eugenia evenly as he shook her hand rather than taking it as a gentleman would. "Niall Pierce," he replied. "A pleasure."

"One hopes," murmured Arabella.

"I expect," stated Aunt Eugenia as she pulled her hand from his, "that you have some vague familiarity with everyone else present. Here is Miss Dowd, my niece's chaperone…"

"Miss Dowd, good evening," Pierce said, accompanied by a quick narrowing of the eyes, the slightest tilt of the head, and an effort *not* to look in my direction. With it came the realisation I'd *not* informed Pierce to expect her company.

"…and you know Miss Lion, my ward…"

I started to object, when Miss Dowd, standing at my side, pinched the back of my arm.

"Miss Lion." Polite but not overly familiar.

"…and here is my daughter, Arabella. She is the Most Beautiful young woman in London, as you see, and I mean to ask you, before the night is out, to take her portrait."

"Miss Spencer," Pierce said with a wry smile. "A pleasure."

"Likewise, Mr. Pierce. I've recently seen some of your work and admit to being curious."

She was referencing the garden rather than his photography, *I believe.*

Pierce was not flustered. "My best work is held in private collections rather than public exhibitions, but I am flattered you approve all the same."

"Oh, I said nothing yet of approval."

But Pierce was already turning back to Aunt Eugenia. "I would be happy to discuss the possibility of a portrait, Lady Spencer."

I drank my sloe gin and considered pouring myself another.

It would not have been sufficient.

~~Somehow, we all made it into the dining room.~~

Miss Dowd shepherded us into the dining room forthwith.

Cousin Archibald had dined at his usual time per Aunt Eugenia's insistence, ~~poor man~~, which left Aunt Eugenia to sit at the head of the table, Arabella to her right, Miss Dowd to her left. I, sitting right of

Arabella, found myself across from Pierce in our accustomed manner.

I'd like to believe we were both clever and careful in our interactions.

I wager we were simply lucky.

Miss Dowd spoke with Pierce as if they had an appropriately distant yet more than passing relationship already established. He had no difficulty following suit. Aunt Eugenia spoke of *The Season*. I tried to appear oblivious to most things.

Arabella watched Pierce.

He did not watch her in return.

I, surprisingly, enjoyed the soup course more than I thought possible, given the circumstances.

The conversation moved with an even measure of Absurd Assumption from my aunt until, near the end after pudding was served, she decided it was time to Establish a Time for Arabella's Portrait.

Aunt Eugenia, of course, opened with, "There is the matter of your limp."

Pierce stilled. "My limp?"

"It's distracting, and not at all what I expected. If one wishes to work in high society, I think it best one do away with things such as limps. I frown upon any gait that draws the wrong sort of attention. This is my being helpful, Mr. Pierce."

Silence from us all.

I was horrified.

Angry.

Even Arabella broke her laconic elegance to utter, "Mother."

"What?" Aunt Eugenia defended. "Infirmity of any kind is grossly inconsiderate, let alone one of long standing. I don't see why he shouldn't settle for a steep case of the ague and be done with it."

I expected impatience or counter coldness.

I did not expect Pierce to throw his head back and laugh.

Now it was Aunt Eugenia with the wide eyes.

"Lady Spencer, forgive me for saying that I don't care what anyone in high society—as you call it—thinks of my limp. Now, I've a full schedule for the next three weeks. If you would like to settle an appointment in April, I would be happy to oblige. But you're wrong about taking Miss Spencer's portrait in my studio. We will achieve a more authentic photograph in one of your houses, be it in London or the country, I've no preference. Miss Spencer? Where do you feel most at home?"

Arabella's perfect lips parted a fraction. "I have no preference—" she began. Then, in rare assertiveness, "My favourite rooms are at Spencer Court, in Berkshire."

"Then that is where we should take the portrait."

I looked back at Aunt Eugenia. She was sitting at the head of the table as if in a strange sort of paralysis. Her right cheek, however, twitched.

"Aunt Eugenia?" I said hesitantly.

She turned her head in my direction, eyes still frozen in disbelief.

"I think he's broken her," Arabella murmured.

It was then Miss Dowd set down her fork and said to Aunt Eugenia in a long-suffering tone, "We must do our best, Lady Spencer, to accept the occasional imperfection, as we've a desire to keep our own unjust opinions, too dear with which to part."

Aunt Eugenia moved her indecipherable expression from Pierce to Miss Dowd, taking a moment for the words to settle. "You are quite right, Miss Dowd," she began slowly, gaining her accustomed speed as she continued. "I feel vexed, however, that this fellow won't even try. How difficult could it be to straighten a leg? Why, I know a man who used a cane for years, and then one day he dropped the cane and fairly *sprinted* away from his wife. Next we heard, he was in Spain."

"It's been known to happen."

"Quite."

This was the moment that Pierce and I locked eyes.

I had two thoughts. The first? I could not wait until we had the dining room back to ourselves, Pierce impolitely reading the newspaper, me happily slouching in one of my old dresses. The second? I would not mind kissing Niall Pierce in his evening clothes.

Meaning, he would be wearing them.

Not myself.

"I don't accept your schedule excluding my wishes," Aunt Eugenia ~~said to~~ mandated at Pierce. "I think you should rearrange your Monday."

"I've a commitment out of town. I'm leaving London Monday morning." Pierce took a drink of his wine.

"You are?" I blurted out.

Everyone at the table looked at me.

Miss Dowd even broke a sliver of disguise as she widened her eyes in alarm.

Pierce swallowed.

"That is to say," I cleared my throat, "you are not thinking of leaving before settling rent with Mr. Flat for your lodging, are you, Mr. Pierce?"

"Certainly not, Miss Lion," Pierce replied with formal ease. "I'll be sorting everything with Mr. Flat."

"Good heavens, Emma. How ghastly!" This was, of course, Aunt Eugenia. "A man should never be *accosted* by a woman younger than himself in the dining room. It's very bad manners and a great inconvenience to those of us with every right to take him to task." She looked at Pierce. "I apologise, Mr. Pierce. Only because you are highly regarded with the Vancotts. Otherwise, you would be beneath my consideration, as I'm sure you understand."

Pierce did his best to keep his expression one of professional indifference. (I wonder if I will come to discover this is actually Pierce in a blind panic?)

Aunt Eugenia continued. "Emma's pagan ways aside..."

"Pagan?" I mouthed at Arabella.

I swear Miss Dowd swept a smile beneath the rug of her aghast manner.

"...I am perfectly within my rights to ask—to demand—you accommodate me on Monday."

"I am afraid, Lady Spencer," Pierce replied, "I am unable to do so."

"Who? Who is pulling you away from the God-given responsibilities I've set before you?"

Arabella sighed with contentment.

Pierce pressed his lips together. "Unfortunately, there is a bridge opening in Wessex, and I've been asked to photograph the event."

Aunt Eugenia slapped her hand on the table. "A bridge? You are throwing me over for a bridge!"

"Not at all, Ma'am." Pierce tapped three of his fingers idly on the table. "Who is opening the bridge is the important question."

"Who is?" I asked, before anyone else at the table could.

Pierce took another sip of his wine—his grimace was an internal prayer for something stronger, *I believe*—then said, "The Prince of Wales."

I will go to my grave convinced that the stifled snort belonged to my fictional Miss Dowd.

Aunt Eugenia again slapped her hand on the table. "The Prince of Wales, you say? Little Bertie?"

"Little Bertie?" I mouthed at Arabella. A shrug my reward.

"So you see why I cannot adjust my schedule," Pierce finished.

"No, I should think not. Few people's privilege surpasses my own, but I'll allow Bertie the pleasure. If no one were to be privileged, there would be no privileges, and that, Mr. Pierce, is a world we *must* avoid at All Costs."

Pierce gave a long-suffering smile. He tapped the table again.

He's a champion, really, for how he handled it all.

I opened my mouth to finagle a dismissal, but Aunt Eugenia beat me to it.

"I think the ladies must go through to the drawing room. Mr. Pierce, I trust you are quite capable of enjoying port and a cigar in your own company."

"I am." Pierce stood as Aunt Eugenia did. "This evening, however, I will be joining friends at the club, so I will excuse myself, with your permission."

"Which club?"

"Brooks's."

"You have friends above your station, I see; moderately acceptable in a man, abominable in a woman."

A sentence for which Pierce had no ready answer.

"Good evening, Mr. Pierce," I said, standing. "Thank you for joining us."

"Miss Lion," Miss Dowd said sternly. "One must not talk across the table in such a way."

Pierce, who had opened his mouth to speak, closed it again, returning his attention to Aunt Eugenia when she said, "Do try, Mr. Pierce, to take my advice."

"Which advice, Ma'am?"

"Why, all of it!"

The party crossed the hall to the drawing room while Pierce was handed his hat and gloves by Parian.

"Good evening, Mr. Pierce," Parian said. "A pleasure to see you, as we usually don't."

It was sweet of Parian, really, and after Pierce nodded and walked through the opened door with nary a glance back, I gave Parian a small smile.

He smiled in return.

Who would have supposed a year ago that we would be in cahoots?

Life is not all disaster.

March 9th

How wonderful that Aunt Eugenia refused to attend church.

She kept Arabella home as well.

"I never trust an hour in a church I've not experienced personally. And I've no desire to see that vicar of yours. He's a perfect heathen."

He is, according to Aunt Eugenia's standards.

Blissfully so.

As I sat in my pew well before the start of the service—"You see, Aunt, I believe God is calling me to arrive early that I might consider all the ways I am to be of use *This Season.*"—I saw the Sabbath day and called it good…as an excuse to leave behind one's most trying relatives.

Islington arrived at ten to the hour and, after a few niceties with fellow St. Crispians, sat beside me.

"Pierce was at the club last night," he said. "He told me of your, ah, guests."

"So *you* are the friend he was going to meet."

"Yes."

"You do remember," I grumbled, "that one of the basic Ten—Commandments, that is, not Reprobates—is Thou Shalt Not Covet?"

"Yes…?"

"I don't feel heaven will count you blameless for trying to incite a covetous riot in one Emma M. Lion."

"What, that Pierce and I were at the club?" Said with incredulity.

"I answer in the gloomy affirmative. The two of you have all the freedom in the world. To spend half the night at a club without anyone remarking on it one way or the other? Imagine!"

Islington said nothing at first, but then, "My sister was always divided in regard to her majority. 'It only counts, Henry, when one is a man,' she would say."

The way he said the words, apologetic for the truth of it, caught between us somehow, like shaking the hand of a comrade who has delivered bad news.

"So she eloped and avoided the whole thing?"

"Ah, no." A crease appeared between his eyebrows, and he smoothed his gloves for distraction. "Spoken by a different sister."

I said: "How many do you have?"

Just as he said: "So you've found your Miss Dowd?"

The service began.

Neither question was answered.

Later

A trying afternoon. However, Miss Dowd continues steadfast. "Your black coat has been mended, Miss Lion," she said during tea, "and has been left on the banister. Also, your reticule is on the stair. Hop to it now and put them where they belong."

"Yes, Miss Dowd," I answered, with a silent thanks to Jack.

Aunt Eugenia was pleased. "If I weren't convinced Emma did not need your steady hand, I would claim your wisdom wasted, Miss Dowd. You would do very well in a post of authority at a women's prison."

"Your praise is too high, Lady Spencer. Shall we discuss the most effective bedtime routine to keep Emma looking sweet and subservient?"

I can't help but notice that Pierce has kept himself away from Lapis Lazuli Minor all day.

I left him a note.

I'm nearly certain a sainthood is being prepared in your name.
Niall Pierce, Patron Saint of Those With Unfortunate Relations.

March 10th

A wagon came near dawn, and I wrapped myself in my blanket and watched as Pierce loaded his supplies. Once all was settled, he exchanged a few words with the driver, then re-entered Lapis Lazuli Minor. I could hear him come up the stairs and enter his room. The closet door was opened—for Tybalt access, I imagine—then came the scrape of his chair on the floor.

A minute later, this:

> *I'LL BE HOME ON THE THIRTEENTH OR FOURTEENTH. NOT CERTAIN WHICH.*
>
> *CHAMBERS WILL FEED TYBALT.*
>
> *YOU LOOKED CHARMING THE OTHER NIGHT, BUT NOT AS CHARMING AS YOU LOOK NOW IN YOUR WINDOW.*
>
> *I WOULD MAKE A TERRIBLE SAINT.*

He stood, crossed his room, and left.

I returned to the window, flushed, I am certain, and did my best to look ~~charming~~ natural.

Pierce lifted a final carrying case up to the driver, then, as his hand gripped the wood, he turned and looked up at me.

I swallowed.

Raising his hand in the slightest salute, Pierce pulled himself up beside the driver and said something which made the man laugh.

He did not look back.

I did not look away.

Later

Due to my aunt's ~~instruction~~ rather militant orders, I spent a good deal of the day in my room reading *Mixing in Society*. I am pleased with this development, for I only heard from a distance Aunt Eugenia yelling at Parian for how he opens doors, and the small battle that happened on the stair when Cousin Archibald was attempting to slink out of the house unnoticed. As for what I've learned about good breeding?

MIXING IN SOCIETY
Select Quotes

> *Fluffy knitted things and gaudy pieces of wool-work should be abolished by Act of Parliament.*
>
> *Trifling as many of these little rules may at first sight appear, they are by no means unimportant. Trifles in the aggregate become great social forces.*
>
> *Long hair is never indulged in except by painters and fiddlers.*
>
> *Economy in gloves is an insult to society.*
>
> *Never recognise a gentleman unless you are perfectly sure of his identity. Nothing is more awkward than saluting the wrong person.*
>
> *Dancers are generally hungry people and feel themselves much aggrieved if the supply of sandwiches proves unequal to the demand.*
>
> *Napoleon is said to have lost the battles of Borodino and Leipzig because he had dined in too great a hurry. What a warning!*
>
> *We now imitate the Romans and cover our tables with flowers—a happy innovation.*

The pages in my journal continue to dwindle, my pens are much abused, and my ink bottle is nearing an end. I'll escape to the Reed and Rite this afternoon.

Later

As I set five bottles of ink and two sets of fresh nibs on the counter, the shopgirl—a niece of Jape's come to stay for a few months, if I've heard the gossip correctly—was visibly surprised.

I shrugged my shoulders as if the purchase were inevitable. "When one's life is threatened by the abysmally ridiculous, one needs large quantities of ink."

After paying for my purchase, I left.

Later

It is late now—very late—and I've given myself permission to rejoin Theseus. We've just left the island of Crete where he has saved the youth and killed the Minotaur.

The truth of the matter is I find myself thinking of him. Pierce. Not Theseus.

Often.

~~I like Niall Pierce.~~

~~I am more than fond of Niall Pierce.~~

~~When he walks into the room, I want him to come stand beside me.~~

It's only getting worse, isn't it?

I should have simply ended with, *I like Niall Pierce*, and saved myself the embarrassment.

March 11th

Aunt Eugenia has gone!

We were sitting in the drawing room, I reading, or rather pretending to be.

"Have you made a monumental effort to finish *Mixing in Society*, Emma?"

"Not monumental, no, Aunt."

"Go on then! You will do nothing else until the last page is read."

Praying silently for deliverance, I was feeling very book of Exodus by the time my aunt's footman came with the message all was restored at Spencer House. I held my breath from the moment she said, "We shall have you bring our trunks down" to the minute the carriage was fully loaded, with Aunt Eugenia standing in the hall waiting for Arabella, pulling gloves onto her fingers as she looked about with a sniff.

"You may tell The Photographer that I will write to him regarding Arabella's portrait."

"So you'll engage his services despite the limp?"

"I shall endure. I will not play second fiddle to a *Vancott*, limp or no limp, thank you very much."

"He'll be *thrilled*, I'm sure."

With a harrumph, Aunt Eugenia began to direct Parian and her footman.

It was then that Arabella descended. "What a jolly summer we're going to have, darling," she said as she came up behind me, wrapping her arms around my waist as she rested her chin on my shoulder. "Cheer up. By the end of it, I'll have selected a husband with massive amounts of money."

"If it weren't for you," I replied, "I would abandon your mother."

"If it weren't for me, I would abandon her too."

I leaned back against Arabella. "You owe me a ridiculously expensive tea."

And like that, the clouds parted.

Lapis Lazuli was quiet and blessedly empty.

"Parian?" I said as I stood, arms crossed, at the threshold of the front door, looking out onto Whereabouts as the carriage drove away.

"Yes, Miss Lion?"

"Would you ever have supposed that having only Cousin Archibald would feel so peaceful?"

"No, Miss."

"If you will shift the chiffonier back to the dining room, then see to it that Mr. Flat has his tea and something to keep him occupied in his rooms, I'll give you the rest of the day off."

Parian visibly brightened, standing a bit straighter than he had been. "I'll do my best."

It was then that Miss Dowd descended with her dour hat pinned securely in place, carrying case in hand.

"Miss Dowd! Leaving so soon?"

"I find"—she stepped onto the checked marble floor of the hall, her accent more elevated than it had been—"it best to keep most endeavours to a minimum. All the best, Miss Lion. It has been a delight."

And she was out the door, walking down Whereabouts without a second glance.

"Well!" I said to an equally stunned Parian.

Coming back up to the garret, I changed into something more comfortable before inspecting myself in the mirror. I re-pinned my hair and pulled a few curls loose, thinking about ~~Pierce~~ abstract, philosophical concepts.

By the time I'd returned to the hall, the chiffonier had been returned to the dining room and Pierce's door stood like a soldier at ease. Biting the inside of my cheek, I approached and tested the doorknob. It opened. He must have unlocked it before leaving. And so I peered in.

It was tidied, still, and empty of Brooding Photographers. There were two days of newspapers on the table before the sofa and a wrapped parcel on his worktable. With all this came the sense that though not here now, Pierce would be coming home.

I released a long sigh of relief.

March 12th

Smudgy clouds in the sky and rain—the kind that threatens to be dreary but is not because one's aunt has gone.

Later

I went down for breakfast.

Parian was eating at the table. As I joined him, a prattling Agnes placed a bowl of porridge before me. Parian slid the sugar bowl in my direction.

I accepted the gift happily. "Is it nice to have the kitchen back to normal, Agnes?"

"Yes, Miss," she said. Then unexpectedly, "Only it was thrilling to organize a dinner with five courses for a *lady*."

"Hmmm. Are you coming down with a fever? Perhaps you should put your feet up."

Agnes—stove door opening so she could check on some bread—turned with a creased expression. "Miss?"

"Never mind, Agnes."

But Parian appreciated the comment.

I could see him smiling to himself as he stirred more sugar into his porridge.

Later

I've cleaned both rooms on the third floor, leaving the linens for Agnes. Parian cleaned the rooms on the fourth floor. All the while, I thought of Theseus.

And nothing else.

March 13th

I am experiencing the dissatisfaction that comes after weeks of barrelling at such a pace one can't keep one's feet on the ground. But when a perfectly blank day presents itself, one is too out of sorts to make heads or tails of it.

March has been such a gallop.

The quiet should be restful but feels maddening.

Even the tea tastes stale.

My entire life digresses.

Pierce did not return home today.

March 14th

This afternoon, when I returned from The Keep—Agnes had found a velvet slipper far too large for anyone in the house—I saw that Pierce's studio door was open. My heart felt like one hundred birds suddenly flown in every direction.

The lamps were lit and curtains open, the room as welcoming as ever. No Pierce to be seen, but one of the bureau doors was ajar, and the dartboard looked like a dangerous, flattened pincushion. I walked towards it, trailing my fingers along Pierce's worktable as I went. Standing before the board, I pulled the darts loose, then retraced my steps several paces and let the first dart fly.

Then the second.

And so on.

Thus I was admirably focused when Pierce entered, hands in his pockets, black waistcoat buttoned over his shirt, sleeves rolled up. I threw another dart before greeting him, hoping it would lessen the impact of that man walking into a room.

It did not.

And his absence had only increased the unspoken tension.

Dear me.

"Hello," I said, placing my hand that was not filled with darts on my hip, blowing a loose curl of hair away from my face.

"Nice throw," he said.

"Yes, well…"

Pierce walked over to the board, removed the darts, reached his hand into the back of the bureau shelf for another dozen, then came to stand beside me. He smelled of balsam wood. It was rather nice and tremendously inconvenient. An unfair playing field.

"How was the bridge?" I deflected.

"It was there," Pierce replied. "Job done." He threw a dart. "Your aunt has finally left?"

"Miraculously so." I threw a dart.

"And Agnes Dowd?"

"Gone within the same quarter of an hour. All sorted. One hopes."

Pierce nodded. "Mind my asking where you rustled up such a

character?"

Mind? A little. Yes. "My friend Jack is in the business of getting people what they need."

A frown, but thoughtful. "Have I met Jack?"

Certainly not.

He'd seen Jack. Once.

But was never introduced.

A great triumph on my part.

"You've not had the pleasure," I replied. "We don't see one another often."

He threw a dart.

I threw a dart.

"It looks like we've found our opportunity to talk," he said, throwing a dart.

I threw a dart. "Yes, it does."

He threw another dart. "Do you wish to lay out your qualms first, or shall I?" It was asked in as middle a tone as possible. But it was not the tone that stuck, rather the word *qualms*.

Qualms.

Fine then, yes.

Qualms *are* to be had.

I've my own, to be sure.

Only, qualms so often feel like butterflies. It is not always simple to tell the difference.

"It shouldn't matter who goes first," I said, sounding for all the world as if I were comfortable. I was not. And Pierce knew it. His eyes glanced off my face before, without a word, he walked to the dartboard and removed those we'd thrown. Then he opened the other door to the bureau and retrieved a box from the bottom shelf. Walking back to where I stood by the table, he set the box down and removed the lid. I looked down into a dizzying number of throwing darts, most of them old, some missing a fletch, but all still with their points.

"Sometimes I throw to clear my head. A handy distraction. Shall we begin?"

We were standing ~~fairly~~ ~~rather~~ very close.

"If you don't mind, I've decided you should," I said, fiddling with the dart in my hand. "You see, I've had a great deal of time to think about what happened—as have you. I'm not implying you haven't—I only think it would be—" I took a breath. "Please, Pierce." I threw the dart. I hoped he hadn't seen how my hand was shaking. "You go first."

Pulling his bottom lip between his teeth in the briefest moment of internal thought, Pierce reached for a handful of darts, setting them all in the same direction in his hand. "I have a list in my mind, reasons why I shouldn't kiss you again," he said, deftly throwing a dart, his expression giving way to a frown. He had hit just off centre. "Reasons why I should beg your pardon and not entertain any other course."

I swallowed. "Such as?"

"Our ages, for one."

I threw a dart. "You think I'm too young."

"No, I don't actually. I think perhaps my age is a deterrent for you. *Should* be a deterrent for you."

"The Accord of Parameters, drawn up in Dormitory A at Fortitude, sets the boundary based on the age between one Elizabeth Bennet and Mr. Darcy, with five years reasonable accommodation," I answered. "I signed it with all the rest of the girls—and the horticultural mistress, who I now realise must have been no older than I am now. I digress. As to their ages, Elizabeth is not yet one and twenty, Mr. Darcy is twenty-eight." I threw another dart. "That is eight years. The addition of five years leaves thirteen of reasonable possibility. And you are thirty-three?"

"I'm just turned thirty-four."

"When?"

"December."

"You didn't tell me!"

"No," he said. "I didn't."

"Pierce!" I slapped his upper arm with my handful of darts. "What day?"

He took a breath that wandered into a smile. "Aren't we drifting from our aim?"

"Pierce."

"The twenty-sixth."

Niall Pierce was born on Boxing Day. My mouth opened and closed twice as I resisted the urge to thwack him again. "I could have done something! Agnes might have—"

"There was no need." A shrug. "I liked the day we had. You were reading that mutilated dictionary—"

"Begging your pardon, my dictionary is near perfect."

"—and I was reading the paper. We had a lazy tea. Ideal, one would think."

"I'm going to call you out on behalf of my dictionary's honour."

"Find yourself a *K* section and I'll retract."

There are moments in life when one is standing rather close to the man one kissed in the drawing room, and as he looks down at one's face—absently spinning a dart between his fingers so the colours of the fletching catch the light—one braves a return glance. Often these moments are accompanied by, "What was it we were saying?"

This was my first of such situations.

Pierce answered my question. "That I suspect the difference in our ages presents a problem for you."

"No, we were arguing over your not having told me Boxing Day was your birthday." And then without thinking I moved towards him a fraction of an inch, the slightest start. Pierce held his ground. At first.

And then he carefully took a half step back.

As did I.

Miserable geometry.

"Regarding disparate ages," I cleared my throat, "I've laid before you my contractual obligations on the subject. Our ages are no barrier. However, I would perfectly understand if you were to think me young and too inexperienced—"

"Don't do yourself the disservice." He turned away from me and threw the dart in his hand. He missed the board entirely. He swore. "You've paid your dues, Emma. Any fool can see you've not swum in the shallows a long time now. Setting the question of our ages aside, you still have a reputation to consider."

This concern struck dead centre.

As did the next dart I threw.

"I consider my reputation often enough. For better or worse," I covered. "What about yours?"

"I'm trying my best not to have one," he replied. "In London, anyway."

"Wonderful. We both endeavour to exist in pleasant anonymity."

"We live in the same house." He threw a dart.

Yes. A very present problem. I approached it as a verbal exercise. "To be fair, there are walls. And doors. You are a tenant, I, a property owner. If every landlady were required to only let rooms to women, there would be a disastrous number of men sleeping in Hyde Park. Though I daresay that would make the park good fun, like walking through a catalogue of eligible gentlemen."

Pierce paused, half shook his head, threw a dart, and released a breath. He looked at me in an unfortunate manner (i.e., directly) and said, "I know you have a witty thing to say about every absurdity, a trait I enjoy, but surely you understand the hazardous ground we tread. I am your tenant. We are both unmarried. We have kissed, inside this house. To say nothing of the fact that you are very comfortable in my studio, while I make myself at my leisure in your drawing room and frequent your dining room table on the regular. We have been seen in the neighbourhood in one another's company more than a few times."

He threw a dart.

I threw a dart.

He threw a dart.

I let my own sigh catch before forcing it out. "Yes, it could very easily look untoward."

He made a humoured sound and threw a dart. "It could very easily *be* untoward. It *is* untoward."

"Cousin Archibald does live here," I said. "He is seen as the head of the household by the neighbourhood. It was he who engaged the contract with you in the first place."

Pierce shrugged a shoulder. "How much respectability can a man like Archibald Flat honestly command when the rumours start?"

"A rather unfair question as we both know the answer is depressingly little."

"If anything were said…"

I grimaced. "The Watchers of Whereabouts Lane are already measuring my friendships with all of you."

"Who?"

"The women who watch us from their windows and gossip. Mrs. Morrow is the head of the snake. I quite like her. But she has been asking me questions."

Pierce looked uneasy. "About me?"

"About all three of you." I threw a dart. "I managed it well enough. There is no scandal noised abroad. Yet."

By the sound he made, he was not comforted.

"What are your other qualms?" I asked, pressing my finger against the sharp point of a dart.

"Your parents wouldn't like me. Not for you. Not that I'm saying we— That is, I'm confident the last thing they would want for their daughter was for her to entertain any notion about a man with my past."

I didn't know—I still don't know—how to unravel the feelings of what my parents would think about a great many things. So I kept that to myself and pushed back against his last sentence. "What past exactly? That you came of age during a war? That you learned a difficult trade? That you capture death?"

"I have too many ghosts."

"We all have ghosts."

"Not as many as I do."

It's not often that words sound haunted, but these did.

I threw my last dart.

He threw his last.

The board was riddled and mismatched.

"Care for a drink?" he asked.

I gave no response.

Pierce pulled two glasses from the sideboard and set them down on the table before he poured what I soon discovered to be whisky.

I took mine, suspect at the colour, and walked over to the sofa. Sitting down, I tested a sip.

"Oh dear," I coughed. "That's very nearly wretched."

"Strong."

I left the glass on the table before me. "What other qualms do you have?"

"Age, reputation, parental disapproval, and a problematic past are not reason enough for us to pretend nothing happened?" He swirled the whisky in his glass, then walked around the worktable, setting his glass down before leaning back against the table and crossing his arms. This was grim business. "I feel I've made a strong start. What of your worries?"

Sitting on the edge of the sofa, I leaned forward, my arms also crossed. While his qualms were listed in a clear, coherent manner, my own thoughts were not—some I understood, some I didn't; some were tied to my past, some, my uncertain future.

As fraught as the situation could become, I admit I am more distracted by what is actually and tangibly between us and that it makes me feel both exposed to the elements and given cover at the same time. But how exactly was I to tell Pierce that we both knew the kiss was not due to the mesmeric time of day or the light and shadow and rain. That I can still feel it ringing through my chest. That it feels like the ends of my fingers carry the marks of a lightning strike.

My hesitation had welcomed a nervousness into the room. Pierce finished his drink, set the glass down, then placed his hands on the edge of the table he leaned against.

He frowned. "I'm sorry, Emma, but I think—"

"No." I didn't intend to slap the word between us, but I did. Pierce raised both his eyebrows. As for myself, there was no stopping the flood of words. The torrent had rained down and the water had to go somewhere, consequences be damned. "If you're going to apologise or dismiss what happened, please—" I raised my hand as he moved again to speak. "Lying won't sort this out any sooner than truth, but always with more consequences. You don't know what I'm trying to say. Neither do I, for that matter, but that's beside the point as we are both soon to find out." I took a deep breath and dove right into the mess of my thoughts. "A door has been flung open. Blissfully and overwhelmingly so. The sheer electricity of *you*. I didn't mean to say that in such a way. Aloud, at least. Let me try again. Only it felt brand new, you see? And yes, I might have hidden in the pantry longer than is advisable, but there are certain things we hide from, no matter how they feel. Or rather, *because* of how they feel. You have always been a storm, rolling in from a far-off place, with such strength that even the ground registers the thunder. Clearly you have experience that I do not—"

"Clearly?"

"—but you cannot tell me that afternoon in the drawing room was not *something* to you as well. And yes, conflicted feelings arise in my chest because you were there when I buried the body of the only boy I've loved. The only boy I'd kissed. Maxwell and I were so young, and you are someplace else entirely, having grown up far too fast. What I am trying to say is— What I *mean* to say is, I have said goodbye, and offered my thanks, and made my peace that he is never going to walk through the front door, the door that was always going to be open. That door, that life.

"I say all this only because I was taken off my guard when you— When we—" I lifted a hand to half cover my face. "This might be going very badly. Let me try again." I dropped my hand. "I find you handsome, I always have. Well, not with the beard the day you arrived because you looked a bit wild, and not in the good way. Rather like you had been eating locust and honey in the wilderness. Dear me, this has gone rather pear-shaped."

Pierce was tense through the shoulders, waiting.

"Go on." His tone was patient.

"All this incoherence leads me to say that I believe I was ready… for you. That I am. But it's a tangled thing and I don't understand all the reasons why. I feel like a jumble drawer inside. You know the sort. The drawer where every odd thing is placed because you're not certain where it is to go? I need time to sort it out. Both what is past, and what is present—tremendously, shockingly present. I mean that in a very good way, as I have daydreamed that kiss—" I lifted a hand to stop myself. "All this to say, I would not change what has happened, but I'm doing my best to sort it all out.

"As for you? I know very little of your life, and you seem to have no desire to tell me. How did you injure your leg, I wonder? Is it painful every day or only on occasion? Where have you been besides America? For the names on your boxes of photographs draw an insufficient map. You admit to your ghosts—demons, more like—but I don't know where you found them, or what you do about them besides—" I looked at the empty glass on the table.

"I was stabbed," he answered bluntly. "Several times, with bayonets."

My gaze snapped back to his face. "What? You were attacked by soldiers?"

"British soldiers, as it happens."

"Why?" I asked in disbelief.

"I don't want to tell you."

I lifted my hand to my face, rubbing the bridge of my nose. The image of it in my mind—

I winced.

"Emma."

"Who would do such a thing!"

"It's done." He waved a hand. "It's past."

"But you live with it."

"I do, and I don't know if I'll ever want to speak of it again. Which might prove your point that there's much of my life you don't know. And if we… If you and I decided… There may be things I'll never speak of. Could you be reconciled to that?"

"I don't know."

For half a minute the only sound was our breathing.

And in the caution between us was the dazzling moment that had brought us here in the first place. The human mind is an odd thing under pressure, for I, well, I laughed. "You!" I exclaimed. "And your brooding past and limp, quoting Whitman! Who has any defence? You, untranslatable?" I lifted my hands. "Yes, you are. Like the Rosetta Stone. I can't figure how to tally the light and shadow you use as currency."

He was trying not to smile. "The Rosetta Stone *is* translatable. That's why it's significant."

He was, of course, correct.

"Well, not to me. I can't make out a word of it."

Pierce's shoulders were looser now, his face relaxed. "I've shared my qualms—some of them—and you have articulated your jumbles—some of them. But you are right that it would not be honest to dismiss the reality of what we are both feeling. So."

"So."

"Where does all that leave us?"

I laced my fingers and placed my hands over my knees.

One could not simply ask to repeat the event that set everything in motion, so I said, "We enter into Formal Considerations."

"Meaning?"

"We consider. We sift, we clarify. Yes, clarify! That's the word. And once we've sorted our hesitations or qualms, we decide if we abandon ship or brave seeing where the two of us might go."

He pushed away from the table and walked towards where I sat, sinking into his brown leather chair, arms on the armrests, right ankle crossing over his left knee. He let his head fall back. "You wish to clarify."

"Yes."

"You want the both of us to see if we can sort out more of what we think, or feel, about all this."

"The Great Considerations of 1884."

"The *Great* Considerations."

"It adds consequence."

"Consequence to our considering if we abandon ship or venture into unknown waters."

"Yes."

"Haven't we just done that?"

We had, in part, but I couldn't help feeling—*can't* help feeling—that we'd opened a door but still needed to look from the threshold before stepping outside. And so I replied, "With the cyclone of the last fortnight, I don't see how it counts towards the aforementioned clarification."

"What," he moved his head to look at me, "are the protocols of said time?"

I certainly hadn't gotten that far. It felt as if I were grasping for driftwood in flood waters. And so I answered with, "If you have any suggestions, the committee would be more than happy to consider."

"The obvious suggestion would be for us to act as normal as bloody possible."

A fine idea.

"Protocol one." I ticked it off my finger. "Act as normal as possible. A fine start. Protocol two?"

Pierce shrugged. "Do we need a second?"

"Protocol two, we don't have to say everything we feel if not ready; however, anything spoken aloud must be honest."

"Agreed."

Determined not to embarrass myself, I did anyway. "Ought there be something surrounding…?"

"Surrounding what?"

"Regarding, rather."

"Regarding?"

"Ought we kiss one other!" I blurted out.

There it was.

Flung into the open.

Pierce was so surprised that he started laughing; it sounded almost boyish. "That part we've managed," he said. "Quite thoroughly."

I lifted both of my hands to cover my face. "Yes. Only I meant during The Great Considerations of 1884."

"From which you and I are to gain clarity," Pierce clarified.

"Yes." I dropped my hands and looked at him.

He considered my face, then his gaze dropped to my lips before looking away with determination. "One might argue it could muddy the waters."

"True." One might indeed. "Only…"

Pierce put both feet on the floor and leaned forward in his chair, elbows on his knees. "What do you honestly expect me to say to that, Emma?"

"All right," I determined, sitting up straight and clenching my fists. "Protocol three. Any physical, ah, affection is to be thoughtfully executed— No, that's not what I mean to say. Any physical affection is to be appropriate…to…" I waved my hand. "…the time! That sounds official enough."

"Any physical affection is to be appropriate to the time?" Pierce repeated.

"Exactly. Not *dis*couraged, not *en*couraged, simply appropriate to circumstance."

"Not terribly clarifying."

"Better than an outright ban."

Head bent forward, hands loosely knit, Pierce looked at me with a narrowed gaze. "Are you trying to get me to kiss you, Emma Lion?"

"I…"

"I invoke protocol number one." Pierce stood. "The sun is out, some air would be nice. I need to go to The Keep. Care to come along?"

"That— Yes. Good idea." I stood as well. "I'll go up and—"

But Pierce had taken my hand, bent down as he pulled me just off my balance, and kissed me.

Twice.

"It seemed appropriate to the circumstance," he said in my ear, before releasing my hand. "I'll meet you out front in, say, quarter of an hour?"

Later

We mostly managed protocol one.

March 15th

Miss Lion,

Would you consider throwing caution to the wind and joining me this evening? Mr. Penury and I often frequent the Crystal Palace; however, he has found himself unable to attend tonight's performance. We will hear Miss Thudichum sing and Joseph Joachim play the violin. I believe Mozart will be present in some form. If you are amenable to the plan, I shall arrive by carriage this evening at a quarter to six. We will dine at Claridge's first.

Mrs. Penury

Mrs. Penury,

I would love to attend the performance with you this evening, with a firm hope that Mozart is present only through his music. I've a so-so response to the séance as I've no great opinion of spiritualism.

Yours,
Emma M. Lion

Later

Mrs. Penury and I had a wonderful time. Helped, I would like to believe, by my constant asides and Mrs. Penury's resulting attempts to maintain composure. I did see Annalise Clifford across the way. We waved to one another, but our paths did not cross as Mrs. Penury does not remain after a concert to mingle. As wonderful as the performance was—truly—it was the quiet drive from Sydenham Hill to St. Crispian's that I enjoyed most.

I made a sound of relief and Mrs. Penury glanced my way.

"Mrs. Penury, this has been a treat. Especially after the fortnight I've just endured. You wouldn't believe me if I told you."

The passing expression on Mrs. Penury's face said she might very well believe anything, but the driver pulled up short on the reins and then called down an apology for the jostle, and we moved past the moment.

I found Agnes, Parian, and (to my unhappy surprise) Cousin Archibald in the kitchen. They were playing draughts. Cousin Archibald glanced in my direction, muttered something about tainted enjoyments, and then proceeded to triple jump over Parian's pieces. He smirked at me as if it were a triumph of his person over mine.

"How was the Crystal Palace, Miss?" Agnes asked, rising to offer me a cup of tea.

"Beautiful, Agnes. I've firmly decided that most people's talents surpass my own. There was no séance, thank heavens, so Mozart could not be asked any impertinent questions."

Parian hopped one of Cousin Archibald's pieces just as Cousin Archibald opened his mouth to—I would wager—give his opinion on the art of the séance. Or Mozart.

I wished to avoid both.

"Has Pierce returned home?" I asked before he could speak.

"Yes, Miss," Agnes answered. "But he went out again."

"He went out, you say?"

"Yes, Miss."

"Did he…?" *Did he ask after me?*

"He did come in for dinner first; he'd even changed his clothes."

"And had a fresh shave," Parian said absently as he studied the board.

A fresh shave.

"Well," I said to Islington's portrait.

Cousin Archibald skipped over three more of Parian's pieces.

I sighed. "Goodnight."

And I couldn't help but feel a little disappointed that I was at the

Crystal Palace this evening when Agnes had made such an effort over dinner.

Much Later

They were trying to be quiet. Had I not abandoned Plutarch to slink down into the kitchen for a cup of after-midnight tea and a plate of Agnes's lemon shortbread, I might have missed them altogether.

Not that they could hide the bruises.

From the kitchen, I heard a commotion. Something being knocked over. The sound of hushed voices. One not-so-hushed voice swearing, followed by an answering laugh.

I was in my nightdress and robe, my mother's shawl over my shoulders, with my hair twisted into an unruly knot against the nape of my neck. This After Midnight State of Dress was enough for me to think that, yes, I would stay in the shadows of the pantry and nose about unseen.

However, curiosity.

Taking the kettle off the stove and setting it aside, I crept up the kitchen stairs and into the hall. I could hear talking in Pierce's studio.

"On the sofa there. Yes."

"I'm bloody fine. You don't need to— Damn. My hand."

"Have you broken it?"

"Are you trying to insult?"

A laugh.

"Head back. Give me that cushion. No, not Emma's. The other one."

"Is there a rag about, Hawkes? We should get him cleaned up."

"It's slowing. That's a good sign."

"There's still a tremendous amount of blood."

That was the comment that sent me through the door, regardless of my state.

"What on earth is going on?"

The men froze.

A tableau of the absurd.

Half lying on the sofa was Pierce, bloodied, and with what looked like a thoroughly broken nose. Islington was in disarray, the skin on his right cheek swelling purple. Hawkes had a split lip on the left side of his mouth. Although he had no other visible marks, his breathing was laboured and he looked very awake.

"Have you all been... *fighting*?"

Pierce shifted himself, enough to face me but not for the bleeding to increase.

"Hello, Emma," he said.

I pressed my lips flat. "Hello. I would ask after your evening, however you've blood all over your shirt."

This seemed to set them back in motion. Pierce laughed, then grimaced, falling back against the cushion. Islington was arranging his own clothes into some semblance of ducal order and studying a split knuckle on his hand. Hawkes walked straight to where I stood, took me by the arm, and guided me from the room.

"Hot water? Clean rags? Medicine cabinet?" he asked quietly as we went back towards the kitchen.

"Yes, yes, and in the pantry."

We came down into the kitchen, where I poured the water from the kettle into a bowl and then refilled the kettle (quietly, so as not to wake Agnes) while Hawkes assessed whatever was in the cabinet. I watched him from the corner of my eye as he examined tinctures and remedies, pulling a few items from the shelf.

"I've prepared the hot water," I said. "The bandages are just there, with some clean cloths. Have you found what you need?"

Hawkes's blue gaze met mine, cheeks looking too hollowed out for his own good. (He needs more sleep.) A wordless nod, then the tilt of his head as he indicated we should return to the studio. "I'll see to his face," Hawkes spoke quietly as we crossed the hall, "if you would attend to his hands."

"What happened to his hands?"

Entering the studio, we found Pierce still recumbent on the sofa, a bloodied hand lifted to the bridge of his broken nose. Islington was standing a few feet off, tenderly touching the edge of his bruised cheekbone.

I raised an eyebrow when he looked in my direction.

While Hawkes began to clean Pierce's face with a cloth, I took my own rag and went around to the back of the sofa where I could reach his left hand. The knuckles were bleeding, but it was the swelling along the back of his hand that caused more worry. He jerked when I tried to clean the blood away.

"...broken nose," Hawkes was saying. "Best let me set it now."

"Do you know how?" Pierce asked.

"He's a Reprobate," I answered, coming around to his right hand, not knowing one way or the other. "Of course he does."

"Of course he does," Islington echoed from across the room.

"Hold still, man," Hawkes muttered as he put his hands on Pierce's nose and gave a sharp twist.

It was the most horrible crunch I'd ever heard.

Pierce swore.

My stomach twisted unpleasantly.

Then,

Hawkes: "Better?"

Pierce: "Surprisingly, yes."

"Really, Hawkes, this is more ridiculous than the duel."

"What duel?" Islington asked, studying his face in the glass of a framed painting.

One would think he'd never engaged in fisticuffs before.

After I had seen to Pierce's hands—a bandage wrapped round the split knuckles on his right—and Hawkes had seen to his face—which looked fiercer by the minute—I gathered the bloodied rags and left them by the bowl of water. "I'm off to set the fire in the drawing room, after which we are all going to sit down for a cup of tea while you explain the barbarity of this after-midnight interlude. No sneaking away," I said, glaring at Hawkes. "Honestly, the three of you."

I left to go set the fire. Islington accompanied.

"Are you going to tell me what happened?" I asked, handing Islington the matches, wordlessly asking him to set the fire.

He took them with a stiff hand. "I don't wish to spread unfounded rumour."

"Is that what you call an unfounded rumour?" I indicated the bruise on his cheekbone.

Islington struck the match and lit the kindling. "We were sitting at a table near the back."

"Of The Cleopatra?"

"Of The Cleopatra. Pierce had gone to the counter for another pint and was talking with Gibbs when a handful of men—already well inebriated, from the looks of things—entered. Soldiers. They recognised Pierce from a campaign. He gave them a cold shoulder, turned back to Gibbs, no love lost. But they wouldn't let it pass. Things escalated quickly, and they set upon Pierce. Five against one. We thought it best to help."

I looked down and heard Pierce's voice in my head. *I was stabbed. Several times, with bayonets. British soldiers, as it happens.* "Why would they have?" I asked, without looking at Islington.

"They seemed to hold Pierce responsible for something. I couldn't quite make out what. Things moved rather quickly. Others came to our aid. Gibbs had the men tossed out, and we brought Pierce here. His leg was, well, one of them took a deliberate, cheap shot, and it dropped him to the floor."

My lips parted. I pressed my tongue to the roof of my mouth, taking a long, slow breath. Fortitude taught no courses regarding how to react to a cheap fight. "I'll go and fix the tea," I said. "None of you need anything stronger, *I imagine*?"

"*Ah*, no."

"*Ah*, I thought not."

"Are you always such a mimic after midnight?"

"Are you always such a Reprobate?"

Islington lifted a hand to his heart in an uncharacteristic manner. (Which, with his bruised cheek, did make him look terribly Reprobate.) "You wound me."

"'Twas not I who took a swing at your ducal face. Keep the fire happy. I don't want to wake Parian for our incapacities."

The three of them were present and accounted for when I returned carrying a full tray of tea things and biscuits, Pierce and Islington on the sofa—the former having changed his clothes with the help of Hawkes, I later discovered. Said Hawkes was, of course, reading in his chair.

I set the tea tray on the table between my chair and Hawkes's.

"I assume you will all take some of everything?" I asked.

"Please," from Islington.

Hawkes turned a page.

A nod from Pierce, who was grimacing over his left hand. "Do you have something less pedestrian than tea?" he asked.

Hawkes stilled.

Islington cleared his throat.

I gave Pierce—who yes, had freshly shaved when he believed his evening would be in my company—a look. "In view of your having crossed my threshold bloodied from fighting at a public house, I have prepared a rather pedestrian tea."

Pierce pressed his lips together and gave a slow nod. "Pedestrian tea will be fine. Thank you."

There was silence while I prepared our tea things until Pierce leaned forward, head bent as he ran his bandaged hand over the back of his neck. "I'm sorry about the mess, Emma."

"Yes," Islington added, shifting his pose. "Apologies are warranted."

Then Hawkes said, "Beware the Ides of March."

And I burst out laughing.

It was late. Islington and Hawkes prepared to leave, while I gathered things onto the tray to take back to the kitchen. I pretended not to notice that Islington discreetly helped Pierce to his feet. Sorting the dishes, I put water on to boil for the wash, then pulled it back off again. Lifting my hands to my face, I took a shaky breath. I hadn't realised how strongly it raced through me—electricity or nerves, or perhaps fear.

When I returned, the door to Pierce's studio was open, a lamp lit within, so I was able to see Pierce's form sitting on the stairway in the hall. Slowing my step, I wrapped my arms around myself as I came to the base of the stairs. I looked down at him, but I could not see the expression on his face until he shifted out of shadow. He looked terrible, the cuts matching the darkness of the hall.

"I'm sorry that I wasn't home this evening," I said.

"Nothing to be sorry about," he dismissed. "You enjoyed your concert, I hope?"

"If I'd been here, you might not have gone to The Cleopatra."

"Bad timing is all. Ill luck."

"Ill luck?"

A shrug. "Ill past, more like."

"Islington said they deliberately hurt your leg."

He stilled. Then, "Don't look so bothered. It isn't the first time."

Angry and unnerved, I pulled my arms tighter against myself and spat, "*Hitherto fore*," like it was a curse.

Pierce cocked his chin an inch to the right. "I'm sorry, what?"

"Oh. My father always said that when things were looking all uphill, *hitherto fore* was as good a thing to say as any. Makes one feel like something can be done."

Pierce gave an unhappy smile, then lifted a hand to his face, gently touching the bridge of his nose with his fingers. It looked painful. The bruise beneath one eye was darkening. He cursed and said, "I thought of you, in the middle of it all. And on the way back from The Cleopatra. I kept running our conversation through my head, thinking we had had one day of a chance. But now—" It was the way he moved his bruised hand, dismissing possibility with such a casual motion.

"But now?" I repeated. "Pierce, you were set upon, unfairly, I might add. You defended yourself. How does that alter anything?"

"For many it would. This would be the end of any consideration. Look at me, Emma."

I did. Directly. "I believe we've established I'm not like many. Very possibly to my detriment." I meant it as a self-deprecatory quip, but my words came softer than I intended. "I don't—"

"Mind if we stop?" he interrupted. Something in my expression must have caused his grimace. "I don't want to ruin anything," he restated. "My hand hurts like hell, my face is a bloody mess, I look like a villain, and I've had too much to drink. I don't want, in this moment, to make a mistake."

"Pierce—"

"Emma."

I shivered as if I were cold.

I was not.

He reached out his right hand and I took it. First with my left hand, then with my right, as if I needed to hold him from getting swept away. A moment passed. He squeezed my hand and I nodded, pressing my fingers lightly into his palm—mindful of his bandage—before letting go.

"Goodnight." And I stepped past him, up the stairs, my robe brushing against his shoulder as I went. I don't know why I didn't continue up to the garret. I started to, the quiet creaks beneath my feet marking my path. But I paused and turned where I could just glimpse the shadow of Pierce on the stairs.

He'd let his head fall forward.

Then, after a long breath, he forced himself to his feet.

I watched what he'd wished to hide from me, how difficult it was for him to stand and take a step. His knee gave out, and he gripped the stairwell, cursing until he could right himself. He then stepped quickly towards the wall, hitting it with his shoulder, using the wall for support until he reached his studio.

He closed the door behind him.

I sank onto the floor and wrapped my arms about my knees, praying he would sleep in his studio. When I'd returned to the garret, I listened for the sound of his compromised gait. A relief, really, that it never came.

March 16th

Hawkes stood to give this morning's sermon and did not speak for a full minute. Needless to say, the entire congregation waited on pins and needles. "Friday I prepared a sermon on Christ's counsel to turn the other cheek." He lifted his fingers to lightly touch his split lip. "Seeing as how a number of you were at The Cleopatra last night, I think we can all agree that sermon will have to wait for another time. Let us turn our attention, then, to the cleansing of the temple, shall we?"

The Reprobates on the back row—Night Watchman included—all gave a polite clap, to Hawkes's chagrin.

Islington, nursing his bruised cheek, was not in attendance.

Pierce spent most of the day sleeping. I did not see him.

March 17th

Dr. Fairchild came late afternoon to look at Pierce's left hand.

I only knew because I'd come back from the Philosopher's Sole with a fresh pair of bootlaces and had gone straight to the kitchen.

"Would the doctor like tea while he's here?" Agnes asked.

"Pardon?" I replied, having just ~~gracefully sat~~ collapsed onto a kitchen chair.

"Dr. Fairchild has just gone in to see to Mr. Pierce's hand. Would you ask if he's had his tea?"

I stared at her. Rather, I was staring past her, asking myself for the hundredth time *why* Pierce had been set upon in The Cleopatra.

"That is to say," Agnes rearranged her request, "if it pleases you to invite him, as the *lady* of the house."

"What, Agnes? Oh." I waved her aside. "No, I was thinking of something else. I'll go ask."

I could hear the two men talking through the door. Pierce saying something. Fairchild replying.

I knocked.

"Come in."

I did, to see Pierce sitting in his brown leather chair, his injured left hand set gingerly on the arm of the chair closest to Fairchild, while his right hand dangled off the right arm of the chair, a half-filled glass between his bruised fingers. Dr. Fairchild sat on the plum sofa, his doctor's bag on the floor beside his feet, his own drink on the table before him. He looked relaxed and tired in equal measure. Which is why I waved him off quickly as he began to stand.

"Don't rise on my account, Dr. Fairchild. I have come with strict Agnes Instruction to enquire if you've yet had your tea."

Dr. Fairchild consulted his rather fine pocket watch—I looked on with a pleasant twinge of envy—"Almost five o'clock already!"

"I take that as a no. Shall I bring in a tray?"

"You'll join us?" Pierce said. It was asked with uncertainty.

I noted the bruising on his face, now two days old. Worse under his right eye. "Of course. Let me tell Agnes," I replied.

A fine interaction.

A simple one.

Only, I wasn't expecting to see the shape of all our unspoken questions between us. And that he was still unsure of what I might be thinking about the fight.

When I returned, I found Pierce sitting forward in his chair while Dr. Fairchild gingerly moved his fingers around Pierce's left hand.

"Why didn't you send for me on Saturday night?" Dr. Fairchild was saying.

Pierce shrugged.

"It's well Agnes called me in from the street this afternoon."

Agnes! Calling a doctor off the street without Pierce's permission. This Society of St. Crispian's Senior Servants is proving to be a touch high and more than a little mighty.

"I'm sorry, Pierce," I said, sitting on the far end of the sofa.

"Don't be," replied Fairchild for him. "Just because Pierce is a stubborn jackass, doesn't mean—" he corrected himself. "Apologies, Miss Lion. I forget myself. Pierce and I have seen one too many military campfires together." Fairchild had returned his attention to inspecting Pierce's hand. "I'd wager there's a small fracture, but nothing more. You'll need to be careful for the next few weeks. Do you have someone to assist in your work?"

"If needs be," Pierce replied.

"Good. Don't be foolish, and it should heal soon enough."

Pierce made a dismissive sound.

"Next time you're in a fight—"

"I did not," Pierce said with a measure of distaste, "break a bone throwing a punch. A bottle came down on the back of my hand. Thankfully, it was full and didn't shatter."

This made Dr. Fairchild grin. "An important clarification."

"A damned important clarification."

"Now, Miss Lion." Dr. Fairchild turned towards me. "Have Mr. Flat's bunions recovered?"

I wrinkled my nose. It was unfair to burden me with such information. "He's up in his rooms on the second floor if you wish to ask him," I supplied. "I warn you, however, he might be terrible."

"I'll be back before Agnes brings tea, with any luck."

"Oh, you'll need all of it."

He left the door into the hall standing open.

I looked at Pierce, who was already watching me. It felt like the starlings flying about my chest had settled with a thud in my stomach.

"Thank you," he said to me. He said the words calmly despite our joint uncertainty.

"For?"

"Your help with all of this."

"Of course."

Agnes came in with the tea. "Has the doctor left?"

"He's gone up to see Mr. Flat."

Agnes set the tray down. "Mr. Flat has been reading to me from that book, Miss. It's very kind of him, so very informative."

Uncertainty pricked. "Oh? And what book is that, Agnes?"

"*Mixing in Society*, Miss. I love it more than any story I've ever heard!" She curtsied and left us with a very tempting tea, steam rising from the teapot. I, however, was trying to keep myself from boiling over.

"Won't you excuse me a moment, Pierce?"

I left the studio, marching up to the second floor with my hands clenched. I came to Cousin Archibald's personal room and knocked on the door. It swung open.

"What, what?" he said.

It was in this moment that Dr. Fairchild made his escape. "Remember what I said about soaking your feet, Mr. Flat." And he was past me and down the hall before he could be recalled.

Cousin Archibald watched him go with displeasure and then looked at me and sneered, "Away with you, harridan," and began to shut the door.

I put my foot between it and the door jamb. "Cousin Archibald, are you reading my book?"

"No."

He tried to close the door again.

"Agnes said you've been reading *Mixing in Society* aloud."

"That isn't your book!"

"It is. Were you up in my room?"

"Of course not! I found it!"

"Where? On my desk?"

"In the drawing room."

And then I remembered having set it there when Aunt Eugenia left, and my fears abated.

"Ah. Yes, well. I don't mind you borrowing this particular volume, but—as bizarre as this request sounds to my own ears—I would like it back once you're finished."

(It strikes me now that this was a measure of goodwill I might call upon at some future date, when I ask if I might see his library.)

After withdrawing my foot, the door was slammed in my face. Promptly. I went downstairs and would have walked through the door to the studio with little to no thought had I not been stopped by the temperature of the conversation into which I was about to walk.

Not meaning to eavesdrop, I...well, I did.

"They won't come back," Pierce was arguing.

"You don't know that," Fairchild said firmly. "The five of them weren't so drunk they don't remember in which pub they found you. I wouldn't be surprised if they asked around and know exactly where you live."

"They're cowards, Fairchild. Give it a rest."

"Cowards who all but accuse you of—"

"I know what they say." Pierce's voice cut his off like flint on steel.

A pause. Then, "I've never asked you if it's true."

The silence preceding Pierce's response was unsheathed, sharp edge out. "What is it you want me to say?"

"Pierce—"

"I have nothing *to* say, and you very well know why," Pierce spat. "I live with ghosts every day, true or not. But you don't have to. Leave off, Fairchild. Drink your tea and let me worry after my own bloody skin."

"I see they made a mess of your leg."

A grunt.

"I've never called you a fool, Pierce, but—"

"Don't start now," Pierce interrupted. "Have some cake and stop making a fuss. Here, put this in your tea. It will go down better."

Feeling that the hammering of my heart was loud enough to give me away, I stepped back until I was near the base of the stairs and then practically stomped into the studio with a sentence at the ready. "Mr. Flat ought to be the subject of a farce. Ah, the tea looks lovely. Agnes makes such a fine cake."

Pierce and Fairchild recovered well. Had I not heard their exchange, I'm not sure I would have seen the unease between them. Tea was populated with stories from Dr. Fairchild, mostly humorous, regarding his work. I asked enough questions—such as, "And had the dog swallowed only the one spoon?"—to help the stories roll along. Pierce was quiet; sometimes I wasn't convinced he heard what we were saying.

When Dr. Fairchild was about to leave, and we three were standing over the crumbs of our conversation, he looked at Pierce. "I'm telling you this as your doctor—drink less of that."

Pierce gave a practiced smile. "What, tea?"

Fairchild was not amused.

When I returned to the studio after seeing Dr. Fairchild out, Pierce was standing at his worktable sorting through a stack of letters, one open in his right hand. As he reached across the table, he was ginger with his leg but moved more easily than what I'd seen on Saturday night. Wordlessly, I placed the remnants of tea on the tray.

I thought to let sleeping dogs lie.

Not ask questions.

However.

Wisdom to let well enough alone failed me.

I rested the tray on the worktable. "Are you feeling yourself today?"

Pierce slowed his sorting but did not stop. "More or less." He glanced up at me.

"Only you look…"

"Like I've been in a bar fight?"

"Worried. Over something."

He gave me the sort of nod that doesn't confirm what one said, only that one said it. "Jonathan Revel has written to me three times asking I invest in the expansion of his stables. That's been on my mind. Fairchild was also fussing over the men at The Cleopatra, but…" He dismissed it with a shrug.

"Are they dangerous?"

"To people who can't defend themselves." He tossed the letter onto the table before him. "I'll never see them again."

"I hope you never do."

I wanted to reach for his hand or give him a reassuring smile. I wanted to tell him that despite not knowing all his past, I knew his character, and that it was good.

I did neither.

"I hope you enjoy your evening."

He made no suggestion that perhaps we spend it together. Only, "You as well."

And I left.

What does one with a limited library read when melancholy?

One attempts to read a dozen chapters from Leviticus for perspective (I wouldn't say Leviticus was particularly helpful), a passage of Whitman for hope (hope and impatience, more like), and a soliloquy or two by The Bard (*What a piece of work is a man*, indeed!) before circling back to Isaiah, if necessary.

It was necessary.

March 18th

Mary came by Lapis Lazuli shortly after lunch. "It was an unexpected half day at the telephone company," she said as she collapsed into Hawkes's chair. "So I thought I would take the chance to pay a visit."

"Unexpected how?"

"Someone brought a python to work."

Tybalt looked over from where he was bathing himself on the green sofa.

I doubted. "I'm certain that doesn't happen in actual life."

"One would think," Mary replied.

"Did it eat anybody?"

"Not yet, but Mr. Jenkins—perpetrator of the glorious crime—said it has been a fortnight since he's fed it any rats. He brought it with him today as he was worried for the family dog. And then it disappeared. The secretaries, Miss Strain and Mrs. Plum, both smallish women, were rattled. Uproar ensued."

"What on earth is Mr. Jenkins doing with a python, of all things?"

"His brother works in trade and found the thing in one of his shipping crates. He gave it to Mr. Jenkins as a birthday present."

I considered, and decided, "That's rather wonderful."

"Our gifts to one another pale in comparison."

"So it seems." We both drank our tea in contemplative silence. Then, "And your other source of employ?"

Mary, setting her cup and saucer on the table, slumped dramatically in her chair. "Professor Fletcher has asked if, once *A History of the East India Company* goes to press, I will help research for his next book—The economy of the Netherlands from the years sixteen something or other to sixteen and so on—which means seeing him more often than I do now."

Tybalt and I both thought this wonderful.

We wisely kept it to ourselves.

Not long after Mary left, I received the following:

Miss Lion,

It was a happy thing to see you at the Crystal Palace. Pity we couldn't talk. May Northgate overheard your aunt and her aunt discussing the first event of the Season, and so we expect to see you there. If not, we will present ourselves to your door unannounced and shock the world.

Annalise Clifford

A greater acquaintance with Miss Clifford and Miss Northgate is a cheerful thought, one I've hoped for myself. Only, if arriving at a door unannounced is a shock to the world, I daresay I'd jolt them on the daily.

Later

My second visitor of the day was not so delightful as the first.

I was at the round table in the drawing room, reading the final chapter of *Mixing in Society* (having found it in the kitchen), my left hand firmly holding Plutarch for moral support, when someone knocked on the door. I awaited the pitter-patter of Parian's little feet.

No pitter.

Little patter.

It was up to Emma M. Lion to answer the door.

My efforts revealed a depressing, one-eyed pirate.

"*Ah.*"

"The same enthusiasm with which I greet you," he snapped as he ~~walked~~ hobbled past me, a satchel under his arm.

"I— Excuse me— I—"

But he had already gone into the drawing room.

"Welcome," I muttered to myself as I closed the door. "Right this way. Won't you have a seat?"

Fortifying myself, I followed him into the drawing room. He was sitting at the table in the chair I'd just abandoned. Perspiration could be seen at his temples.

"Would the sofa not be more comfortable?" I attempted.

He shook his head.

"Really, you might find—"

"This chair, Miss Lion, is of a better height for when I wish to stand. If you don't mind."

"Oh, of course."

We both ignored his accompanying grimace.

(Question: Does Lapis Lazuli have a propensity towards gathering wounded men?)

(Second Question: But truly, does Lapis Lazuli have a propensity towards gathering wounded men?)

I sat across from Mr. Chambers, clenching my jaw when he looked down at my opened *Mixing in Society* and made a dismissive sound. I reached across for the offending article and snapped it shut, pulling it and Plutarch towards my person. "I think you'll find that the Plutarch reflects my own reading choices, while *Mixing in Society* reflects my aunt's. How might I help you?"

I don't think he believed me.

However.

Lifting the leather satchel he'd brought onto his lap, Chambers withdrew a book.

"This," he said, placing it on the table, "you will recognise as the binding for your custom library. You'll notice marbled paper of green, sky blue, and brown, with the dark green spine and corners. But *this* is what I propose for your personal journals." He withdrew a square of leather, deep black, along with a few samples of vivid marbled papers, and laid them between us.

I reached across the table, hesitant at first, thinking he would slap my hand away.

He did not.

The leather was so soft I could cry.

Expensive, I thought.

"Beautiful," I said.

"The journals will be bound in black leather, but the endpapers will change with each year."

I liked the thought. "Yes, I approve."

Chambers reached across the table and took the samples back. "I will do this for you on four conditions."

"Conditions?"

"Firstly, you must allow me to bind your current vanity project to match."

"Vanity project?"

"Secondly, I want to know you're not buying cheap ink."

"The ink I choose to use is none of your business!"

"I don't wish to be kept awake at night by the sound of your journals weeping, Miss Lion. Thirdly, we will bind each journal by year. Which of these papers, by way of example, feels most like 1883?"

I looked at the Italian paper before me, a variation of patterns and colours. I liked them all a good deal—the dratted Pirate has excellent taste—but one in particular caught my eye. It was in a traditional peacock style using a light blue, soft green, warm purple, and a gentle red; gold ink mixed throughout.

"This one, I think."

"Good," he said with a businesslike clip. "Fourthly."

I groaned.

"When you come into the shop, you will *try* to annoy me less."

"I find your own mood usually dictates my annoyance."

He said nothing.

"Are those all your conditions?"

"Four, as I told you."

"Well, I have a few of my own."

He guffawed. "Do I look like I'm seeking your custom?"

"First—"

"Firstly," he corrected, before I'd even finished speaking the word.

"First," I repeated, determined to say it ~~however I liked~~ in the way that would irritate him the most. "We must both agree that you have been unfairly sour in regards to my person."

"I won't deny it."

"Second."

"Secondly."

"Second! I want an assurance that, after all this silly fuss you've made, I can rely on you to make my journals in the future."

"I've no plans to leave St. Crispian's, Miss Lion. Do you?"

"I'm trying my level best not to, Mr. Chambers, however fate may be against me."

He snorted.

I resisted a sneer.

"Third—don't you even think about opening your mouth further, Mr. Chambers! Third, I want to be able to buy books from your shop if I have the funds to do so. Without complaint. Without comment. Do we have a deal?"

Chambers began to gather his samples and put them into his satchel. The book in my personal fiction binding he left on the table. "Deal," he said. "Bring that ghastly exhibition—"

"Ghastly?"

"—to The Hound once you've only a dozen or so pages left." He stood, his face white as a sheet for the effort.

"Mr. Chambers—"

"Good day, Miss Lion." He started towards the door.

I grabbed the abandoned book from the table.

"You forgot this," I said, following him into the hall.

Twisting halfway to face me, he gave a mock bow. "Compliments of The Hound."

And he let himself out.

I thought three unpleasant things and then looked down at the book in my hand.

It was the second volume of Dr. Johnson's dictionary, *L–Z*.

March 19th

This morning I began my day by cleaning the one and a half windows in my room as well as in the west garret. I don't know why that moment required the action—me still in my nightdress, braid falling over my shoulder—but I woke feeling a need for light. And so I took the basin of yesterday's water and an old handkerchief and cleaned the windows, the fine texture of dust giving way to smooth glass.

That sense of clarity seemed to permeate the entire house, for when I came across Pierce reading a newspaper in the breakfast room, he looked better than I was expecting. Yes, his face was still a mess—the fading cuts all dark lines over mismatched bruises—but his general demeanour was buoyed. As if he'd glanced out of the window and been pleased to see sunshine.

"Good morning," I said.

An authentic smile in return. "I was wondering if I would see you this morning," he said.

I noted his polished appearance. "Are you off somewhere?"

"Back to the British Museum."

"Ah."

Pierce looked at me, his silver gaze even. "How do you think they'll take my appearance?"

"You will be gifting them a diamond's worth of gossip."

His smile deepened. "Such is life."

"You seem better, lighter. I imagine you slept well?"

"Hawkes didn't leave 'til late, but after I slept well enough."

"Hawkes?"

"We were having a drink. Talked a while, is all." He set his paper down. "I see that amuses you."

Amusement?

The thought filled me with unfettered delight.

For reasons of both happiness and high entertainment.

"Not in the least!" I said. "Only, yes, it does. In the very best way. Did Islington join?"

Pierce shook his head. "Just Hawkes."

My grin would not be contained. "No wonder you look restored to your proper self."

"How's that?" he asked, folding his newspaper to read the next section of news—favouring his right hand.

"It's one of the miracles Hawkes performs. He picks you up, dusts you off, and gives you whatever is needed before he disappears into thin air."

Pierce was looking at the paper, the frown of not really paying attention to what one was reading on his face, and then said, "In my case, he simply walked down the street."

"Yes, well, I imagine he didn't wish to unsettle you."

This brought a quick smile. "No doubt." He glanced back up at me. "I think you can claim at least some of the credit."

Pleasant embarrassment is the common name for what I experienced then.

The Latin equivalent being bashful.

Pierce did not notice. "I meant to ask, if I paid his wages for the day, might I borrow Parian? I've a lot of equipment to move. But my leg is still stiff, and with my hand…"

"Of course. Though you will owe me something delightful for removing Cousin Archibald's handler."

"I'll agree to that."

March 20th

Is there anything so intoxicating as wandering uninterrupted through The Dalliance?

No.

There is not.

I expected, upon my slipping into the bookshop, to receive a gruff dismissal from Mr. Graves. But when I closed the door behind me, the brass bell chiming in welcome, I heard nary a word. The bookshop was empty. No one perusing the shelves. No one behind the counter. It was still, freshly dusted, and smelled of wax and vanilla.

It was the first vision of my life, for I'd swear it was heaven.

I wasn't there to buy a book. Not yet. But I wanted to daydream a bit. What if I found steady employment and was not only able to cover the household expenditures each month but had something to put into the accounts? Could I not, then, find something to go towards my library?

This afternoon the bookstore felt cosy, darkened by grey clouds, but sunshine was trying to break through from the west, and when it did, all the book spines looked like gemstones. I was in the poetry section, having pulled a volume of Wordsworth from the shelf…

> *Dreams, books, are each a world; and books, we know,*
> *Are a substantial world, both pure and good.*

…when a voice said, "There now, dear, what have you picked for yourself?"

And I looked up to see a woman—well-kempt, kind eyes, old enough to be a grandmother, a saucer in hand with a cup of tea balanced contentedly—watching me.

"Hello," I replied. "Wordsworth, actually. Although I'm afraid I can't buy anything today."

I expected a polite but pointed invitation to leave well enough alone what I didn't intend to purchase. But instead, she took a sip of her tea and then set the cup and saucer on the counter.

"Wordsworth? Let's see. What was the line? '*How blest the Maid whose heart—yet free from Love's uneasy sovereignty—beats with a fancy running high, Her simple cares to magnify.*'"

My lips parted, but I had no reply.

Those were the words—some of them, at least—for this question Pierce and I hold between us.

Love's uneasy sovereignty.

Some ramifications understood, others not.

I closed the book and slid it back onto the shelf.

"My favourite thing to do at your age," the woman continued, "was to wander through a shop as if I had the power to buy any book and was simply being selective. But my mother was insistent that ribbons caught more husbands than novels."

"I hope you told her many novels have a ribbon, to mark one's place."

She laughed. "Well now, I didn't think of that."

"Did your ribbons catch a husband?"

"My mother thought so," she replied, "but he and I had already met, when I'd found a well-worn copy of *Kenilworth* dropped in a field and sent a letter to the address pencilled inside the front cover."

"Is that true?"

She nodded. "'Tis. We wrote for half a year before we met in person."

My answering smile was the quiet one I kept for private moments of reading. "Now *that* is a romantic way of meeting one's husband."

"I thought so."

"Are you Mr. Graves's…?" I left off, not knowing what she would be to him.

"Oldest sister. Half-sister, if truth be told. He's twenty years younger than I. My name is Mrs. Lewis."

"A pleasure, Mrs. Lewis. I'm afraid if I tell you my name, you'll have to banish me from the shop, as Mr. Graves is none too fond of my person."

"So. You've made Thomas angry over something?"

"I didn't sell him my father's library."

"A capital offence!" she laughed. "I bought the latest Thomas Hardy in Bath, and he wouldn't speak to me for a month."

"If that be the case, I'll trust you with my name. Miss Lion."

"Well, Miss Lion, I am keeping the shop this afternoon, so I tell you to dally all you like. Take whichever books you wish down from the shelves; sit and read. We'll neither of us tell Thomas that it happened."

I lifted a finger to my lips to seal the secret between us.

And so it was I passed not one, but two hours. Admiring gilt edges, beautiful fonts, chasing down words, and smelling the inked paper as if it were expensive perfume.

A good afternoon.

A much-needed daydream.

I returned to Wordsworth so I might commit to memory what I had begun to read.

Dreams, books, are each a world; and books, we know,
Are a substantial world, both pure and good:
Round these, with tendrils strong as flesh and blood,
Our pastime and our happiness will grow.
There do I find a never-failing store
Of personal themes, and such as I love best.

March 21st

I am in possession of knowledge hitherto fore unknown.

It is perplexing.

This afternoon I decided to seek out the seclusion of Jacob's Well. The aim being Consideration brought about by Contemplation. On my near arrival, however, I paused. For there was Hawkes, sitting on the bench just inside the brick arch.

He was ~~occupied~~ absorbed by the contents of a letter he held in his hand.

I watched longer than is strictly polite—one ought not spy on their vicar, even if they have entered into Friendship. (Said Friendship strictly reinforced by the embroidery of a cushion in Latin, among other things.) I know this. Yet as I was opening my mouth to make myself known, a wind raced by. The letter was stolen from his fingers, flying into the sunshine of Jacob's Well.

Instinct prevailed.

I gave chase.

Past Hawkes. Into the small park. Across the grass. The errant letter was like a painting in motion. It blew across the entire park and threatened to fling itself right over the stone wall into a private garden. I, however, was determined. I stretched out my hand. It was just at the edge of my fingertips. I reached and ran and reached. And then grasping it, I fell forward, the momentum carrying me into a tumble.

The sky, from the damp ground of early spring, was very blue.

Ascertaining that nothing had been damaged, I sat, then stood, brushing my skirts before considering the object in hand. It was the loveliest script I've ever seen. Smooth as silver. The paper alone must have cost a small fortune. Deliciously soft. As I turned back, the faintest scent of pear lifted in the air. Expensive perfume.

Heavens, she must be lovely.

Hawkes was standing at the entrance of the garden, an indiscernible expression on his face. My hair was coming undone beneath my battered hat, but it was no matter. I walked to where Hawkes waited and held out the fugitive letter.

His gaze did not leave my face as he took it and slipped it gracefully into the envelope—none of that awkward business of the paper getting caught on the rough, open edge.

"Thank you," he said.

"Of course," I answered.

A thousand questions came to mind. Who is she? Is it an attachment of long standing? *Is* it an attachment? Why is Everything Hawkes part of a riddle?

I bit my tongue. However tempting the questions.

This was Hawkes, after all. Not one of those run-of-the-mill dukes or photographers that one encounters these days.

"You look pleased, Miss Lion."

"Mildly triumphant." My breath was short from the unexpected sprint. "I've always wanted to do something heroic."

Hawkes gave me his slow half-smile. "The world needs heroic deeds."

"It does. Cousin Archibald declares it all gone to the dogs, but I've still hope. '*I guess it must be the flag of my disposition, out of hopeful green stuff woven.*'"

Tilting his head, Hawkes said, "Extra marks for the Whitman. How are you two managing?"

"Whitman and I?"

"I was asking after you and Mr. Flat."

"I've been praying a good deal," I answered. "That he falls into a hole where he's forced to subsist on mushrooms and rainwater."

Hawkes took the opportunity to tuck the letter into his jacket, but I swear it was only to cover his amusement. I decided then that—in this fallen world of ours—*one* heroic deed might equal *one* impertinent question. "Is she lovely?"

It was as if I'd thrown a pebble into a deep, deep pond. Internal stillness encountering mild surprise. This ripple caused a change only in his eyes. Which might very well be Hawkes for besotted. Or surprise at my lack of manners. Really, how is one to know?

(Besotted: a strong word, and possibly the result of Emma M. Lion's imagination operating in a generous manner. But in my defence, could one ever consider Hawkes's feelings less profound than the poetry he reads?)

(I think not.)

(What he feels romantically surely must accommodate a measure of besot.)

Hawkes said, "Do you sincerely wish me to answer you?"

"I'm acting the part of Marianne Dashwood, who knows she's been abominably forward and should talk only of the weather and the roads." I paused to see if he understood the reference. The subtlest nod to indicate he did. "But I hope she is. For you are lovely, Hawkes."

Again, only the slightest ripple of a response.

"She is," he replied in all sincerity, like a string of white clouds in a blue sky.

I nodded. "How wonderful for you."

He looked right at me. Smiled. His bearing shifted. And I could see—I *knew*—Hawkes was about to perform one of his disappearing acts—the kind where he would simply walk away.

I decided it was my turn to make a premature exit.

"Well sorted, Hawkes." I clapped my hands together. "Good afternoon." And I strode (yes, strode) out onto Whereabouts. Before I could take three steps up the lane, Hawkes—having followed me out—spoke at my back, "Are you trying to best me, Emma Lion?"

I glanced over my shoulder. "If there is one thing I've learned from my vicar," I replied, "it's that I do not have to explain myself to anyone."

Let it be recorded that Hawkes's grin is an unapologetic thing.

He flipped his collar against the breeze, glanced at me sideways, and stepped past me, disappearing down the lane.

I turned towards Primrose Hill, having done my duty to God, if not to country.

Later

I've been sitting at my window the last hour, telling myself I was watching for The Roman. Really, I've been thinking. I don't believe I approve of Hawkes writing to a…what would one call her? Sweetheart feels too sentimental for Hawkes.

Whoever she is, how can I trust her not to ruin everything?

March 22nd

It was a day of housecleaning.

As I scrubbed the checked floor in the hall, Agnes came through.

Twice.

"Is something on your mind, Miss? Only, you seem preoccupied."

I looked up, my rag full of suds. "Do I?"

"You've been going over that same spot a quarter of an hour."

"I suppose," I sighed, blowing a wild lock of hair from my face, "I am considering the mysteries of God."

She nodded as if to say, *I see.* Then her nose twitched, and she asked, "What *are* the mysteries of God, Miss?"

"Hawkes, Islington, and Pierce, of course."

Agnes scrinched her eyebrows in perplexity.

(Scrinched: Likely not a word.)

After Agnes returned to the kitchen, I resumed my contemplations, a version of which I record forthwith.

EMMA CONTEMPLATES the MYSTERIES

An approximation of my thoughts while scrubbing the hall.

Hawkes is exchanging letters. And looking absorbed while doing so. I am troubled. And not in the lovely biblical way where the angel runs a hand through water, and someone is healed. (I've always loved that account. So did Father. When a visiting vicar said something or other about it being a sign of this or that, and not in a good way, Father complained to Mother all the way home that the clergy were doing their level best to poke holes in the poetry of God. "Really, Declan," Mother had replied.)

Perhaps I submit a Formal Complaint against Hawkes. For rogue communications of the ardent variety. Not that I don't wish Hawkes well. I do. I do! I wish Hawkes constellations, and poetry, and wonder, and much more sleep than he presently finds.

But who is she?

Does she love him?

Ought I attend service wielding a sword?

Was he with her the day Jack and I were at The Langham?

To think I could have caught Hawkes in the wild. Instead, I minded my own business (tea with a confidence man). Priorities. I must sort my priorities.

I wish this elegant, pear-scented young woman all happiness.

Only, perhaps, not concerning Hawkes?

Wildly unfair.

But he's Hawkes. Brilliant, elusive Hawkes. Who spends his days hiding in St. Crispian's preaching poetry and speaking elysian sermons.

Sigh.

Islington's secrets are rather like a dark corner of his mahogany library, the light not able to illuminate the titles of the books hidden there. He's said nothing to enlighten the meaning of his aunt's cryptic quips. Or his own admission to secrets—and painful secrets at that. And what of what Hawkes said that day when I'd left Islington's library (the actual library, not the metaphorical library mentioned above) after our reading tea? Why do I remind Hawkes of her? And who is she to which they were referring? Question: How nefarious can the past of a duke be if it is not yet common gossip? I've heard nary a scrap on the Official Circuit as Aunt Eugenia's pawn, other than he's very rich and endlessly proper. Then again, I've done my best to avoid most upper-class gossip. How foolish. This Season I'll take care not to mind an inch of my own business.

One learns as one grows older.

Wisdom must be earned.

As for Pierce. I suppose he arrived from the unknown to begin with, looking up at my window that first night, secrets kept carefully and beyond scrutiny. Then our lives were thrown together. Comings and goings, small exchanges. The first months of our acquaintance he was not profuse by any means, but still mentioning this person or that, speaking of places well-travelled, friendships in various forms. I've so enjoyed the earned ease between us. More than that, I think how he kept the course on my behalf when it came time to bury Maxwell.

Still knowing little to nothing until that night at Islington's, where the sense of all Pierce wasn't telling us hid in every shadow of what he did. If I had to give a reason, I would say that he doesn't want to drag his past into this present. He doesn't want to talk about what he's endured. Rather, he's given himself to the novelty of home. He has a studio, half a cat, and a grocer's bill. He has friends scattered throughout London. His work is seen in a favourable light. He's been lauded in the paper and kept busy with clients. Who wouldn't want to choose this life over memories of dead men and boys buried too young in too many places?

Only, some of those memories became flesh and blood on Saturday night at The Cleopatra. "I don't want to tell you," he had said when I'd asked why. But what am I to think? Or feel for that matter?

Pierce.

He's markedly better after his evening with Hawkes. And this morning, when I delivered his post, there was our usual ease—only we've underlined our previous camaraderie with a more complicated set of emotions, haven't we? With every possibility, on both sides of the measure.

March 23rd

I was kidnapped by the Reprobates before today's service could begin, particularly by Night Watchman, who handed me a calico ribbon of purple, "In honour of services rendered."

"Oh! Thank you. I shall…think of something to wear this with."

Night Watchman beamed.

"Is your arm mended?"

"Better than I'd hoped, dash it all. Can hardly tell a bullet blew a trough through the thing!"

"Unfair," I consoled, "when one has rightfully earned the scar."

"Just what I was telling Mastiff last night!"

Sitting on the back row with five Reprobates on one side, four on the other, I felt genially irreverent. It was, by all portents and signs, going to be a wonderful sermon.

When Islington entered—his face almost returned to respectable, only a tinge of faded yellow on his cheek—he paused upon seeing me on the back row.

"Are you minding this litter of whelps at church now?" he asked.

Only to be met with: "Islington!" from eight of them. The Boy simply nodded.

"Finest specimen known to man!"

"True form!"

"The king of White's a fortnight running!"

Reading perturbation in Islington's tightened jaw and pursed lips, I—sagely—said nothing.

(My full grin was all the representation I needed, by any measure.)

Sitting in the pew before us was the woman who accosted me outside the cobbler's last July. She turned and sneered at my person, as if I were responsible for all Reprobate activity.

By the time the organ began to play, I had felt my Sabbath well spent indeed.

That was when gloom descended.

For was it Hawkes who stood to deliver a sermon worthy of a Sunday in March?

No. Rather, a curate who visits from time to time. A man of

middle age, thick and thin in odd angles, who decided to speak on the Garden of Eden.

Less than two minutes and the natives were growing restless.

"He didn't warn us," Charlie Cross hissed.

"Hawkes swore he'd be back in time," said Mastiff.

The Boy lit a cigarette.

(At which point even I felt their behaviour had crossed ~~a line~~ several lines.)

Quality Jones was the one who began the exodus. "Sorry, gents," he whispered (loudly). "I don't do snakes."

And just as Adam was to be tempted by the slithering serpent, Quality Jones stood, followed by the remaining Reprobates. They filed out both sides of the pew, leaving me sitting dead centre and alone. One of them had the good grace to pat me on the head before making their escape.

After the church doors closed behind the Scoundrels Recently Departed, two things happened.

The visiting curate gave a sigh of what could only be relief.

And most of the congregation began to laugh.

"For those of us who don't mind snakes," the curate said, ears pink, "let us continue."

"It seems," Islington said after, as we were walking around the graveyard, taking advantage of the afternoon sun, "Hawkes warned the curate."

"Where is Hawkes? One feels slightly abandoned when he's away."

"He is visiting his parents, from what I understand."

This piqued my interest.

"He went home then?"

"Yes."

"Where is that?"

"I've no idea."

I searched Islington's expression, but he seemed in earnest. "*No* idea?"

"His family lives near the sea. Somewhere."

"But haven't you been friends since he came to St. Crispian's?"

"Much longer. We were at school together."

"School? But aren't you— You're much older!"

Islington gave me a sideways look. "Yes, as three years Hawkes's senior, I'm practically ancient."

"That's not what I implied, which you perfectly know."

His expression confirmed my statement.

"Go on," I ~~politely invited~~ prodded. "Expound."

Islington processed an internal thought or two before answering, "You're right in that Hawkes and I certainly improved our friendship when he came to St. Crispian's, but he was admitted to Eton the year I was, on account of his sheer brilliance. I knew who he was, kept a loose eye on him until he got his sea legs. Needn't have worried. He managed the lads just fine. Came to Stonecrop twice with half a dozen school friends. We were off to Oxford the same year, I at eighteen, Hawkes fifteen, and as I'd finished my first of two years, he'd already claimed a degree—Divinity School—in one year before moving to Cambridge to read classics for a second. I don't think he slept, doing more than double the coursework as the rest of us."

That is what he said. The extraordinary nature of the entire statement gave me pause. Islington half turned and waited.

"You mean to say he studied at both Oxford and Cambridge? And in the time it took you to gain one degree, he took two at the most prestigious universities in the world?"

Islington simply looked at me. *I believe* it was to be interpreted as a nod.

"I'm *all* envy."

And I was.

I *am.*

"I didn't realise they even *allowed* boys to begin early at Eton."

"When I tell you Hawkes is brilliant, it might be an understatement. It was a deal he made with his father: begin Eton early so that he be allowed to claim two degrees at the schools of his choice in half the time before studying the profession where his true gifts lie. Suffice it to say, he's a tremendous scholar. He would have left Eton early if his mother hadn't put her foot down."

Now it was my turn to return the side-eye. "Hawkes intended a different profession from the church?"

No answer.

"Is it such a secret?"

Islington—hands clasped behind his back as we began once again to walk—frowned. "Not so much a secret as a part of his past about which I make a point neither to discuss nor enquire."

"I see." And despite having more questions, I allowed Islington to change the subject.

(Subject being? One of his hounds is expecting a litter next month. Honestly.)

Returning to the subject of interest, I *do not* see.

I am baffled.

Am I surprised having Hawkes's genius confirmed? Certainly not. Only, no one of my acquaintance has taken degrees at ~~two universities~~ the two most prestigious universities in the world. And quickly! I don't run in the most academic of circles, and for all I know there are several geniuses following the very same course, all while memorizing the most beautiful poetry ever written.

(I am not one of them.)

(The great sorrow of my life.)

But to not speak of the profession he'd intended to follow to such an extent that Islington will not breach the subject with Hawkes?

I cannot understand.

Unless he studied piracy and is under threat of being flogged and publicly hanged, then certainly discretion. By all means!

That would also account for his gifting me *Treasure Island*.

I'm dreadfully curious.

Later

I lit a candle for Father tonight.

And asked him if he'd known any of this about Hawkes.

He gave no reply.

March 24th

Emma,

You are expected at Spencer House at eleven o'clock tomorrow morning for a strategic meeting regarding The Season. *This is a direct order.*

Your Aunt

Agnes came to find me late this afternoon with the above note. I read it before she could quit the drawing room. "Really, Agnes, one would think we were trying to defeat Napoleon."

Agnes frowned. "But, Miss, my mother said we'd already defeated Napoleon well and good."

I pinched my smile and nodded with grace. "Agnes, in this instance, your mother is correct."

My reading this afternoon has been Plutarch's comparison of Theseus and Romulus. I found this observation to be interesting,

> *Both Theseus and Romulus were by nature meant for governors; yet neither lived up to the true character of a king, but fell off, and ran, the one into popularity, the other into tyranny, falling both into the same fault out of different passions.*

March 25th

There is no worse evil than a bad woman.
–Euripides

When Aunt Eugenia sends a missive, run far, far away.
–Emma M. Lion

I reported at Spencer House on the hour.

A stern-faced maid took me into the second drawing room.

Bad omen.

However.

When God locks you in a second drawing room, he provides an archenemy. For there sat Roland with a pink waistcoat beneath his charcoal grey coat.

"What force, pray, has brought you crashing down to earth?" I said in lieu of hello. "And in the *second* drawing room, no less."

Roland looked up at the sound of my voice and smiled. "The enemy lies waiting in the tall grass, I see."

I sat down on a chair across from his. "Has Aunt Eugenia mandated your presence as well?"

"I am being enlisted to aid in *The Season*. It was she who ordered the waistcoat. Not quite my shade of pink, but I'll oblige. She's my mother's cousin, after all."

"I would have selected a warmer hue." I sat back and looked around. The second drawing room. A room I know ~~well~~ too well.

"I thought there used to be a palm over there?"

Roland's eyes followed my lazy gesture. "Moved to the conservatory, I think, before the dinner last week."

I frowned. "What dinner?"

"One of her prelims."

"Pardon?"

He looked at me. "Lady Spencer's Preliminary Dinners. Believe it or not, they are a popular ticket."

I've never heard of Aunt Eugenia's Preliminary Dinners—something I've been clearly barred from attending—and wondered if I ought enquire or leave the dead buried. I chose excavation. "Why was I not invited?"

Roland—Sun God gracing a mortal with his beatific presence—smiled. "Before *The Season* is underway, the old girl invites the top tier of society to be sated at her table. It's how she ensures the correct levels of snobbery are in place before *The Season* begins. Says it keeps people from Getting Ideas."

"You've been roped into dinners all month while I've happily been home?" I burst out laughing. To think how I've been spared! I ought to have thanked my mother a great deal more for running away with an Irishman. "I'm feeling much better now, thank you," I said.

"You're welcome."

A pleasant sigh. "I've always liked a good conservatory. Do you have one, Roland?"

He leaned forward, counting conservatories as one might count cousins. "Three, actually."

"You do not!"

"I do! One in London and two in the country."

I made a distasteful face. "Roland, you are the very worst."

"But I thought you said you liked them?"

"Of course, I do! Only three is so excessive. Is there no end to the indulgence of your class?"

Here Roland took on a rather stern expression. "*My* class? You mean the class you were more than half born into on both sides? Even your dear Irish papa was half English aristocracy."

To which I replied, "My comment was less about class and more about conservatory envy, Roland. Don't get on your high horse."

When Aunt Eugenia arrived—Arabella resting in her rooms as "the best bloom must be coddled"—Roland and I found ourselves on the long end of a lecture.

"This will be the most important five months of our lives," she declared, surrounded by her flock of cushions. "It is imperative that each do their part. Events are on every horizon."

"Every horizon, Aunt?"

"Every horizon, Emma! You must commit yourself, body and soul."

This did not make me think of *The Season*. Rather a different ~~person~~ question entirely.

"Roland," Aunt Eugenia continued, "you must be dispensable upon my order. We will practice the signals"—a quick flick of her hand accompanied with a squint—"as needed. I do not wish you to make Arabella's approved suitors despair, but I expect you to intimidate all the rest. As for you, Emma, whereas last year you were meant to look miserable and possibly consumptive—a thing you never quite managed," said with accusation, "this year I want you to look like someone worth having in the family." She turned to Roland. "Last Season she was Arabella's foil. No one who saw her thought her anything but the opposite of perfection."

"You're welcome, Aunt," I said.

Roland, wisely, kept his amusement to himself.

"As for your wardrobe, Emma, I've had Madame Tasset make over a handful of Arabella's old dresses for you. I will send them back with you today. Now." She ordered her maid to hand us each a handwritten sheet. "If you reference the schedule before you, you will see our First Event, Lady Harlow's ball on April the Fifth. And below the schedule, I've also made up a list of the eleven candidates we are considering, with basic information I thought would be helpful. Please Review."

I glanced at the paper she'd pushed across the table.

"Your task is to assure they are smitten with Arabella within the first month. Which is not so very much to ask."

I glanced it over, seeing all the expected names.

And then.

"Oh no, Aunt!"

"Do I hear the unpleasant tone of dissent?"

I looked at the list, then to Roland, then back to Aunt Eugenia. "You've added the Duke of Islington!"

Roland frowned down at his list and visibly flinched.

"So I have. Provisionally." Aunt Eugenia sniffed. "He's a good deal handsomer than I wish and not as malleable as I would like; however, his portfolio is one of the best in the country, to say nothing of his sheer arrogance. Any children would inherit both."

"But this—"

"Emma, I can't imagine God giving you an acquaintance He did not mean for me to make use of. Please, close your mouth. Let us all pretend you're not as dreadful as we know you to be."

Roland did not manage to stifle his laugh.

I gave him a death stare.

"Speaking of using your acquaintances," Aunt Eugenia continued, "I demand we address your photographer."

It felt like she'd shot a cannonball through my chest.

"Mr. Pierce?" I squeaked.

"His idea to photograph Arabella in Berkshire is absurd," Aunt Eugenia replied. "He will take them here, at Spencer House. Please give him this card. He may select one of the dates written on the back. I expect to hear no later than the day after tomorrow. Once a date is settled, you will need to arrive two hours early so that the maid will have time to do something with your person."

"My person?"

"Of course! I am having a portrait taken of the pair of you. Arabella *insisted*."

"*Ah*."

What a lovely rat she can be.

And so now I sit in my garret discussing the ~~merits~~ aspects of each potential suitor with Tybalt.

Except Islington. I've already crossed his name from the list.

"Ah, here's George West. A lord, I should add. Unthreatening but not exactly right in the mind. Do you approve? I thought not. Here's one I was not expecting to see: Lord Abernathy. His wife died only a year ago, if I recall from the papers. Lord Brexton, the Earl of Toll! The man has seven children, all older than Arabella! Miserable. What would your fellow felines say? What? You would burn the entire empire to the ground?"

ARE YOU TALKING TO YOURSELF?

I'm speaking with Tybalt about eligible men.
For Arabella.
How was your day?

TAXING

Did you see Agnes saved you a plate?

NO, I DIDN'T.

She's gone to her meeting with St. Crispian's Senior Servants, or whatever it's called, but I know where she's put your dinner, if you're hungry.

I'LL SEE YOU IN THE KITCHEN.

March 26th

Agnes, Parian, Cousin Archibald, and I held a household council in the kitchen this afternoon. The topic? Ought Lapis Lazuli House acquire a plant.

It was Parian's idea. And as he asked me about it when Cousin Archibald was crossing through the hall—"What, what!"—we had no choice but to involve him.

"What sort of plant were you thinking, Parian?"

"Nightshade! Monkshood! Hemlock!" This from Cousin Archibald.

"Cousin," said I, "one would think you were trying to poison someone."

"I've no idea of what you speak," said he, a finger moving across his scar. "Foxglove!"

"The Society recommends a variety of fern," Agnes said, sitting primly with her hands laced before her.

"That's what I was thinking," Parian said. "A fern. I heard a doctor speaking about it being healthy."

"Ferns?" asked Agnes.

"Houseplants. Something about the atmosphere, or the soil, or..."

"Who would water said plant?" I asked.

"I don't mind," Parian answered. "I like the thought of something green."

"Will you be able to keep it alive?" asked Agnes. "It's a serious responsibility, taking charge of a living thing."

"I've no idea," Parian answered, beginning to look nervous. "But I'd like to try."

Agnes furrowed her brow. "I hope it doesn't make a mess."

"The government of this house is a mess." This from Cousin Archibald.

"Thank you, Cousin Archibald." I turned back towards Parian. "I don't see why you shouldn't try. Why don't you conduct an experiment. Keep a plant alive in your rooms for a few months, and if it does well and you feel you are up to the task, we'll adopt a plant for the drawing room or the hall. Mr. Pierce has several plants, and they seem to do quite well."

And so it was decided.

Parian is going to care for a trial fern.

March 27th

There is no contentment like that of sitting at one's window, reading a book, with the sounds of birdcall and the promise of spring.

Ah.

Look there.

Someone has arrived in a carriage.

What on earth are Lord and Lady Braithwaite and their spawn, Victoria, doing at Lapis Lazuli Minor!

This house ~~will not~~ cannot abide more unwelcome visitors!

Later

I've gone down to the hall twice, pausing before Pierce's door. The second time I heard Victoria say something and Pierce laughed. Lord Braithwaite followed it up with a remark of his own.

I can't honestly think anything would be So Very Amusing as to warrant Pierce's appreciation. Perhaps he is just being kind to the aggravating, as the Bible asks us to be.

They have been in there over an hour now.

I feel upset. And invaded.

Cousin Archibald hasn't even stirred from his rooms. Inconsiderate. A small, well-timed catastrophe would not go amiss.

Later

When Pierce came to find me, I was in the drawing room ~~pretending not to have just run back from the window after watching Victoria Braithwaite and her parents creep into their carriage~~ reading a book.

"Hello," he said. Pierce crossed his arms and leaned against the doorframe, wearing his very proper "I've just had a wealthy client" attire.

I flicked my eyes upward and looked over the top of *Latin Phrases for the Unrepentant*.

"Hello."

"I was thinking the Reed and Rite for something to eat. We could sit in silence and consider."

"Were you going to invite Scylla and her spawn to join us?"

Pierce paused, then his eyes narrowed, even while the corner of his mouth lifted in confusion. "Excuse me?"

"The family you have just paraded through my house—"

"Hardly paraded."

"—was the family I was forced to live with for six months after my mother died."

"Lord and Lady Braithwaite?"

"Yes." I let my book drop and snapped it shut. "And you opened the gates of my personal Troy to the infernal Greeks."

"I take it you and the daughter did not get along?"

This was one of those moments where one might take the moral high road.

I chose to dig a ditch.

"Victoria Braithwaite is one of the three people I dislike most in the world, and now she's invaded the inner sanctum. I blame you for this. I'm certain I'll find something disagreeable left behind, like a cockroach."

Now Pierce actually did smile. Unfair advantage. (Something to consider.) "Am I to run my list of clients past you for approval?"

I may have looked towards the window and made a face. "Clearly not."

"Were they very unkind to you?"

I said nothing.

He waited three steps' worth of time before saying, "I'm sorry."

"Yes, well, so am I. And peevish, apparently."

"Anything I can do?" Pierce uncrossed his arms, putting his hands in his trouser pockets.

Emma wished to say: Let's throw a basket of eggs at something (a Braithwaite, preferably).

Emma said: "Shall we go, then, for tea?"

And thus it was that Pierce and I found ourselves at our corner table at the Reed and Rite. "Have I mentioned how nice you look today?" Pierce said, taking a sip of his coffee.

EMMA PAUSES IN HER NARRATIVE

To infom the record that she does not always think before speaking.

One would think my many faux pas would have given me renewed determination to mind what I say.

With diligence.

However. I return to the moment.

"Have I mentioned how nice you look today?" Pierce said, taking a sip of his coffee; his long fingers, wrapped around his cup, shared a scar. For someone who is supposed to consider the merits and risks of a possible relationship, it was too much.

"Different hands would do," I muttered to myself.

"Pardon?"

"Your hands, Pierce. Your hands."

"My hands?"

"That very attractive scar that corresponds along the back of your fingers."

He glanced down. "Oh, archaeological dig outside of Damascus."

"In between wars?"

"In between wars," he replied, taking another sip of his coffee.

If the purpose of our period of Contemplation and Clarification is so rational thought prevails, he's cheating by placing an attractive finger on the scales in his direction.

We followed the first protocol to the letter. Very nearly, at least. But when Pierce half-laughed at something and shook his head over it, I had had enough.

"You mustn't do things like that, Pierce. It breaks all rules."

He looked up. "I'm breaking a rule?"

"Most likely several, but yes to one in particular."

He narrowed his eyes in uncertainty. "How?"

I frowned. "We're supposed to be Considering."

"I remember," he answered.

"Exclusively."

"Yes. Consideration. Clarity. Protocols. I understand where you and I stand, Emma."

"Then why are you casting your charms about the room?"

Pierce made a baffled noise. "What?"

"You're casting your charms."

"How the hell does one do that?"

"Like so. Now, I am going down to The Keep. When I return, we neither of us will remember what I said just now."

Pierce's answer was a slow smile.

I stood. "I recognise that silent expression of amusement. You've been spending too much time with Hawkes."

As if it were a slight.

As if it even could be.

"That I refuse to confirm or deny," Pierce said.

March 28th

Saffronia March, whom I've not seen all month, came by with an invitation. "Would you like to accompany me to the Dulwich this afternoon?"

"Yes!" I replied. I'd never been. Father had meant to take me, but there is never time for what one plans to do, only what one does.

"Then it's settled," Saffronia said, pleased. "Should we beg Agnes for some tea before we set off?"

We spoke of things about which Saffronia was trying to make up her mind—i.e., should she accept the invitation from an Austrian count to the opera? ("I don't understand why it's a question," was my reply.) Should she deliver the commissioned portrait to Lord Cross herself? ("I wish to strangle the man," she'd stated. "Twice over.") Was it going to rain? ("Likely.")

The Dulwich Picture Gallery was a feast, with Saffronia and I moving from one gallery to the next, sitting on the occasional bench while she sketched an idea in the generously sized portfolio she'd brought for the express purpose.

And then something neither of us was expecting.

Lo and behold, there stood Hawkes before Reni's painting of Saint Sebastian.

Shoulders tensed, head tilted forward despite his gaze being raised to the painting before him, hands clasped behind his back, left hand holding right wrist in an artistry all their own against his blue coat.

Saffronia and I saw him—and recognised him—at the same moment and reached for one another. "We should leave him be," Saffronia whispered.

"Yes."

Then Saffronia's face took on what my father called "the unholy gleam of the heathen artist." With a lift of her eyebrow, she directed me to the nearest bench. We sat, and Saffronia opened her portfolio to a fresh piece of drawing paper.

While Hawkes studied Reni, we studied Hawkes.

Saffronia's eyes darting from our *modèle vivant* to the lines on the page before her. Swift, practiced lines. Lifelike despite the sparsity, this Hawkes might have walked off the drawing paper and I wouldn't have thought anything of it. It was nearing five o'clock by the time Saffronia finished. All that time Hawkes had not moved, had not turned his head, neither shifted his balance. He simply stared at Saint Sebastian.

We left in silence.

When we were out on the street, Saffronia showed me the completed sketch.

It was beautiful.

"It looks like Sebastian will collapse onto Hawkes's shoulders!" I said.

Saffronia let out a breath and closed her book. "Hawkes always spurs me to examine my life, whether he speaks to me or not. It's vexing."

We returned to St. Crispian's by hansom cab, talking of the various pieces seen, neither speaking more of Hawkes. But when we'd disembarked at Lapis Lazuli, Saffronia opened her portfolio and withdrew the drawing.

"For you, I think," she said. "I could hardly do anything else in good conscience. If I keep it, I'll paint it, which Hawkes might not like. And you will take good care. I've an old frame that should just about fit the size. I'll send it down with Toff. Feed the boy, if you would. Word is he's growing out of everything and hungry all the time."

Later

Toff arrived just now with a gold frame, chipped in the best sort of way. I sent him through to the kitchens and went up to the garret—Tybalt following along—to introduce the sketch to the frame. I've placed it above my bookshelf.

It feels right.

March 29th

From what I gather, number 34 and 36 Whereabouts Lane are now empty.

Other than the young family Mrs. Morrow spoke of, who else will move in, I wonder?

I think I'd favour someone disreputable and loud, who could take all unwanted attention away from Lapis Lazuli. This person would cause such Byronic Uproar that the thought of a studio door opened on the daily would not register as untoward. The idea of two individuals who only technically live beneath the same roof ~~courting~~ investigating possibilities would not cause *Scandal!* to be noised abroad; rather, a feeling of goodwill and unspoken support for the unfortunate orphan and sharp, but kind photographer with a limp.

Now, if a Dissolute Viscount were to settle across the way, that might prove fatal to our Considerations, as I might have to explain to Pierce that the man is likely my future husband.

Such are the conundrums of life.

March 30th

When Hawkes began his sermon this morning, the sun shone through the stained glass.

I could almost swear there was a halo.

Later

Cousin Archibald is in the drawing room "for the duration of the day."

Therefore.

Pierce and I are going to take sandwiches out in the wilds of the back garden.

March 31st

I feel almost sick. And angry.

I went to Hyde Park to meet Roland, fully imagining a lark.

I was not expecting him to say within three minutes of walking, "You've heard about Victoria, of course."

"The Queen? Has she done anything remarkable of late?"

"No," Roland replied, his tone weighed down. "Victoria Braithwaite."

Here, I behaved as I normally would.

I gave Roland a dismissive expression, the kind I would despise on someone else, and said, "Victoria Braithwaite is a rather unfortunate reality."

"Emma," Roland said, his uncomfortable smile doing a poor job at covering his censure. His cheeks turned red. "Her parents have only just died."

It felt like falling from a second-story window.

"What?" I managed.

"Saturday night. The two of them were returning to London. Something about a large coach whose lamp had gone out, a collision, and an axle breaking on their carriage. It was in the papers yesterday. Father dead at the instant, mother sometime during the night."

"And Victoria?"

"From what I've heard, she's here in London, having stayed behind."

The rest of the walk we had very little to say.

Truth be told, there are things one wouldn't wish on one's worst enemy.

April 1st

Apparently, Cousin Archibald has found—or been given—a religious pamphlet from America. I know this because he has sat himself at an open window of the second floor, and any time I come or go, he jeers out a line about damnation, hellfire, and the lost state of my soul.

"You will have a clear remembrance of—what what!—*all* your sins…against me!"

I feel he inserted the last part.

I entered the hall with a heart burdened by the sin of wishing to push my relation out a window.

The studio door was propped open.

~~I went like a moth to a flame.~~

I thought, perhaps tea? And went in. "I am afraid we have our very own April fool," I said, taking off my gloves. "Have you yet been called to repentance from the second floor? I have four times already."

Pierce was cleaning a camera with a white cotton rag. His answer came with half a smile. "I suspect he doesn't wish to lose the rent."

I sat down on the plum sofa. "Or he thinks you're beyond saving."

Rueful storm-cloud laugh.

Gaining Pierce two points in The Great Considerations of 1884.

"I was wanting—"

"There was—"

We both began at the same time.

Pierce set down his work. "You first."

It was uncomfortable to speak of. "Do you remember— Of course you do. Your clients, the ones I gave you such trouble over. The Braithwaite family?"

Pierce let out a breath. Taking a portrait waiting on his worktable carefully in hand, he walked over, placing the image before me, and then dropped into his leather chair. Leaning back, his elbow on the arm of the chair, he rubbed his temple with his fingers. "I was going to bring up that very thing. I read about the accident in the papers. Horrible mess."

"I only found out yesterday."

"From all accounts the daughter was not with them?"

"No, she was here in London."

He nodded and ran the back of a finger along his jaw before looking at me with that uncomfortably open stare. (I blame his years in America.) "It was what I wanted to ask you. I have their portraits ready. I don't think I should deliver them."

My stomach tied in knots. "Pierce."

"I know." He held up a hand. "You have a past, a complicated past, but it would be inappropriate, I think, to take them myself. The daughter will have begun full mourning, and her visits will be under the damned scrutiny of her neighbours. An unmarried tradesman?" He shook his head. "I thought it best you take them, as you know the family. Unless it's too difficult, which I would understand."

I looked at the portrait. It was of the three of them, the father sitting, hand on a cane, the mother and daughter standing behind, their arms around one another's waists, Victoria's hand on her father's shoulder. Smiles all, a happiness for their shared company. It was like never having seen them before. He appeared as a man who had not given up, who had decided innovation and fight would see him through. Lady Braithwaite also looked strong, as if a lifetime of insecurity—of knowing that her personality caused barbed words to trail behind—had forced her to lift her chin, regardless, and that she possessed courage. As for Victoria, I could see there had been happiness with her parents, and an almost naïve confidence that she would find the same in her own future home. Pierce had done beautiful work.

I leaned forward, resting my elbows on my knees and my chin in my hands, watching him watch me. "My hesitation isn't that we have a complicated—*very* complicated—past. Only what do I possibly say?"

"One would think you, of all people, would have an acute idea."

I closed my eyes. "That is how I know I will fall short."

He made a sound of understanding. "I'll send them with a delivery service," he conceded. "It will be difficult, regardless, and she may not want to look at them now, or ever. But I think she should have the option. I'd only thought it would be best for her to receive them from someone she knows."

I opened my eyes. "If you prepare them, I'll take them tomorrow."

I could tell he was pleased by the way his eyes narrowed slightly, as if part of a smile. "Thank you."

April 2nd

I was standing in the hall, waiting for Pierce. His studio door was open six inches, and he was writing something. I took a deep breath, not looking forward to the visit ahead. Pierce came out into the hall a moment later, a flat grey box held between his two hands. It was tied with a charcoal grey silk ribbon, an envelope tucked beneath.

"A note of condolence," he said as he followed my questioning glance.

"Will there be one waiting for me when this goes terribly wrong?" I asked as he handed me the box.

Pierce, placing his hands in his trouser pockets, looked both amused and down.

A confusing sentence.

That is to say, I'd amused him. And he looked down at the checked floor of the hall before again meeting my eyes. Pressing his lips together and raising both his eyebrows, he looked around the hall, back towards the kitchen, and up the stairs.

It was quiet.

Nary a soul about.

He then took a step towards me and, hands still in pockets, Pierce leaned forward and kissed the left corner of my mouth.

"My condolences for the task ahead," he said, close enough that had I moved a quarter of an inch, my cheek would have brushed his lips.

Upon realising I'd quite forgotten the use of my lungs, I took a breath—it stuttered as it went in and quavered as it went out—and then I swallowed.

In that moment, that sterling, bright, and almost unbearable moment, my interior landscape suffered a small quake. And so I resorted to whatever was at hand. Which—and this is unfortunate—was impeccable politeness. Odd, as that is a foreign country for one Emma M. Lion.

"Thank you," I said. "How very kind."

Am I perhaps remembering wrong?

Alas.

I am not.

That is what I said when Niall Pierce acted in a manner worthy of awards and accolades in the daydreams of Dormitory A.

Thank You.

How Very Kind.

(I am not worthy to read Jane Eyre for a month. Possibly three.)

Needless to say, there *is* such a thing as a lost moment.

Pierce gave half a laugh. It was sharp. Then he stood up straight, which was the equivalent of taking a step back. It was not a self-deprecating smirk on his face, but something akin to one. I stood there gripping the box that held the portraits of my archenemy's deceased parents.

Romance, thou art ~~elusive~~ possibly dead.

"That's not what I meant to say," I blurted out. "I panicked."

Pierce ran his fingers through his hair, his smile having found his usual ease.

And I just barrelled on. "You see, at a point in every life, the training of one's mother will actually take hold. And a perfectly polite answer will roll—or tumble—off the tongue. This is usually a token of good breeding. In my case, however, it doesn't seem to indicate such, does it? I can see by your face that I have now wandered into irredeemable ridiculousness, so I simply say, wish me luck, and I will see you after. If I haven't shipped passage to Australia. Booked passage to Australia, that is. On a ship."

Box firmly in hand, I marched myself up to the garret without looking back.

Later

I intended to take a hansom cab to Lyall Street. Pierce had given me the money earlier in the day—"You're on an errand of business." But I decided to walk and let my fluster evaporate, as if I were a scientific experiment.

A successful one, I hope.

It took over an hour, and by the time I turned the corner onto Lyall Street, I was feeling less silly and more stalked by dread.

There was a large black crepe bow on the front door and all the curtains were closed. The house was too large, and terribly sad. I pulled the bell cord and tried not to think how I despise bell cords—we would all be better to remain a nation of people with enough confidence to bang on a door—and waited.

It took a long while, but I was determined to leave the neighbourhood *sans* box.

Finally, the door opened.

It was a maid with a black armband.

I straightened my shoulders. "I've come to see Miss Braithwaite and bring her…something important."

"She's not seeing anyone, Miss."

"Ah, well, in that case, if you could give—"

The door swung open wider and not under the maid's power. It was the housekeeper, one I did not know (and, regrettably, who did not know me either).

"Have you come to see Miss Braithwaite? Please, come in. The child hasn't seen anyone in three days. I've been hoping against hope a friend would come. Please, Miss…?"

"Lion," I said.

"Miss Lion, do come in by the fire and I will coax her down."

That moment confirmed my fear this was the very worst of all ideas.

The drawing room was dark and stuffy, a fire burning and a few candles, the barest shreds of natural light hesitant to come through the curtains.

Grim.

Very grim.

I waited quarter of an hour.

Then half an hour.

The maid brought in some tea—admittedly very good—and I sat sipping in the dark room, unsettled.

When the door opened, Victoria entered in all black. I stood. She looked at me with purple smudges under her eyes, hair pinned back severely. The click of the drawing room door as it closed was ominous. She stared at me. Then walked across the room and stood before the chair opposite me. "I've promised Mrs. Marsh five minutes," she said flatly. She sat.

I sat.

She said, "You've come to confirm the gossip?"

"No," I answered, my cheeks flushed, "I've come to…say I'm terribly sorry and see how you are."

"Why?"

"We have a shared past and…and your parents were kind to me," I said.

"No, they were not," Victoria pinched out the words. "You were an unwanted charity case."

No, I could have repeated, *they were not.*

Instead, I offered, "I had no place to go, after…well, and Lord and Lady Braithwaite took me into their home. I thank them for it, and I am sorry."

Victoria gave her head a shake. "Do you feel bigger now? Do you feel superior, like always?"

"Superior?"

"You were, quite frankly, a misery to us all. It was a great imposition on the family." She had begun to shake, clasping her hands to smother the visible evidence.

"I'm sorry," I said softly.

"Do you know how many enjoyments and pleasures were denied me because of you?"

Having a clear recollection of outings and holidays and visitors for which I sat in my room, I felt no twinge of remorse, but held my peace.

"He said you had nothing, the vicar who begged my parents to take you in because no one in the village wanted the burden. Which wasn't true. Lady Spencer came to fetch you, eventually; I understand her delay. And there was that dreadful woman who wrote Mother endless letters asking if you were well and could she visit? I swear the inconvenience of it all put Mother half in the ground."

"Pardon, what woman?" I asked.

But I was never given an answer.

"Pauper, indeed. You were a minx, and my parents felt the same. Here I've been left with a single relative, a lunatic I scarcely know, all the while you had the Duke of Islington in your pocket."

Ah.

My chickens come home to roost.

Or is it pigeons?

I forget.

"Connections are not always as glamorous as they seem," I muttered.

"You were a bother. A bother and a nobody."

How can a nobody be a bother? I might have said.

I rested my hand on the grey box at my side. "The photographer, Mr. Pierce, is my…neighbour. He meant to bring these to you this week but thought it inappropriate as you are beginning your mourning. He also wrote a note of condolence."

I lifted the box and held it out in the space between us.

She sat stiff a moment before quickly taking the box away and placing it firmly on her lap in a protective manner. I understood, but I tried not to show any sympathy on my face. It would only make her angry. Glaring, Victoria removed the envelope and practically ripped it open. She looked at Pierce's script dismissively at first, then a trace of pain moved through her expression, the smallest glimpse of tears inside out, a dark landscape illuminated by lightning for the briefest, bluest moment of storm, then going dark again.

She folded the letter, carefully now, and cleared her throat.

"I think you should go," she said.

I gave a single nod. "If there is a day you need to speak, or yell, or shout, you can come to me. I will listen."

I took my card from my reticule, left it on the sofa, and stood. She looked away towards the fire, her fingers holding the box so tightly they were white with the strain. I crossed the room, the carpets absorbing my footsteps, and only when I had put my hand on the door handle did I turn back towards Victoria.

"It feels like all the pictures have been taken out of their frames," I stated.

She glanced in my direction, her eyebrows in an angry knit. "What?"

"It feels as if you are wandering the empty house that was your life, the rooms so familiar you can't deny you once inhabited them, but everything is sparse: bare windows, naked floors, and all the paintings are gone from their frames. It is the loneliest feeling I know, and I am sorry."

Victoria set her face stubbornly against my words and looked past me.

I left.

I tried not to think on it. But the image of the three, captured so well, so compassionately by Pierce, crossed my mind again and again. Poor Victoria. Two parents in one dark slice of a night. Even I was spared that by a handful of brittle months.

Upon returning home, Pierce's studio door waited ajar, but I came up to my garret. I needed my most secure walls; I needed to gaze out a window that did its best to be very good to me. I needed to write out the demons of this day's work. I'll go down for dinner, and Pierce will be there, and he will ask. I'll be honest about the feeling but keep the words lying where they were spoken, only between Victoria and myself.

I will do my best not to be too polite.

Perhaps I will watch for The Roman tonight.

April 3rd

I HAVE IT FROM A RELIABLE SOURCE THAT THE REED AND RITE IS SERVING SCONES WITH CLOTTED CREAM AND YOUR PREFERRED STRAWBERRY PRESERVES.

Is this an invitation?

IT IS A THANK YOU FOR TAKING THE PORTRAITS TO MISS BRAITHWAITE.

You thanked me last night.

I DID. AND LATER AT THE CLEOPATRA I ASKED HAWKES FOR A LINE OF SHAKESPEARE I COULD ADD TO IT AND ALL HE SAID WAS, "I CAN NO OTHER ANSWER MAKE BUT THANKS, AND THANKS, AND EVER THANKS." AND I HAVE NO IDEA WHAT THE HELL THAT MEANS SO INSTEAD I'M INVITING YOU TO SHARE IN THE PROMISED SPOILS.

I am excessively pleased such a conversation took place. I am pained to not have witnessed it myself. As for the spoils, these must be very serious baked goods.

CHAMBERS THINKS SO.

Not a reliable source, then.

WHY NOT?

To a pirate, everything tastes good.
I'll fetch my hat.

Later

I concede, the scones were very good. Pierce and I sat in our usual corner. When we were almost finished, he informed me that

Islington had invited us to his house this evening. "Your aunt has no nefarious plans, I trust?" I could feel some strawberry preserves on the corner of my mouth and ~~lifted a napkin politely~~ wiped it away with my thumb. Pierce watched, his eyes following the movement. Our eyes locking briefly before we both looked out of the window.

I did not abstain from his face too long, however, and was enjoying his profile when I answered, "Day after tomorrow is when it all begins. I'll only need to speak with Agnes."

"I mentioned it to her this afternoon." Now Pierce looked back at me, a slow release of his breath and quick shake of his head.

He smiled.

I smiled.

And then we both tried not to laugh but did.

He said something I couldn't quite hear, something about ridiculousness.

"Islington's," I said, taking firm hold of the situation. "Tonight. Wonderful."

And it was.

A relief, as the first half of the week was draped in cobwebs. Hawkes was present and accounted for and we all decamped to the library to await dinner, Islington sending a footman to abduct his aunt who was supposed to have already arrived.

"They never do what you tell them to do," Islington said.

"What," I said, "females?"

This earned me an even stare. "Aunts. Particularly those of the novel-writing variety."

That did make me laugh.

"Have I mentioned," Hawkes said, from where he sat on the sofa by the fire, arms crossed behind his head, legs crossed at the ankles, and eyes closed, "that I rather enjoyed *The Pharaoh's Curse*?"

This from the man with degrees from both Oxford and Cambridge.

Islington rolled his eyes. Then, "Pierce, I brought down the architectural renderings from Stonecrop. They're over here on my desk."

While they retreated to marvel over architectural renderings, I happily sat across from Hawkes, my aperitif in hand. "I'd like to read *The Pharaoh's Curse*."

Hawkes smiled and opened—albeit narrowly—one eye. "How did Pierce manage his Shakespeare?"

I'm certain I looked like a candle newly lit (i.e., pleased). "He wrote Sebastian's line beautifully, though I suspect he thinks you said it wrong."

Hawkes closed his eye. "Infidels, Miss Lion. We are surrounded by infidels."

"A toast to that."

And then, because I could not help myself without helping my curiosity first, I said, "Islington very discreetly mentioned your remarkable scholarly history, and I'm desperate for you to tell me about it, having done good deeds all this week to ensure I deserved such confidence." I could feel my brow wrinkle, as I bit my lip and waited.

Hawkes moved nary a muscle.

Still I waited.

Finally, he said—eyes still closed, mind—"Ask me no questions and I'll tell you no lies."

Taking my remaining drink in one gulp, I lifted a finger in rebuttal.

But the door opened, and dinner was announced.

Our dinner conversation moved smoothly between us four. My favourite moment being when Islington, rather at random, asked after my employment efforts of late winter.

"Haven't I already told you I handed in my notice the end of February? Or was let go. I'm not exactly certain which is the more accurate statement. Mutual agreement that it was an untenable situation perhaps?"

"Was that because you killed an already deceased canine?" Islington said before taking a bite of the very well-prepared fish we were eating.

Hawkes took an interest.

"No," I answered slowly. "It had more to do with my being required to use a poker as a cricket bat and desecrating an ancient Chinese urn filled with the ashes of several family pets."

Islington grimaced.

Pierce grinned.

Hawkes raised both eyebrows.

"So there is little chance they'll ask you back." This from Islington. It was not a question.

"Even if they did, would Emma wish to return?" Pierce said.

"What a very American question, Pierce," I replied.

He shook his head at me, a twist in his smile. "It is not."

I looked around the table. "Who in this room feels that Pierce's question had the tang of an American?"

Islington, Hawkes, and I all raised our hands.

After a dismissive sound and a sip of his wine, Pierce asked, "Why were you swinging a poker in the first place?"

"Ask me no questions and I'll tell you no lies."

When the conversation moved on, Hawkes discreetly raised his glass in my direction.

April 4th

I am not an ancient Greek historian, but it seems to me that if one wishes to instill confidence in one's reader, one does not begin by writing,

> *Concerning Lycurgus the lawgiver, in general, nothing can be said which is not disputed, since indeed there are different accounts of his birth, his travels, his death, and above all, of his work as lawmaker and statesman; and there is least agreement among historians as to the times in which the man lived.*

Now I'm reading the subsequent paragraphs on Lycurgus and doubting them all!

Later

> *Miss Lion,*
>
> *Due to your recent return to unemployment, I thought perhaps we might meet one day next week? I'll be in my office, so you might stop by at your earliest convenience.*
>
> *Sincerely,*
> *Mr. Penury*

Sigh.

Time for my monthly rush to the bank to ensure I'm not going to lose everything I own.

Although I do look forward to seeing Mr. Penury. And his mustache.

April 5th

Tonight, Roland and I were launched like a warship into *The Season*, the name of Arabella painted on our bow. "EmMA!" Aunt Eugenia said. "You are to keep the undesirables from your cousin. Intercept them and dance with them yourself. We must not waste Arabella's strength."

Arabella winked at me.

I glared. "You realise I will look quite forward, Aunt."

"Don't be silly. I'm more worried over your looking quite backward."

"But how am I—"

"Use," she slapped me on the head with her fan, "this. Why else would God have given it to you?"

"Yes, Emma, why else?" Arabella said smoothly.

"You," I hissed at her, "are nothing but a gilded lily. All gleaming gold and sparkling gemstones. But beneath it all? Rot and damp."

"There's my Irishman's daughter," she answered, kissing me on the cheek.

On the whole, it *was* a jolly evening, the first start out of the gate. To quote Aunt Eugenia, "Anyone who matters was present and many who don't."

Crystal and brocade silks and men in sharp black and white. Alas, the number of mustaches has increased exponentially. Roland even dared sport one.

I was aghast.

"All the chaps at the club wear a mustache or a beard, you know. I thought I'd give it a go," he explained the one time we danced.

"But Roland," I tried, "have you ever, ever seen a Greek statue with a mustache? Don't say a bearded Zeus. Being a god comes with privileges."

"I thought it turned out well enough."

"You all think that!"

"Aunt Eugenia gave her approval yesterday at tea."

"Does it not bother you?" I asked.

"Hardly know it's there."

"No, not that *thing* above your lip. I mean Aunt Eugenia's approval."

Roland shrugged, still charming. "I'm not looking for a wife at present, and I like to amuse the old girl."

I snorted.

May Northgate was there with her sister Fanny. "Annalise meant to be here, but her cousins are in from Bombay." We caught only a moment of conversation before Aunt Eugenia called me back into service—I danced three dozen times, I'd swear it—but there was amusement enough to finish the night with good grace.

Afterward in the carriage, Aunt Eugenia said, "Emma, while not infallible, you were serviceable nonetheless."

"All we need to do is break a bottle of champagne over my head and weigh anchor," I replied.

This earned a harrumph. "You speak such nonsense."

"No Lord West this evening," I diverted.

Another harrumph.

Then from Arabella, "He and his sister travel down next week."

"How will his sweet peas bear it?"

Arabella laughed. And I could testify in court that the gaslight revealed a smirk on Aunt Eugenia's face as well.

April 6th

I kept nodding off during the last half of Hawkes's sermon.

On Palm Sunday!

It was unconscionable.

Only I was so very tired from last night. Maybe I'm coming down with something. Like a cold, or an allergy to people in general.

The subject of Hawkes's sermon was grace.

April 7th

This morning, on my way to the kitchen (i.e., sustenance), I passed the open door of the breakfast room. There sat Pierce, reading a newspaper.

I retraced three steps backwards, and said, "Hello."

In response, Pierce folded his newspaper and set it on the table. "Do you make a habit of walking backwards?"

"Only when retracing my steps. Might I join you?"

My question was rewarded with a smile. "Please."

"Oh, Miss!" Agnes rushed in just as I sat down. "You would not guess! Parian dropped the egg basket just as the toast caught fire! Mess everywhere and smoke, and then the rag I had tossed onto the stove when the eggs had splattered also went aflame."

"You sorted the eggs before putting the fire out?"

"Oh, no, Miss. I mean, yes. Only because Mr. Pierce was at the table, and he managed the fire. Then I sent Parian to fetch more eggs and told Mr. Pierce to come eat in the breakfast room where there was no smoke." She wiped a hand over her brow as she set a stout plate of food before the amused photographer. "And here we are, Mr. Pierce. You would do well to keep up your strength."

"Um, thank you, Agnes?" he replied.

I could not have composed a superior beginning to my day.

"I'll bring your breakfast, Miss, if you would be so kind as to keep Mr. Pierce company for his heroics in the kitchen."

She left.

I leaned back against the chair, my delight barely concealing the smirk crawling beneath. "*Heroics*! How very Greek. Need you reference my Plutarch for anything now that you're in the business of Hercules and Perseus?"

"Nothing of the sort," he said, lifting his fork and eyeing the mound of food before him.

"You saved Lapis Lazuli from burning down entirely."

A look as he stabbed his eggs.

"You deserve a medal. To think how you've won Agnes over so completely. Why, she used to shake at the very thought of you."

"Am I going to eat this entire meal taking your verbal spars or should I have let the house burn?"

"Niall, I am only doing what Agnes asked."

He seemed pleased when I spoke his Christian name, pausing only just and smiling to himself. Then he changed the subject. "I am back at the British Museum today." ~~Sounding less enthusiastic than he looked.~~ ~~Looking less enthusiastic than he sounded.~~ He sounded and looked less enthusiastic than I thought he ought.

"Are you?"

A grunt in response. "I'm being supervised by Miss Kingsnorth."

"Oh, I quite like her."

Another grunt.

Agnes brought my breakfast, set it before me, then said, "Is there anything else, Mr. Pierce?"

He looked at her in surprise. "I—uh, no?"

I'm sure my expression was disapproving.

Agnes was bothered by neither reaction.

"He's fine, Agnes," I said. "As am I. Thank you."

She beamed and then left.

I shook my head. My own cook.

"One would think," I said, turning the conversation back to antiquity, "that respectful handling of artifacts would be something you enjoyed, or believed in, at very least."

"I do, on both counts. Only, she gets under my skin."

This I found delightful. "A point for bluestockings everywhere."

He sipped his coffee, then looked disappointed it was cold. "And your day?"

"Plutarch and my banker."

"You're reading Plutarch to your banker?"

"Of course not."

He sat back in his chair. "Teasing, is all." He waited until I had finished my breakfast, reading his paper, making a comment or two, and then when I was finished, Pierce gathered our plates and silverware and took them into the kitchen.

A thing I tallied under The Great Considerations of 1884.

Later

MISS LION AND MR. PENURY

A Review

Mr. Penury: "What new avenue of employment have you brought today, Miss Lion?"

Emma Lion: "None."

Mr. Penury: *Perplexed expression.* "Miss Lion, it was my understanding we drew a clear timeline regarding the vital nature of adding to your accounts at a rate exceeding—"

Emma Lion: "Mr. Penury." *Dramatic pause.*

Mr. Penury: "Yes, Miss Lion?"

Emma Lion: "My work in the Whitaker household, as you know, terminated at the end of last month."

Mr. Penury: *Nods in a bankerly sort of way.*

Emma Lion: "Since the beginning of March, I have been witness to a duel, unceremoniously hosted my upper-class aunt and cousin, cavorted—but not in that way—with a confidence man, hidden my tenant from the aforementioned—the aunt, not the confidence man—argued with a pirate over book bindings, managed the back end of a drunken ambush, consoled an archenemy, and have been forced to socialize with the *crème de la crème* of society so that my cousin might become engaged before *The Season* is out. To say nothing of other personal matters, rather pressing all. There is also the sad fact that Archibald Flat does exist. As disappointing as my progress may be to you, I honestly do not know how I might have found employment in March."

Mr. Penury: …

Emma Lion: …

Mr. Penury: "I have a friend who is a director at the South Kensington Museum. Here is his card. He said you were welcome to come by and speak about a possible position."

Emma Lion: "Wonderful!"

Mr. Penury: "Miss Lion."

Emma Lion: "Yes?"

Mr. Penury: "You do know that duels are illegal and very, very dangerous. Not at all the thing for a young woman of…any circumstance."

Emma Lion: "Never fear, Mr. Penury, he was only winged." *Stands.*

Mr. Penury: "Miss Lion?"

Emma Lion: *Pauses near the door and raises her eyebrows in question.*

Mr. Penury: "I think it best not to cavort at all, regardless of the way."

Emma Lion: *Pretends to tip her hat with a flourish and leaves the office, card in hand.*

April 8th

I went to the South Kensington Museum this morning.

To no avail.

"To be honest, Miss…?"

"Miss Lion."

"I don't have anything for you to do at the moment." The man fashioned a most apologetic expression. "We've had to let a few staff go, as we rely on…"

"Oh dear," I sighed. "Has Mr. Penury mentioned the Chinese vase?"

The man paled. "What Chinese vase?"

"Nothing. Nothing at all."

"Albert Penury—"

Albert?

"—is a good man. I've known him many years. We're both part of the same club, you see. But as of right now, I have nothing for you. If, however, you leave me your card, I would happily send 'round if in need of someone with your qualifications."

Meaning, someone with no qualifications.

"I understand. Thank you for your time."

I left the museum ~~resigned~~ ~~dejected~~ hungry, really.

As I walked towards Kensington High Street, wondering if Agnes had a meat pie at the ready, I heard my name.

"Miss Lion?" came the call a second time. I looked up. There, not five feet away, stood Professor Fletcher, mountain of a man with a satchel (a few papers threatening to fly out from beneath the leather straps), horrendous glasses still in place and—

"You haven't cut your own hair!" I exclaimed.

As any barest acquaintance would.

Professor Fletcher pulled back slightly, his eyes blinking in ~~panic~~ question. He absently lifted a hand to the back of his head. "Is there something amiss with my hair, Miss Lion?"

"Nothing," I stated. "That's the problem. You look quite dashing. Did a barber cut it for you?"

"My sister?" He said it like a question.

"She did a wonderful job. You are almost irresistible, what with your brain and all." I lifted a hand as if signalling him to stop. "I state that in a purely platonic way, but you put the other women in your life in a very difficult position."

"I beg your pardon, but I don't follow. The other women in my life?"

"One in particular," I sighed. There was no stopping myself. "All this to say, it is nice to see you, Professor Fletcher. I'm happy you're still wearing your appalling glasses. They're the only thing saving anyone from your overwhelming, masculine charm."

At this point, Professor Fletcher seemed perplexed to no end. I felt sorry he'd encountered me at all.

"It's only a theory, Professor Fletcher," I attempted.

Honestly, Emma. You muddle with the best of them.

"I see." He rubbed his chin absently with his free hand, then adjusted his glasses. "Is this Miss Bairrage's theory?"

"Oh, mine entirely," I covered. And to my horror, continued. "Your self-inflicted hair and glasses were the only two forces keeping the female population safe. Now you've done away with full half the safeguard. If anything happens to your glasses, I would worry." This was the moment that my rational thought caught up with my irrational tongue. "And now I am feeling mortified. Perhaps because I'm quite hungry. Desperation, and all that." I took a deep breath. "Let us part, for as much as I would like to see you again, this measure of chagrin will not likely be dealt with in this lifetime. Here's hoping for reincarnation, where I will be reborn a mute. Good afternoon, Professor Fletcher. It truly was *wonderful* to see you. In a platonic way."

"Miss Lion," he said, "I was going to walk a few streets over to the Britannia and have a spot of lunch. As you're so very hungry, would you care to join me?"

"*Ah.*" One can't claim the man doesn't know how to rally. My stomach growled loud enough for us both to hear. "If you can promise to forget the last five minutes, I would be happy to accept. I like you very much. Platonically."

He was making great effort, I believe, to keep a straight face. "Platonically," he repeated solemnly. "Two colleagues in the vast search for truth, breaking bread."

And so we fell into awkward step, crossing the street and turning left. Having never been to the Britannia, I let him lead while I attempted to engage in normal conversation. "And what brings you to South Kensington?"

"I was lecturing to some of the young women who will be attending the new Ladies' Department to be established by King's College London next year. They'll be in Kensington Square. My sister is to be an administrator."

"Capital!" And it was. "I read about the new Ladies' College when I was living in Bournemouth. What I would do for such a chance!"

"It is a fine thing, with many bright young women. They were a good deal more attentive this morning than usual."

I opened my mouth to make a comment.

I closed my mouth.

Grateful for my ofttimes-elusive but occasional ability to do so.

There was a table near the back recently cleaned, and that is where we seated ourselves. Professor Fletcher, a regular it seems, received welcome and quick service.

"This one of your sisters now, love?" the woman serving us asked, leaving before he gave answer.

"My apologies," he said, his eyes distorted by the spectacles to disappointing and wonderful heights.

"It is an honour to be mistaken as one of the Fletcher sisters," I answered. "If I were so educated, I would feel qualified to argue with Plutarch, who I think biased although not wrong—tricky balance, that—in his comparison between Theseus and Romulus. We'll see what he does with Lycurgus and Numa Pompilius, I suppose."

"Plutarch," Professor Fletcher repeated. "*For the very spring and root of honesty and virtue lies in the felicity of lighting on good education.*"

I had never heard the quotation before.

Owing to my dismal time spent at Fortitude.

No felicity, no lighting.

Professor Fletcher was curious. "Are you endeavouring away on a scholarly work, Miss Lion?"

"Yes. No. That is to say, I've been *reading* Plutarch. He keeps comparing great men, trying to decide who is best. It may sound like a novel concept, but clearly the man never attended an afternoon tea. While academia might, and *should*, be impressed with such a work, I've listened to more expansive treatises in many a London drawing room."

Bemusement, then understanding on the professor's face. He laughed. "Arguably without the burden of sifting through historical records."

"Oh, don't think the mamas of London couldn't cite entire family trees from memory—with associated bank accounts and estates, mind. As for my studies, I'm attempting to learn history. For myself only. No great academic work in the offing." Then I added as an aside, "Other than a current study of photographers."

"Photography, you say? A fascinating, modern field. From what I understand, once one catches a passion for the thing, there is no giving it up."

The blush on my cheeks was like a flash pan of powder igniting. "That question being the very thesis of my study."

"Wonderful. You will have to keep me abreast of your research."

I thought of my less than scholarly response to Pierce's half kiss.

More research needed, I should think.

When our food arrived, it was solid pub fare. I tucked in immediately, while Professor Fletcher was staring at the gravy spilling over his plate. He gave his peas a contemplative nudge with the tines of his fork before saying, "I confess I asked you to join me so I might put a question to you, Miss Lion. Do you know how Miss Bairrage fares?"

It took me a moment to answer ~~as I was chewing~~ for I was chewing. (Important distinction.) "Mary fares well, professor. She's a force to be reckoned with. Why do you ask?"

"Only the other day, after the whole business with the lamp post. And when I tried to ascertain if she was all right, she ran off."

"Pardon? Lamp post?"

"The debacle with the lamp post. She didn't tell you?"

"She most certainly did not!"

"I've been more than a little worried."

"Professor Fletcher," I said, placing both hands flat on the table. "Please, start from the beginning and tell me the whole."

So Professor Fletcher told me how he and his sister were walking along the Bayswater Road yesterday when he looked across the street and saw Mary.

"She must not have recognised me, despite her looking so intently in my direction. Just as I waved my hand—I meant to introduce her to Alice, you see—she sneezed, rather forcefully, and hit her head against a lamp post."

I lifted a hand to my face.

"It was a busy time of day, quite congested, and I had to wait for a few carriages and a wagon to pass before I could run across the street. By the time I did, she was gone."

"You don't say."

It was not a question.

It was a statement.

Professor Fletcher did not read my less than innocent meaning. "I asked the college secretary to send an enquiry around to her address—he handles my manuscripts, so he's the one with the information—but have heard no reply."

"I'll go to Miss Lamb's and ascertain the injury."

He nodded, his mind elsewhere. Then, "Is Miss Lamb's a boarding house?"

"Er, yes," I replied, wondering what information one imparts to a nearly forty-year-old widower professor who is the father of three boys, no matter how dapper his hair looks. "Miss Lamb is a stickler for rules," I added as a safeguard. "Determined to keep her boarders on the straight and narrow way." Then, "Mary tests the bulwarks on a regular basis."

"I'd wager she does." He smiled to himself. "I admire your friend. She has a tenacity of which most are fearful. I was hoping to introduce her to my sister yesterday. Alice was wishing the same. They all—the sisters, that is—refer to her as Martin." He looked up with uncertainty. "Out of admiration, to be clear. They are educated women of some standing, and when I recounted the switch and bait business there was general approval all around."

I smiled brightly.

Perhaps his three boys shouldn't be such a deterrent after all.

As soon as Professor Fletcher and I had finished our lunch, we parted ways with a nod, he to King's College London and me directly to Miss Lamb's.

Miss Lamb was busy dusting. Which was wonderful as she was atop a ladder and could not physically stop me from going up the stairs.

"I haven't seen Miss Bairrage at all this morning, but she is usually absent this time of day," she wobbled out, careful not to fall.

"Yes, usually," I confirmed. "However, her future guardian has asked I make certain she is feeling up to snuff today, so I thought I would check. If there's no answer, I'll quickly see myself out. Good day, Miss Lamb!"

And I tromped up the stairs before she could stop me.

I banged on the door. "Mary, are you there? Mary?" I waited a moment. "I know you smashed into a lamp post yesterday. I've come to ascertain the damage."

I heard a moan.

I tried to hide the sound of my smile when I added, "Professor Fletcher is worried."

Now came a groan. "Please go away," her voice hobbled to the door. "I'm in a state of self-loathing."

I grinned. "Is the door unlocked?"

"Mmm hmmm."

I let myself in.

Mary was lying on her bed fully dressed, as if she'd intended to go to the office that morning. Her hand was covering her face.

"Did you, by chance, break your nose?" I enquired with some concern.

"Worse," she replied. And taking her hand away from her face, Mary managed to prop herself up on her elbow.

I gasped.

It wasn't because of how rumpled her clothes were—yesterday's—or the state of her hair—a magpie's nest of the first order—but she had a goose egg between her eyebrows and dark puddles beneath each eye.

"Good heavens, Mary! You've been bludgeoned!"

Her face crinkled as if she would cry. Mary let herself collapse back onto her bed. "He saw it all," she said miserably.

"Not exactly," I replied, walking over to sit in her chair.

She rolled over on her side. "What do you mean?"

"Professor Fletcher and I met in the street and went for a luncheon, a meeting between colleagues in search of the truth. At a pub. He told me he was worried after he saw you run into a lamp post, but that before he could make his way across the street, you had fled. He is most concerned."

Mary's face scrunched and her eyes filled with tears. "Then you've seen his hair?"

"I have."

"How cruel is fate. He looks *wonderful.* Even his glasses are not so silly as before."

"They are doing their best to hold the line, the last man standing, to be sure. But if you were to have been seated across from him today and had seen him blink behind those lenses, you would have been comforted. It was adorably grotesque."

"She must have done it."

"She?"

"The woman he was with. They walked arm in arm. She was making him laugh. I should be pleased on his behalf. He deserves happiness. Not that he's for me. The man must be nearly twice my age. Twice my age, Emma! What is one to do with that?"

"It *is* outside the parameters given in the Accord drawn up in Dormitory A—"

"Which I didn't sign."

"What?" I said.

"That was the week I was at my brother's house with a toothache."

"Ah. Ah! Good fortune then!"

"He's still twice my age, Emma!"

"Wasn't Colonel Brandon in that neighbourhood?" I countered.

"He is so intelligent and...and...and certain. And he wants me to help research and edit his next book. All well and good, except he'll soon be married and have no interest in the history of Dutch commerce, and it won't matter how he cuts his hair!" It ended with a wail.

I was all sympathy. "Mary."

"Woe is me."

"That was his sister."

Mary's eyes flew open. She looked like a haunt in a graveyard. I winced.

"His sister?!"

"He does have eight of them."

Mary sat up.

"You look like you've been in the grave a week," I said.

"His *sister*?"

"Alice. Who was disappointed not to have met you. Apparently, they—The Sisters—call you Martin, with great affection."

Mary's eyes went wider. If possible. "How lucky I was to have bolted! Can you imagine," she lifted her hand and pointed at her face, "if he had seen THIS?"

I defend.

My laugh was one of sympathy.

Mary collapsed back onto her bed.

"His sister," she repeated. "I feel like Mr. Thornton."

"Who?"

"You remember, from Gaskell's *North and South*."

I winced. "My father had that one. Alas, I've not read it."

"Oh, Emma!"

"Vicissitudes."

"There's an old copy at my brother's. I'm sure Mable won't mind. It will be yours, in thanks."

"Thanks for what?"

"Delivering a troubled mind from one horror to another."

"What horror are you delivered to now?"

"Clearly I care for the man to some small degree."

"Now that my dictionary extends beyond the J section, I will look up the word *understatement* and read it aloud to you, Mary."

She grimaced. "I've let my feelings run away with me. When he sent me the galley proofs—there they are over there, going to print next week—I saw what he wrote. 'Special thanks to Miss Mary Martin Bairrage, for her invaluable skill, consideration, and grit.'" Staring up at the ceiling, she placed a hand across her heart. "I am in danger, Emma. Retrench, I must retrench in all feeling. For if I don't, I won't be able to work with the man ever again, and that would break my scholar's heart."

"It might break all your other hearts as well, but we won't dwell on that now. Suffice it to say, the man was with his sister when you encountered the lamp post and has been worried."

Silence between us for the space of a half minute. It was very biblical.

"I have to go to the telephone company tomorrow," Mary said stoically. "I can only miss one day's pay."

"What will you tell them about your face?"

"Oh, something to arouse their sympathies."

With the promise that I would have Agnes make soup and send it over, I left Mary to rest.

I had thought to tell Mary about Pierce and perhaps engage her opinions on The Great Considerations of 1884, but one must be sensitive to circumstance. No woman languishing with a goose egg and two blackened eyes wants to hear of a romance that is not her own.

Heavens, I just called it romance.

April 9th

Rain, rain, rain.

With a note from Aunt Eugenia reminding me to humbly prepare myself for the ball tomorrow evening—"*Submissiveness is next to Godliness, for your type of person.*"—and to give Miss Dowd her regards.

I've not thought a great deal of Miss Dowd since she took her bag and disappeared down Whereabouts Lane. Neither have I seen Jack. When I do, I mean to ask him where he found such a glorious woman.

With the pages of my journal dwindling, I might as well admit that the inevitable moment has arrived. Time to pay a visit to The Hound.

Perhaps it won't be so very bad.

Mr. Chambers did gift me the second half of Dr. Johnson's dictionary.

~~The man can't be all bad.~~

~~The man may have ulterior motives.~~

I go with an expectation of goodwill.

Later

One can only feel so much goodwill when greeted with: "Did I do something in a former life to deserve this?"

I halted, my gloved hand still on the door I'd just opened. I looked across the shop to The Pirate behind the counter. "Likely you did. However, I don't understand your complaint when you were the one who told me to come to the shop when I'd only a dozen or so pages left."

"I thrive on pain," was Chambers's reply. Then he looked at the young man who was dusting the displays. "Mind the counter, Stevens, won't you?" And he disappeared past a red and black patterned curtain.

I waited.

And then, "Are you coming?"

"Oh! You wish me to follow?"

I could swear his response was a growl.

Navigating around the sharp edges of the counter, I lifted my gloved hand and pushed the curtain aside.

I ~~gazed~~ gawked.

It was the oft spoken but rarely encountered love at first sight.

One expects a shop's storeroom to be either sterile in its order or a jumbled, dust-filled shadows sort of affair—most are fighting the war of attrition found between the two.

But this!

This was an atelier!

So beautiful I couldn't hide my adoration.

The large room was clean and clear, no scraps or tools strewn on the wood floor. Everything had a place, and often that place was unexpected but right—a bespoke order. There were shelves filled with merchandise on the right and back walls, some unpacked, some not, but the left wall, which jutted out five feet like a sunroom, was all windows, allowing the warm light to bathe the space in daylight rather than always requiring lamps. In the corner of the glass extension was a small hob with a kettle, a black chair, and a side table with tea things. In the centre of the room were worktables, each dedicated to a different craft. One table was covered with leather gloves in all stages of make, another for leather carrying cases and satchels. Best of all was the largest table, where everything one could want to bind a thousand books was laid out in satisfying glory.

It was here that Chambers stood, selecting whatever items he deemed necessary for his task.

If his atelier is a reflection of his mind, I could like him—given half a chance.

I approached the bookbinding table. "This is—"

"No," he said.

"But I—"

"Take a step back."

"You won't even—"

"Miss Lion, I have broken my steadfast rule of ill hospitality. There is a comfortable chair only waiting. Please sit, have a cup of tea—fine tea, I might add. Is handing me your journal, reading that Plutarch you've brought with you, staying out of my way, and not speaking unless spoken to so much to ask?"

"I—" I closed my mouth.

Dubious, my being given half a chance to like him.

"Don't we need to—"

"Sit," he commanded, holding out his hand for my journal.

"You promise you won't read it."

A scowl. "I won't read it."

His words carried insufficient weight, but the way he said them gave me confidence. With an expression of Rebellion Quelled by Choice, Charm, and Maturity, I handed over the Record of My ~~Life~~ Last Year, walked to the chair, and sat, looking about the corner to which I'd been banished.

It was endearing.

There was a basket with kindling for the hob, a copper teakettle, a green teapot with cornflower blue and gold teacups, five different canisters of tea, a tin of biscuits. To the right of the black wingback chair was a carved table the perfect height for tea and a book, while over the left arm of the chair was a folded Kashmiri blanket in middle green.

"Now,"—the Pirate interrupted my observations—"I am going to dismantle your shed snakeskin of a record—"

"Such humour."

"—separating all of *1883* to be bound in the custom binding upon which we've agreed. The remaining pages will be bound to fresh signatures with a temporary cover; still black, serviceable. We will estimate as best we can how much we think you will indulge yourself. Once *1884* comes to an end, that journal will be rebound in its permanent binding."

"Is that not a good deal of extra work?"

"What should that matter?" he said as if slamming his words against the table. "We have an opportunity to create order from chaos. One book, one year. Simple. Elegant. Certainly it's extra work! Fine things, fine ideas, fine people, require work! This entire age is indulgent and selfish and shortsighted, complaining that easy things are not as easy as they'd like." He lifted a hand before him, half shake of a fist, half artistic passion. "If you want quality, you must work for it. You wake and you strive and you make decisions to sacrifice. An easy life will never bring the kind of satisfaction the soul craves. I despise people who lounge all day as if there weren't more important ideas than comfort, complacency, and appetite. Stretch yourself! Be industrious! Do something!"

He was perspiring, his strong grip on the words just shy of a yell.

I sat agog.

A deep breath, then a deep release, Chambers leaned against his worktable and wiped the back of his hand across his brow. Thinking it might be time to contribute to the conversation, I said, "I think you would be pleased with how often I dust my drawing room."

Chambers threw his hands in the air.

I settled into the chair with my book, half-watching as Chambers began his work.

He stood with his back to me, using a penknife to dismantle my lovely, companionable, faithful journal. My heart twinged at regular intervals, like a mother watching her child beneath the surgeon's capable but impersonal hands. Once the pages of *1883* were—carefully, I acknowledge—separated from the rest, Chambers set them aside and began to construct a new and temporary journal.

"I will do a better job of it if you aren't watching like a circling vulture," he said.

I harrumphed (like Aunt Eugenia). "I wouldn't eat you in any case, carrion or no," I replied, turning to fully sit in the black chair and opening my Plutarch.

~~It was not long before…~~

~~A short time later…~~

~~Sooner than I'd anticipated…~~

I had no idea how much time had passed as I had fallen asleep, but I was unceremoniously jolted out of sleep by, "Miss Lion, your *1884* journal." Chambers was standing before me, my new-old journal in hand—black leather, serviceable, just as he'd said. He placed it on the table to my right and looked pityingly at my open but unread Plutarch, as if I were a dog owner who refused it a walk. "Careful with it for a day or two, open it as little as possible. I'll bring *1883* to you the day after tomorrow."

This brought me wide awake. "I'd rather you didn't," I said. "I'll wait until—"

"Miss Lion," he insisted, "I have made provision for you to scribble away without interruption—despite the fact that this journal *should* dry for two days, not that I think you capable of such restraint. As I have done this favour for you, please let me take my time to create your *1883* journal and allow it to dry properly."

"With me present, yes."

His nostrils flared with his intake of breath. "I've already promised I won't read it."

"Someone else might."

"I will lock it in a cabinet."

"What if you accidentally read a page. It happens. It happened to me! I found myself in possession of a journal and read the entire thing. Twice."

I'd swear the twitch on his face was one of amusement rather than utter disapproval of my person.

(I may also be wrong.)

"Miss Lion, I do not want to rush this piece of art."

I beamed.

"I refer to the binding, not the contents. I will return it to you the day after tomorrow, once the journal has cured."

"Cured?"

"Yes."

"Like a ham?"

He scowled. "Like a book."

"I can't risk you reading anything on these pages."

"I won't."

"But I—"

"Do you think I lack discipline?" he shot back.

I bunched my lips together, not wishing to call his honour into question.

However.

He surprised me when he said with irritation, "I swear to you on the man who saved my life, that neither I nor anyone else will read your journal while it is in my care."

Closing my mouth, I considered.

Swearing on a life means a great deal.

"All right, then," I said.

Looking ready to argue, he opened his mouth, then closed it when my words struck home. "Good," he recovered.

"No other way," I replied, "*apparently*. But I expect you to place a white feather on it when it's not in your hands."

"No need."

"Mr. Chambers. I insist on the white feather. Were this to disappear from your shop, my entire life would be over. Metaphorically, if not in actuality."

"Things don't disappear from my shop, Miss Lion."

"This is St. Crispian's, Mr. Chambers. Do you expect me to believe that?"

The way he waited to answer was almost solemn. "I have never had so much as a thread disappear from my shop. If you leave an item here, it is safe. I promise you."

He was so serious, I looked down. "I believe you, Mr. Chambers. But a white feather would not go amiss."

"Unbelievable."

"Yes, well." I looked at the temporary journal in my hand, the first fifth with my already written pages. I moved to open—

"Careful!"

I started. "What?!"

"Don't open it for hours, and then only with consideration. Be gentle. Massage the spine."

"Massage the spine, Mr. Chambers?"

"Tonight, write only what you must," he said with anticipatory censure. "I can't believe I let you talk me into such a slapdash job. That book is a near-disgrace."

"By the time I'm done with it, Mr. Chambers, I certainly hope it will be." I stood, stretched the tweak in my neck to the side. Twice. And said, "Good afternoon."

The journal looks perfectly fine to me.

In fact, Mr. Chambers's slapdash job is better than my original binding.

I don't know if I've been properly massaging the spine, but I have been complimenting it a fair amount.

April 10th

"Remember, Emma, creativity gives way to vulgarity."

This was said as I stood in my dark blue gown before the tall mirror in Arabella's room ~~preparing for~~ being prepared for the Salisbury Ball.

"I only meant, Aunt, that any necklace should look fine with this colour of gown."

"*Any* necklace? One would think you were intent on a life of Venetian beads and nothing more."

"Perhaps."

"How vulgar of you. Only I'm disturbed by your selection for this evening. Dark blue is acceptable for dinner with a politician, but not for the Salisbury Ball. You look too serious by half, positively disinterested in society of any kind. Close your mouth! I've no need of an opinion from you on the matter."

Well!

"You will wear Arabella's single strand of pearls."

Arabella, herself wearing diamonds, was admiring her reflection in the mirror above the dressing table.

I frowned at her, then turned back to Aunt Eugenia. "I think her jade beads would look *lovely* with dark blue."

"Do you wish to look like you've drowned?" she snapped.

Yes. Yes, I did wish to attend a ball feeling like Elaine of Astolat.

I said as much.

"For heaven's sake, child! It is *not* done."

"I think *I'm* rather done," I replied, moving towards a beguiling chair.

"Don't! You! Move! An! Inch!" She threw each word emphatically.

I sighed and turned back towards the mirror while Aunt Eugenia consulted her lady's maid. It had taken an hour to ~~set~~ attempt to set my hair. The end result was no small amount of pleasing madness.

Which I enjoyed.

Aunt Eugenia did not.

"You might as well see how Emma looks in the jade beads,

Mama," Arabella said, still admiring herself.

Aunt Eugenia went through the great show of pretending she was not going to give in, but in the end did, me standing the entire, painful time. (My heels pinched.) "You don't wear anything with the same distinction your mother did." She motioned the lady's maid in my direction. "However, the jade can do nothing but improve your aspect, and so we press forward. We cannot expect a prize like Charles Goddard to wait for your charms alone."

A prize like *Charles Goddard*?

I bit my tongue, refusing to lengthen the ordeal.

The Salisbury Ball began with the following conversation between Arabella and myself as we entered the ballroom arm in arm.

"Arabella, how do you truly feel now that *The Season* has arrived?"

"You worry over trifles," Arabella replied. "I'm much more enamoured with my new gowns from Madame Tasset than the rather pedestrian business of selecting a husband."

I raised a disapproving eyebrow. "If you decide to find a soul between now and then, do tip your hand on which hapless male you prefer, and I'll do what I can to secure the victory."

Roland was soon present—joy of all joys, he had shaved his mustache—and we both received our orders for the evening. He was to dance with Arabella at The Crucial Juncture—when the most eyes were on the ballroom—while I was to dance with six of the men deemed Eligible, the only approved conversation being Arabella's beauty. With acceptance, I began my task.

Seeing as how I'd not known he was in attendance, I was surprised when Lord West appeared at my elbow.

"Miss Lion," he said, looking at me with as blank an expression as ever.

"Lord West! Good evening. How nice to know you're back in London. Have you seen that Arabella is—"

"Would you dance with me, Miss Lion?" he asked, oblivious to his interruption.

"I— Why, yes."

It was a waltz, of course. I tried to ignore Lord West counting under his breath until he had found the pattern of the thing. Once he did, he said, "I have thought of you all winter, every time I read the germination records of my departed Elizabeth."

"A sweet pea much missed."

"You also feel a keen absence, then?"

"Why, I… It was an afternoon I'll never forget."

"I knew you possessed a horticultural profundity. Now I only wish to clarify something he told me."

"He?"

Lord West nodded, not realising I was requesting a name. I cast my mind back. Cousin Archibald? Hawkes? "Do you mean Islington?"

"Yes, he made it very clear that—"

Speak of the duke and he appeareth, for just as Lord West was to clarify something, Islington cut in politely with a, "Do you mind, Lord West?" and claimed the waltz.

Lord West, likely never having had another gentleman cut in, was at a loss for words as Islington and I spun away.

"I didn't realise you were here tonight," I said, adjusting to Islington's far more confident style. "Only, poor Lord West. He doesn't seem to know how to get himself off the floor."

"He'll manage," Islington said smoothly, glancing at my face a moment before he looked past me. "You look rather nice this evening. The jade is an artful touch." Islington looked rather nice this evening himself, his hazel eyes leaning towards the green. I almost told him so but thought I should give my Mild Outrage on behalf of poor, hapless Lord West another sentence or two before giving compliment.

"You are in a position of immense privilege and assumption—"

"Assumption, is it?"

"A man like Lord West has gathered all his courage to ask for a dance, and you—"

"Lord West was only just telling his friend and fellow horticultural enthusiast that he'd painted a portrait of you and placed it next to Elizabeth's casket in his library. He added that if he ascertained you were open to an alliance—despite what I'd told him last November—he would ask for your hand as you waltzed, with the hopes that the entire Season might be relegated to the past while you and he made plans for a new greenhouse. I fear, Lion, he also has thoughts for a nursery."

"I..." All ability to speak ceased.

"Now," Islington continued, "I thought perhaps you should be given a chance to choose between a waltz with me, followed by a walk out on the terrace, or to return to your pending and botanically sound proposal. You can name your first son Mendel, or Gregor, for that matter."

"You're lying. Surely! Arabella—"

"I quote, 'Miss Lion understands the hierarchy of the *flos familiae* and the requisite honours due. The other does not.'"

"Oh dear."

"Indeed."

"You've no need to look so very serious, Islington. It's not you to whom he's wishing to propose!"

This comment delivered Islington's full smile just as the music stopped.

He offered me his arm. "Shall we escape, Lion? Or is it a life of sweet pea and trowel?"

I took his arm, careful *not* to glance at Aunt Eugenia, and we soon found ourselves outside.

"How dreadfully inconvenient," I stated as if it were Islington's fault. "I already have one unintended intended."

"Who is also present this evening."

"Charles Goddard?"

"He's not dancing due to a blister, *I believe*."

"How could you possibly know all this?"

"I was playing cards with Lord Salisbury in the library. Charles Goddard was sitting at a table doing"—here Islington's lips twitched—"a children's puzzle while explaining the whole to Lord Salisbury's mother."

"Did he mention my name?"

"Not specifically, no." Islington straightened his cuffs. "He did, however, mention a clandestine betrothal before speaking of the wedding breakfast in great detail. Lord Salisbury threw the game early to escape the nonsense. I won a thousand pounds."

"One thousand pounds!"

"I'll use it to buy your wedding present."

"I very much—" What promised to be an excellent set down was interrupted by a messenger from Mount Olympus. "Oh, hello, Roland."

"Emma. Oh, I say, Islington!"

"Sutherland."

They shook hands.

Then Roland said, "I'm beginning to think the two of you more acquainted than I realised."

"Unfortunately." We replied in unison. Upon which I made an indelicate sound and Islington smiled, pulling at his cuff. "Family friends," he explained.

Roland, standing in the light of his own golden existence, wore a bemused expression.

Which is to say, Roland was confused.

"Now this turns awkward, Islington"—Roland flashed his smile—"as I was sent out by Lady Spencer to rescue Emma from the clutches of a most distasteful individual."

"I can imagine," replied Islington.

"Especially as I was hoping to see you at the club later for whist and draw poker. Are you playing?"

"Yes, I believe I'll be playing tonight," Islington replied, removing his pocket watch (how I want one) and tilting it towards the light. "Leaving within the hour, I should think."

How casually they spoke of what they would do, and when.

My resulting expression was one of annoyance.

"Well sorted," Roland replied. Then he looked expectantly at me, waiting for me to extricate myself from the balcony and save him the embarrassment of ordering me about in front of a man he would like to impress.

I, wishing for three minutes off my aunt's leash, dug in my heels and said, "Aunt Eugenia will not forgive you for leaving early."

"She won't do anything too drastic," he said without a care in the world. "She can't, really."

I bit my tongue at our differing realities. "Thank you, Islington," I said. "You have done me a great service this evening. Now I'll try not to impale Roland, so he has the strength to make it to the club where you will gamble away the carefree hours of your life."

Roland smiled gleefully. "Don't kill the messenger, Emma! To borrow from Shakespeare's Benedick, '*Against my will I am sent to bid you come in to dinner.*'"

"That wasn't Benedick," I growled as I walked past him towards the ballroom. "That was Beatrice."

"I expect you to remain at my side the rest of the night, unless I give permission for you to dance," Aunt Eugenia said through a frozen smile. "You should not be dancing with Islington, let alone leave the floor in his company. If anything, you should direct him towards your cousin now that he's on the list. Provisionally."

"I am twenty-one years of age, Aunt," I said, watching every man in the room watch Arabella as she danced with a younger gentleman who wore expensive clothes. (Not on the list, *I believe.*) "I am allowed the occasional dance."

"Yes, and your cousin Damian is just turned twenty-five. Yet my solicitors have managed to keep him from his inheritance barring he does what I say. Don't cross me, Emma. You've promised me *The Season*. Next year will be your turn. We will see you happily settled on the Goddard estate in Surrey."

"I don't—"

But we were interrupted by Lady Sheridan. "Have you seen Lady Rolling's daughters?" she whispered behind her fan as she came to stand beside my aunt. "Shameless flirts."

"Lesser standing often leads to the grotesque," replied Aunt Eugenia. "Take the Crays. The oldest two married last year, and they all think themselves wonders. I hear the third is now hunting for a husband."

I sighed, which brought Lady Sheridan's attention to me. "Good evening, Emma. How is the Duke of Islington?"

"I am fine, thank you," I replied.

Ignoring her questioning expression, I looked stupidly over the ballroom.

Like a mindless cow.

Against all obstacles, such as blisters, Charles Goddard rallied and asked for a dance.

I make no record beyond stating it as fact.

On the drive home, Arabella nudged my arm. "Don't tell me you mean to be this glum all Season."

"I'm not glum, I'm tired, and I've been trampled upon by that giraffe of a Goddard. My own life is far more pleasant than evenings like this," I added.

Aunt Eugenia, sitting across from us in the coach, gave a rather musical snore.

"Your own life is far more interesting *because* of evenings like this. Speaking of, how is your photographer? You know he wrote to Mother and they've selected a date."

"Shh!" I motioned towards the sleeping gorgon.

"Oh, this is Mother's Sleep of the Dead. I can say what I wish, and she'll not hear a thing."

Another snore.

I grimaced and looked out the window.

"Regarding your photographer," Arabella continued, "I suspect you've not confessed to me the whole."

This from Arabella, who tells the whole world she cares about nothing that happens to her as long as she has comfort and money.

Turning away from the window, I looked at her.

She gave an even stare in return.

It was beneath me, but I was tired.

And I wanted to push back against Arabella's easy beauty and expensive assumptions she could well afford to keep. Prudence might have counselled me to say nothing; however, I was looking to shock.

"His kisses," I said, "make the very ground shake. To say nothing of his hands. If you can imagine."

Arabella tried to keep her expression fixed in disinterest, but her lips curled up at the end, and something in her eyes seemed to pull back and rush forward in opposing and equal measure. "In the plural?"

I lifted my chin just so.

And as much as I wished to be peevish, the thought of Pierce did make me smile.

Arabella linked her arm through mine and pulled me close. "You are a scandal."

"And you're insufferable."

I did not add, "And please don't marry any of the men on your mother's list. However horticulturally inclined."

April 11th

That it was my fault Charles Goddard stepped on my toes while dancing does not make the pain any less today.

Later

I was standing in the queue at the Reed and Rite to purchase polish before returning home to consume half a dozen hot cross buns, when someone spoke at my back.

"No Maundy Thursday services for Miss Lion."

I swivelled half around. Two steps away, waiting patiently, was Hawkes. His words were not said in accusation, more like how a friend would say, *I looked to see if you were there, and you were not.*

Still, I felt some discomfort.

"Hello. Er, no. I'm afraid I was preparing to attend a ball yesterday and…forgot. With the other heathens."

Hawkes said nothing.

"But now that you bring it to mind," I attempted to right the ship, "I do mean to join you today for Good Friday. What time is the service?"

The queue moved a step forward, we with it.

"The Liturgy of the Lord's Passion was at midday."

"Midday," I replied with a nod. "I'll be there with bells— Oh, I've missed it! I'm sorry, Hawkes. I don't suppose you might give me a condensed version of the service?"

The queue moved a step forward, again, we with it.

"You wish me to recite the Liturgy of the Lord's Passion in the Reed and Rite?"

"Only your favourite lines, really. We've just three more people before we reach the counter."

Hawkes looked past me and said softly,

> *All the ends of the world shall remember and turn unto the Lord: and all the kindreds of the nations shall worship before thee. For the kingdom is the Lord's: and he is the governor among the nations.*

It was a Psalm. I couldn't remember which.

But everyone in the busy shop had paused. And listened.

Eternal God of unchanging power and light:
look with mercy on your whole creation;
and bring to completion your saving work,
so that the whole world may see the fallen lifted up,
the old made new,
and all things brought to perfection
by him through whom all things were made,
our Lord and Saviour Jesus Christ. Amen.

Silence.

Even Jape at the counter had paused, hand over his till. Then a ripple of amens.

"Amen," I said.

The silence settled, spreading out along the floor, then movement tentatively resumed. Hawkes, fingering the book he'd stowed beneath his arm opposite, looked about as if he desperately needed to take flight.

"If you'd like to stop by Lapis Lazuli, Agnes has fresh hot cross buns just coming out of the oven."

"Thank you," he replied, "but all I need are candles." Handing me a few coins before turning on his heel and walking back out onto the street.

The queue moved, and I was now at the counter.

"What'll it be?" asked Jape.

"Ah, candles?"

"How many?"

I put the money on the counter.

"Anything for yourself?"

"I can't now remember. I may have to come back. But wrap those candles in that blue paper. I think that is what Hawkes will like best. Thank you."

I stepped out of the Reed and Rite feeling in a bit of a daze, a parcel of candles in my hand. Was Hawkes expecting I keep the candles until he came to fetch them? Was he wanting me to leave them at the church? Or his flat? Or The Cleopatra?

In that moment, Toff came running down Whereabouts. He stopped before me, breathless.

"G'day, Miss Lion," he said.

"Hello, Toff."

Opening his fist, I saw two wrapped peppermints waiting. "For you. In exchange for candles."

"Oh! I see." I handed Toff the parcel and took one peppermint. "You may have the second."

He doffed his cap. "Thank you, Miss Lion."

And off he shot back up the lane.

I only remembered later, as I was sitting at the kitchen table licking the sugar from my fingers, that Hawkes was likely fasting for Good Friday.

And so I ate a hot cross bun on his behalf.

We must all do our part.

April 12th

Arabella and I went for a walk in Regent's Park this afternoon.

There was no escaping.

I'd opened Pandora's box and now she'd delivered herself to my door to demand answers in long form.

"Now," Arabella smiled, and sunshine rolled over the green lawn as a result. "We are without supervision of any kind, slumbering or sonorous. Please enlighten your dearest cousin. Are you and Mr. Pierce…courting?"

Arms crossed, I fussed absently with my sleeves as I enjoyed the view of the park coming into bloom.

Spring gives us more than we deserve.

The light breeze twining about the frothy blossoms.

I digress.

"A better word, I think, is negotiating."

Arabella made a sound I'd never heard from her before.

I gave her a sharp look. "Did you giggle just now?"

"I did. The first chapter of this book reads very promising, Emma. Please continue."

"Niall, that is Pierce, *Mr.* Pierce and I— Well, he kissed me at the end of February."

"Emma Lion. You never said. I demand the whole of it!"

"Well," I said, recalling the rain and early evening, "I kissed him back."

"Why am I suspecting this was not a simple, chaste peck?"

I sighed.

"And so?"

"So we agreed we needed to discuss our situation. And the first week of March was a ridiculous series of events, culminating in—"

"Mother and I descending on Lapis Lazuli House."

"Agony for us all."

"Oh, I quite enjoyed myself."

"And then we spoke to one another about it, the day before the fight at The Cleopatra."

"Isn't The Cleopatra the public house in St. Crispian's?"

"Yes."

"Why on earth were you fighting there?"

I rolled my eyes. "I wasn't fighting anywhere. And neither were they, really. Only Islington and Hawkes joined in when they saw Pierce surrounded."

Arabella slowed her step—if such a thing is possible. "The Duke of Islington was in a fight at a public house?"

"In the letter of the law, yes. Though I deny he fought in spirit."

"You, Emma," she gazed about in utter contentment, "bring havoc wherever you go."

"I won't deny my life is comprised of odd happenings."

"Returning to the point at hand, you and Mr. Pierce are in negotiations?"

"...yes."

"It's clear as day that the two of you should simply marry and be done with all the speculation."

I felt my eyes widen. "Arabella Spencer."

She grinned.

Wickedly.

"I'll be serious for a few moments only, Emma, so please don't hedge your answers."

"You've not asked any questions."

"Does he have any hesitations in courting you?"

I lifted my gloved hand and ticked off the reasons, "Our ages, my reputation, my parents' disapproval, his past—which he won't speak of. More, I believe, but we've begun there."

"I don't think he's too old for you in the least."

"It doesn't bother me, either."

"As for reputation, your marrying a photographer shouldn't alter a thing. You're not a staple in the upper classes—I mean that in a good way, darling. I think the eccentric middle class is where you truly belong."

"Thank you?" I said.

"Clearly, I understand why he's worried about your reputation. You must marry, Emma, even in the middle class, if you decide to go on living with this man—"

"I'm not living with him! There is a shared door."

"Used daily and with abandon, I would guess. His worrying over your reputation could be valid if you think this courtship might limp on for a year. If someone were to discover the whole, you would be dropped from nearly every class forever, which would be a pity as it would make it harder for my husband and I to have you as a guest. Not on my account, but on his. I have the dreadful feeling that I may marry a stubborn man who makes it hard to have my way."

I was taken aback by Arabella's confession. Usually, her easy confidence assures me that there isn't a husband in the world whom she can't bend to her desires. But as I didn't wish her to retreat behind her laissez-faire exterior, I replied, "Nothing ~~untoward~~ so very untoward has or will happen. Besides, we've Cousin Archibald in the house."

"Hmmm. Tread with care, dearest. As for your parents, they lost all say by abandoning us to my mother years ago. If they roll over in their graves, they can thank us for the exercise."

I could hear she honestly felt abandoned by them.

Two personal feelings in a row.

"Are you feeling quite yourself, Arabella?"

"Yes, darling. Now, what are *your* concerns? His mysterious past? I would have thought that an asset. It would keep marriage from becoming frightfully dull. His looks are no obstacle, neither is his voice. He works, there is that, but in an intriguing profession, and we neither of us pictured you married to a man of independent means."

I opened my mouth and closed it again while delivering an angled glare. "You should know I'm in the market for a dissolute viscount."

"Is he cruel? Pierce, I mean, not the viscount we both know you'll never accept even if you do find him."

"The opposite. He is kind."

"Then where do you hesitate?"

"I'm not hesitating. We're very nearly courting."

"You're negotiating a courtship. It's almost sad."

"Arabella, I wish for us to know one another. To feel that, yes, this is a person that— And then also— Oh, never mind."

"I think you worry that in your attempt to fall in love with someone else, you might stumble upon the wreckage left behind by Maxwell, and you won't know how to move forward."

I stopped in my tracks.

So did she, after circling gracefully to face me.

"Have I hit the centre of things?" she said.

She…

She had.

In a way I'd not known to articulate to myself.

"I've said goodbye to Maxwell," I stammered.

"And I couldn't be prouder." Arabella looked me directly in the eyes. "You have let him go as he has let you go. You have both done one another a great kindness. But what I am referring to—and you are desperately afraid to admit—is that the sovereign kingdom of Emma Lion's Heart might not have recovered, and you are fearful of what you will find if you allow another to again enter the terrain. What ruins await?"

Nonsense.

Silliness, really.

Yet it was perfectly fitted to the sharp-edged labyrinth of my chest. And possibly the most correct thing anyone has ever said to me.

I swallowed and looked towards the sun on the lake.

"No need to answer, my dear Irishman's daughter." She took my arm in hers and began walking. "I now revert back to my usual self and tell you only that as long as the man you marry is handsome, I have little care who he is or what he does."

We made our way back to St. Crispian's.

"Will you stay for tea?" I finally managed. "It's almost five o'clock."

"Happily. I've told Mother to send the carriage after tea, in any case."

Neither of us spoke of what Arabella had said, nor did we need to. There is a lightness that comes after truth is spoken plainly, and into that we leaned, conviviality surrounding our conversation as we entered the hall and removed our hats.

"Give me your afternoon coat, and I'll lay it over the banister," I said to Arabella, and then I called towards the kitchen. As we heathens do. "Agnes, is tea ready?"

"Hello, Miss Lion," she said, coming out of Pierce's studio. "I'm just fetching the rest of the tea. Oh, Miss Arabella! Oh dear!"

"Is something wrong, Agnes?"

"Only *He* is expecting to take tea with you."

"*He*? Do you mean God, Agnes?"

"No, Miss—"

"*God would also like to have a chat, no doubt…*" Arabella drawled under her breath.

"I mean Mr. Pierce, Miss." She was fiddling with her hands. "And I've already laid half the tea in ready and told him so. He's in the back garden but is soon to come in."

"Wonderful. I think we three will manage just fine."

Agnes's cheeks pinked, her panic moving from her fiddling hands to her expression. "But he isn't properly dressed for tea with *a lady*, Miss."

"Do you mean to say he's not fully clothed?"

"Oh no!" Agnes nearly perished at the thought. "He's wearing all his clothes, but no jacket. I wouldn't think he should be…seeing as how Miss Spencer is…and everything…"

Arabella could not have been enjoying the moment more.

"Your thoughtfulness does you credit, Agnes; however, seeing that Arabella has been warned Mr. Pierce may appear *sans* coat, and you've already told Mr. Pierce tea is waiting, it is our Christian duty to allow the poor man to enjoy his tea without making a fuss."

The phrase Christian Duty sprung Agnes into action. She straightened her shoulders, nodded stoically, and in a repentant tone said, "I shall invite him in now, then fetch the remainder of the tea with diligence and haste, like Christina."

"Who?"

"*Pilgrim's Progress*," murmured Arabella.

"Oh," I answered. "I must have missed that one."

"Faulty education," she replied. "Shall we? I expect the next hour to be marvellous."

"Possibly catastrophic," I answered.

Now having endured the hour, I can say while it was not catastrophic, it was not comfortable.

We entered the empty studio. The tea tray waited on the table before the sofa and chair.

"It smells heavenly," Arabella said, her eyes travelling around the room, resting on the photographs displayed.

"I wonder what Pierce is doing in the back garden," I said, looking out towards the street.

"He's been reading letters, Miss," Agnes said, returning with an extra plate and saucer and additional sandwiches, "but will return shortly. Now, will you pour, or should I?"

I wanted to tell Agnes that she has been riding a very high horse as of late when it comes to household management.

I said, "I'll pour, Agnes, thank you."

We were left alone.

"Who is this?" Arabella pointed to the woman dressed in white from the photograph of people by the pond.

"An acquaintance, I think. I don't know her name."

"Speaking of mysteries."

"Hello," came the sound of Pierce's voice. We both turned. He stood leaning against one side of the doorway, hands in his pockets.

"Pierce." My smile felt like a triangle, all awkward angles. "Agnes…" I waved a hand. "Tea…"

"She told me, before mentioning something about Christian Duty. Has the church elevated tea to spiritual ritual?"

"Heavens no," I replied. "We English have done that all on our own."

He nodded, then, "Hello, Miss Spencer."

"Mr. Pierce, a pleasure, once again."

"I'm coming to Spencer House this coming Tuesday, if I'm not mistaken."

"You are not mistaken."

"Too bad your mother insisted on staying in London," he said, pushing away from the doorway and stepping into the room, his limp a somewhat easier gait than it has been since the fight.

Arabella sat down on the far side of the sofa, resting her arm and taking lazy command of the room. "You can't manage to capture a decent photograph in London?"

"I can manage just fine," Pierce said, coming to a stop at my side. "But clients are often happier when their photograph is taken somewhere they care for."

Arabella gave him one of her smoothest smiles.

He didn't respond.

She blinked her eyes and pursed her lips in a way that drove most men to distraction.

No response.

Arabella could not move Pierce across the board like a pawn.

A thing she noted.

A thing I noted.

And enjoyed.

"Would you prefer we take tea in the drawing room?" I asked Pierce in a quieter tone of voice. "It looks like Agnes has assumed. Again."

He looked at me, silver eyes direct. "I'm happy to have you here."

Moving to sit on the sofa beside Arabella—who was studying the two of us—I began to sort the tea while Pierce retrieved his newspaper and came back, easing himself down carefully into his chair. Had we been alone I would have asked after his leg.

Only a minute passed before Arabella's games and Pierce's resistance to such settled into a polite exchange. She asking him a question, he answering in return.

For Example

Arabella: "How fares the world today, Mr. Pierce?"

Pierce: *Eyeing his newspaper.* "Falling apart, per usual."

Arabella: "Are you always such a pessimist?"

Pierce: "Pessimist, no. I'm a realist."

Arabella: *Laughs.* "A realist, and yet you live in this silly pocket of London?"

Pierce: *Gives Arabella an indiscernible, steady look.* "Sometimes what saves us are the things opposite our own view."

Arabella: *The scaffolding behind her eyes becomes unsteady. She braces it quickly with a dismissive air.* "No philosophy over tea, Mr. Pierce," she said, sitting back into the corner of the sofa. "It's rather tiring."

Emma: "More cake?"

After Arabella left, as I was putting everything back on the tray, Pierce said, "I almost forgot. Chambers came by and asked me to give you this."

My heart fully somersaulted in my chest.

I'm sure of it.

I jerked my head up to see Pierce holding a book in his hand.

Wrapped, thankfully.

And tied with twine.

A white feather beneath the twine, with a slip of paper that read, "Private! Miss Lion Only!"

"Are you all right?" Pierce asked, measuring my reaction.

"Fine!" I straightened, brushed my hands together, and ~~took~~ practically ripped my parcel from Pierce's hand.

"Dare I ask?"

"It's nothing. Nothing at all. Only my year, my journal, that is. *1883*. Absolutely nothing of interest to anyone else."

"You trusted Chambers with your journal?"

I stared at the wrapped book in my hands. The white feather affected me more than I was willing to let on. As if Chambers understood every inch of my trepidation and was honouring the fact. "Would you not have?"

"I would trust him completely. Only you and he can't seem to stand one another."

I looked up at Pierce. "Well, he swore on the man who had saved his life, and I thought it enough to trust in his discretion."

Pierce's reaction was slight, but still a reaction. He nodded. His eyes were no longer looking at me, rather a memory of something else. "Right," he said. "Glad he could help."

"Do you mind?" I asked, holding my journal to my chest. "I'll send Agnes in to fetch the tray."

"Go," he waved me off. "I can take these into the kitchen."

"Thank you."

I rushed up to the garret, two steps at a time, and collapsed onto the window seat, gripping the journal in my hands. Once my breath was caught, I pulled the twine loose—setting the white feather to the side—and unwrapped the paper.

It was perfect.

It was more than.

The black leather had a glorious sheen, not too bright but neither dull; the front and back cover stamped with a gold foil pattern of flowers and vines stretching out from each corner. And on the bottom of the spine it read,

EML
1883

The endpapers inside the journal were lovely and all the interior cream pages filled with my writing, familiar.

A note was placed just inside the front cover.

Miss Lion,

As promised, I did not read a word of your journal. Nor did anyone else. I kept it with me the entire two days.

Send Parian to settle the account. The bill of sale is enclosed.

Ben Chambers

April 13th

Easter Sunday.

Hawkes at his finest.

He began with John of Damascus, something I've heard many an Easter.

> *Now the queen of seasons, bright*
> *with the day of splendour,*
> *with the royal feast of feasts,*
> *comes its joy to render.*

The service was part liturgy, part Hawkes being Hawkes, moving from scripture to poetry and back again—an elysian masterpiece. His most careful reading came from Jeremiah,

> *And they shall be my people, and I will be their God: And I will give them one heart, and one way, that they may fear me for ever, for the good of them, and of their children after them.*

All wonderfully well and good.

It was near the end of the sermon that I was delivered a shock.

For when I glanced over my shoulder, I saw Victoria Braithwaite—of all souls—in mourning black, sitting on the other side of the chapel.

Wondering if I was being haunted, I looked again.

And again.

No, she was there. And looked very, very sad.

My heart twisted.

"What do you keep looking at?" Islington murmured.

To be fair, I was unduly distracted. Here was Hawkes giving the sermon of his life, and I found myself fixated by this strange appearance.

"Miss Braithwaite, Miss Victoria Braithwaite. What is she *doing* here?"

Now Islington glanced over, then returned his gaze ahead. "She moved in with the general last week."

My mouth fell open. "The general? General Braithwaite is her uncle?"

"Great-uncle, I believe."

No.

It couldn't be.

There I was, Victoria Braithwaite on one hand and General Braithwaite on the other, never dreaming that the two of them were connected In Any Way.

"What was that?" Islington asked.

I shook my head. "I was only thinking. Aloud, apparently."

"Do you know her, then?" he whispered.

"Yes. Since we were children."

"She'll be glad to have a friend in the neighbourhood."

Here I sighed the sigh of the damned. "Friend is not the word either of us would use."

Islington, quiet for enough of a moment to conjure several reasons why this would not be the case, bent his head and rubbed the bridge of his nose. "I am assuming this story could wait until the sermon has ended?"

"She's the most prominent name on my Enemies List."

He elbowed me.

In all honesty, it was more of a nudge.

Or a hint of one.

It may simply have been Islington moving his arm.

Regardless, I glared.

The stream of Hawkes's divine discourse had stopped.

"Amen," I said. Then looking around, I realised Hawkes was still standing at the pulpit before the congregation, watching Islington and me with—what I defend to be—an affectionate impatience.

In lieu of elbowing Islington good and hard in the ribs, I folded my arms and tried to look like the penitent ~~I struggle to be~~ Islington prevents me from being. It could not have been longer than five seconds, but so relieved was I when Hawkes's all-knowing gaze left us and the sermon continued, my sigh was *quite* audible. Several around us turned their heads.

"You really are dreadful in church," Islington whispered.

I glared.

Hawkes ended his sermon with an amen.

"Amen," I murmured again with the congregation. I did not look over my shoulder towards Victoria Braithwaite.

However much I wished to.

Toff sidled up to me soon after the service. "Young Hawkes has asked that you wait in his study."

Islington looked smug.

"You *and* the duke," amended Toff.

"Ha!"

Thus Islington and I waited while the church emptied of its worshipers.

"Your elbow is rather sharp," I complained.

"Can a man not shift his arm in church?"

"Not with an accompanying scowl. It gives the wrong impression. One of these days I'm going to jab your ribs in retribution. All sanctioned by God, of course. Eye for an eye, tooth for a tooth, and all that."

"Have you not read the New Testament?"

"You and I are fixed squarely in the Law of Moses."

He laughed out loud.

It was so unexpected that I couldn't help but give a begrudging smile.

When we entered the old vestry—empty of Hawkes, who had walked Mrs. Ribbits out into the churchyard—Islington stood by the window, holding his hat, while I perused the bookshelf. It is such a delicious mishmash of novels and history and science and languages and religion and poetry.

All loved, if their wear indicates anything.

I almost said as much, but Hawkes entered.

Crossing the room to stand behind his desk, setting the books he carried down, Hawkes removed the cassock he'd worn for Easter service from over his suit of clothing.

"I have no illusions," he spoke evenly, moving things about his desk, "that my sermons are worth rapt attention and find it perfectly reasonable that someone might carry on a conversation in lieu of listening." He looked up, first at Islington and then at me. "Even on Easter Sunday. But I quoted from *Devotions Upon Emergent Occasions* as the crowning passage to this morning's sermon, a passage I have held especially because I thought you, Miss Lion," he looked only at me, "would enjoy."

Disappointing him was surprisingly painful.

"Hawkes—"

"We're terribly sorry—" Islington began.

But Hawkes quieted us with a mild, almost unattached smile. "It doesn't matter, really; only John Donne deserves better from us all. Now," he released his breath, "how was the rest of it?"

I had never heard Hawkes ask a question with such a vulnerable tenor.

"The rest of the sermon?" I asked.

"I wasn't certain pairing Wordsworth and Hosea gave the words enough room to breathe."

"Oh, Hawkes, it was perfect. Truly. I've never heard the like."

"Well done, Hawkes," Islington said, frowning. "But you know it was."

"I'm feeling a touch sideways, is all," Hawkes said, mussing his hair. "If you'll excuse me, there is a sick parrot whose owner has asked I read it some poetry."

He selected a volume of Dryden and left.

"Dryden," I said, glancing at Islington. "For a parrot?"

But Islington was looking down, expression pensive. "Unusual. For Hawkes."

"What does he usually read exotic birds?"

"No, not the Dryden. Rather the fuss, the uncertainty."

"Is he not usually so protective of John Donne?"

"No. That is to say, he *is* protective of John Donne, but something else is bothering him."

"What?"

Islington lifted his head and released a breath through his nose. "Would she—?" he quietly asked himself.

"She?"

A single *tsk*. Then, "Never you mind."

My mouth opened in insult and injury of its own volition. "You, Islington, are such a snob."

"Which is much less a problem than a brooding Hawkes." He walked out of the old vestry.

"Is *she* to whom you refer the one who writes him letters on rather expensive paper spritzed with a pear scent?"

A ducal step hesitated, giving me room to catch up. "How do you know that?"

"I saved one such letter. In a most heroic manner."

Islington raised an eyebrow as he opened the church door and motioned me through. "Yes, it is *she* to whom I am referring."

"*She*," I imitated his tone, stepping out into the weak sunshine. "Who is *she*?"

"When Hawkes wants to tell you, Hawkes will tell you."

"One of these days we will all gather in Baron's Square to stone you," I said.

"What, you and your bloodthirsty Old Testament penchants?"

"Precisely. If your Islington offends you, cut him off."

Here Islington laughed again.

Later

Hawkes,

I send Parian with this excellent cake as a peace offering. Or rather, a piece offering. I meant to send the whole but have found that Cousin Archibald ate full half. And then Tybalt had a go.

All this to say, I'm sending you a third of a cake, with an extra candle and my sincerest apology. I hope you don't make me wait forever before quoting John Donne.

~~*Emma M. Lion, newly committed to reverence in church.*~~
Emma M. Lion, newly committed to not *sitting beside Islington in church.*

April 14th

Victoria Braithwaite has moved into St. Crispian's. Her great-uncle is General Braithwaite, who lives in Baron's Square.

I'M NOT SURPRISED. WHAT WITH ALL THAT BUSINESS IN THE PAPER.

Clearly I need to read the paper. What business?

THE USUAL. HER FATHER WAS IN DEBT. DIDN'T TELL THE FAMILY. NOT ENOUGH MONEY TO SATISFY CREDITORS. EVERYTHING SOLD. I USUALLY HAVE LITTLE INTEREST IN SUCH STORIES, BUT I FEEL TERRIBLY FOR THE GIRL.

Later

After Pierce sent his message, I put on my worn boots and went for a long, winding walk. I did not stay in St. Crispian's, but I ended back at the crest of Primrose Hill all the same. A few others moved about the park as I sat rummaging through the emotions of the day. There are two tracks of feeling running through me, deep and knotted. Victoria Braithwaite and I seem to be on corresponding paths, fate or fey nonsense or trial sanctioned by God? I've no idea. But our early lives crossed, and since then we've both been away to school, both come to London, both lost father and mother, both found our financial securities taken through selfishness of others. Both ended up here, in St. Crispian's. Disparate circumstances and different orders, but a pattern nonetheless.

As for how we've varied, I would take my path a thousand times over in a thousand lives, however difficult—the art, the colour, the way that light bends gold around my memories, even the unhappy ones. I have known love and lost. I was gifted so much.

And here I come to the second feeling, so overwhelming I'm not certain what I am to do. St. Crispian's is mine. It is the corner of

London given to me by my great-aunt, the original Emma Lion. My strange, small kingdom of quirk and delight. St. Crispian's was not meant to house the Victoria Braithwaites of the world. Unfair to think so? Certainly. Yet it is how I feel. But the thought of all her losses, coming one after the other without reprieve, is breathtakingly painful. I think, of course she should be here.

Why not?

Why not this gift for her also?

My feelings are a tangled knot, stiff and impossible. And I've a stomachache trying to figure it out.

I don't want to see her in St. Crispian's.

I don't want to *prepare* myself to see her in St. Crispian's.

I don't want to be a small-minded, petty human being.

"There's nothing worse than someone who would shrink their generosity for the sake of keeping what they want," is what my father would say.

No, St. Crispian's is not mine alone.

And alone is not what Victoria Braithwaite should be now.

April 15th

The photographs have been cancelled.

Ha!

Aunt Eugenia and Arabella have both come down with Tremendous Head Colds. "*Of the very worst sort and kind,*" my aunt wrote to Pierce.

"How wonderful!" This was my contribution, leaning forward, my elbows on his worktable, my chin in my hands.

Pierce was searching through one of the bureaus on the far end of the studio. "Hmm," he replied, as he lifted something heavy (I've no idea what, but it looked like an anvil covered in black fabric) and shifted it to the side, before reaching behind a crate, and making a subdued but triumphant noise. Standing up straight, Pierce turned. In his hand was a pair of brass binoculars with a cover over the lenses.

"Are you brushing up on your ornithology?"

"No." He didn't smile, but the edges of his eyes crinkled (Is crinkled the right word? Possibly not.) in amusement. "I thought I would do some personal work, as my schedule"—he waved his hand—"has cleared for the day."

"Spectators at the racetrack?"

"Street urchins. At the docks."

"*Ah.*"

"Speaking of, Islington is going with me."

I made a sound like a snort. "Is he really?"

"Yes." Pierce walked towards me and set the binoculars down beside Aunt Eugenia's letter. (Doctor's report, more like. She'd used the word phlegm. Twice.)

"You've not invited me on any of your expeditions," I said, straightening up, my hands on the edge of the table. Pierce leaned back against the table just around the corner from where I stood, folding his arms, turning his head, and looking down at me.

"For obvious reasons."

"You don't think I'd be strong enough to help carry your equipment?"

"No. I think you'd do just fine with that." His voice always sounds like a rain cloud when he's speaking quietly. "I'm going to a part of London that isn't particularly safe. I don't want to take you there."

"I'm a crack shot."

"Oh you are, are you?"

"I would be if you'd given me that pistol for my birthday."

"It would have suited," Pierce replied. Unfolding his arms, he reached out his hand and lifted the gold chain of my lion pendant with his finger. "So does this."

I swallowed. "Yes, well, it's less lethal."

Pierce looked like he would argue a moment, then pressed his lips together in a questioning expression. "If I were to kiss you, like I did last week, would you insist on being so damn polite about it?" He pulled his hand away and the chain fell back into place.

"I— That is to say, I was rather— Nothing could have— I can guarantee nothing."

Pierce, already turning towards me, allowed himself an uneven smile—a rare bird, and one of my favourites. He leaned in.

I closed my eyes.

It was not, however, the kiss he gave me last week, teasing and halfway.

It was careful, it took its time.

It asked a question.

When he hesitated, and began to move away, I pulled him back.

In response, Pierce lifted a hand to the side of my face.

And then.

Pierce stilled.

He looked past me.

His hand fell away. "Good morning, Parian. Can I help you with something?"

They say that in moments when one's butler finds one kissing one's boarder, time does not rush; rather, it stretches like a judgemental cat, giving ample space to consider how absolutely foolish one has been, and that the only way to carry the day is with misplaced confidence.

I can now confirm this to be true.

From my own experience.

I turned around—my heart beating oblong and loud—cleared my throat, and said, "Yes, Parian?"

He was standing stock still. Dust rag in his hand. Mouth *quite* unhinged.

Pierce stepped away with an ease I admired, picking up the brass binoculars from the table and walking across the room to continue preparing for his day at the docks.

I resisted the urge to wipe the flush from my cheeks, absently smoothing my skirt instead. "Are you dusting, Parian? How industrious of you, as we are all trying to be. Shall we take our conversation elsewhere? Mr. Pierce is busy."

Without looking at either man, I walked past Parian and into the hall.

Dazed, Parian followed. I had to close the studio door behind him.

A stone had fallen from my heart into my stomach, landing atop the knowledge that if Parian spoke one word regarding what he had seen, I would pay a higher price than I could afford.

I felt ill.

"Is there something you needed?" I asked Parian, brushing my hands as if I were the one dusting.

He shook his head.

"Parian, if I might ask you to keep your mouth closed in relation to—"

He closed his mouth so quickly his teeth made a sound.

"No, well yes, you look much better this way. What I mean was 'metaphorically' only not quite. That is to say, I'm asking you to not say anything in regard to— Nothing untoward has happened, Parian, absolutely nothing, but I need you to not say a word. To anyone. Do you feel you can do that?"

A nod—a shingled, stiff affair. I've never seen an expression of such shock on his pointed face.

"Now that I think on it, why don't you ask Agnes if there is anything she needs done before you take a half day. Yes, that should suit. You go out and wander London to your heart's content."

Later

I decided to spend a ~~vigorous~~ virtuous hour walking Regent's Park.

Penance.

For not having closed and locked the studio door.

And my walk turned into Penance indeed, for who did I encounter but Lady Frankland and her niece Leah. I'd only met them at Lady Sheridan's tea a few months past and had not spoken to them since.

"Why, Miss Lion," said Lady Frankland.

"Why, Miss Lion," echoed Leah.

"Good morning, Lady Frankland, Miss Frankland."

"You're walking alone." Lady Frankland ruched her smile like an expensive gown. "How intrepid you are."

"Intrepid," Leah said.

I tried not to quirk my eyebrow in a Hawkesian manner as a lacklustre smile rose on my face. "Not as intrepid as I'd like. My chaperone, Miss Dowd, is somewhere—" I interrupted myself. "Are you both well?"

"Very well," said Lady Frankland.

"Very," said Leah.

"And what a rush of busyness!" said Lady Frankland.

"A rush."

"Remarkable," I answered, "for April."

"Yes," they both echoed.

"Well, enjoy your constitutional," I said cheerily, primed to step away.

There was a conspiratorial look between them.

I sensed danger.

Before I could make good on my farewell, Lady Frankland took my arm. "Miss Lion, Saturday evening we have a *To-Do.*"

"Ah," replied I.

"A very great *To-Do. A ball,*" emphasized she. "Everyone in London will be there."

"How very crowded."

They both laughed for an over-polite four seconds. "We expect some acquaintances of yours. Lady and Miss Clifford, Lady Sheridan, among others. The Duke of Islington, of course."

Ah.

Lady Frankland reached for my gloved hand, giving it a good shake. "Why don't you throw caution to the wind, Miss Lion, and join us."

"Do join us," Leah repeated.

My smile, at this point, had gone rather rictus.

"I don't believe I am able," I began. "You see, my aunt being ill and my chaperone being…unfit for such occasions, I find—"

"Miss Lion," Lady Frankland leaned in conspiratorially, "I simply propose you be accompanied by another guest. Islington, perhaps!"

"Islington!" said Leah.

I could not hide my shock at the effrontery. For them to invite me to invite myself to be squired by Islington! Absurd.

"Being such a close family friend, I am sure all will be good and proper," Lady Frankland assured. "We're so *happy* to have you."

"Thank you," I managed.

"Wonderful!"

"Wonderful."

I sighed. "Quite."

April 16th

Islington,

I expected a quiet Saturday evening at home reading Plutarch. Now I'm being trotted out for the dog and pony show of Lady Frankland's To-Do. I wholeheartedly blame this turn of events on my association with you. She had the effrontery to suggest you squire me to and from, as my aunt is ill. I think it a ploy to ensure you accept the invitation. Or stay the entirety of the ordeal.

Lion

Later

Lion,

My apologies for the grievous weight my friendship imposes. I, however, am pleased to have your company, as I was dreading the affair, my private secretary having errantly accepted on my behalf.

I would be happy to convey you to the Frankland's unless you have made other arrangements.

Islington

Later

Islington,

Grievous weight, indeed.
I accept your offer.

Lion

P.S. You've a private secretary? Where do you keep him? In the garden?

Later

Lion,

I have no overwhelming need for a private secretary—I've a steward for most affairs and prefer to keep a solid handle on everything myself—and so it is only once a week that my aunt lends me hers.

Perhaps they were conspiring against me.

Islington

April 17th

I don't care for the word conjunction.

Con. Junc. Tion.

Conjunction.

There is nothing about those three sounds that makes one believe (even remotely) they are spending time together of their own free will.

And while I don't particularly find a word like incorporate to be any lovelier, one does get the sense that the syllables do take a slight interest in one another.

However, the word digress is all charm running backward, and I approve.

Oh dear.

There is Parian coming up the lane from The Keep—he is carrying the poker to our fireplace set.

(We've not spoken since my fumbled attempt after The Event.)

(Is there anything else, truly, to say?)

April 18th

Dear Emma,

Mama is still horribly ill. As for myself, darling, I'm pretending to be worse than I am so I can stay in my room, sleep, eat sweets my maid brings me from the kitchen, and read whatever silly novels I have on the ready.

Lady Frankland sent a note saying she'd invited you to her ball tomorrow night, to be accompanied by the Duke of Islington. Mama turned an impressive purple. Well done.

Arabella

Later

Islington and I had tea at Everett's this afternoon.

It was not in joint battle plan, but rather a happy accident, as we met on King Henry's and decided to move our conversation within comfortable reach of Bavarian cream.

"You're looking extraordinarily hungry today," I remarked as he let his usual conversation dwindle in favour of a very good sponge cake.

"Crosby is visiting a cousin's anniversary celebration, and I told him to stay on; but then Mrs. Knowlls, having discovered her niece's baby had come early, left the day before yesterday. My aunt and her entire household are visiting Stonecrop. I've a footman to ensure the house isn't ransacked but no one with any sense in the kitchen. Seeing as how I can take my meals at the club, it isn't too much of an imposition, but yes, this cake is exceptionally good."

"Lapis Lazuli is not the height of culinary excellence, but you are welcome any evening. Agnes would be thrilled."

"If needs be, I'll throw myself on your generosity."

After tea, we walked Primrose Hill, and Islington made a comment about my appalling love of strawberry preserves.

"There is nothing wrong with an appalling love of strawberry preserves. Now you're only looking for something to fuss about. I know you don't disapprove of me half as much as you would lead me to believe."

"What on earth gave you that impression?" Islington replied.

We passed a couple and then two men, Islington lifting his hat and giving appropriate greeting, me smiling like an escapee from Bedlam, before I answered.

"You've welcomed me into Thursday."

"What was that?"

"Thursday, Islington. Thursday. *Dies Sanctus*. You've shown your hand."

Islington surveyed my face, then looked out over the park. "Who was it, I wonder, who gave you the key to that particular door? Was it in my journal you so ungallantly read?"

"I was every inch gallant when I read it," I argued. "I even fancied myself half in love with you."

His side-eye was of superb make and quality. "Why does high doubt come to mind."

"That was before I'd met you properly," I said. "You are very irksome in person."

He smiled (smirked?) and then returned to the question of Who Gave Up His Secret.

"Hawkes would never say anything without reason."

No, he wouldn't.

"You have no correspondence with my sisters," Islington continued, then paused before adding, "Has Maggie been writing to Pierce?"

"He has received one letter that I know of, and she mentioned nothing about Thursday."

"What did she say? That her brother is a stick in the mud?"

It was not far from the truth. "Nothing so harsh," I answered. "Only that you were such a stiff collar she couldn't see how you had time for friends, let alone Pierce. The image gave her delight."

"The image made her laugh with diabolic glee," Islington coolly corrected.

He had almost quoted his sister verbatim.

"I take it the two of you are not close?"

"We siblings are close. We can't help but be. We do, however, have our differences." He paused. "It was my aunt, wasn't it?"

"Remember you yourself sent me, as penance."

"I thought you would enjoy the encounter."

"I did!" I exclaimed. "She's a modern marvel, a countess who smokes like a sailor. And yes, she did tell me how you keep your Thursdays holy."

"I expect you to hold that secret, as it's not something I delight in others knowing. I like having my day, my *one* day I refuse anything I don't expressly wish."

"I accept your compliment."

"What?"

"You usually invite Hawkes, Pierce, and myself to dine on Thursdays."

Islington tipped his hat at someone, then looked back at me. "Correct."

"Which circles us back to my point. You don't disapprove of me half as much as you would like me to believe."

To which he replied, "I'll bring the carriage round at eight o'clock tomorrow for the Frankland's ball."

"We none of us escape this life without tribulation."

"No, we do not. I am on the May Day Committee, and I'm positively going mad."

It was a most delightful image. "The May Day Committee?"

"Baron's Square is hosting the fête. *Ah*, you've never been? An all-day fair. I should think it just the thing for you, Lion."

"But why wasn't I aware last year?"

"It's biannual."

"You celebrate the first of May twice each year?"

"Biannual, as in every other year. Last May there was no fair, this year there is."

"How confusing."

"Don't lay the foibles of the English language or St. Crispian's at my door."

"What are your responsibilities on the May Day Committee?" I asked.

"Legion."

I laughed.

April 19th

ARE YOU STILL PACING?

My apologies. Am I keeping you awake?

NO. I DON'T IMAGINE I'LL SLEEP FOR HOURS.
ARE YOU WORRIED ABOUT ISLINGTON?

FAIRCHILD EXPECTS THINGS WILL BE BETTER IN THE MORNING.

Yes, I am worried. I should have insisted we leave the Frankland's early. But he seems well enough settled. Parian is keeping watch, and Agnes, thankfully, cleaned the entire fourth floor last week, so the room is not in total disgrace. Is your leg recovered?

IT WILL BE FINE.
IT'S BEEN BOTHERING ME SINCE THE FIGHT, IN ANY CASE.

I SUSPECT PARIAN COULDN'T HAVE CARRIED ISLINGTON UP THREE FLIGHTS OF STAIRS.

Physically impossible, I daresay.

April 20th

Feeling need of divine intervention, and knowing I left the situation at Lapis Lazuli in Agnes's capable hands, I went to church. While waiting for the service to begin, Toff sidled up next to me.

"Vicar wants to see you," he said. "Before the service."

"Does he?" I asked, trying to stifle a yawn. I had not slept well, twice checking on Islington.

Toff nodded, his chin pointing towards the old vestry. "In his study."

I stood quietly, trying not to draw attention to myself as the church was already quite full, walked back to the old vestry, and knocked on the door.

"Come in."

I pushed the door open, then half closed it behind me.

Young Hawkes, standing behind his desk, was fussing with his collar with his right hand, while turning the pages of a book with his left.

"Emma," he said in greeting without looking up.

"Good morning, Hawkes," I answered.

"I hear rumours from time to time," he said.

I raised an eyebrow and replied cautiously. "I'm certain you do…although often untrue or exaggerated, I imagine. The thing is, Hawkes, if Parian were to have considered—"

Now Hawkes looked up, enjoying my attempt to mitigate whichever of my many sins he was laying at my door. "Don't mind the rumours I hear about you. A wonderfully curious and odd collection. No, I'm speaking of another."

"Oh?"

"Did Islington take ill at Lapis Lazuli House?"

"Heavens. How was that noised abroad?"

"Very easily, you'll find."

"Yes. Well, no. He was ill before arriving at Lapis Lazuli. Unbeknownst, as it happens. I blame the entire episode in the servants' corridor. Which, by all accounts, can only be considered a significant disaster to my young life. But we were outside Lapis Lazuli House when he— That is to say, yes."

Hawkes—shifting a few books to the side before lifting one in his hand—looked at me as I finished. "I'll come round after the service."

"Please do. He asked after you last night, but Parian couldn't find you."

"Fairchild saw to him, I expect?"

"Yes. He came by again this morning. Islington is sleeping. Fairchild said it was a good sign."

"Good," Hawkes nodded. Then again, "Good."

And he walked past me, out into the chapel, and the service began.

I was effectually stuck, as I could not walk out of Hawkes's study mid-service.

Speaking of starting rumours.

So I did what any self-respecting Christian would do, I half listened to the service while nosily introducing myself to Hawkes's books.

It was a wonderful sermon.

Agnes said Islington woke once while I was at church, asked only for something to drink, then fell back asleep.

I suppose I ought to record the events of last evening before he again wakes.

A Full and Partial* Account of Last Evening

**Partial meaning biased*

The fact that I wore one of Arabella's remade gowns—a cobalt blue velvet with silk brocade—bears no importance other than that Islington paid me a compliment. As for what Islington wore? Quality, of course. Deep black. Crisp white. Hair combed into an immovable place with pomade. Hazel eyes more gold than green.

"I barely managed to pull myself together," he answered. "My footman was called to his grandfather's funeral."

"You're fending entirely for yourself?"

"Which a man ought to be able to do," Islington parried. "On occasion."

The *To-Do* was larger than I'd pictured. A full ball and quite crowded.

"A lavish stable filled with pedigreed specimens of English society," I said.

Islington nodded but did not reply. Upon reflection, he looked a little flushed.

I was happy to see Lady Trewartha—"Miss Lion, lovely. I need some young blood about. I'm stealing her, Islington. Go find yourself some champagne. Let me introduce you to my friend, Lady Harrington."

After a spate of introductions, I was asked for a dance.

I acquiesced.

I was asked to dance again.

And again. Some absurd gallop I pretended to know.

How much I enjoyed a ball without Aunt Eugenia was not lost on me.

As for Islington, for the first two hours I'd only seen flashes; he danced very little, mostly speaking with acquaintances, looking too serious by half. I told him so when he claimed a waltz.

"I don't believe I look overly serious."

"You were glaring just now."

"I was squinting. The lights are very bright. Don't you think the lights are bright?"

"Not particularly," I replied, trying to match my mediocre skills to his more graceful talent.

And then, rather unexpectedly, Islington stumbled.

Unnoticed except by me. I gave a small hop, we righted our footing, and continued. When I glanced up at Islington's face, I saw he was perspiring.

"Pardon my clumsiness," he said.

"Are you feeling quite well? It's too warm altogether, but you look especially—"

But then—horror of horrors—I looked past Islington to see Charles Goddard standing at the edge of the dance floor, watching me with all the adoration he could gather inside that tall beanpole of a frame.

"Cruel, cruel fate," I hissed.

"You don't *have* to dance with me, you know."

"Not you! Only I've just sighted— Dear me, he's on the move. You must do your best to guide us to the other side of the room. Yes, please hurry. We can go out onto the terrace and possibly slide down a column."

"Why in the name of—"

"No battlefield arguments, Islington."

The scheme was successful, the unwanted interaction avoided.

We were off the floor and through the crowd.

The terrace looked as popular as the ballroom, so Islington and I found ourselves in the room where supper had been laid out.

"Enough flummeries and jellies to make one sick," Islington said as I was contemplating a rather tall specimen of the former. I gave it a poke with a clean knife and Islington looked away. "Please don't, the room is moving enough as it is."

I resisted giving the flummery another poke and turned instead to my ailing duke. "As you're not well, I think we should—"

Then Islington went absurdly pale—an effect having nothing to do with his physical health whatsoever. "Emma, I beg of you, get me from this room as quickly as you possibly can."

"What?"

"Please," he whispered, setting his empty plate down on the table. "Please, do it now."

I placed my own plate—a slaughtered point of a Brunswick Star jelly wiggling in abandonment—and played my part. "I am feeling unwell. Will you accompany me? Thank you." Gripping Islington's wrist, and with nary a glance over my shoulder, I marched from the room, Islington in tow. We did not turn back into the ballroom, nor did I take him into the adjoining salon, but turned into a hall, then a corridor, where I found a door.

Opening it, I pushed him in.

It was then that Islington noticed we'd found ourselves in the servants' corridor.

"Why on earth are we in here? You of all people could have found the library," he said, lifting his hand to his head and grimacing.

"You told me to help you escape. Pale as if you'd just seen one of the four horsemen of the apocalypse, I might add."

"Of all the ridiculous— Yes, I needed to quit the room in haste, but I gave no indication hiding in a closet was necessary."

I frowned. "It's a corridor. Now tell me what, exactly, we are hiding from?"

Islington at this point had returned to his flushed state, pressing his fingers into his left temple. "There was someone in that room who thinks we should be, ah, married."

I think I physically recoiled. "Thinks that *we* should be married?"

"No!" His reaction mirrored my own. "Another young woman. *Quite* another."

I felt a smile walk itself across my face. "*You* have an Unintended Intended?"

"Most certainly *not.* I have a young woman who is doing her best to force me into such a situation. Her mother has already married off two sisters in such schemes, and I only just escaped their snare at a dinner party last week—"

This.

This was the moment of my fatal decision.

I should have forgone chivalry and let him crash to the ground.

If *only* I'd let him.

I could have claimed that Islington, the Duke of, was a drunkard.

All would have been well.

Alas.

In that moment, Islington closed his eyes and began to sway.

"Islington?" I reached out to steady him, but he stumbled. I grabbed his shoulders as he fell against me, his head bent near mine in pain.

The door swung open.

Standing before us was a wide-eyed footman and Lady Frankland.

Lady Frankland, high colour rising in her cheeks, could not keep the triumph from her eyes. She had caught the Duke of Islington in the servants' corridor with an unattached young woman. In what, I admit, looked remarkably like a desperate embrace.

Disaster.

We would likely not recover.

And Lady Frankland would wear the moment like a feather in her cap the rest of her life.

Something had to be done.

"Lady Frankland," I swallowed. "Thank heavens. Islington is—"

I pushed us apart just as Islington was attempting to right himself. "He stumbled."

Islington lifted his head, attempting to draw himself to his full height; but as his face was flushed, he looked as intoxicated as the best of them. "I did. We were simply…"

"We were discussing—" I began.

"Yes." Islington rallied. "Miss Lion had a very pressing question."

"I wish to travel to Europe with friends," I blurted, grasping for any explanation, "but Islington doesn't approve of the scheme! Have you ever seen such a bully?"

"I've been trying to talk some sense into Miss Lion," Islington inserted. I glanced sharply at him and found him more put together than he had been only a moment before. Only his high colour gave him away.

Lady Frankland's expression could only be termed as dubious.

It was, in short, a catastrophe for us both.

Our honour and dignity deserved one last attempt.

"You see, Lady Frankland, I often confer with Islington, because…"

"Now that Miss Lion is turned twenty-one years of age," he continued, "she has left the guardianship of her aunt, Lady Eugenia Spencer."

"Yes," I rushed hastily, "which means—"

"It just so happens—"

"Islington is…my…"

The duke at my side closed his eyes briefly. (In prayer I now suspect.) He then straightened his shoulders and pulled at his cuff. "You see, Lady Frankland, now that Miss Lion has left the guardianship of her aunt, she is considered my ward until she marries." And then muttering under his breath, "Whenever that blessed disaster takes place."

Dread thunked into my chest like an arrow.

"Oh!" Lady Frankland's eyes went wide.

Islington cleared his throat, "Miss Lion's parents arranged it thus. A *joy* for us all. And now she has been wishing to travel to Europe with friends, but I don't approve of the scheme."

"I don't approve of *this* scheme," I stated in panic.

But with a grim determination to find his way out of the corridor,

Islington continued. "Miss Lion was put out; I, more than .a little annoyed. She accused me of being heartless, I declared her willful, and we found ourselves needing to, ah, find, a place to discuss the issue."

"Especially as Islington has had more than enough to drink and is unsteady on his feet."

Islington glared at me.

I glared in return. "I should very much like to flee to Europe now, if at all possible." It was desperation that came out as sulk.

"Perhaps you ought," snapped Islington.

Let me note that at this miserable juncture, Lady Frankland was kind enough to display all internal thought on her face. Surprise. More triumph. Self-satisfied snobbery. Suspicion. Incredulity. Then a wavering disbelief as the story sounded only a shade less ridiculous than if we'd declared that the pair of us had joined the Welsh circus.

(Is there a Welsh circus?)

"A young lady of spirit always pushes against the restraints she's given." Lady Frankland gave her head a knowing tilt. "And I shouldn't think it too hard to explain your rather—shall we say French?—situation when I opened the door just now?"

Islington set his mouth in a hard line.

"Aaahhh," I said, as if it had only just occurred to me that we'd been discovered in unusual circumstances. "I *see*. You thought…" I began to laugh. "You thought we—" I made a motion with my hand. "Islington and I?" I punched him fraternally in the arm.

"Heaven help us," Islington muttered, lifting a hand to his face.

"No, Lady Frankland," I continued. "I was trying to persuade him. Like so." And I grabbed Islington by the shoulders. "Henry, what a dictator you are! You must let me go! Please." I shook him once, then twice, and he lifted a hand and gripped my arm, prying my fingers away.

"Emma, if you don't stop shaking me, I am truly going to—"

But his threat went undelivered. "Goodness me," Lady Frankland interrupted. "You bicker quite like my own children. As for the overindulgence, Your Grace, I'm surprised at you. I've always believed you to be a man of reputation and sense. Perhaps you ought not enjoy yourself *so very much* when acting as chaperone to Miss Lion. She is young and impressionable. It would have been best if

Lady Spencer had continued her guardianship."

Islington's expression tightened further, wound by a quiet but growing fury.

"Oh, no, Lady Frankland," I protested, stepping out to take her arm and lead her away. "My aunt has Damian to worry over; you've heard he is in Paris chasing an actress?"

I led her away.

Of all the ridiculous, mad, stupid messes to have stumbled into.

By the time I had procured my coat and found Islington—he was waiting wordlessly by the door—my expression was foul.

His was no clearer.

We entered his carriage without speaking, both of us staring doggedly ahead.

Until.

"Damn," Islington muttered to himself.

I could think of nothing more appropriate, so I blessed the sentiment with my silence.

We fumed most of the way home, but a verbose pugilism was inevitable.

"Islington, how could you possibly claim you were my guardian!"

"Isn't that what you yourself were driving at?"

"No!"

"You said, and *I quote*, 'Islington is my…'"

"It was inadvertent! A mistake. You should have steered us aright!"

"What exactly would you have had me say?" he snapped.

"Anything else! Unless this little joke suits you."

He scowled. "Believe you me, I don't take pleasure in having perjured ourselves to save our reputations, your reputation in particular."

"*My* reputation!" I exclaimed.

"Yes!" he winced. His head likely pounding. "A man speaking privately with his ward is a far cry from a duke hiding in a servants' corridor with an unattached young woman whom he will be escorting home!"

"Certainly! But why do you emphasize *my* reputation as the one having been saved!"

He winced at my volume. "Please—"

I pinched my lips. "Islington, my autonomy has been effectively stolen in one false claim."

"The only alternative would have been to propose marriage," he snapped back, his hand still covering his eyes. "Is that what you want? For us to spend the next fifty years raging at each other because we were caught in a servants' corridor together, *quite* together?"

"You wouldn't have had to propose!" I half hissed, half shouted. "An explanation of you not being well and of me trying to help and getting confused would have settled—"

"Absolutely nothing! You know how gossip can be. That situation could have been solved in one of two ways. Had I claimed neither guardianship nor engagement, You. Would. Be. Ruined!"

"I don't want a guardian! I've just crawled—"

"Quiet, please!"

"*Crawled*, Islington, crawled out from under the thumb of my aunt. And I've done so through determination, grit, and a very robust lie named Agnes Dowd."

It was here he leaned his head against the side of the carriage. "I'm not, in all actual fact, your guardian! You are not my ward!"

We came to a stop before Lapis Lazuli House.

"But all of London will hear of it because it's *you*! It will be printed in the society pages, mark my words! The Duke of Islington having an adult, female ward—"

"Adult?"

Oh, I wanted to wring his neck.

I settled for crossing my arms and glaring. "Islington, I have owned my house, my accounts, and my life outright, for three months. One hundred blissful days. And now I'm to be known as YOUR WARD. Until I am MARRIED. Do you have any idea what my aunt will say?"

He closed his eyes with a grimace, shifted as if to exit the carriage, swayed, and fainted.

I had to move quickly to catch him, flinging my arms out and half falling to the floor.

"Ho there!" I called out to the driver, as if I were a sea captain.

And then Parian was there, opening the door of the carriage.

There I was with Islington in my arms.

The poor man.

In a flurry of activity, I ordered them to bring Islington inside. Agnes was calling for Pierce. She then ran up to one of the fourth-floor bedrooms, lit the lamps, and pulled down the bedclothes. All while Islington was being carried by his driver, and then Pierce—who had stepped out into the hall—said, "Bloody hell," and then went about carrying the unconscious Islington up the stairs. Parian was following behind holding one of the duke's shoes. I'm still not certain how that came about. I snatched it from him and sent him to find Dr. Fairchild.

Islington began to come to just as we'd laid him on the bed.

"What—? I'm— I should be going home," he managed.

"You can't," I said, standing there holding his shoe. "Your cook is away, as is your butler and your footman, and your aunt's household is also gone, if you recall."

He looked monumentally confused, his gaze focusing on my hands. "Why are you carrying my shoe?"

I handed it to Agnes, who left the room nattering about boiling something or other for a compress.

Pierce was attempting to check Islington's pulse. "What the hell happened, Emma? His heart is racing."

But I was giving direction to the driver. "...yes, the doctor has been sent for. You go and see that the horses are fed and stabled. We will keep the duke here until further notice."

When I finally turned back to Islington, he was once again unconscious.

"What happened?" Pierce asked again, loosening Islington's collar.

"I'm not sure. He wasn't feeling himself; he was flushed. He stumbled while we waltzed and wanted me to stop prodding the jellies. And then when he needed to make an escape, I took him into the servants' corridor, but we were found out just as he fell into my arms, and rather than offering his hand in marriage he claimed to be my guardian. And then we argued."

Pierce at this point was looking at me in utter bafflement.

"I didn't realise he was so very ill," I added, feeling my voice dip in a feet-out-from-under-oneself manner.

Pierce gave his head a single shake, as if deciding it was no time to sort out my story. "He's burning up, that's for certain. Go on and look out for Fairchild while I make him more comfortable."

I nodded and slipped out of the room.

The stairway was dark, but I managed to find my way down to the kitchen where Agnes was boiling water and considering an assortment of dried herbs. Her eyes were wide, her hands trembling. "I am at the ready for seventeen eventualities."

"With any luck, we will just need one."

"Do you think it's," she swallowed, "the pox?"

"I don't think so, Agnes, no. However, we'll know more when Parian brings—"

And then three things happened simultaneously.

Cousin Archibald came howling downstairs in a morning robe.

The front door opened, with Dr. Fairchild following Parian.

And somewhere in the pantry, something exploded.

Agnes shrieked.

Leaving all kitchen disasters to Agnes, I ran to exorcise our demon before he disturbed Islington.

Parian was taking the doctor up the stairs as I was trying to contain Cousin Archibald, who was following them, screaming, "What what what! What is the meaning…the meaning of any of this!"

I dragged our household demon through the hall and down into the kitchen, where I forced him into a chair at the table and ordered Agnes to make the man some tea.

"Agnes," I whispered, "do we have anything in the house that would render a man unconscious?"

"Such as a frying pan?"

"No." I closed my eyes. "Not blunt force, rather something like laudanum or chamomile tea spiked with…well, laudanum."

Her face went pale. "My mother says…"

"Agnes, there is a very ill duke upstairs. It is in his best interest to have peace and quiet. If you can think of something, anything, that will give my dear Cousin Archibald a swift and prolonged night's sleep, you will be serving the better good of society, the peerage, and the Queen. Do you understand?"

"…yes?"

"Can I leave you to it?"

Agnes straightened her shoulders and nodded. "You may, Miss Lion. I won't let our beloved Islington down."

Our Beloved Islington.

Dear me.

"See that you don't, Agnes."

It was then I returned upstairs and—

Ah!

Hawkes has come from the church!

Later

Islington's fever from last night has returned with a vengeance. Hawkes is worried. He hasn't left the room. Pierce only to refill his glass. Fairchild has returned twice more. He's given Agnes careful instructions and gone for more medicine.

Later

Everything is quiet. Pierce has gone to bed, as has the rest of the house. I do not know if Agnes drugged Cousin Archibald again or not.

Hawkes and I are sitting by the low fire while Islington sleeps.

An hour ago he woke, speaking through the fever. I couldn't understand the words. When I went to his bedside, he blinked and looked at me in the dim room. "I've been waiting and waiting, Hannah."

Hawkes looked up swiftly from his book.

I shook my head once as I took the hand he was reaching towards me. It felt like it was burning my skin. "It's Emma," I said.

"I'm so sorry. Can't say it enough."

"Islington, it's me." I paused. "Henry?"

His eyes went wide when I said his Christian name. "*Angels and ministers of grace defend us*," he said, as if the words were poison on his tongue. They startled me; I tried to pull away. For in his delirium, Islington had quoted the line that Hamlet utters when he first sees his father's ghost.

"Islington, it's Emma."

He shook his head. "Always on the edge of my mind."

"What is?"

But by then Hawkes had come to the bedside and asked me to hand him the waiting glass of water. I did and then retreated to the fire.

Dr. Fairchild has returned. Now I'm listening to them discussing Islington in low tones, shivering a bit as the line from *Hamlet* repeats itself in my mind.

Who is Hannah?

Later

The fever has broken.

Hawkes has sent me to bed.

April 21st

He's awake and coherent!

What a relief.

A blessed relief!

"I don't see what all the fuss should be about," Islington said, his voice thick.

I frowned in irritation.

Fainting.

Fever.

Delusion.

There was plenty to fuss over, the stubborn imbecile.

"You fainted mid-lecture, Islington. I was gravely concerned."

He looked haggard, his appearance—usually so carefully crafted—at the mercy of two unsettling nights abed. He was only just sitting up, sunken against the pillows. From the way he lifted his knuckles to his jaw, I'd wager he dearly wished for a shave. His hazel eyes were red-rimmed. "Of all the places I might have taken ill, it had to be in the clutches of Lion."

"You're such an ingrate," I said.

Hawkes, sitting near the window, morning light illuminating the page of his book, gave a sleepy smile.

I sat in the empty chair near the bed, saying nothing of what he'd uttered at the height of his fever. "I hope you find the room to your liking."

"Very comfortable," Islington replied with his uneven voice. "Thank you, Lion."

"You're most welcome. Now," I laced my fingers together. "What did Dr. Fairchild have to say this morning? I just saw him in the hall, but all he said was you were awake."

"There seems to be nothing out of the ordinary—"

Hawkes closed his book and interrupted, staring out the window as he spoke. "Islington appears to be suffering from an infection, an unwieldy malady that has likely reached his brain and has the potential to do great damage if he doesn't lie still and cooperate with his medical superiors."

Islington closed his eyes in a bid for patience.

(Remarkable, how very like a duke he manages to be from a sickbed.)

Setting his book on the window seat, Hawkes looked towards me. "It was providential he fell ill with you in the carriage. Had he been home by himself, things could have taken a turn for the worse. What he needs now is rest, a great deal of it, and to avoid adding any strain until this can be sorted. He's healthy, his body should rally."

Ah.

Strain.

There came an uncomfortable flood of memories.

"Strain, like lying to all of London, you mean?"

Islington's swollen eyes narrowed in cautious thought. He seemed to be experiencing a momentary confusion. (A state, I would argue, he lives in on the regular.) Then remembrance yanked realisation into the room. Like blooming lightning. He lifted a hand to his face with a groan. "God save us all."

I sighed. "Amen."

Hawkes, with a frown, came over and checked Islington's pulse. "Dare I ask?" he said evenly.

It was then Pierce knocked lightly on the door as he let himself in, newspaper beneath his arm. "Well met, Islington. You're awake."

"Have *all* of you been playing nursemaid?"

Pierce sat in one of the chairs by the fireplace, half turned towards the bed. "You look like hell," he said.

"An apt description of yesterday evening with Lion."

"Har har," I said flatly. "Besides, last evening you were delirious. It was the evening before we wove our 'tangled web' and set London on its head."

Islington rubbed his eyes. "Has it been two days?"

By this point Hawkes had returned to his window seat. He did not pick up his book, rather he sat on the edge with his arms crossed, legs crossed at the ankles, his head bent.

"Oh yes," I replied. "You've missed all the excitement. You fainted, Islington. In my arms, as fate would have it. Agnes concocted two dozen poultices, only one of which Dr. Fairchild would let her use. It was Pierce who carried you up all those stairs."

"*Ah.*" Islington was not enjoying having been the unconscious centre of attention.

"No bother," Pierce said as he snapped his newspaper open, eyes scanning the headlines.

"My apologies, nonetheless. How's your leg?"

"Same as before."

"Yes, well," I inserted, "I wouldn't be surprised if we are splashed all over the society pages this morning."

Jaw clenched, mouth a line of resignation, Islington closed his eyes briefly. "Remind me that we had no alternative."

"You insisted it was that or marriage," I retorted.

Pierce looked up with a raised eyebrow.

Hawkes tapped his finger against the side of his leg.

"By the time Lady Frankland opened the door, we were practically in each other's arms," Islington snapped. He then closed his eyes. "My head. Is pounding."

Pierce turned to the society pages, scanned halfway down the page, then threw his head back in laughter.

Islington and I groaned in concert.

"*The Duke of Islington's Secret,*" Pierce read aloud. "*If you've not heard the gossip from Lady Frankland's ball, you'll not yet know that the Duke of Islington—whose youngest sister recently married an American racehorse breeder—is supposedly the guardian of one Miss Emma Lion, niece of Lady Eugenia Spencer. Miss Emma Lion, who is one and twenty years of age, a side character at most in upper class society* ('Rubbish,' Pierce inserted), *was under the guardianship of Lady Spencer until she came of age, whereupon the responsibility of reining her in—*"

"Reining her in?" I repeated.

"*—has allegedly been transferred to a friend of the family, our own eligible Duke of Islington. The pair were found arguing in a servants' corridor over a European tour, a source tells us, likely fuelled by the duke having availed himself too freely of the night's intoxicants and Miss Lion's youthful if misguided enthusiasm for getting her own way.*"

My mouth fell open. "The gall!"

"I was not intoxicated," Islington said to the ceiling.

"*Our source tells me that Miss Lion is to remain under the guardianship of Islington until she marries. If this be the case, we will see how soon our handsome and elusive duke notices that his young ward is very pretty.*"

"That is the most absurd thing I've ever heard," Islington stated.

"Emma is very pretty," Hawkes said quietly.

"Why, thank you, Hawkes."

His returning smile was quiet.

"Not that," Islington practically snarled. "The whole damnable mess."

"It's poor writing." Pierce folded the paper and tossed it aside. "Are either of you going to explain what happened, or are Hawkes and I to be left in the dark?"

"It all began when I was prodding the jellies," I explained.

Islington made a sound. "It began when we were escaping the man who thinks he's your fiancé."

"This wouldn't be Charles Goddard, would it?" Pierce drawled.

Hawkes uncrossed his legs at the ankles and recrossed them and listened.

"Yes," I replied. "We were dancing—Islington and I, not Charles. But the entire thing happened because Islington, who was clearly ill, is being hunted by a fortune hunter."

"That is a redundancy," murmured Hawkes.

"After I asked Emma for assistance in leaving the room," Islington continued, "she dragged us, not onto the terrace like a normal human being, but into the servants' corridor, where we began to argue."

"Islington, in his great animation, was overtaken by illness and stumbled forward—"

"She raised a hand to catch me—"

"Which resulted in a partial embrace—"

"Just as Lady Frankland opened the door with a tattling rat of a footman at her heels," Islington finished. (That footman ought to fear Islington's wrath.)

"She said our situation looked quite French."

"*C'est la vie*," muttered Islington, followed by a sigh of the quietly bitter.

"*C'est la guerre*," said Pierce, accent less refined.

"*C'est les carottes d'hiver*," I added.

And then.

Hawkes burst out laughing.

We all turned our heads.

It was like magic happening for the first time.

Lifting a hand to cover his face, morning limning his tired frame, another laugh escaped Hawkes. When he managed to gain his composure, he cleared his throat, banishing Puck as he resumed a contemplative expression. Though it couldn't be denied his eyes were still lit by the untoward humour of it all.

"Needless to say," I continued, "we bungled our way towards an explanation ending with Islington claiming to be my legal guardian. Admittedly, I did my part in leading us down that primrose path."

"*I am afraid to think of what I have done*," Islington uttered.

I gave him a hard look. "You do realise it's my independence that has been stolen by all this nonsense?"

"You do realise that my reputation is now chained indisputably to yours?"

"You do realise that people will expect me to answer to you!"

"*What's done cannot be undone*," he said in a bitter tone.

"Why are you quoting *Macbeth* at a time like this?"

It was then that Hawkes, arms once again crossed, lifted a finger.

Our Shakespearean argument fell by the wayside.

"To clarify." He tousled his own hair with one hand, staring at a fixed point on the carpet. "The two of you were found in a servants' corridor, alone, Islington falling into Miss Lion's arms."

Pierce snorted.

"As unlikely as it sounds," I said, "that is the basest summary, yes."

"Your explanation to Lady Frankland being that Islington was your guardian, so as to avoid announcing an engagement?"

"Clearly," stated Islington.

Hawkes bowed his head more than it already was, pinching his lips almost severely as his shoulders began again to shake.

I gave Hawkes a blank expression.

Islington was less genteel and told Hawkes where he might go.

Pierce leaned to one side of the chair and grinned.

"It's a small mess," I said. "That may end in one of us murdering the other."

"Payment for some deed of butchery in a former life, no doubt," Islington said, mangling the word butchery.

"If Islington is perceived to be your guardian in the eyes of polite society," Hawkes said, "you can come to Stonecrop in June for the full duration of our stay, without raising untoward speculation."

"Stonecrop?" I looked from Hawkes to Islington. "In June?"

"You've not yet invited her?" Hawkes asked.

"Am I invited?"

"I meant to on Saturday night. In person," Islington said matter-of-factly. "Hawkes will be there, and Pierce hopefully is coming for the first week or two."

"If work allows," Pierce said, watching my face from across the room.

"Why didn't you say anything sooner?"

"An invitation to Stonecrop," Islington took a breath, "is something to be done with gravity."

I looked from Islington to Hawkes and back. "Is a month at Stonecrop such a prize?"

"It is," Islington and Hawkes replied simultaneously.

Islington, collapsed into his pillows, was expected to fight for the honour of his ancestral home. But it was the way Hawkes closed his eyes. In reverence. In rest. And I thought I would very much like to know this place that gave Hawkes his ease.

"I'm only surprised none of us thought of this charade before," said Pierce, fingers laced behind the back of his head.

"Are you quite mad?"

Pierce answered with a shrug. "Islington doesn't have any real say in what you do or don't do. You'll have the cover of a respected guardian. So spending time with the three of us becomes a much simpler equation. Be it at Stonecrop or in London. I think it's bloody brilliant."

I fell back into my chair. "Yes, but it has the potential to go horridly wrong."

Islington took a tired breath. "It already has."

Once the three of us had gone downstairs, Pierce going straight to his studio, I turned to Hawkes.

"You'll be back later, then?"

He gave a nod. "The fever breaking is a sign he's fighting the infection, but he must take time to recover."

"So says Dr. Fairchild?"

Hawkes paused. Then, "So says Dr. Fairchild. I'm going to consult with Agnes before letting myself out the back door. I think it best she not kill Islington with much cherishing."

He had begun to walk towards the kitchen, but I was so chuffed over his ease of mingling Shakespeare into his commentary that I continued with the scene. "'*Parting is such sweet sorrow.*'"

Hawkes paused, half-twisted, and looked at me over his shoulder.

He has a dimple I've never noticed before.

And he was gone.

I then followed Pierce into his studio. "I'm going to go for a walk, or to study Latin insults, or something. Is there anything you need before I do?"

Pierce, who was unrolling one of his "horrible backdrops," looked up at me. "An odd request."

"Is it?"

"You've never made it before."

I shrugged. "It feels strange to disband into the separation of our normal tasks."

"I would happily propose I join you on the walk, but I have two clients this afternoon."

"*Gladiator in arena consilium capit.*"

"Is that an insult?" Pierce said, placing his backdrop onto two hooks secured into the wall, and slowly letting it unroll.

"No. It's Seneca, according to my book."

I turned to leave and was almost out the door when Pierce said, "Embracing Islington in the servants' corridor, huh?"

I spun around. "No! As was explained—"

He laughed, anchoring the bottom of the backdrop—a country scene, complete with a gate and flowers, a sentimental if not saccharine display.

"Are you teasing me?" I demanded.

"No," Pierce said. It sounded more like a yes.

Turnabout.

Fair play.

And all that.

And so, "Are you jealous?"

Pierce stood up and wiped his hands, studying his work before turning towards me. "Surprisingly, I did feel a twinge or two."

"Oh." I didn't know what else to say. For he didn't seem bothered.

Pierce began moving a few stools into place. "One of my Considerations, if you'll allow, is that you could very easily walk away with many a finer gentleman than myself."

"I don't think that—"

"It's true," Pierce said lightly, shifting a stool. "But I'm not bothered. I'm far below your level." He rummaged through the second armoire and pulled out a parasol, a basket, and—horror of horrors—a stuffed rabbit. "I've been telling myself that I can—and will—easily walk away from any thought of *us* if required, and I've believed it too. So when I heard you and Islington were caught in a passionate embrace—"

"It was nothing of the kind!"

"I had"—he paused and straightened his shoulders, lifting his hand before him like he were Hamlet (Alas, poor Yorick.)—"a moment of envy. Jealousy, if you like. And it felt bloody good. I haven't felt that in a long time. Thank you."

Envy.

Jealousy.

Well. Not knowing what else to say, I answered, "You're welcome."

You're welcome?

"I might," he continued to fuss over his abominable props, "even try to convince myself, and you, that we could actually be something more. I'm considering it, at least. In the meantime," he paused to look at me, "I have to photograph seven children for Easter; my own small hell."

I couldn't help but laugh.

The strain of the last two days, I suppose.

I lifted the back of my hands to my face, catching the tears close to the source. "You deserve it."

"You think so?"

It felt the most natural thing to close the distance between us and kiss him on the cheek.

I did not.

"Yes, well, '*God moves in mysterious ways, his wonders to perform.*'"

"Don't you have a park to terrorize?" he said, a smile getting away from him.

"Don't you have small children to frighten with that creature there that looks like it died seventy years ago?"

"Likely it did."

"There is only one problem, Pierce. Easter has already passed."

"Don't remind me," Pierce almost growled. "The mothers wish to mark it anyway."

With the knowledge that Pierce was taking photographs with a taxidermy rabbit and Islington was resting well, I took my Plutarch to Primrose Hill and spent a lovely two hours with the end of Lycurgus, where I learned (according to one account) that when his bones were returned to Sparta, his tomb was struck by lightning. This was taken as a sign of favour, as the only other person to whom this happened was beloved Euripides, buried in Macedonia.

What a curious detail.

In some ways it feels as if my life has been struck by lightning.

April 22nd

All Present and Accounted For

Islington slept well last night and has spent the day reading Pierce's newspaper and thumbing through my Whitman, claiming he would be leaving before the day is out.

Parian has stopped looking at me like I'm every scandal known to London. Mostly.

Dr. Fairchild has come. Twice.

Hawkes stops by with uncanny timing so that he might confer with the doctor and confirm that Islington will *not* be leaving before the day is out.

Agnes is so happy to be "Coming to the aid of the duke in the depths of his agony" that she won't stop baking.

Pierce asked me for a walk between his clients. (Fairchild and Hawkes were with Islington, so I accepted.)

Cousin Archibald had to be told Islington was very contagious with a Fever that afflicted Bachelors of a certain age and meant Doom so he should Stay Away!

Tybalt brought a grass snake into the house!

As for Myself?

I supplied Islington with both newspapers and Whitman, then later read him the first chapter of *Treasure Island*. He kept it with him when I left.

I told Parian he had been exemplary and to remember—to save Islington any embarrassment—that anything witnessed in Lapis Lazuli House was strictly confidential. Nothing was to be shared elsewhere.

Nothing.

Dr. Fairchild told me in the hall that he thinks Islington needs some beef stock. "He's weaker than I'd like, due to the fever having been so strong. But I've every hope that he will improve quickly if he stays abed."

After Hawkes conferred with Dr. Fairchild, he spent an hour reading in his chair. I record here that his jacket carried the scent of pear. I am slowly crumbling inside from curiosity.

I told Agnes that with her cooking, Islington, Duke of, could never be in the depths of any kind of agony. She puffed her chest in pride, giving his portrait a look of devotion as she released a wistful sigh.

The walk with Pierce was needed, and quite wonderful. We found ourselves smiling over little things and watching one another's faces more than was required. ~~If only I could shake all my uncertainties.~~ I think one feels many things one does not always understand.

I told the lie to Cousin Archibald. Outright. I asked Hawkes—as he sat reading in his chair—if God would require my repentance for an act of clear communal good. He looked up, offered a sleep-deprived smile, turned a page, and returned all attention to his book. I am left without spiritual guidance in the matter.

I removed the grass snake from the house.

Pierce, Islington, Hawkes, and I spent an hour in conversation after dinner. Islington sitting up, shaved, and in fresh clothing his footman (returned from…where was it the footman had gone?) had brought.

I am ready now that sleep has come for me and will go gladly.

April 23rd

Islington has been taken home by his cook, who'd returned once she'd heard The News.

I will not claim she kidnapped him.

I will not *not* claim she kidnapped him.

I will say that Hawkes thought it was a day too early for him to have been moved but there we were, silent Hawkes tapping his finger on the kitchen table while Mrs. Knowlls insisted that when the carriage came to fetch the duke, it would be with all due speed and consideration.

"Mr. Crosby returns this afternoon. We can take care of our own. His Grace will be more comfortable in his rooms."

"His comfort isn't the pressing question at hand," Hawkes murmured, turning a page.

"Young Hawkes," she tsked. "You may know a great many things, but I'll take it from here, thank you very much!"

Hawkes closed his book and set it on the table.

"And when you come by, dear," she couldn't help herself saying, "I'll drizzle everything in chocolate three-fold. Now, be a lamb and help him down the stairs once the carriage arrives."

Hawkes did so.

But from the set of his face, I would not claim him to be a lamb.

After Islington was on his way, Hawkes pulled a candle from the inner pocket of his coat and handed it to me. "For my part," he said.

Then he left.

I am thoroughly confused as to what he meant.

Later

"Oh, Miss!" Agnes said just after Hawkes had gone. "This came for you yesterday, and these three this morning, only I wasn't thinking and left them all in the pantry!"

She handed me four envelopes.

Ah.

Responses to the society pages.

"This, Agnes, is called one's chickens coming home to roost."

"You've ordered chickens, Miss! I'm so glad. We kept chickens at home!"

"No chickens, I'm afraid. Only consequences."

I removed myself to the drawing room.

Emma,

The secretaries at work have been gawking over the society pages. I couldn't help but overhear. They all think it is a secret love affair. Hearing you gossiped over by women who've never even seen your face makes me feel slightly better about the lamp post. I expect an explanation when neither you nor I are being run off our feet. If I didn't know your tendency for falling into a good scrape, I would have thought it was a printer's error.

Mary

Emma,

Mother has forced me to sit in her rooms, embroidering, while she complains abed. Which has led me to reading the society pages aloud. You have been delivered for now, but it will be only a matter of hours (don't hope for days, dearest) before a friend pushes her way in to discuss the fact that Islington is your guardian.

I know for a fact he is not.

Explain, dear one. I'm desperately bored.

Arabella

Bavarian cream,

What angle could you possibly be working with this scheme?

Jack

And, most ominously, an envelope I do not recognise with the clipping inside drawn over with a large black question mark.

Nothing else.

What am I to do with that?

Later

I've just realised the purpose of Hawkes's candle.

It is the twenty-third.

April 24th

With my house emptied of ill dukes who spuriously claim to be my guardian, I allowed myself a long walk, Plutarch and journal in hand, fountain pen in coat pocket. Despite a brisk wind, I went to Regent's Park first, wandering, wandering, wandering, and then crossed to Primrose Hill, where I climbed the hill and settled on a bench somewhat near the top.

My life's current disaster required a good deal of philosophical consideration.

I am moving into a perplexing state regarding all and sundry.

In the midst of such elevated concern, I heard, "I'm sitting down. Hope you don't mind." Said with a manner which indicated *I don't care if you mind or not.*

The Pirate sat beside me.

"Oh. Hello, Mr. Chambers."

His reply was a sound. There was perspiration on his temples and his lips were pressed white.

"What?" he snapped.

"Did I speak aloud?" I asked. "I'm making great efforts not to do so."

"No. You're staring."

And I was. "Pardon." I looked ahead at the view of London. "I wasn't staring at you. I mean, I was staring, but only because I'm perplexed."

"What's so perplexing? Half my leg was blown off and it hurts like hell."

I flushed. "You misunderstand—the perplexations are my own. You've nothing to do with them. I am, however, very sorry about your leg."

A grunt here.

How elegant.

~~I almost offered to move to a different bench~~.

That's a lie.

Part of me did not wish to cede ground.

Petty, I think. And below who I aspire to be on Mondays and Thursdays.

He looked at my journal, noting where my pen lay between the pages.

"How could you possibly have written so much in two weeks' time?"

"I've endured a ridiculous sequence of events. It had to be recorded."

"You state that as fact, but it isn't."

My eyes narrowed in challenge, and I was almost going to reply with something clever when I heard a familiar voice say, "Well met!" I looked up to see Saffronia March.

"Hello!" I said in response.

"Hello, Emma. Hello, Ben."

Ben?

"Saff," he replied.

Saff!

She sat to my left and leaned forward to look around me at Chambers. "Game leg making a fuss?"

That's *exactly* what she said.

I expected a deadly expression in return. I was surprised to find our resident Pirate had a good-humoured tilt to his scarred lip. "It doesn't like the cold wind, but what can you do?"

"My studio is very warm."

"No."

"And comfortable."

"No."

"Your recompense would be anything you could wish—except a whole leg, of course. That is beyond me. I'm dying to paint you."

"No, you're not."

Needless to say, I sat AGOG. And quiet—not wanting to insert myself into an exchange so terribly interesting to observe. Also, I did not wish to startle *Ben* from his cantankerous mood. Better he be ornery than dripping with contempt.

"Emma, is it true you've been caring for the Duke of Islington?" Saffronia asked.

"He took ill at Lapis Lazuli. Well, outside Lapis Lazuli. In the carriage. Not that we left him there. He was carried inside. But he's gone home now."

"And the other rumour?" Saffronia was looking at the view, but her words were staring me in the face.

"Other rumour?" As if I did not very well know which one.

"Yes, the one reported in the paper about Islington being your guardian?"

"*Ah.*" I thought how to best reply in the company of The Pirate. "A conversation over tea, I think?"

Saffronia eyed me. "I'm finishing a commission this month, then I'll have you up for a *tête-à-tête.*"

We, none of us, said anything for a few minutes.

Until.

"How's Dr. Johnson?"

Saffronia pinched my arm.

"Ow!" I looked over to see The Pirate glaring in my direction.

"You're speaking to me? Voluntarily? Remarkable. He's well."

"You better not be putting undo stress on the spine." It sounded very much like a threat. "No stacking, always return to its shelf, and don't stuff the shelf too tight. Open with care. Do not leave the book lying open for any reason except in short instances where one wishes to write out a passage."

"You're such an old woman, Ben," Saffronia said wryly.

"If a person has enough of a brain to read, they can take care with a book spine. And Miss Lion here, with all her perplexing thoughts, surely must be capable of that."

"I take great care with my library, no matter how perplexed."

He made a dubious sound.

"Why so perplexed, Emma?" Saffronia ~~asked~~ fished. "Your tenant giving you trouble?"

"Certainly not," I said, delivering truth by half.

"Leave Pierce out of it," Ben said.

"You know him?" Saffronia leaned forward so she could see Chambers.

"It was me who recommended him to Mr. Flat."

Saffronia gave Chambers A Look. "So if he compromises Miss Lion's reputation, I'll have you to thank for it."

"Saffronia!"

"I recommended him to Mr. Flat, not Miss Lion," Ben said.

"A senile old man," she replied. "Wasn't there something about a fight at The Cleopatra?"

I was now quite impatient with being talked of. "There is no better tenant than Pierce, Saffronia. He pays twice the rent as he keeps a studio and is a valued friend—fights, or no fights, at The Cleopatra. I'm very grateful to you, Mr. Chambers."

He scowled at me in return, but when his expression shifted to Saffronia, it went awfully smug.

"Well, I'd better be off. I promised myself only a short walk before returning to work." Saffronia stood. "Enjoy the view."

"Good afternoon, Saffronia."

"Emma," she replied. "Ben, do try to be human today."

"Get a real profession," Chambers replied.

Saffronia looked down on him—it was very well done—then reached out her gloved hand and patted his head. "I do have a real profession, Jabberwocky."

Heavens!

I cleared my throat in an effort not to laugh.

He said something I ~~wouldn't~~ shouldn't write down and watched Saffronia leave.

"Have you two known each other long?" I ventured.

"What do you think?"

"Mr. Chambers—or ought I call you Jabberwocky?—if I were to go through this life exclusively on what I think, I would not get very far. However amusing it may prove to be."

He did not reply.

Immediately.

Then, "The Hound was a general mercantile shop owned by my uncle when I was a lad. I worked for him when not helping my parents. While I did not live in St. Crispian's, I grew up here, so to speak. Saff and I have known one another for almost as long as we can remember."

I resisted the urge to stare at him open-mouthed.

What had it been? Three, maybe four full sentences said without irony, sarcasm, snap, or profanity?

A record, to be sure.

He lifted his hand to below his eyepatch and absently traced the pencil-thin scars shattered across his face. "I like Saff," he said.

"She's one of the few people who doesn't fuss. Direct. She doesn't—" Chambers then proceeded to use several words no gentleman would say around a lady.

I swallowed my shock before saying, "We all need one friend like that."

His wordless response was dismissive as he stood, a hiss of pain in accompaniment. I thought he would leave without saying anything more, but he glanced in my direction. "We both know you've no need to call me Jabberwocky as you already call me The Pirate."

Now my mouth did fall open. "Did Pierce tell you that!"

"Good day, *Chit*."

Now my eyes widened. "Is that what you call *me*?"

But he was already limping away.

I sat another fifteen minutes in silence.

Chit, indeed.

At least *The Pirate* carries a sense of romance and adventure.

Bah, say I.

April 25th

Cousin Archibald and I were sitting in the drawing room ~~reading~~ doing our best to ignore one another while reading. The complete indifference being as much a sign of mutual respect as we could muster. I was crawling along with Numa Pompilius while he (Cousin Archibald, not Numa Pompilius) was reading a pamphlet put out by the Morning Robe Appreciation Society.

Into this picture of domestic bliss, there came a pounding on the front door. Parian arrived just as I'd come out into the hall—

("What what! What?" from the drawing room.)

—and he opened the door.

There stood a breathless footman. "Miss Lion?"

"Yes?"

He gave me a note. It was a call to battle, written in Islington's architectural (albeit shaky) hand.

> *Lion,*
>
> *Lady Spencer is currently sitting in my drawing room. She refuses to leave. I think it wise if you were also present to explain our unfortunate new reality.*
>
> *You cannot abandon me to this.*
>
> *Islington*

Astonishing, how similar amusement and dread feel at such a moment.

Despite wearing my walking skirt and a blouse, I threw my coat and hat over without changing, grabbing my red gloves as I ran from the house.

It was when I was racing up the Diagonal that I ran into Toff.

This is not a figure of expression.

I crashed into a doorway as he went tumbling towards the street.

Both of us kept our feet.

Well done.

"Good day, Toff," I said, breathless. "Are you quite all right?"

"Fine, Miss," he said, picking his cap off the pavement.

"I'm sorry to have trammelled you nearly into the street."

A nod. "In a hurry, Miss?"

"Yes. To Baron's Square." It was then that the idea of steady reinforcement entered my mind. "I say, Toff, could you get a message to Young Hawkes rather promptly?"

"Of course, Miss. He's only just returned home."

"Wonderful. Tell Hawkes that my aunt is at Islington's. He'll understand."

He was off like a shot.

As was I.

When Crosby opened the door—displeased with the turn of events—I rushed past him into the drawing room where Islington—fully dressed, shaved, dignified, and fatigued—stood with his hand resting on the back of a chair. Aunt Eugenia was sitting imperiously with her walking stick, a man wearing depressing black on the sofa beside her.

Had I known Aunt Eugenia had brought someone with her, I would not have blown into the house out of breath, hat askew, and face red from running.

Upon seeing my dishevelled appearance, Aunt Eugenia smiled.

Terrifying.

"Here she is, Doctor."

Doctor?

"Hello," I said brightly. "A nice day, is it not?"

Islington quirked his mouth regretfully.

"Observe," Aunt Eugenia said, "wholly inappropriate clothing, the hat awry, gloves whose very colour are an affront. Oh, Emma, look at you, rushing about like one of those newfangled carousels."

"I came rather quickly," I explained. "Good morning, Islington."

"No honorific," Aunt Eugenia said to the man.

He was taking notes.

"Miss Lion," Islington replied, his patience a thin wire pulled taut.

"Your aunt has come to pay me a visit. This gentleman with her is a doctor."

"Are you still feeling unwell, Aunt?"

"Emma!" she said. "I don't know what ruse you and this second-rate duke have concocted—yes, concocted—but I am here with Dr. Trout to prove you unstable of mind, therefore needing to remain in *my* guardianship until I see fit. How Islington came into things, I've no idea."

"He was a friend of my father's," I said, stepping forward and sitting in the chair beside the one where Islington stood, his expression one of utter disbelief at what was transpiring.

"I do not believe your father arranged for you to be in Islington's care, and neither do I think you fit to care for yourself."

"Yes, you've said that already."

"Miss Lion is of a perfectly sound mind," Islington interjected. "I assure you she is a capable and intelligent young woman."

The doctor wrote something in his notes.

It felt we were all being subjected to a poorly written farce.

It was then that Hawkes appeared.

He did not look hurried in the least. Annoyed, I dare claim, upon seeing my aunt, but not hurried.

"Hawkes," Islington said, the tightness around his eyes releasing a touch. "You remember Lady Spencer? Dr. Trout, let me introduce our respected vicar, Young Hawkes. Young Hawkes, Dr. Trout, brought to assess Miss Lion's mental state."

Hawkes nodded to both the doctor and Aunt Eugenia.

"I will not have him here, I will not!" Aunt Eugenia declared.

"Hawkes is welcome in my home," Islington said smoothly. "Now, Lady Spencer, let us conclude our business as I assume we, each of us, have much to be about."

Eyebrows in a flat line, face set in distaste, Aunt Eugenia glared at Hawkes. "A single verse of scripture from you, and I will report you to the Archbishop of Canterbury. Wardie and I go very far back. I have *influence* in the church."

"To make up for the influence the church has not had on you," I muttered.

The doctor wrote something in his book.

But Aunt Eugenia was back to Islington. "You are no sooner Emma's guardian than I am a hippopotami."

Hawkes, who had walked to Islington's side by this point, smiled at the accidental plural.

He also discreetly slipped Islington a folded letter.

I was amused at the first and bemused at the second.

"I don't know what game you play, Islington," my aunt continued, "but I suspect you of wishing to steal my niece's fortune for your own. I will not have it."

I laughed.

Dr. Trout made a note.

Islington glanced towards me as if to ask how his life had possibly come to this point. "That is not the case, Lady Spencer."

"Yet to be determined," she said. "Why then are you claiming to be my niece's guardian? And from the inside of a closet!"

"There was no closet involved," Islington stated. "Merely a corridor for a private conversation."

"You see, Aunt—" I attempted.

"Corridors notwithstanding, I assure you Emma is under *my* guardianship until she marries Charles Goddard."

"No, that isn't—" I tried again.

"Dr. Trout has testified before my solicitors that Damian is unfit to receive his inheritance, a result of Mental Weakness from his father's side. It was not difficult to arrange. I intend to do the same now. Until Emma is a Goddard, she cannot be trusted."

"Aunt Eugenia!"

By now Islington had unfolded and read the letter Hawkes had slipped into his hand.

His furrowed brow did not relax, but he looked relieved.

"Aunt Eugenia, I was in your care until I turned twenty-one years of age. My banker can attest to that. I thank you, but I no longer—"

"Your father did *not* make the Duke of Islington your guardian! The idea!"

Islington cleared his throat. "If you would allow me to read this letter, witnessed and signed by a solicitor."

It was beyond Aunt Eugenia's pale.

"You? Read a letter at me?" She stood and held out her hand.

"I will read the letter myself, young man."

Hawkes by now had circled back to the door and was leaning against the wall.

The doctor made a note.

After a second reading, Islington handed Aunt Eugenia the letter in question.

She cleared her throat and began to read, "*My dear…*" Aunt Eugenia's eyes bulged, and she drew her head back. "What is that abominable name?"

"It's written in Irish," Islington said.

"Declan was always one for hysterics." She cleared her throat and began again.

"'*Until my daughter, Emma Mirabel Lion, is twenty-one, she is under the guardianship of her aunt, the trying Lady Eugenia Spencer.*' Trying? What is that thieving Irishman going on about? '*It is often the practice for guardianship of a woman to continue until she is married, even after she's come of legal age. Absurd, yet true.*' Absurd? Rational, I say! What else has this barbarian written? '*Therefore, I make my desire known that after Emma comes of age, you are her rightful guardian until she is wed.*' What ridiculousness! He can't have been thinking at all. '*If Lady Spencer gives you any trouble, simply remind her that I know what I know, even from beyond the grave.*'"

Aunt Eugenia stared at the letter in hand. Affront met with an unexpected trepidation.

The doctor made a note.

"Why, I never," she attempted, but her usual zip and verve were punctured through. Miffed, she began to fold the letter and slip it into her reticule.

"I'll have that back." Islington stepped forward, whisking the letter from her fingers before she could abscond with (and destroy?) the evidence. "You'll recognise the hand and the signature," Islington said smoothly to Aunt Eugenia.

She did.

One could tell by the way she tried to strangle Islington with her gaze.

I record this all as if I were merely an interested observer; this was someone else's life mandated on the page. But I watched the scene play out with an ill-fitting feeling in my stomach.

Was it truly in my father's hand?

Had it been forged?

Was Hawkes a forger?

A supposition which would explain so very much.

(A forger and a vicar; grand way to spend a life.)

Aunt Eugenia sat again on the sofa, grasping her walking stick. "I could refute this," she stated.

"Aunt Eugenia, honestly," I remember saying, but I was staring at the folded letter in Islington's hand.

"I could have Dr. Trout write her up of an unsound mind and find a judge to side with—"

Islington ran his finger along the edges of the letter before sliding it into the inner pocket of his coat. "Lady Spencer, let me make myself quite clear," he steeled his tired voice. "I have read this letter. You have read this letter. We both know what it clearly states. If you've a mind to question Miss Lion's sanity and challenge me in court, I will come at you with all the means at my disposal—financial, legal, and social. They are no small amount. Your friends—many of whom still have daughters attempting to wed—would be forced to choose which side to support. I believe I have every advantage were I to press the matter. I could apply the same pressures to the medical establishments. Therefore, Dr. Trout, I suggest you leave. Thank you. My butler will see you out." Islington drilled the doctor with his gaze.

Dr. Trout stared back at Islington in assessment.

Dr. Trout looked at me and closed his book.

Dr. Trout turned towards Aunt Eugenia and said, "Good afternoon, Ma'am," and skulked out of the room.

Islington watched as the man closed the drawing room door, listening for confirmation that Crosby had let him out of the house. He glanced at Hawkes, who was still leaning against the wall in the corner, book open, then looked at me, the edges of his eyes rising in question. I couldn't tell if he was asking my permission to continue but reading it as such I gave a quick nod. Islington then returned his attention to Aunt Eugenia.

"I suggest, Lady Spencer, you and I agree to a truce. Emma, I know, is aiding you this Season. I am happy for her to continue if she so desires. *If*."

That caught Aunt Eugenia's attention.

"If you will acknowledge that I have the right to veto on the rare occasion it is in Emma's best interest."

"Might I say that I'm the only one qualified in the subject?" I inserted.

"My plans *are* Emma's best interest," she snapped.

"Let me rephrase," Islington said, sitting down in his wingback chair. His hand was shaking, he should have been lying down. "I intend to claim Emma's time when it suits either her or myself. Which is why I make it a point to tell you now that Emma will be staying the month of June at my family home in Derbyshire."

"She will not—"

"Yes, she will," cut in Islington.

"Yes, I will, Aunt."

"It is to be a private gathering of family and"—Islington motioned towards me without looking my way—"those friends tied to the family. You shall have her help, if she so chooses, throughout May and again in July and August."

"Why I never!"

"I don't see there being anything else we need to discuss," he dismissed.

Left eye twitching, lips twisted like a piece of dried peel, Aunt Eugenia weighed her odds. She granted Islington's threat validity, that was clear enough. What she had seen of the letter was formidable. To say nothing of my father's ~~threat~~ posthumous threat.

One would think that mystery would be driving me mad.

Only, it's what came after that has preoccupied my thoughts.

Aunt Eugenia had regained her footing. "There is yet much to discuss, young man. Over tea, if you've any manners."

One look in my direction conveying a buckled-down exasperation, and possibly regret at ever having met me, then Islington motioned to his waiting—and disbelieving—footman.

"Let us have tea, Lady Spencer," he said.

"No longer than quarter of an hour," Hawkes said from the corner. "Then Islington is to return upstairs."

Then the current of What Makes Hawkes Hawkes began to stir,

and I looked to see him tuck his book beneath his arm and slip out the door.

Heavens, no.

Not while Emma M. Lion drew breath.

I didn't care a fig about tea. I wanted to ask questions.

"I've just… I'll only… A moment." And I rushed after Hawkes into the hall, just as Aunt Eugenia pronounced, "I suppose it is up to me to tell you what Is and Isn't appropriate for a male guardian."

The door closed behind me.

In the hall, I ~~gracefully caught Hawkes's attention~~ practically launched myself to grab Hawkes's arm before he could escape out of the front door.

Startled, Hawkes looked back at me, then down at my hand gripping his blue coat.

Bold of me, I know.

Alas.

I have courage enough to tangle with my own fate.

"A word, Hawkes," I said, gripping harder and dragging him across the hall and through a doorway. It felt like trying to hold a wave on the shore, but I managed, closing the door behind us.

Hawkes cleared his throat.

In that wandering way of his, he had placed himself on the other side of the table.

Impressive, how quickly he can find a barrier and establish physical and philosophical self-separation. Only this time there was a wariness in the shadows. His eyes marked my movements.

"The Rabbit Room, Miss Lion?" His tone was light, as if he were barely touching the words.

I looked about me—on my right, the portrait of the hounds on the hunt, then to the left, the rabbit huddled inside its frame, the green paper of the room growing around us like a forest—then back across at Hawkes. His very nature excused himself from the hunt. Too wild to be a hound. Too strong to be a rabbit.

"Hawkes the fox, indeed," I said.

He watched, unmoving.

I swallowed. "That letter: in my father's voice, written and signed by his hand, from all appearance. Where did you get it?"

He looked out of the window a moment.

"You cannot think I'm not owed an explanation," I pressed. And then my dratted voice betrayed me as it cracked along a line of my heart. "You, of all people."

Hawkes closed his eyes, as if the sound caused him pain. He bent his head, released the slowest of breaths, and looked up. "You have *every* right, Miss Lion."

I waited.

I waited while Hawkes considered me. It was uncomfortable, heart-wrenching even, as if there was tremendous beauty in the world, but it always came with a difficult price.

Reaching into the pocket on the inside of his blue coat, Hawkes removed a second letter. Carefully, his eyes on my face the entire time, he set it on the table between us.

I had to spend three steps to reach it. I did. Picking up the letter, I unfolded the familiar paper—torn from one of my father's sketchbooks, his scrawl inked across the page.

Mo bhuachaill daor,

I send this letter with little anticipation it will be necessary. My Emma has the spark of the gods in her blood, for good and ill, as well as a strength I envy. But as I've no intention of trusting her fate to the gorgon that is her aunt, I've made a few provisions. I send this to you, trusting you will honour a most solemn request. You see, F, I will not last the month. And Emma doesn't yet know this, but Mirabel is not strong. I worry my going will sweep her away with me. Mirabel insists her sister, one Lady Eugenia Spencer, take charge of Emma until she comes of age. I can do nothing to dissuade her. I don't trust that woman to act in Emma's best interest. It fills my chest with the fury of a thousand warring angels. But I must believe that Emma is made of sterner stuff.

I worry for both Emma's financial security and her autonomy.

This is why I've written the enclosed document, signed by myself and my solicitor, despite hoping you'll never need to use it. It gives you authority to claim guardianship of Emma until she is married (painful, beautiful thought—may she choose well). I shore up Emma's freedom in this manner as I do not trust Lady Spencer; it is to prevent any damnable meddling. It is one of the two precautions I've taken for her future. I pray it will not be necessary, but there are times we build doors, just in case.

You would give Emma nothing but freedom.
I trust you in this without reservation. I can give a man no higher compliment.

Give your parents my love and take care,

Declan Lion

P.S. I used your Irish name. Call me superstitious, but it is my blessing upon your head, a blessing that the uncanny winds may blow in your favour all your life.

I don't know how many times I read the letter, only that when I finally folded it upon itself once again, holding it in my hands as I looked up—"Hawkes?"—he'd taken a step back, two steps, leaning against the wall, his book still secured between his upper arm and ribs despite him having crossed his arms, head bowed, gaze looking up at my face.

"So while the farce," I tested the steadiness of my voice, "is with Islington, it is you, truly, who is my guardian."

He pressed his lips together. "No. You are your own. Wholly. Your father sent this to be used only if you were left without recourse. Only as someone you could call on if the wolves closed in."

"Why…? Why have you never said before?"

"This ruse with Islington is advantageous to your not being left behind, but an actual guardian?" Hawkes shook his head. "That isn't what you need."

"What is it you think I need?"

He looked as if it were obvious. "To remain undaunted."

My heart stilled a moment, then tumbled back into its regular rhythm.

Hawkes returned my stillness only with a fixed gaze.

I cleared my throat.

"Why you?"

Pain? Apprehension? Caution? What was it that cast the shadow behind his eyes.

"Hawkes?"

"He trusted me."

"Clearly. He trusted you with my life!"

"It was a letter sent"—he lifted a hand—"by a dying father that brought him peace. I have never once entertained any action would be needed."

"How long in the length of our friendship would you have gone without telling me of its existence?"

He did not answer. But I could almost swear I heard his voice in my mind. *Forever, I think.*

"Why?" I pressed. "How did you know him? He mentioned your parents. It sounds as if— Will you answer me?"

It was then my aunt Eugenia's voice could be heard in the hall—Islington's replies clipped. It could not have been more than twenty seconds before my aunt was dispatched.

(Dispatched meaning she was maneuvered out of the house, and the door was firmly shut behind her. And locked, likely.)

(No, she was not finished off in Islington's hall.)

And all the while, Hawkes and I stood looking at one another—he with his hair tousled, cheekbones more pronounced than they should be, weary, while I held the letter in my hand.

"I will answer any question you have," he said, "honestly and completely, if you ask it of me." Hawkes measured his next words against a thousand invisible weights. He ran his tongue across his bottom lip. He looked at the door over my shoulder then back at my face. He was not afraid, but there was fear, and I am not certain how to explain the difference. "There are forces at work in my life, Emma, and the only way I can see how to manage them, the only way I can keep those I care for safe, is…to keep a certain distance. You have every right to ask the questions. I will answer them if you do. Only I wish that you wouldn't."

Later, when Islington and I were sitting in the library, I told him what Hawkes and I had said to one another.

"I am as taken aback as you are by the whole thing," he replied. "Uncanny, how it served its purpose." That was the word he used. *Uncanny*.

"*Uncanny winds will blow*," I murmured.

Islington sat staring out into his back garden, despite the fact I'd already told him twice he needed to go upstairs and rest. "It makes sense. A single young woman has two distinct vulnerabilities—her finances and who, if anyone, has the right to dictate her life. My own father held those two things over my head like the sword of Damocles. But upon his death?" Islington lifted a hand. "Freedom. Not so for you."

I pressed my knuckles against my lips. "Was I right?" I wondered aloud. "To let Hawkes go without asking?"

Islington frowned, leaning his head back against his chair. "Do you know what he said the night after he pulled you from the fountain?"

"On St. Valentine's?"

"Has he pulled you out of the fountain any other night?"

I grinned for the first time in three hours. "No."

Islington made a You've Answered Your Own Question sound.

"What was it he said, then?"

"He stood by the hearth there, drank an entire glass of brandy, filled it again, and said, 'I've been too careless.'"

"How?" I asked.

"'Careless with Emma,' he replied. And then he said something I've wondered at ever since. He said, 'Only she blew into St. Crispian's like a four-leaf clover, and I've trusted in that.'"

I blinked at Islington. So unexpected, I could only think to ask, "What did he say next?"

"He drank his second glass of brandy, slammed the glass onto the mantel, and said, 'Tell Crosby I'm going upstairs to have a bath.'"

I looked out at the back garden as Islington continued. "What he feels for his small tribe is a deep thing. Fathomless. He's always been so, but he was changed after a summer he spent in Ireland. When I saw him again, he'd shouldered a caution I'd not seen before."

I glanced back at Islington. "He said there are forces at work—I don't understand what he meant—but that he can only keep those he cares for safe by keeping a certain distance."

Islington blew the air out of his chest. The day had done him in. "So I've gathered. And why it's incumbent upon us, the few who know, to do our best by Hawkes."

"So you think it good I didn't ask Hawkes any more questions?"

"For now. The answers are, by rights, yours. Only, I think it— I think it kind."

I *hadn't* asked. I had looked Hawkes directly in his blue eyes and seen the tide going out, and that he was trying to hold on despite it all, and I'd said, "*Keep thy friend under thy own life's key.*"

And Hawkes had nodded, unease slipping from his expression. He'd walked around the table as if to leave, then stopped near me, placing his left hand on my right shoulder, his thumb naturally resting against the side of my neck. I could feel my pulse against it. "*The purpose you undertake is dangerous, the friends you have named uncertain, the time itself unsorted, and your whole plot too light for the counterpoise of so great an opposition. But I tell you...out of this nettle, danger, we pluck this flower, safety.*"

I knew the passage.

No matter that Hawkes had rearranged the words.

"You've quoted *Henry IV* out of order."

"Shakespeare will forgive me."

"Shakespeare might, but will Hotspur?"

Hawkes smiled, slant thing that it was, and gripped my shoulder more firmly before letting go and walking out the front door.

I went to the window to watch him leave. Hands in his trouser pockets, book under his right arm, shoulders bent beneath the nameless weight, but still spring was all about him. Not until he'd disappeared down Sterling Street did I leave the window and find Islington in the library.

April 26th

Mary and I sat on a bench near Southwark Cathedral this afternoon, eating sandwiches and boiled eggs prepared by Agnes.

"So what you've just told me is," she took a bite of her sandwich, chewed a long while, swallowed, and then continued, "while I have a fake cousin for my freedom, and you've a fictional chaperone for yours, you've now added a flesh and blood duke who is pretending to be your guardian."

I had. I had told her ~~everything~~ nearly everything.

"Your sums are correct, Mary Bairrage."

"Until you marry?"

"That is how it came out in the wash, yes. We're both still more than a little put out by it all."

She polished off her sandwich and cracked her egg against the bench, peeling the shell away with the ponderosity of a philosopher. "What if you never marry?"

It was, I admit, a large fly in the ointment and—as incredible as it may seem—had never crossed my mind. "*Ah.*" A frightening detail. But no, nothing I can't manage. I suppose I either flee to America or claim *carte blanche* at Islington's table whenever I wish. Or wait for Aunt Eugenia to grow feeble or die altogether.

Mary was still frowning. "When you say *embracing* in a servants' corridor?"

"Full stumbling into my arms."

A *tsk* of frustration. "They would have burned us as witches."

"A statement we've repeated a hundred times."

"So it pains me deeply to say—"

I eyed Mary with a wary expectation.

"—he was correct in this one thing. Pompous, but correct. The two of you unmarried, embracing in a closet."

I cracked my own egg on the bench. "Corridor."

"Either you confirm an engagement or suffer social death. Not a flimsy exclusion. I'm not worried over your being banned from an earl's table but accepted at a clerk's."

"Do I know any clerks?"

"My point, Emma, is References. The closet—"

"It was a corridor!"

"—is the kind of debacle that would make a respectable reference nigh impossible. How would you find work?"

I peeled half my egg before saying, "I don't suppose they pay particularly well at The Drunken Duck?"

Mary's guffaw diluted the moment, and we both grinned. "Not well enough to keep Lapis Lazuli," she said. "I'm only amazed you've managed this guardian ruse."

"It's far too early to know if we've managed anything. For now, we can only debate if it's a tragedy or comedy?"

"A tragic comedy?" she proposed.

"A comic tragedy, rather."

"There should be a subset of drama called a Calamity. That would account nicely for most of your life."

"Agreed." I polished off my egg.

I'd told Mary neither of the letters nor of Hawkes's supporting role in the ~~tragic comedy~~ ~~comic tragedy~~ calamity.

I'd not told Pierce either.

I am not certain why.

I've sat in my garret, staring at the drawing of Hawkes before Saint Sebastian, asking myself that very question. I think, perhaps, it is because the one person I wish to question above all others is my father—my first death—and I cannot. And the second person is Hawkes, who would answer any question I ask, but asked me not to.

I stray from the record. For it was at this juncture that Mary dropped an anchor.

"And in the midst of this fiasco enters your romance with Mr. Pierce."

"I did not call it a romance."

"Hmm," was Mary's reply.

I had also told Mary about Pierce.

~~Everything.~~

Almost everything.

"Emma." She wrapped the eggshells in her napkin and placed it in the basket I'd brought. "You know I'm not a prude."

"The woman who dressed as a man to attend a club with Jack Hollingstell? Certainly not."

"Finest moment of my life."

"We all need one."

Mary bandied her agreement in a beautiful, piratical smile.

And then she sank my ship.

"You do realise the fall is just as far if you and Mr. Pierce take a misstep?"

The bells of the church rang.

"Emma?" she said.

"Yes, Mary," I said with the impatience that only comes when advice is perfectly on point. "I am well aware. Reputation ruined either way, references beyond reach."

Mary raised an eyebrow. "You're only that peevish when you're uncertain."

I laughed. I couldn't help it. "The bane of someone knowing you well."

"Fortitude forever," Mary quipped, looking towards the street. "What is it like?"

"What? Being peevish?"

Now Mary grinned. "No. Your dalliance with Mr. Pierce."

A question came to mind. "Have you ever kissed anyone before, Mary?"

"Albert Charles from Stoicism. It was rushed and in the school barn."

"You kissed Albert Charles!"

"It inspired no confidence in the practice."

"Ha! Never fear, Mary. There are better practitioners than Albert Charles."

"Mr. Pierce among them?"

"Pierce is… He's so very…"

"Now look at you," she said.

"What?"

Mary shrugged her shoulders. "You know those rare afternoons when sunlight is slanting across the fields but it's raining? It always feels like such a thing should be impossible, and no matter what else has happened that day, you feel absurdly happy? That is how you look now, thinking of him."

It was an apt description.

Sunlight in rain.

April 27th

I can't claim to have had any expectations walking into church this morning, only that I was nervous about seeing Hawkes.

The occasion proved unexpected.

Relievedly, delightfully, so.

For Pierce was in attendance for Hawkes's sermon.

A wager lost, from what I understand.

He dropped onto the pew beside me, dark grey suit, hat in hand, scowl firmly in place.

"What on earth are you doing here?" I asked. "Is everything all right? Has Cousin Archibald finally killed someone?" A pause. "Have you finally killed him?"

Pierce, slouching just enough to look defiant, glanced my way with a hard smile. "Lost a bet to Hawkes. Cleopatra. Friday night."

"Marvellous."

"Is it?" he said, glancing up towards the stained-glass windows. "I told him that if he stretched this nonsense out, I would wait for him in a dark alley."

A smile walked onto my face. "What did he say in return?"

Scratching his jaw before crossing his arms, Pierce replied, "*Of all base passions, fear is the most accursed.*"

I whistled—receiving an over-the-shoulder look from the man in the pew before us—and said, "Someone who quotes *Henry VI* in response to a threat is not one I would wait for in a dark alley."

Pierce grunted and settled in for the duration.

When Hawkes stood to give his sermon, he looked troubled and at anywhere but me.

I could feel my face tighten, as if in pain.

"We begin with Genesis chapter one, verse four," Hawkes said quietly, "where we stare into the abyss before us, dividing light and darkness with the grace of God. Light begets light. Light begets life. 'I am come,' said Christ Jesus, 'that they might have life, and more abundantly.'" He swallowed. "It can be a terrible task, that of learning to divide the light from dark, for we agonize beneath the weight that someone we care for might be caught in the twilight of our indecision, our ignorance, our selfishness, or our fear." Finally, he looked at me. "But when I recall that with the light of God comes the abundance of God, I take courage. *Virtus Apprime.*"

I lifted my hand, enclosing my lion pendant.

Hawkes saw, then looked away and down, repeating, "*Virtus Apprime.*"

After his sermon, Hawkes was not to be found.

I hadn't seen her sitting in the congregation. Neither had I thought to look for her, but after the sermon, when I was exchanging pleasantries with Mrs. Killoran and Pierce was standing out in the churchyard staring at a tall gravestone, hat still in hand, Victoria Braithwaite, wearing all black, broke from the path and approached him.

She said something.

He looked up, the expression that accompanied his words, earnest.

A response from her.

A half smile, his eyes narrowing as he answered, then a nod.

She turned, walked back onto the path, and left the churchyard alone.

"What was it Victoria Braithwaite said?" I asked as we walked down the Diagonal.

"Hmm?" he broke off from his own thoughts. "Oh, she thanked me for the condolence I sent with the photographs."

I nodded. "I think," I said, looking up, "it's going to rain."

"Divine retribution for my having entered a church."

"That's simply ridiculous, Pierce," I said. "It's likely for *my* having entered."

April 28th

The Great Considerations of 1884 have come to an end.

Pierce and I spoke yesterday afternoon.

Parian and Agnes were both away on their half days.

Cousin Archibald had gone to spend the afternoon with The Ericksons of Great Pulteney Street, who are visiting London from Bath and are apparently in need of a court jester. I suppose there are those who suffer fools gladly.

The first fact was confirmed by Archibald Flat.

The second fact was assumed by Emma M. Lion.

Luncheon was long over—Agnes had laid it out in the kitchen—and the rain had come and gone and come again. Whereabouts was all wet stone and buoyant spring flowers in the occasional front garden along the street. Pierce had opened one of the windows in his studio so he could hear the rain.

"My heathen nature is finding solace," he'd said of his second glass of whisky as he lay stretched out on the plum sofa with an American newspaper, Tybalt curled on his stomach like a feline paperweight. I, having changed into one of my oldest dresses, sat in his brown leather chair, a cup of tea for warmth, Plutarch in hand.

"*Seeking to quench a cruel tyranny*," I quoted in reply.

Pierce made a sound, then tossed his paper onto the table as he shifted—Tybalt jumping onto the carpet and claiming refuge beneath the table. Sitting up, Pierce took another drink from the half-empty glass before him. "Do we," he mused aloud, "revere the past too much?"

"It's Sunday afternoon, Pierce. Are you really coming for my Plutarch?"

Two raised eyebrows, another swallow, and he set the glass down with more force than I was expecting. "I think we've considered long enough, Emma. We need to talk. Settle this matter between us. Courage, wasn't that what Hawkes said?"

What a jolt in my chest. My heart froze and lifted in the same breath.

Numa Pompilius glanced up at me from the page, and I—thinking he should mind his own business—shut the book.

Pierce and I looked at one another.

We both moved to speak at the same time.

We stopped ourselves in unison.

Pierce fussed with his hair in a manner I could accuse of being Hawkesian, stood, snagged his glass between his fingers, and walked to the sideboard behind his worktable before pouring himself another drink.

He silently offered me one.

I declined. And thought one of us had jolly well better say something.

"I don't mind our ages," I said.

Pierce nodded, taking a sip before setting his glass down and folding his arms. "The least of our worries, I'm beginning to think. Did you ever speak with Parian?"

"I tried." I pulled Plutarch to my chest. "A rather fumbled attempt, I'm afraid."

"Right." Pierce looked down, lifting his hand. "I should have been more circumspect."

Circumspect.

The word had never felt more like a boundary.

"As should I have," I said, both for and against the feelings inside my chest. "Cousin Archibald may be a flimsy excuse for respectability, but he is what we have, unless you propose to lock the door between hall and studio, move from Lapis Lazuli Minor, and come for tea and chaperoned dinners, courting with bouquets of flowers—"

"I hate that bloody word."

"Bouquet? I think it lovely."

He grimaced and took another drink. "*Courting.*"

"As in: to court? As in: they were courting?"

"As in so awful I wouldn't know where to start."

"No matter how you feel about the word," here a smile caught up with me, "there lies our reality nonetheless."

"Hmm." Pierce moved around to the front of his worktable, setting his drink down.

"You mentioned my parents, last time we spoke."

"I did."

I thought of my mother and father arguing over where I would go once they died. "I can't speak to what they might think of all this, but they would have liked you, as an individual, I'm sure of it. My father would have met you at some soirée of mutual friends and invited you up to Cambridgeshire."

Pierce looked up at me. "Cambridgeshire? Is that your home county?"

"It is."

"You've never said."

"No, I haven't." I moved past a homesickness so deeply buried it was like a stone one could not dig out. "My mother would have fussed over the obligation, but I think she would have taken to you immediately."

Pierce leaned back against his worktable and folded his arms. "And neither of them would have said, 'Here is my daughter, just twenty-one years of age. You're a man with a knotted past. Why don't you *court*.'" He spat the word out before taking a drink. "I do hate that bloody word."

"Yes, well, in my narrative, you and I do not speak much over the meal, but afterward my mother suggests we take you to the meadow past the stream." I set Plutarch on the table before me and settled back into my chair as if I were telling a story. "Father is soon distracted by something he'd like to sketch, and you and I begin to speak of overlapping interests. I would have already read Whitman, of course. You would take an interest. And mention your time in America."

Pierce looked out of the window while I spoke, and I am not certain if he was seeing what we might have been or something else. "I've been honest about the fact that I might never want to tell you certain things from my past. Would that become a barrier for you?"

I had no ready answer, but I refused to paint over the question. Pointing first to Pierce's drink, which he picked up and brought to me, I took one burning swallow and handed it back.

He returned to his post.

"I don't know," I answered truthfully. "Some bridges one can only cross *when*."

Pierce again looked out the window, his expression tight before asking,

"What of your own jumbled thoughts? Have you sorted anything?"

I thought of Arabella and I speaking in the park.

I thought of the line from Wordsworth, *Love's uneasy sovereignty*.

"I think I found a way to say something, yes."

"Go on."

It must have been my speaking of Cambridgeshire and the cottage, but I felt younger, almost as if the weight of a braid still lay over my shoulder. I brought my legs up beneath my skirt, wrapping my arms around my knees. His eyes followed the lines of my body. My hands, my shoulders, up to my face. "For what it's worth," Pierce said, "I would have thought you beautiful had we met in Cambridgeshire at your parents' cottage."

I smiled but couldn't hide my nerves.

"Go on," he prodded. "What do you wish to say?"

"What I wish to say is— The best way to understand— Dash it all." I cleared my throat and pronounced, "I am a country, Pierce."

"You are a country," he repeated.

"Yes. That is, I am. A sovereign country of my own. And I mean my heart." It was then I noticed my hands were shaking. "These last three years I've guarded all the borders, not trusting anyone to wander too far in, because I had yet to let Maxwell leave. Now I have, but I do worry about what was left behind. Worried what I might find—or what *you* might find—if I were to trust you inside the walls. But these few weeks, I've been thinking that not only do I wish you would step across the border, but I want you to do so. I've been telling myself that the wreckage won't bother you. That you would be rather patient but present while I sort it out."

He leaned back against the table, one hand wrapped over the edge, the other around his glass. His silver eyes were intent on my face, waiting for me to continue.

With a steadying breath, I forced myself not to bury my face against my knees. "But the territory in the very centre of my being is one I am not yet willing anyone enter just yet. I have loved with all my heart before, and I'm wary of trying to do so too soon. I want to board this ship and see where we find ourselves, I truly do, but I need to throw this first game of darts without aiming for the centre, until…until I'm ready. Mixing metaphors with horrible abandon, apparently."

He smiled. "Sovereign territory, ship in the harbour, game of darts. I think it was clear enough."

I knew the last line waiting to be said, and so I rushed it out before I could think the better of it.

"In short, I need to ask you to take part of my heart but not all, not until I know I'm ready. But how does one say that without it seeming…?"

"Just as you have," Pierce answered. "Keep your centre. Give it away to no one until you've decided exactly what you want. Exactly what you can stand."

"Including you?"

"Especially me."

I shifted myself deeper into the chair, for comfort, or confidence, I suppose.

Pierce's expression was as serious as I've ever seen it. He pushed his hair back with one hand then lifted his glass, staring at the last swallow for one thoughtful moment before setting it down untouched. He did not relax his pose but pushed himself away from the table. Standing without anything to lean on, he did not hide a single corner of his self-doubt. "Here is the truth of what I think," he said. "We could talk through a thousand things, but this is what I want to say now, what I can say. This—you and I—could be a triumph, an unexpected, miraculous"—he hesitated, as if the thought were so painful, he dared not breathe through to the other side—"triumph. Or it could end in disaster. Utterly gone up in flames."

I waited.

His jaw tightened, his hand a fist. "I have endless concerns. Some shared, others that I need to hold close to the chest a while; things to work out on my own. But I need you to understand"—he moved his hand to cover his heart—"this is high stakes for me. If we are going to say yes, if we are going to play this game, I've no *intention* of folding. I want to see this through to the end. And maybe we win. And maybe we lose. But I promise I will do my best."

He looked me in the eye as he spoke.

It was one of the most painful shared looks of my life.

"So we're going to try." I meant it as a question. It refused to be anything but a statement.

A deep breath on his part. "If you say yes, I say yes."

"Despite not knowing…"

"Yes."

I looked away, lifting my right hand to the side of my neck. Breathing through the weight of his words, I tested a smile. It was tentative. Hopeful. "I wanted us to be brave enough," I said, not quite having the courage to look at his face.

"So did I," he said, "But there is one more thing I have to say."

I gave a half nod, curt and careful, and without dropping my hand, I looked back at Pierce.

His words were deliberate. As if he'd practiced them more than once. "If I hurt you. If I leave a mark on that indomitable soul of yours—"

"You just said there's a possibility this could end in disaster, Pierce. I know the risks."

"I'm not speaking of bruises, Emma. I'm speaking of scars. If I hurt you in such a way, I walk." He lifted both his hands in surrender, taking a half step back, increasing the distance between us. "I will not leave you worse than before you met me."

"Impossible."

"That is the clear line I have to draw," he reiterated. "Some people are given a permanent place, no matter what comes. You have that with me, Emma. You have a place in my life. I hope—" He broke off the sentence, running the fingers of his left hand down his jaw in thought, then tried again. "I hope I have one in yours. But the moment I hurt you in that way is the moment I walk from any attempt at being one another's future."

It was so raw, I think both of us were too pained to say anything else.

I nodded. So did he, a single nod, decisive, before finishing his drink and setting the glass back on the table. He nodded again, but to himself. Pierce walked to where I sat, placing his hand on the side of my face as he bent down and kissed my forehead, his thumb moving just so across my cheekbone. Then he pulled away and left. Leaving me alone.

I was glad of it, for I hadn't realised I'd still been shaking.

The afternoon grew late before I excused myself from the empty studio, retrieved my coat, gloves, and an umbrella, going out into the crossroads of day ending and evening beginning.

I took my tentative hope with me.

April 29th

I am as shocked as anybody else. None of us ever considered the possibility. I suppose it is because we've seen the other young ladies—Arabella's inferiors in terms of beauty, position, and wealth—and assumed that *The Season* of 1884 was hers for the taking.

I'm getting ahead of myself.

Tonight was the Fouquet Ball.

I did not know if Roland or Miss Northgate or Miss Clifford would be in attendance (Roland was not, May and Annalise were), but I knew that Islington would most certainly not, sparing us the need to field questions in tandem like a pair of comedic actors from a theatre troupe.

Aunt Eugenia, having been ill and bested by a duke in the same fortnight, was chomping at the bit.

Arabella was looking to amuse herself at everyone's expense.

As for my state of mind? It is difficult to parse.

My mind having been so full of Pierce, Islington, and Hawkes, I'd not thought overmuch of Aunt Eugenia's antics. It was ridiculous and crass, her threat, but having grown used to her manner of being over the years, I've taken the absurdities for granted. Nothing I couldn't manage.

But when I walked into Spencer House—her carriage having brought me from Lapis Lazuli—it felt as if something had shifted, like part of a cliffside trail had given way. The housekeeper and maids fussed in their usual way. Greeting Arabella, who lay draped across her chaise longue in her room, was no different. It was when Aunt Eugenia entered that I understood. Aunt Eugenia looked the same, sounded the same, blamed me for causing her grief in the same manner, only there had been a slight hesitation when she first saw me. She had tried to claim more land in this war over my autonomy and instead had lost a swathe of what she'd already had.

We both knew it.

"Why you insist on looking like a rustic is beyond me, Emma. One would think you were vying for a life on the farm."

"It is wonderful to see you as well, Aunt."

"Hmph."

Arabella, sitting with her eyes closed, smirked.

"Tonight, we are going to put Arabella on the highest pedestal with every man in the room. Visibility being the aim," Aunt Eugenia pronounced. "You, Emma, are to direct everyone's eyes to your cousin. And please don't slouch. No man wants to marry into a family that can't sit properly in a chair."

As expected, Arabella's appearance caused a stir. Men stood straighter. They fussed with their neckties. Those sporting a dreaded mustache smoothed the edges from habit. And Arabella was invited to dance. And again. And again.

Things seemed to be going well, *very* well.

She blessed all her partners with a smile, graceful while aloof and untouchable. A garden rose one dares not cut for the table.

She was perfect.

Every man wanted her favour.

Then halfway through the evening, a party arrived.

They were late. Uncouth if one is middle class, perfectly acceptable with wealth and status. They were a party of the latter. A dowager, an older couple, a younger couple. But it was a young woman that gave us all pause.

So beautiful, it was almost painful to look.

We held our collective breath.

If Arabella were the premier bloom in the garden, this young woman was the one found in a dream. Arabella may be the perfect rose, but this young woman was a star, fallen to earth.

She wore a pale gown of embroidered silver, all grace and aloofness. Her eyes were large and distant and certain. Ethereal, I thought. And something about her grace pricked a memory.

Amid the stiffening of Aunt Eugenia and the merest shade of uncertainty beneath Arabella's placid and proud expression, I remembered where I had seen her.

Twelfth Night in Knightsbridge, when she came to claim Oberon on his throne.

Whispers were going around the ballroom, and Lord and Lady Fouquet stepped up to welcome the guests. The young woman waited with her party.

She surveyed the room.

She seemed to be looking for someone.

She was disappointed.

The whispers around me took more volume and form.

"That's the Countess of Ellam, Lady Silver."

"Down from Norfolk, a rare occurrence."

"Her sister and brother-in-law, yes."

"Lady Silver? Gold, more like. They've one of the greatest fortunes in the country."

"That's the nephew and his new wife. There's a son as well, no idea where he is…"

"The young lady? Lady Eloise Silver. No, not married. Rarely comes to London. Most beautiful girl in all England."

Arabella's cheeks were a high colour of pink. She accepted an invitation to dance. But all eyes were on Miss Silver as she, too, accepted an invitation for the pending waltz.

On and on the whispers, as I watched the girl with whom Oberon had danced.

"She's not his Titania," The Boy had said with an edge.

But watching her in a ballroom of mortals, I wondered.

It is not to say that Arabella was forgotten. She wasn't. She was danced attendance on, brought drinks, and given one distracted smile after another, but there was a rarer air in the room, the elusive tang of twilight after a long day of sun.

Aunt Eugenia was not pleased.

Waves of displeasure rolling out despite her rictus smiles. I was sought once or twice, but she told my partners, "Emma is no longer dancing tonight. Sore ankle, you see," and kept me close.

"Aunt Eugenia—"

"Not now, Emma. Not a word from your mouth, *I beg you*." Said more in the tone of, "I *will* cut out your tongue if you say One. More. Thing."

The night seemed to stretch forever.

Arabella, for all her dismissive smiles and easy expressions, looked wilted in a way I've never seen before. Smaller. Nothing too noticeable, no, but the shine of Mount Olympus was not as bright. Perhaps it was because Lady Eloise Silver had come from an older deity; a titan, or even Gaia herself?

My feet were aching. I was wishing the night would end.

When it finally did, Aunt Eugenia was all smiles and opinions as we said our farewells. But upon entering the carriage, she was silent, stone-faced, and cold.

"Dear Mama, don't look so dreadful," Arabella drawled, followed by a yawn. She was running her finger absently against the ornate edge of her sleeve, something she would do when she was younger and her parents were arguing.

"Arabella. Emma! We have worked too hard, planned for too long, to let some country upstart—some country *hermit*—create a stir. Of any kind! We will not shrink. We will not fade quietly into second place."

"No one could claim you were ever quiet," I muttered.

"We will face this with all the cunning I possess. Emma, we will not be attending Lady Harlow's tea on the third. We will cry off. Come to Spencer House on Monday for a Council of War."

"Mama, really," Arabella dismissed.

"A Council of War," Aunt Eugenia articulated at Arabella. "This is YOUR *Season* and no one else shall intervene!"

Nothing else was said.

What a relief to be home, curled up in my own window seat, a warm cup of tea brought by Agnes after she helped me peel myself from my dress. I've not felt sorry for Arabella in a long time, but I do tonight. And as I was leafing through Whitman a few minutes ago—one does not read Plutarch on such a night—I came across a line fitting, not only for this evening but so many things.

I and this mystery, here we stand.

April 30th

My life does not seem to be operating according to ~~plan~~ any plan.

I've just received a disappointing letter. One I was not ready for.

I went to find Pierce in his studio.

He was out.

I left the letter on his table with a piece of black crepe I found in the west garret.

> *Miss Lion,*
>
> *I hope my letter of some months back reached you and that you haven't been left wondering how long you are to care for Tybalt. I am pleased to tell you we are returning home. My husband and I will be in London the second week in May and hope to come and fetch Tybalt at your earliest convenience. I will send a note round to make certain the day is suitable. You will always have my thanks.*
>
> *Sincerely,*
>
> *Jane Stone*

I paced around the back garden for half an hour, then hunted down our resident cat—he was in the kitchen watching Agnes bone a chicken—and gave him every attention.

After which I dusted the drawing room and tried not to weep over the whole thing.

Later

Pierce found me in the kitchen near midnight, a cup of tea for company as I listened to the rain. I'd just finished sewing a pocket into one of my walking skirts for the May Day fête in the morning. Tybalt was curled near my feet. Saying nothing, Pierce sat down on the chair beside me. He reached his hand out and brushed a strand of hair from my face just as thunder sounded.

It was my favourite moment of the day.

He stood, poured himself a cup of tea with the remaining water in the kettle, and sat back down.

"We'll find another cat," he said.

"Not in front of Tybalt!" I said. "Dreadful thought."

A lightning flash exposed every corner of the kitchen for one brief, blinding moment, then was gone, leaving only the lamp I had lit on the table.

Pierce picked up a scrap of the calico fabric I'd used for my pocket and said, "Islington asked I take photographs tomorrow, for The St. Crispian's Historical Society. They are very serious about May Day here, which is terrifying on some level."

I laughed, the weight of the last few days not quite so heavy. "Is he still on the committee? Despite having been so ill?"

"He's intending to go."

"Hmm. I wonder what Hawkes will say to that. Do you think we'll be stuck with rain?"

Pierce looked towards the window, raindrops in long lines down the glass. "It's a moving storm, so I'd wager not."

We sat in silence a while longer.

"Anything I can do for you?" he asked at length.

I shook my head. "I'm fine, really. Sad about Tybalt, is all."

"Anything else on your mind?"

Yes. Beginning with Pierce, drawing a straight line through Islington, and ending with Hawkes. These lives that are now woven with mine.

"Not in particular," I answered.

He nodded. "Goodnight, then."

"Goodnight."

When I finally returned to my garret, I slipped Whitman from the shelf and opened my window to the sound of the storm.

> *Long have you timidly waded holding a plank by the shore,*
> *Now I will you to be a bold swimmer,*
> *To jump off in the midst of the sea, rise again, nod to me, shout, and laughingly dash with your hair.*

THE PERSONAL LIBRARY *of* EMMA M. LION
As It Currently Stands

The Complete Works of Shakespeare by *William Shakespeare*
Illustrated by Declan Lion

The Holy Bible

Jane Eyre by *Charlotte Brontë*
Gifted by the Jane Eyre Society of Fortitude, A Preparatory School for Girls

Shakespeare's Comedies, In Full
Gifted by Roland Sutherland

Jane Eyre by *Charlotte Brontë*
Gifted by Roland Sutherland

Latin Phrases for the Unrepentant by *Barclay Stafford*
Won at The Dalliance Bookshop

Self-Reliance by *Ralph Waldo Emerson*
Gifted by Niall Pierce

Essays by *Ralph Waldo Emerson*
Gifted by Niall Pierce

Meaning of Flowers
Found in the breakfast room

Vermilion and the Flaming Sword
Purchased without a cover at The Dalliance

Treasure Island by *Robert Louis Stevenson*
Gifted by Young Hawkes

Plutarch's Lives by *Plutarch*
Gifted by Islington

Song of Myself by *Walt Whitman*
Gifted by Niall Pierce

Ireland: Myth, Legend, and History
by *Alistair T. Moddle* and *Jonathan L. Kirk*
(Rapscallion Commentary by Declan Lion)
Gifted by Young Hawkes

Dictionary of the English Language A – J by *Dr. Samuel Johnson*
Purchased from and bound by The Hound
(The entire K section is missing.)

Mixing in Society by *The Right Hon. Countess of* *******
Foisted by Aunt Eugenia

Dictionary of the English Language L – Z by *Dr. Samuel Johnson*
Miraculously Gifted by Ben Chambers

Dear Reader,

As incredible as it seems, here we are in 1884. It's been an eventful journey, to say the least, and life in St. Crispian's shows no sign of slowing down.

Beth would first like to thank you, The Reader, for wandering into the neighbourhood and deciding to stay. It is a particular life we live here, good if not ridiculous. And there is much ahead.

Thank you to Beth's family—Kip, parents, siblings, nieces & nephews—who reside in the very centre of her heart. She loves them deeply and is forever thankful for how they cheer her on.

Thank you, Spy Cat Grey. You deserve all the treats.

Friendship is a gift Beth has received in abundance. Thank you, all. You know who you are. An especial thanks to Mary Ann, for traipsing through England, and to Angie, for wielding a sword against discouragement, and holding up a light.

Thank you, Kimberly, for always being the first to read anything. Thank you to her Mother, her Father, Alena, Lorien, Natalie, Caitlin, Jenesse, Rob (look who finally showed up), and Lori. You have faithfully read these journals in-process and Beth cannot express her gratitude enough.

As for the Rhysdon Press team who bring these books to life, you are a marvel.

Thank you, Tyson Cantrell, for allowing your beautiful design to grace the covers.

Thank you, Jennifer Lerud, for your brilliant copy editing, talent, and kindness.

Thank you, Ashley Lloyd, for appearing out of thin air to become Beth's trustworthy assistant.

Thank you, Ben Unguren, ever the magician, who creates time when he has none.

Thank you, Allysha Unguren, substantive editor, board member, and fellow in near-hysterical laughter. You have sacrificed so much for all of Beth's books, and it is recorded in her heart.

Thank you, Kip. The one who is the only.

A note concerning the presumptuous Beth Brower, who thought it a good idea to put my journals into the world. She lives with the aforementioned Kip, her chemist husband, and their cat, Spy Cat Grey.

Beth enjoys citrus scents, books, handwoven rugs, and walking in any weather. She listens to songs on repeat. She feels rather fiercely about the ones she loves and needs windows for light and walls for art.

Beth Brower has written the following books:

The Queen's Gambit
The Ruby Prince
The Wanderer's Mark

The Q

The Beast of Ten

The Unselected Journals of Emma M. Lion

You can find more information on her website and Instagram.

www.bethbrower.com
@bethbrower

You can also subscribe to Beth's newsletter and find short fiction about the characters of St. Crispian's on Substack.

Beth Brower Scribbles Away
bethbrower.substack.com

The Unselected Journals of Emma M. Lion: Vol. 8 is available now.

Sincerely,
Emma

www.ingramcontent.com/pod-product-compliance
Lightning Source LLC
LaVergne TN
LVHW052143160926
848286LV00026B/519
* 9 7 8 1 9 5 7 4 9 2 0 1 8 *